PHILIP A. HIBBERD

GALAXY
AWAKENING

novum pro

All rights of distribution, including via film, radio, and television, photomechanical reproduction, audio storage media, electronic data storage media, and the reprinting of portions of text, are reserved.

Printed in the European Union on environmentally friendly, chlorine- and acid-free paper.

© 2022 novum publishing

ISBN 978-3-99131-212-3
Editing:
Roderick Pritchard-Smith, M.Litt
Cover photos:
Alexandr Mitiuc,
Nuttawut Uttamaharad,
Martijn Mulder | Dreamstime.com
Cover design, layout & typesetting:
novum publishing

www.novum-publishing.co.uk

CHAPTER 1

ARRIVAL

Consciousness awoke within a dark shroud. A blackness that was void of light surrounded him, infinite silence within this dark realm, deafened. He felt as though he were floating inside an enclosed room, no light, no sound and – as he discovered – no feeling. He was numb, paralysed to all senses, and yet, he knew he was alive.

Slowly, the darkness gave way to a lighter shade of black, darker greys now flickered and merged, lighter greys swam within the mix, like sunlight clawing its way through a dark foggy dawn. Pale distant colours emerged from the greys. However, he felt nothing, just a spectator with no apparent emotion.

Sight was returning to him, a myriad of colours exploded silently before him, still, he could feel nothing, no fear, no panic, just ... nothing.

He knew that his eyes were open, but he could not focus on the images in front of him, dark grey shapes mingled with pastel blues, yellows, greens and reds, a dark shadowy shape moved across the confusion of colours, it lurched from his right to the centre then seemed to turn towards him. It hesitated for a moment and then loomed nearer to him, it was close and seemed to sway one way then another before retreating into the now solid pastel colours.

The absence of sound, should, he thought, be un-nerving, but he felt relaxed and at ease with the situation unfolding in front of him. He let his mind wonder, far away from the dancing images. How did he get here? He could not remember, where was he. That, was also a mystery.

Who was he? For a second that panicked him, he had no idea who he was, or, where he had come from. He felt the panic swell into his being, it took a hold of him, he wanted to scream, then, as soon as the panic washed through him it was smoothed away and he felt calm and relaxed, floating within the constant blooming of colours and greys.

The dark shape he noticed, seemed to move quicker from one side of his vision to the other, it broke away from the myriad of pastel colours and once again loomed towards him. He watched unconcerned as it came closer.

It stayed longer this time, then he felt something, a touch, gentle and soothing, and then without warning, a noise, it came to him from far away, a mixture of soft sounds entered his hearing, in the distance, various pitches of humming, a melodic sound harmonising at the edge of his senses.

For a while he listened, and his mind followed its hypnotic throws as it moved from one melody to another. Above this were more sounds, more blocks of sound. One close by was deep, another further away higher pitched. Was this language? He wasn't sure but he determined that there were three separate pitches of sound, the third far away. Of course, he thought, three separate people were in the room with him, talking. They were the dark shapes that moved from one side of his vision to the other. He concentrated on the noise, trying to break it down into words, but could not.

A shape loomed towards him again and a block of noise, deep and authoritative filled his hearing, but he could make no sense of it. Once more he felt the soothing touch on ears, forehead and temples and another block of sound entered his hearing, not just one noise this time but small particles of sound, some with inclined pitch. 'Words', he thought, 'I can hear words. I don't understand them, but they are definitely words.'

The dark grey shape moved away from him into the blurred regions of the pastel colours. Another shape moved to the same position and he heard the language being spoken again, one deep, almost guttural voice, the other softer, higher pitched. 'Male and female', he thought. One grey shape moved away and came back towards him. He felt the gentle touch upon his temples again, a shivering feeling washed through him, not un-pleasant, not unpleasant at all. 'Almost sexual', he thought. He bathed in the sensation, feeling light and calm. Then he heard a noise. Not heard exactly, more sensed.

'Barralama ka delim derom. 'Words', he thought. Separated from each other. 'Syllables', he exclaimed to himself. Definitely syllables, it was definitely a language, but the words held no meaning to him.

Again, a soothing sensation flowed through his mind, the shape moved slightly to one side.

'Barralama to hear derom', the deep voice whispered.

He concentrated. He had heard something that made some sort of sense. He tried to speak but could not. The shape moved back slightly and said something that again, he could not com-prehend, a second grey shape appeared to his right side. They were both leaning over him, and again he was awash with a soothing, relaxing feeling.

'Are you able to hear what I say, close your eyes if you do,' he felt the relief cascade through his mind. 'Yes', he thought. 'I can understand'. He closed his eyes.

'Good ...' said the deeper voice, almost in triumph. The shape leaned over his field of vision to the shape at his left-hand side. A conversation in muted tones passed between them. He could not make out its content. The shape then turned to him.

'Listen carefully, for now, you cannot move or talk. You are in need of a lot of,' he paused, the smaller shape leant towards the larger, whispered voices were exchanged.

'Restoration work,' the deeper voice said hesitantly.

'You are ..., in a very bad ..." the voice stopped. He then heard a deep sigh.

'I am so sorry, but you are not in the best of shapes, I and my team are confident that we can bring you through this. I am Doctor Ghorbany, you are in my medical centre. We are on the Stella ship 'Griffin', we found you in a life pod canister. We are doing everything we can, but ...' his voice trailed away, and the sigh within the 'but' spoke volumes.

'In the meantime, I am passing you over for psychiatric assessment: You will be linked with the Griffin's Med-Comm system. Do you understand? Blink if you do.' He had no idea what the Griffin was, a star ship, maybe, but what type of ship, a battle ship, a science ship, he didn't know. 'Am I crew, passenger or captive? Life pod canister', he thought, but no recollection came to him. And what was a Med -Comm system? It all meant nothing to him. Again, he tried to talk but found he couldn't. He closed his eyes, then reopened them.

He didn't fully understand what psychiatric assessment meant either, but the fact was that he was obviously in no condition to argue.

The pastel colours around him swirled and converged back to various shades of grey, he noticed they were now spiralling around him creating a tunnel of dark and light. He felt no sensation of movement, although the vision before him gave him the impression of falling.

Then, without warning, the grey dissipated, all he could see now was unbroken blue, and warmth, he could feel warmth.

CHAPTER 2

ISLE IN THE TROPICS

A warm breeze ruffled his hair and he could smell the sea salt within it. He looked out over a turquoise lagoon, the white breakers exploding onto the white fine sand that he lay upon. The sky above was an unbroken blue from horizon to horizon. Behind him, some hundred metres away, the shoreline swayed with green palms. Above these, towered a large volcano, its steep sides rising to a smoking plateau.

'Hello.' He turned in the direction of the voice. An elderly man in his seventies, maybe eighties was walking down the beach towards him. He wore a white floppy hat that covered his snow-white hair, which was long, pulled back and tied and hanging to his shoulders. He wore a faded blue shirt with sleeves rolled up to his elbows and white shorts. His feet were bare, his skin weathered and tanned.

'I'm Comm,' he said cheerfully, as he leant down and held out his hand.

From his laying position, he reached out and took the offered hand and was amazed at the strength held within it. With ease Comm pulled him to his feet.

'I'm ...' he hesitated.

'I'm not sure who I am,' he said slowly. He delved into his memory, and found nothing. He was starting to feel anger and frustration, but the overriding feeling, was fear.

The old man gently put his arm around his shoulders and led him across the sand towards the palm trees.

'That's what we are here for, to find out all about you, and ...' he said with a smile on his weathered face. 'Until we do, I'll call you ... Sandy,'

He turned to the older man puzzled.

'Why Sandy.'

The old man grinned, showing perfect white teeth.

'Well, it's pretty obvious really. You're covered in it.'

The younger man stopped and looked down at himself, Comm chuckled as he walked on towards the palms. He was covered head to foot in a layer of fine white sand. He brushed it away as best he could, then ran to catch up to the old man.

At the tree line, he noticed a break in the palms, and in the shade a beach bar made of bamboo and wicker. In front, two wicker stools on which they each took a seat and considered each other. Comm seemed to have a permanent knowing smile, his face showing patience in abundance. He, on the other hand, although tall with long unkempt fair hair, wearing a white singlet and white shorts, looked nervous and unsure.

'We seem to have a bar with no bartender,' the younger man said, just to break the silence.

'Oh, I'm sure one will be here soon,' Comm said smoothly.

'After all, you do have quite a vivid imagination,' he said panning his hand across the vista. Sandy followed this indication, taking in the trees, the sand and the turquoise sea.

'Me, oh no, this is your world, not mine.'

'I can assure you, Sandy, if this was my virtual world, it would be completely empty. It may, however, be pale green or blue, and there would be two comfortable chairs facing each other, maybe a table between them. No distractions you see, but this, actually, I like it, and it's all from your subconscious, not from me at all. The reason I like it, is, this is your inner being yelling out at you. All we have to do, is decipher it.'

A noise behind the bar made them both turn in their seats, a two-metre-tall praying mantis unfolded itself and began cleaning glasses.

'Hm, a lot of deciphering.' Comm said with a chuckle. He leant forward towards the mantis:

'A large Callina, please.' The mantis grabbed a hold of various bottles beneath the counter and with dextrous ease poured the drink and offered it to the smiling Comm.

He took a sip and held the liquid in his mouth before swallowing.

'Oh yes, I like your world very much, far better than anything I could come up with.' He put the glass on the bar top and leant back on his stool.

Sandy wasn't sure of the mantis, but slowly asked for his drink.

'Apple juice, please'. He watched the intricate dance of limbs and Fore-legs and soon, a glass of iced apple juice in a tall glass stood before him. His work done, the Mantis reverted his attention to cleaning glasses. Sandy looked at Comm's drink with fascination: The liquid within had started clear, but now as he looked on, swirls of colour exploded within the glass.

'What is that?' he asked, transfixed on the glass.

'A drink from a miner's outpost, the fifth planet of Tau Ceti.' Comm picked up the glass and took another sip.

'The flavours explode onto your pallet,' he continued.

'It looks fantastic, I might try one next.'

Comm studied the young creature that sat before him, humanisque, definitely, he thought, but so different from the bi-pedal human creatures he had worked with on the Griffin. Something was different, a difference he could not quite define, but, early days, he had been given almost indefinite time, this young human was important.

He thought on that, why did the medical team think he was important, who had told them that he was? Curious, he thought. Smiling, Comm leant forward and said, 'I have never seen a creature quite like that,' moving his gaze to the creature cleaning a tall glass.

'Oh, don't get me wrong, I know I don't get out much, being the ship's Com-link, but I have looked in every historical file, not only the Griffin's, but Command files too, nothing, absolutely nothing comes close to it, and this scenario, it's very nice, but what is it, and your accent, I don't think I've heard that accent before, in fact, the medical team did have a problem in getting you to understand our dialect, and I have quite a large data base,' his eyes sparkled waiting for new information. Sandy sipped his juice, and gave a puzzled look.

'It's a praying mantis,' he said watching the creature remove glasses from the back shelf, and then with the intricacies of its forelegs shine the glasses crystal clean.

He smiled, feeling no threat from such a large predator that stood less than a metre away.

'It's not meant to be that big, mostly they are about 5 to 10 centimetres long, and they certainly don't do bar work … well, maybe they do here, they are known, or, the female is known to devour the male after mating.' Comm's eyebrows lifted, he turned to look at the mantis who was still busy cleaning glasses.

'I think we will be quite safe; I can't see us doing any of that', Sandy said. He leant back on his stool and chuckled.

'And this,' the older man cast his arm wide, Sandy looked around at the tropical scene, he turned to Comm, and smiling, said.

'Is a typical tropical island, complete with volcano, and you asked about my accent, I'm sorry, I can't explain that, it's just the way I talk' Comm regarded the young man carefully. He was relaxed and open, it was now time to probe.

'But, from where, what planet?' he asked, and thought that that was a good opening. Sandy slumped down into his stool.

'Well, erm, I, er. I don't know, er, do you mean me, or the island, me, I have no idea, but the island seems familiar, in fact it's so familiar I would say that it's, stereotypical.' Comm once again raised his eyebrows.

'Stereotypical, you are very, very strange. You create a world that no one has ever seen, then use a word that I have never heard before, and I can assure you, I know billions of words.' Sandy frowned, and then shrugged.

'Having the qualities that you would expect a particular type of person or thing to have. This island is a tropical island. If you were to say to someone, think of a tropical island, this, is what they would think of. It is a stereotype, hence stereotypical,' Sandy said, then sipped his apple juice.

'But from where? Comm countered, leaning forward.

'Well from ...the tropics,' Sandy said at last, shrugging his shoulders.

Comm drank the last of his drink.

'The tropics ... many planets that orbit the habitable region of a star have tropical regions, but I have never seen anything quite like this, and I have been the Com-link aboard this ship for forty-seven standard years, and in that time the Griffin has visited over ten thousand planets. Not once have I witnessed anything quite like this, so, be more specific, which planet, exactly?' he demanded, the smile fading.

Sandy was taken aback by this sudden turn in the conversation. It was no longer jovial, more interrogational. He studied Comm, who was now sitting upright, his bright blue eyes boring into him.

'You are after information that you know I have no access to. But I know whatever this planet is, this island is a part of it.'

Comm relaxed and leaned back from the young man, the smile returning.

'Then let's look at the evidence, an island, the mantis, oh, and the apple juice. The first two I know nothing about, but an apple, now this has come up in my findings of over ten thousand searches. It is indigenous to a planet called Earth. The early colonists on a multitude of planets tried to cultivate the apple, and many other fruits and vegetables, but they just could not get them to grow. Now, the strange thing is, how do you know about the apple? I found mention of it in a report whose author is now long gone, like the planet it came from, a planet that was destroyed over five thousand standard years ago. So, tell me, mystery man, how is it possible that you, a person that has no memory, can imagine this whole scenario, with reference to a fruit that you could not possibly know.'

Sandy sipped his apple juice and concentrated on the taste. It definitely was apple, he recognised it as the juice of an apple. If it were to be fermented it would turn into an alcoholic cider, he knew that. He knew that this was an island, although he had not walked its perimeter. The mantis however, was pure imagination, the creature shouldn't be two meters tall, and would never be serving drinks, this was all imagination, with truths and fiction mingled together. But the revelation that Earth had been destroyed, unsettled him. He did not know why, he had never heard of the place, so why should it affect him? He leant back on his stool and studied the old man, a personification of a machine that collects data.

He replaced the glass on the counter. He had drunk two thirds of its contents. The Mantis dropped in two cubes of ice and refilled it with juice before returning to its glass cleaning.

'I don't know, how I know, I just know that it is. I have never heard of the planet Earth, and yet,' he leaned forward.

'Why should I feel somehow upset when you tell me it's been destroyed?'

Comm's seemed to be in a faraway place. His face was expressionless He had raised his right hand to his chin and his index finger tapped the side of his cheek.

'Er … you okay Comm?' Sandy asked with concern.

'Yes, sorry, er, yes. I am just receiving information from the Med lab team: You have just had a massive emotional experience, in a mind that has no memories. You are a fascinating study and I am sure that some of the answers to a lot of our questions are to be found here, in this wonderful place that you have created for us. We still have quite some time left, so, let's go and explore.'

Putting his empty glass on the bar, he stood and walked towards the white breakers. Sandy left the full glass of apple juice and followed him. 'This Comm,' he thought, 'seems to blow hot and cold without hesitation.' Something within him warned him to be wary, and yet, Comm, was here to help him … wasn't he?

He picked up his speed and very soon he caught him up. Comm stood at the water's edge, turned and looked down one side of the beach then turned to look down the other.

'Any preference as to which way?' he asked.

'If this is an island that means, whichever way we go, we'll end up back here. So I don't think it really matters … so, let's go that way,' he said pointing. Comm shrugged and turned to walk down the white sandy beach. Sandy followed two paces behind. After twenty minutes Comm called to the younger man.

'We have been walking for some time, and yet, the sun has not moved. Your island seems to be stuck in time,' Comm said without turning. He walked into the warm water and stopped.

'This is an interesting feeling, very soothing.'

'Paddling,' Sandy said as he followed him into the surf. Comm turned, his face quizzical.

'Paddling,' he repeated, with a shrug of the shoulders. Sandy laughed.

'Walking in water, or the enjoyment of walking in water,'

'We do seem to have a breakdown in translation. Again you offer a word that has no meaning to me, this in itself, is, curious, but I quite like this, er, paddling', he chuckled as he stomped his way through the shallow breakers.

They walked in silence for a while looking for any evidence of an explanation of this imagined scenario. None came.

The white surf aside a turquoise sea, the breakers splashing onto the white fine sand, the palm trees, and the dominating volcano with its small puff of smoke at its vent. It was all too idyllic. Comm walked four paces in front of the young creature who now represented an enigma to him. There were too many icons, nothing fitted anything, he was confused, and decided to relay the information, such as it was, back to the Med lab technicians who were eagerly waiting for his updates.

'What exactly are you?' said Sandy from behind. Comm turned to face him.

'Well ...' he said slowly, 'that's what I'm here to find out. About you, who you are, what you are, er ... Are you dangerous? Are you a threat to the Griffin, and of course to Command?'

Sandy frowned, and slumped down onto the sand, his feet just touching the warm water. He revelled in the sensation as the gentle waves caressed his feet and calves. He leant back, his hands clasped behind his head.

'I don't think I'm a threat, and I'm certainly not dangerous, at least I don't think I am, not to you, or the Griffin, or to,

Command, whatever that is.' Comm walked back to the young man and crouched before him. Smiling he leant forward and touched the younger's hair.

'I can feel that, do you?' asked Comm.

Sandy frowned. 'What, you, touching my hair?'

The older man smiled showing perfect white teeth.

'Yes, can you feel me touching your hair?'

Sandy raised his hand and gently moved Comm's hand away.

'Yes, I feel it, but what does that have to do with what you, or … I, are?'

Comm sat crossed legged beside him.

'It has everything to do with us, I see you and to prove you're here I can feel you, and it is the same for you. But we don't know each other, that is why we are here, in this incredible world that you have created,' he looked up at the towering volcano. 'We are here to find out, about each other.'

Sandy followed his gaze up to the peak of the volcano and concentrated on the small puff of smoke that haloed the summit.

'As I told you, I don't know who I am.'

Comm turned abruptly to him. 'Ah, but all the clues are here, as I said earlier, we just have to decipher them. This is your mind that is speaking to us; we just have to listen.'

'Yes,' said Sandy turning to face the old man. 'We have to find out about each other, so, you start. What is the Griffin and what is, Command?'

Comm leant back and closed his eyes. To Sandy it gave the impression of deep thought, but in reality Comm was in discussion with the Med team and in conclusion to their debate both Comm and the team could see no danger in revealing answers to his questions.

'The Griffin,' Comm said softly as he opened his pale blue eyes and fixed the stare onto the young man who leant forward slightly.

'It is my ship, or I should say that I am an integral part of the ship, the Com-link controls the ship, from its engines to its life support. However, I am a sub-routine of the main Com. I am assigned to the Med lab, although I do have access to the main data bases and antiquity archives. However, the Griffin, like me, is old, this is her last mission. We have just over three standard years left, then we head to Outpost Station 1436, a facility that will break her down into its component molecular parts. They will auction what they can before that, then scrap the rest. This is the end of days for us, but she has had a long and interesting life. Forty-seven standard years ago she was built as Command's flag ship, the biggest and most powerful in the fleet. She has been in battle several times and for ten years was victorious, and then, as with everything, she became outdated. We lost a battle, but, we survived, we were repaired and sent back, but, on our next encounter, we were out manoeuvred and outgunned. The last battle saw seventy-five percent of our crew destroyed. For five days the Captain played dead in space, our enemy never boarded us, they just left us, eventually we limped back to Command and we were decommissioned as a fighting vessel. The Griffin then started a new life as a training ship, and we did that for thirty standard years, but, technology evolves and it was felt that it was pointless training new crews on such an old ship, so, for nearly twenty standard years we have been at the farthest reaches of known space, jumping from one asteroid field to another, surveying and sampling various ores and minerals so that they can be refined and used to create newer and better fighting ships. It is in this asteroid field, the largest we have ever encountered, that we found you.' Sandy shuffled closer to him.

'You found me here. Why was I here?'

Comm frowned. 'We don't know, that's why we are here, sitting on this beach.'

Sandy lowered his head. 'Yes, of course sorry, please continue'

'The Griffin is now home to a squadron of heavy lift shuttles and freighters. They survey the field and then bring back samples to be tested, and if we have a good field, as I think we have here, Command will send a whole flotilla of factory ships.

'It was on one of the larger asteroids that you were found, a heavy lifter was surveying it when an organic alarm was sounded. They couldn't locate you at first, you were in a capsule, set deep within a cavern. How you got there we have no idea, and even the capsule itself bears no resemblance to any Command design. When they finally got you back, the engineers and the Med teams opened up the capsule, what they found, well, you weren't recognisable as a human. You had deteriorated so much, your body had almost completely decomposed. It was only the life support system that had kept your brain and mind alive, for there was nothing else left of you. Our Captain felt it was beyond the reach of this ship's capabilities to save you. The Med team however, felt differently. There was quite a disagreement, but the Med team won the argument, and they are right now trying to rebuild you. It will take some time.'

Sandy frowned and gaped open-mouthed at him. He held up his hand, a stopping gesture that Comm recognised.

'I am being rebuilt, what into, a robot or something?'

Comm did not recognise the term 'robot' at first, but a deep scan of the older records brought up the definition. This was confusing however. The last records that involved the word, robot, were approximately five thousand years old. He sent the information back to the Med team.

'How do you know such a word?' he asked slowly.

Sandy thought for a moment. 'What? 'Robot'?' he asked, puzzled.

'Yes, 'robot', a term that has not been used since the early colonists. Again, along with the term 'apple' these are references that are over five thousand years old. Could it be possible, that you are … *that* old, that you have been in that capsule for that length of time?' He sent back his report to the Med team and asked them to interact with the engineering Com-link that was designated to the study of the capsule that lay in pieces in sub hanger 6.

'I don't know,' Sandy said, shaking his head. 'Am I going to be a robot?'

Comm sighed, then smiled. 'No, not in the definition of the word. Your body will be cloned using the organic matter found in the capsule. You should look exactly as you do here. We did not create this image of you, this is all your own design, so we can only assume that this is the true image of yourself, an image that I have sent to the Med lab. When you awake, this is the body you will awake in,' he said gesturing to the young man seated before him.

Sandy relaxed and leant back, he sighed with relief.

'That's good to know. So, getting back to the story. You're at war. Who with? Some alien monstrosity that is determined to destroy everything you stand for? And you have been fighting them for, how long? Nearly fifty years, that's a long time,' he paused and thought for a moment.

'Are you winning?' he asked slowly.

Comm was confused for a second. This young man's terminology was difficult to follow. He decided he would answer the questions as they were submitted to him, perhaps, he thought, he was looking too deep into the meaning. That of course could come later.

Comm used the 'hand up' gesture that he had seen the young man use earlier. Sandy stopped.

'Aliens,' Comm said slowly.

'Do you mean sentient beings from other cultures, different from our own? Would that be your definition?' he asked matter-of-factly.

'Well,' Sandy said, slightly puzzled.

'Creatures from other planets, er, not human?'

'There are many creatures on many of the planets that we have visited. None, however, capable of waging war on Command. In four thousand or so years of exploration we have never come across any other species that is as sentient as humans, not even a structure that has been left by any ancient race. Humans are the only dominant species in this sector of the Galaxy, of that I am sure.'

Sandy glared in disbelief.

'We are alone, but there are billions of star systems. Surely ...?'

Comm held up his hand. 'I am not saying that the Galaxy as a whole does not contain other such beings, just the ones we have encountered,'

'And how many is that?' Sandy interrupted.

Comm closed his eyes for an instant. 'One hundred and thirty seven thousand planets or moons have either been colonised, or at least visited by remote unmanned probes, so, in the great scale of the Galaxy hardly any. So, to answer your question, we are not at war with an alien race, but as we have always been, with ourselves, or, in this case a supposedly higher caste of human. They believe they are superior, and we have not been at war for nearly fifty standard years. It has been more like four thousand years, and, as to winning, no side has gained any strategic advantage. Ever.'

'So, what is the point?' Sandy asked, slowly shaking his head. Comm smiled.

'That philosophical question has never, ever been totally answered.' Sandy thought for a moment. A four thousand year war.

'How many have died?' he inquired at last.

'Billions', Comm said quickly. 'And probably billions yet will die,' he added solemnly.

Sandy held up his hand, a puzzled look on his face.

'So, I have been rescued by a ship of war.'

Comm studied the face of the young man as he struggled to come to terms with his own predicament. He was aware that there would be a denial to his situation, maybe anger at some stage, but as for now he would answer the questions as calmly as he could.

'As I said, that was many years ago. At her height, the Griffin had four thousand five hundred crew members. They were distributed over Griffin's thirty-five levels, this ship once pulsed with activity,' Comm closed his eyes and his face drooped into sadness. He took a deep breath and his eyes opened.

'We have a crew manifest of one hundred and seventy-five now, all on just six levels, Oh,' he finished, his face brightening and the smile returning.

'And of course, one passenger.'

Sandy leaned forward, his jaw dropping.

'There are thirty-five decks on this ship! It must be huge!'

Comm leant back and looked at the cloudless sky. He calculated its hue, brightness, and contrast in relation to the sun's luminosity. There were many discrepancies but it was, he thought in conclusion, just an illusion, a visual display, imaginary. He returned to the question.

'She is just over 1.3 kilometres long and just under 400 metres wide. She is pretty big, but the newer ships are bigger.' A sadness flickered over his eyes. Sandy thought he could see his eyes glaze with moisture: He leant closer and forced himself to stop reaching out to comfort the older man.

'Most of those levels have been decommissioned now, just empty spaces, even the air has been sucked out of them.' He shifted his weight upon the sand, altering his position. He noticed the concerned look on the younger man's face and slowly shook his head to allay his fears. 'Each time we docked, whether that was a space station or planetary orbital dry dock, Command would order another level to be stripped away.' He glanced away and focused on the towering volcano, the constant cloud of smoke that haloed the vent wasn't right he thought. It hasn't moved, but then, it, like all of this, is just an image. Sandy waited for him to regain his composure. 'Strange,' Sandy thought to himself, that a computer sub routine could feel the pain of the slow destruction of its home.

Comm took in a deep breath and turned back to him. 'The Griffin does not have a glorious death awaiting her. She will die slowly, one piece at a time, a pitiful end for such a courageous entity, it is …'. Sandy now stretched out his hand and gently held Comm's arm, Comm looked down, smiled, and patted Sandy's hand and looked up into the young man's face.

'It is … shameful,' he finished.

Sandy nodded, feeling the pain that Comm's face revealed, he turned and looked along the expanse of sand and surf that they had yet to explore. He turned back to Comm.

'You said that apart from the ship being broken up, there will be an auction, maybe somebody will buy you and you will be installed in a brand-new ship.' Comm suppressed a laugh.

'No, I don't think so, when we get to the auction, Griffin will be fifty-standard years-old, technology that old doesn't sell well.' Sandy frowned.

'Standard year, what's, a standard year' Comm cocked his head to his right shoulder.

'It is how we perceive time, every planet has a different rotation and orbit time, so rather than adapting to local times, we use a standard time, which is, twenty hour days, segmented into five hour work, five hour rest and ten hour sleep.' He answered with a shrug. Sandy thought on this, slowly, he nodded.

'Yes, that makes sense, but, getting back to the auction, you have to hope, you never know. Something might come up.' Comm was impressed with this young man. He had something that he had never seen in a human before. He searched for a definition, again, his search led him to chronicles written thousands of years previously – 'charisma' – that's what this boy has. He passed the information to the Med team. They were confused and asked for clarification. Comm sighed inwardly, I will state it on my debriefing, when I return.

'You have spoken about Command, on quite a few occasions. Is that your military hierarchy?' Sandy continued. Comm closed down the Med link and contemplated the question.

'No ...er ... yes, it's both, its ...' Comm was surprised, the question was simple, and yet the answer was probably the most complex he had ever dealt with. There was no answer, but surely there is an answer. 'What is Command?' He decided to re-establish the link to the Med lab team.

Sandy watched surprised as Comm's face distorted into a frozen glare, his jaw had slackened and had dropped slightly, his face now gave the expression of horror or shock.

'I'm sorry if I have offended or insulted you, I don't mean any offence.' Comm regained his composure and gently took hold of Sandy's shoulder, the smile with the perfect teeth returned.

'No, you have not offended me, Command is such a huge part of our lives, Command is everything, it just seems strange when you question it, it ... doesn't seem to have a definitive answer.' Sandy was again puzzled.

'It ...you mean 'them' don't you.'

'Them,' Comm said, a frown emerging across his face. 'There is no them,'

Sandy leant back feeling the warmth of the fine sand sift through his fingers and the warm sea as it lapped up onto his calves. It was idyllic, the sea, the sand and the sun directly overhead, bathing him in warmth, it soothed him to calmness.

'Command must be 'they',' he said at last.

'A combination of military high rankers telling the lower ranks what to do, and what to expect if they don't do it.'

Comm exploded in laughter, his eyes filling with moisture. 'No ... I'm sorry, you're so wrong,' he said through fits of chuckles and laughs.

'Command is definitely not a 'they', it is an 'it'. It's difficult, it is so entwined into our life, it gives us standards and goals, it gives us aspirations, yes, it tells us what to do and how to do it, but it also gives us rewards, once those goals have been achieved. Command is ... everything ... everything that we are, whether you are organic or synthetic or photonic, Command is the very structure of our lives, which is why it is so hard to define.'

Sandy studied the old man. He was the personification of the Griffin's control system, and, at best, he thought, just a sub routine, but the old weather-beaten sun-tanned face with the impossibly perfect teeth showed convincing emotions, expressions of seriousness, humour, sadness and now, awe.

Sandy realised that Comm wasn't just answering his questions he was excited to answer them – the answer on Command, which Sandy thought should have been the easiest for this sub routine to deal with came across with an element of pride and passion. Sandy softened his voice and smiled as he asked his next question.

'What then would happen if you did not live up to those standards. Are you punished?'

Comm thought for a while, his face blank.

'No,' he said slowly.

'Not punished, re-educated, maybe removed.'

Sandy was shocked. 'Removed, as in, eliminated,' he said quickly. Comm was physically jolted as if the young man had slapped him.

'No, no, removed, as in replaced, taken away from a situation that you possibly do not understand, re-educated then reassigned,' Comm blurted.

Sandy leant closer. 'And the people that you are at war with, they refused to be educated, is that what happened?' Sandy watched as the smile dropped from Comm's face.

Comm sat up and leant towards the younger man. Sandy instinctively recoiled and leant back from him.

'No, you are wrong. Command is our way of life. Yes, it has standards, the humans that decided eons ago to pursue a different lifestyle left us. Command was not in place at that time. We advanced to a peaceful existence: it was they who attacked us. We adopt a defensive strategy, keeping them at bay, we do however push them back to their own sector, but we never attack. I promise you Sandy, we are not the aggressors.'

Sandy re-examined the Comm link. He was part of the ship's systems, a ship that was no doubt designed and built by Command, originally as a craft of war, then later as a training vessel. Of course the Comm would be biased, it was all down to programming. He decided not to argue the point, instead he altered his seating position and relaxed. Comm also leant back. nodding his head slightly in agreement. Sandy continued.

'So, Command has not always been a part of your lives,' he said in a smooth soft voice.

Comm relaxed, whatever confrontation he was expecting had now passed, but he was surprised at why he had been so agitated. It was just a question, why had it evoked such a response from him, he had for a second felt anger. He relayed this back to the Med team, they did not respond.

'No,' he said, the smile returning. 'It has not always been a part of our lives. It came into being some ...' he stopped to activate historical records.

'About two thousand standard years ago. We had been in confrontation with the Breakaways for a few thousand years before then, skirmishes and land grabs mainly, never a full scale war, even now, the confrontations mainly involve border control, nothing, I assure you, this far out, so, we are extremely safe here. However, two thousand years ago we were losing star systems, we were being pushed back, we needed to unify, so the standards or rules were put together, standards to live and to fight for, then slowly they evolved into what we now call 'Command'.'

Sandy looked out to the horizon of his imagined world, this was all so surreal, he thought, why did he want to know so much about this ship and Command, but not about himself? He had dismissed any notion of asking of his own wellbeing and the life capsule in which he was found.

'Something else troubles you?' Comm asked, trying to gauge the younger man. 'Sandy, I am here to answer all of your questions, no matter how painful they are … well, as best as I can,' he finished with the perfect toothed smile.

Sandy stood and brushed the sand from his shirt. He glanced up at the volcano and took a deep breath.

'I feel nothing regarding myself, my memories start at the water's edge where I met you. I know nothing of my past. I don't even know who I am, and yet,' he paused and waited for his older companion to stand.

'And yet, I feel nothing, no remorse for lost family and friends, no frustration from the predicament that I am in, no fear, no anger. I should at least feel fear.'

Comm gently draped his arm around the younger's shoulder and led him back onto the white sandy beach.

'That,' he said with a sigh, 'is most probably our fault.' He stopped and turned the young man around so that they stood eye to eye. He took a deep breath and exhaled slowly. His stature drooped. Slowly shaking his head he said.

'The Med team, under my direction, has buffered out any emotional stimulus. I will allow some emotions to surface as we continue our journey, but do not worry, I will only do this if I believe it is in your best interest to do so.'

CHAPTER 3

PYRAMID OF EVIL

They were now over five kilometres away from the mantis and the bar. The scenery had not changed, one kilometre looked identical to the previous, but onwards they trudged. Sandy followed the older man two paces behind. This trek, he thought, was becoming so monotonous, he kicked at the water and laughed as he drenched Comm. Comm turned and for a while they soaked each other, both enjoying the experience of each other's play. Sandy stopped, his eyes strained to focus on the cliff, its shear wall almost vertical ascended to the vent some five hundred metres above, but, a hundred metres down the beach. Something in the landscape was different.

'What is it?' Comm asked, turning to follow his glare.

'The volcano has a sheer cliff, and it comes right out onto the beach down there.' He pointed to the outcrop further down the beach.

'That's different to what we have been seeing, I mean.' Comm did not need to follow his pointing finger. He could see the outcrop of rock. He turned to look back the way they had come. There was no diversion in the pattern of the scenery that they had walked past, only this. He turned back and strode determinedly towards the cliff. Sandy watched him 'What would they find?' he thought. He jogged towards the distant outcrop and soon caught up with Comm.

'There is something on the cliff wall,' Comm said softly. Sandy looked to the wall and could see nothing, but then small bulges became evident in the otherwise smooth surface of the cliff wall.

'Oh my ...', gasped Comm, and leapt into a run. Sandy found it difficult to keep up, but after a hundred-metre sprint almost collided with Comm as he came to a sudden halt. They both stared in disbelief at the statues that had been carved into the cliff wall. A pedestal, two metres high and half a metre in diameter, stood at beach level. At its centre a large gold embossed 'O', and standing upon it a two metre statue of Sandy. He held a scroll, unfurled, and blank, above him to his right another statue with its right foot on his shoulder, to the left another, with a foot on his left shoulder, above them three others, and above them four others, creating an inverted pyramid of statues all holding unfurled scrolls at their midriff.

'Who are they?' Sandy asked at last. He walked closer to the perfect sculpture of himself.

Comm studied them all in minute detail for some time before he commented.

'They are not the nicest of people, and it's surprising that you are among them. Or, maybe it is not surprising; we do not know exactly what you are,' he said and flashed a glance at the younger man.

Comm sat himself down leaning back on the warm sand looking up at the statues.

'They are dressed exactly as my historical data records show them, and you, at the bottom there, are dressed exactly as you are now. They all hold a scroll, with their names carved within, except you.'

Sandy sat down beside him.

'And the pedestal, the 'O', does that mean anything?'

Comm shook his head. 'I know nothing of you, but I know a lot about the others, and the 'O' does not match any cross records. This is amazing, absolutely amazing. Why, are you amongst them? They stand upon your shoulders, you hold them aloft. Hmm, perhaps, the O is not an O, but a zero, that might make sense, the pedestal is zero, you are 1, then the 2 above you, the 3 above them, and then the 4 could be some kind of code, 0,1,2,3,4.' Comm cocked his head to one side as he pondered the statues.

'Not much of a code,' Sandy interrupted.

'What about a countdown, if you read it from top to bottom,' Comm turned to him, a frown forming on his face.

'That's very astute, and, if I may say so, somewhat disturbing,' he said slowly.

'Who are they?' Sandy whispered. Comm turned to face him.

'You do not know, seriously?' Sandy slowly shook his head, Comm turned back to the statues.

'They are monsters, all of them, some of them have killed billions, others millions, in one way or another, whole civilisations have either been wiped out, or, at the very least altered, Planets in some cases have been left charred or dead. They have moulded us and destroyed us, we are what we are today because of them, but the strange thing about these statues is, they match a timeline. On the top line, the first two, were the first to appear in our history, then the next two, then the next line, and so on all the way down to you.'

'Are they tyrants, war lords?' Sandy asked in awe, looking up at the statues.

'No, some were scientists, others administrators, but billions have died because of them.' Comm turned to look at Sandy directly.

'And they all stand upon your shoulders, so, how many billions will you kill?'

Sandy felt a shiver run through him. He turned abruptly to the older man, his face a scowl.

'None, I would hope,' he growled. "I do not know these people. I have no idea why I am with them.'

Comm did not return the gaze and sat leaning back on his hands staring up at the statues.

'All this, the island, everything, is from your own mind, a mind that is empty of memory. Do you know, I am fast coming to the conclusion that all of this is being fed to you, probably from the capsule that we found you in. There can be no other explanation. It could be that all of your memories were removed and kept in storage, yet our engineers have not found any storage devices, but the fact remains, you are here, this island with all its peculiarities is here, and it all comes from you. I can assure you, I have not had any input into this place.' He then turned slowly to face the younger man.

'You, my friend, are being drip fed information, which is just as new to you as it is to all of us. The question is, why? So let's just take one step at a time, let's find that common denominator – this island, the mantis, the apple juice, this exhibit. Let's take the first two people on the top line of the statues. Can you read the names on the scrolls?'

Sandy turned his head away from the older man and looked up at the line of four.

'Sindra Chandra and Ilya Kowaski,' Sandy said slowly, squinting at the top row of statues.

'And the common denominator is,' Comm said holding his hands out expecting an answer. Sandy looked back at him with a blank face.

'Earth, we come back to Earth again. And yet, it was destroyed five thousand six hundred and twenty-five years ago,' Comm said with a frown, he raised his hand to his chin and tapped his index finger upon his cheek.

'You could not have known the Earth, our engineers say that the capsule in which you were found is only a thousand years old, though as good as our engineers are, they have been known to be wrong sometimes.'

Sandy looked back to the two statues on the first tier. 'Do you know their story, maybe, in the telling of it, I might recollect something.' Comm turned to him nodding his head.

'Yes, that's possible, but what you have to remember, is that reports, or truly accurate accounts of what happened over five thousand years ago, are to say the least, a lot of hearsay. Command, has put together a historical account of the events that took place that day, but they may not be exactly accurate. It was a very confusing time.'

Sandy shrugged his shoulders. 'I think that it's important to try,' he said trying to gauge the frown on Comm's face. Comm thought for a moment.

'There are of course, other archives, diaries, personal logs and journals of the people who were there at the time. These documents are available, but many are incomplete. But they may help to, well, to give a flavour to the events.'

Sandy turned away from the statues and faced the older man.
'Ok, I'm ready; tell their story, as best you can.'

CHAPTER 4

DISTANT PASTS

The sand below Sandy's' feet slowly congealed to become a much harder surface. In a slight panic he looked around him, the statues and the high cliff face slowly melted away, and for a few moments they were laying in a place that had no features, just a greyness that fell about them. He turned to focus on the older man, but Comm seemed to have frozen. Sandy was about to speak when slowly the structure of the beach and the cliff face reformed about them. They were now lying on the floor of a broad carpeted corridor that seemed to run for hundreds of metres in both directions, crowds of people pushing and jostling to be nearer the far wall.

'Where are we?' Sandy asked in a whisper. Slowly, Comm rose to his feet and offered a hand to Sandy, who accepted it and pulled himself up.

'This is the cruise liner 'Orion', positioned fifty kilometres from the Stella portal, which was known as the disc. These people have paid a high price to witness the first interstellar maiden voyage. What they will actually witness is the destruction of their own planet.'

Sandy felt an emotional pang. Was this, his own planet, his ancestral home, no, surely, that was impossible, but the emotion was triggered by Comm's matter of fact description of a planet being destroyed.

'Can we get closer to the observation windows?' he asked, trying to look over the crowd of at least ten deep in front of him. Comm watched amused as he jumped to try a capture a glimpse of the spectacle beyond the enormous viewing windows. He then received a report from the Med lab regarding the emotional spike that had just occurred. Sandy didn't seem to be phased by it, or he was hiding it well, but, thought Comm, this planet Earth definitely means something to him.

'We are not actually here,' Comm said, raising his voice above the drone of the hundreds of people around him. He turned and walked to the back of the pushing crowd. Without conscious thought they parted to allow him access. Sandy watched amazed at how Comm eased his way through the throbbing crowd. Shaking his head in disbelief he caught Comm up and walked alongside him to the window.

Outside the enormous observation windows of the Orion, hundreds of space craft of different sizes and shapes lay in wait above and below them, but they alone had an unbroken view.

The space portal was disc-shaped, concaved in the centre, and it glistened in the sunlight. Sandy could just make out a large ship stationed at its centre. The disc had a diameter of five kilometres. It was, he thought, a spectacular scene. To his left the blue green planet with wisps of white cloud, and just coming into view from behind the myriad of ships on the far side of the disc, the planets satellite, its moon.

Comm was in communication with the Med lab, the science technical team were asking whether Sandy would react to more of the history of the planet. Comm had argued that to go back further into the planet's history would be stretching the validity of the personal journals to their limit and could not guarantee the accuracy of any events they would witness. The Med team then argued that the violent history of this planet's past could trigger some lost memories. Comm thought this through and reluctantly he conceded, and agreed.

Sandy was leaning up against the observation window, transfixed by the spectacle. Comm leant towards him and over the drone of a thousand voices spoke into Sandy's ear.

'We are twenty minutes from the destruction; let us go back to just before the alliance unified the planet.'

Sandy turned puzzled.

'Back ... but ... I want to see what happens.'

Comm smiled.

'Let's build this story from its beginning, then through to its spectacular finale.'

Sandy turned back to the enormous observation window to look at the space portal, just as it started to dissipate. They were again in the non-place, the grey featureless world that he had experienced before. Soon features appeared, and after blinking away the brightness of a noon day sun that had just materialised around them, he realised that they were now standing on the brow of a hill looking down over a deserted, desolate place.

'These are the barren lands, two thirds of the Earth have been taken over by this wanton devastation. It was orchestrated by an organisation called the Elder House. I have very little information on who or what they were, but, before they came into being, it is reported that twenty billion people populated this planet. Two thousand years later, which is the time that we are now witnessing, the population has been reduced to just a few million, planet wide.'

Sandy surveyed the sparseness of the land.

'We are in a desert,' he said, scanning for any manufactured structure or vegetation he could focus on. He could not see any.

'Yes, it is one now,' said Comm slowly.

'We are in a place that was once quite fertile, but the overseers of the Elder House have at this time reduced people to a nomadic existence, the weather satellites in orbit have failed due to non-maintenance. As a result, the solar mirrors are fixed pointing down onto the planet's surface. over the last two thousand years the temperature has risen to create desert conditions on every land mass.'

Sandy slowly shook his head, the desolation of this burnt land was starting to awaken the realisation of the total devastation and the wanton destruction of society. He then slowly turned to face Comm.

'What is the Elder House?' Comm turned away from Sandy's inquisitive stare.

'It is a travesty that they were powerful enough to do this, and I have to apologise Sandy. The personal journals that mention this period of time are very few and far between, most of the history of this time was destroyed in the destruction of the Earth, but I think that what we will see is a reasonable account of what happened. But it will not be exact, remember, these are from the private journals of the survivors of the destruction. I have cross referenced all stories concerning the Elder House, and have come up with this one scenario, I fear it is not complete.' Sandy felt that as Comm was part of the Griffins control system he probably would not like the idea of portraying a history that may or may not have existed in this scenario. As the Com-link of a Stella cruiser he would be called upon to take on trillions of bits of information per second, this, was guessing, and Sandy felt that it would not sit right with him.

'Comm, you're doing fine, I'm sure this is as close to the truth as it could be, after all, I think all we need is a flavour of what has passed, it does not have to be perfect, so, do you know what the Elder House was?'

Comm turned back to him, a smile returning to his face.

'No, I have no reference as to what or who they were, but they ruled for over three thousand standard years. At the time we are standing here is within the last of those thousand years, the Earth is about to change.' Sandy panned his gaze from the furthest east to the furthest west.

'So, where are all the people?' he said slowly.

Comm brightened.

'There is a tribe, a few hundred kilometres away, do you wish to see how they lived?' Sandy frowned.

'Are you going to supply transport or are we walking?' Comm gave a wry smile.

'You can walk if you want, but I'm, going to fly.'

Sandy watched in astonishment as Comm soared up into the sky, arching his back and then dropping softly onto the ground in front of him. The look on Sandy's face made Comm chuckle.

'We are not here in body Sandy. All this,' he swept his arm across the desert that surrounded them, 'is just a program – think up and you will go up, think down and you will go down.' Sandy stared at him puzzled.

'You're telling me, that we can fly? Why didn't you tell me that on the island? We could have explored a lot more, and we wouldn't have had to trudge around the island hour after hour.'

'Ah yes, but ...,' Comm said slowly, 'we could have missed more than we found, we may have missed the statues.' Sandy shook his head, not fully convinced.

Comm set about teaching Sandy how to fly. After an hour or so of tuition he had the rudiments and they set off together westward.

The terrain below was just barren. It never altered. Sandy flew cautiously behind Comm watching carefully every move he made. After a while he felt more confident and started to soar higher into the sky then swooped down towards the ground, rolling and arching before he finally stopped.

'Comm,' he shouted. Comm turned and saw that he was no longer following, but standing in mid-air with his arms folded. Comm turned and flew back, concerned.

'What is it?' he demanded. Sandy stood rigidly before him.

'I feel nothing. This should be exhilarating. I should be getting a rush of adrenaline and I felt nothing. I need something. I know that somehow my feelings are being smoothed out, but I want to be able to feel something.' Comm listened to his rant. He felt that the younger man's pleas were justified, perhaps it was time, he thought, that he should receive more emotions. He contacted the science team, but at the same time spoke to Sandy.

'I agree, I think you should receive more emotional stimulus, but, for now, not too much, we do not wish to over burden you.'

Sandy looked down to the ground, some three hundred metres below him. He immediately felt sickened with vertigo.

'Yes ... yes, that's fine,' he stuttered.' Comm nodded, turned and continued his flight. Sandy followed carefully behind.

'Up ahead! look!', shouted Comm. Sandy looked towards the far horizon, a thin trail of smoke stood out upon the pale blue sky. He watched as the small village of makeshift huts came into view.

'This is what Humanity has become,' shouted Comm. Sandy stared down in disbelief. They were just skin and bone, most of the children were naked. The adults he noticed wore either rags or animal skins. Comm pointed to a hillock twenty metres to the north, Sandy followed him down.

'This is a representation of five private journals, taken from the Techno-Alliance, so, they are reasonably accurate.

'Techno-Alliance,' Sandy whispered, turning to the old man.

'It will be our next port of call, I will explain everything once we are there, but what we are seeing here is almost the extinction of the human race.' Sandy turned his attention back to the tribe. They accounted for about twenty individuals. Three females tended the fire, one stirring a blackened pot that straddled the flames. Further away he could see adult males butchering a small animal, some children looked on eagerly, they all looked starved, this was possibly their first proper meal in a month. The animal was more likely to have been found dead than hunted, Sandy thought. They just didn't seem to have the strength for any hunting activities. Comm tapped Sandy on the shoulder, then indicated the valley between two hillocks some one hundred metres away.

'This next part of the story is taken from one journal. If true, it shows how brutal this life is.'

Sandy looked to the dust cloud to the east of the village that Comm was pointing out to him. He could make out animals within the dust. As they drew closer, he could see they were horses and they were being ridden.

'These are the overseers. They are from the Elder House,' Comm said softly.

'Have they come to help?' asked Sandy, hesitantly. Comm turned to him.

'That's very naïve ... no, they have come to collect taxes.'

The horsemen surrounded the small gathering of the village. They branded whips with barbed ends. Sandy noticed that each rider had ancient daggers and cleavers hanging loosely from their roped belts: The only technology that had survived from a people that had once been the space farers that had put the weather satellites into orbit, thousands of years ago. He watched as they separated the men and children from the females. Sandy then looked on in horror, as the women were subjected to beatings from four of the overseers. One of the male villagers found the courage to step forward and pushed one of the attackers to the ground. The overseers on horseback burst into laughter at their comrade's misfortune, but the merriment was short lived. Two other horsemen pulled the courageous villager back and they whipped him into unconsciousness.

Sandy had to turn away as the poor man's body was ripped to shreds. He fell, and the dry barren land hungrily drank in the free-flowing blood from the fallen hero. When Sandy turned back to the horror, he watched as the incensed overseer that had been pushed to the ground stumbled to his feet. He then attacked one of the women that had been tending the pot on the fire and ripped at her tattered clothing that fell to pieces as he clawed his hands over her. With her breasts bare he fell upon her and as she fell into the fire she frantically fought back, trying desperately to pull herself out of the intense heat, her screams and flailing punches only spurred the other overseers into a frenzy of howls and screeches to jeer their comrade on. As she pulled herself out of the flames, they beat her with their staffs, pushing her back into the thermal hell. A couple of the younger men of the tribe that were being held back by the now incensed and chant-driven psychopaths, found some deep anger that surfaced into pure brutality. It was short lived as they were beaten to their knees and what life they cherished left without looking back. The overseer that had originally been thrown to the ground, now on top of the bucking and writhing woman brutally raped her. But her ordeal was far from over, spurred on by the act, his comrades then took it in turns to hold down the now submissive woman as they all ravaged her.

Sandy turned his head away, sickened at the sight.

'Comm, that's enough, please, I don't want to see any more,' he shouted, but the shout was almost a hysterical sob, and the woman's screams throbbed in his mind.

The image before him vanished. They were once again in the grey non-place. Sandy felt sickened and buried his head in his hands.

Comm was once again arguing with the science team. They had wanted to smooth away his emotion and Comm had argued that it was these emotional spikes that may give an insight as to who this man was. He had won his argument and now turned to Sandy.

'We will take a rest; I think we need to re-evaluate.'

The greyness faded, shapes appeared: They were standing in a cavern, an ice cavern, crowds of people moving in a determined path, not rushing, yet motivated. He sensed that they needed to be somewhere other than where they were. The rape of the woman from the small family tribe still conveyed horrific images to his mind. He felt weak and almost stumbled. Comm took his arm and led him to a bench situated at the side of a large thoroughfare.

'Where are we now?' Sandy stammered, looking down the length of the cavern which covered some five hundred metres. He noticed buildings protruding from the ice walls, people moving at a pace to get from one place to another. Above him small vehicles hovered silently past.

'Just catch your breath, relax awhile. We are a thousand years before the destruction and three standard days after the vicious attack of the family tribe. Only two of them survived, an adolescent boy and a young girl, just a toddler really. They hid for weeks until they eventually were found. They were lucky, especially when we find out what happens next. It was the young boy's story that was put into print and that journal is the basis of the scenario that we have just witnessed. Do you have any recollection of the sights that we have seen, any at all, no matter how small?' Sandy shook his head.

'No, none.' He looked about him, from one end of the cavern to the other.

'The people here seem ... panicky,' he said, almost dreamily, still trying to rid his memory of the images from the previous scenario.

'Yes, yes, they are, they have lived in these caverns for generations, just over two thousand years. These are the Techno-Alliance: When the Elder House came to power their laws were quite simple – do as we say or die. Death was quick and, in most cases, public. A few however, banded together and stood up to them but they could not win.

the Elder House influence was everywhere, the Alliance was easily infiltrated and in a lot of instances their resistance cells were compromised and they were made an example of. So, they retreated, year after year they moved south, other groups joined them. I do not have specific documentation of this era – just a footnote from a command publication – why they were not just permanently removed. I have no idea, the Elder House at this time were definitely strong enough. Whether they were herded or chased, we will never know, all we do know is that they ended up in the frozen wastes of the southern pole. With the technology that they had brought with them they carved a home, until today, today is when they fight back. Many journals mention this day in some detail, they call it ...'

'The swarm,' Sandy whispered. Comm spun around, cutting off the communication from the science team.

'You know it!' He held the younger man by the shoulders and looked deep into his eyes.

'What do you know of this, Sandy? It's important.'

'All I know is that they left this place, and retook the land, and those that stood before them were destroyed, totally destroyed.'

'And how do you know this? Is it a memory? Were you here?' Sandy looked away from him.

'I don't know, I don't think I was here. I think it was a story.' He turned back to Comm.

'I'm sorry, it was just a flash, a fragment, just the word "swarm" came into my mind.' Comm glared into the young man's eyes, trying to look deep within, into the mind of this fascinating individual. Is it the truth that he speaks or a script that he is unknowingly adhering to. The elderly Com-link could not tell.

'It's a start, we have something that we did not have before. We can build on it.' Comm let him go and sat relaxed beside him. The science team conveyed that a memory had arisen where before there had been nothing.

'It is curious that a mind that is completely void of anything, can create, and now, all of a sudden, remember,' Comm communicated back to the science team. 'I still believe he is being fed with information.'

'So why now?' Sandy asked, watching the populace rushing from one place to another. Comm turned slowly towards him, and noticed that he had calmed considerably. He followed his stare, to the people that gave them no notice, just rushing past, determined to get to where they should be.

'It is their time. This is the time that they reclaim their world.'

'But why now, after two thousand years or so?' Sandy asked again.

'The journals, diaries and historical records of the time say that five years previous to where we are now, they had discovered the gravitational beam, a mass of energy that could be manipulated to increase or decrease a gravitational force. This beam, was refined to become an energy field which would eventually make Stella flight possible, but at the moment, they would use it as a defence shield. Oh, and at that time they also developed the first obliterator.' Sandy turned to face the older man. With a puzzled expression, he added, 'Energy field, obliterator.' Comm smiled.

'These people had nothing but their technology. Slowly over the generations that technology had been refined. When the energy field was discovered and they found that they could manipulate it, some used the technology to coat the surface of the cavern, which stopped the many cave-ins, and of course heat loss. Some used it to seal the entrance, others to create the first anti-gravity vehicles, those that you see passing us now, Sandy looked up to the underside of four vehicles as they passed.

'And the obliterators?' Sandy asked, bringing his gaze down to the old man.

'They were developed from the graviton beam, a tool to create new caverns for expansion. It scattered the atoms of anything the beam touched. It was very quickly developed into a weapon.'

Sandy scanned the cavern, the almost silent hovering vehicles, the structures that were seemingly impossibly fixed to the curving heights of the cavern walls, the clothing that the people wore. He scrutinised them all as they passed him by.

'The Elder House had no technology, just whips and ancient daggers, how did they manage to keep these people imprisoned for so many generations? I mean this society is thousands of years more advanced.' Comm followed Sandy's gaze around the cavern, turned to face him, and with a smile shrugged.

'I just do not have enough recorded information to share. I admit, it does seem ridiculous, but, if I were to surmise, the Elder House had one weapon that these people do not possess, and that is, fear, and I mean absolute fear and terror.'

He turned to the enormous cavern entrance some two hundred metres to his left. Sandy followed his stare.

'It has started, hasn't it?' Sandy asked softly, almost in a whisper.

'Yes, hundreds of thousands of them will leave this place and they will destroy everything. The Elder House will crumble in three days, the Techno-Alliance will show no mercy. In just over a year the only people on this planet will be the Techno-Alliance and some of the less fortunate, the Elder House and all that it stood for will crumble before them, including most of the tribes that they encounter. So great was their bloodlust that they allowed almost nothing to survive, they will then make their home on the land masses within the southern hemisphere. The deserts will once again be fertile, great cities will rise, and in a thousand years, it will all be gone.'

Comm stood and turned to Sandy.

'These are bad times Sandy, but ...' He panned his arms around the cavern.

'For all these people, these bad times are over, but we must continue our journey. I am taking you to five years before this planet's demise.'

The ice walls of the cavern seemed to melt out of existence; they found themselves back in the grey non place.

CHAPTER 5

SANDY WHO?

They were on a large hill to the east of an enormous lake. Waterfalls fell hundreds of metres to the great expanse of water below. Islands protruded from its surface, all of them lush with vegetation, even the surrounding hills. From their vantage point, Sandy could see that this was a highly fertile land, north and south of the great lake as far as he could see, greens, yellows pinks and whites of the flowering trees and shrubs, it was in stark contrast to the deserts and ice caves that they had just departed.

'They have achieved much in the short time they have had here,' Comm said admiringly as he looked out over the great lake.

'There are ninety islands on that lake, all inhabited and farmed. All that fresh water and all these farmlands contribute to the incredible wealth of this scientific society. Now, turn around and look eastward to the ocean.' They turned and Sandy gasped, all around them a great city radiated out to the east north and south.

The city was laid in a grid formation, and had a symmetry that was pleasing to the eye; from the suburbs Sandy could see that the buildings were no more than four or five stories, but as the metropolis converged into the centre the buildings grew in height, to what seemed like a staggering five hundred levels above ground. Comm stretched out his arms.

'This, is the city of ...'

'Technopolis,' Sandy said. Comm turned to him, shocked.

'You know of it,' Comm asked, his voice almost a whisper. He had heard the inflection of awe in Sandy's voice.

'I am pretty sure that I have been here. It doesn't feel like some story that I've heard or been fed.' He turned to Comm, and pointed towards the city.

'I remember walking through those streets. I remember … – No. I … it's gone.' He turned back to the city, trying to recapture the memory that was now eluding him.

'Comm. for a moment, I remembered.'

Comm was in full communication with the science team, multiple memory spikes had emerged, and then, as quickly as they appeared, they had vanished.

'He is being controlled,' Comm argued.

'As soon as he gets a personal memory, it is taken away. You have to give him more stimuli … yes, I'm sure he can handle it.' Comm gently turned the younger man by the shoulder.

'Sandy, try not to dwell on that memory too much, I have altered your emotional stimulus, it may come back to you later.'

'I remember this smell, I think it is magnolia, and there is a hint of pine.'

Comm looked confused. 'Sandy, what we are a part of here, is an image within an image, locked into a scenario, designed around the information stored in historical accounts … there are no smells that are detectable to me. However, the scenario has been built within your own imagination. I suppose it is possible that you can detect the aromas around us, but I am afraid I cannot.'

Sandy smiled and tapped his temple with his fore finger.

'I know that the smell is in here; this place is so familiar, I feel I have spent a lot of time here, and it is sad that you can't smell the sweetness that surrounds us.' He turned to survey the great expanse of the city.

'And I am sure that I have spent years here,' he said softly.

Comm pondered this last statement.

'There is somewhere we need to go,' he said casually.

'There is an event that takes place every five standard years, and it happens today. It is about a hundred kilometres from here; we'll fly, it will take us about an hour.'

Without waiting for any reply, Comm took off following the path that led down the hill towards Technopolis.

They had flown through the suburbs and had marvelled at the open gardens. The opulence of the flora was stunning.

They landed a couple of kilometres from the city centre and walked on through the open markets. Sandy stopped a few times to investigate the stalls, a thrilled expression on his face at the fare that the stall holders had to offer. On these occasions, Comm stood back and observed.

'Do you recognise these things?' he asked on one occasion, when Sandy had spent more time than he had on any other stall. Comm studied the two-metre-long furry and flexible tube.

'Tellemyerias,' Sandy stated, smiling awkwardly. Comm frowned, then raised his eyebrows.

'It's a toy: I remember them from my childhood. There is a head set that you place across your temples. This will enable you to control the Myerias in flight. They soared around the buildings. You could get them to dance in the air, turning this way and that, and depending on the direction and speed they would change colour, and the colours would shimmer in the sun light.' Sandy turned away from the stall and beamed a smile.

'My friends and I would have fun for hours, I remember that so vividly.' Comm smiled and nodded.

'It will all come back Sandy, I am sure of it.'

They continued past the stall holders, then into the entertainment sector, theatres, and holographic museums, in amongst restaurants and street entertainers that filled the plazas. The whole district was amassed with an excited populace. Sandy was now well adept at dealing with the heaving crowds and walked through them without a care.

'I remember this place, I remember this place very well.' He span on his heel 360 degrees. Comm looked on, fascinated. The Med lab science team were demanding that the stimuli be turned down. Comm had refused and had overridden the Med team by increasing its sensitivity.

Sandy stopped mid spin and walked towards a restaurant.

'Oh, wow,' he breathed.

'Comm,' he called, not looking around, but Comm was soon by his side.

'What do you remember,' Comm asked softly.

'It was here. I was a younger man and she was beautiful, Lien, yes, that was her name, Lien. That night was the night to remember.' Comm noticed that his eyes were glazed and a strange smile remained fixed across his face. Sandy slowly turned back to Comm. The smile slowly faded.

'It couldn't have happened at this time, not five years before the destruction, that's five and a half thousand years ago. Comm, what is it that I am remembering?'

Comm pulled him gently from the restaurant entrance and guided him away. They walked silently for a while.

Comm led him away from the entertainment district, they walked silently through empty alleyways, the buildings had changed, these were now designed for loans and investment. They carried on through into the main finance sector. The crowds had thinned to almost non-existent. Up ahead lay their destination – the science and technology centre.

'Five thousand six-hundred and thirty years,' Comm repeated to the Med lab science team. For the last ten minutes as they had walked silently through the financial district, Comm had been in communication. This revelation of Sandy's vivid memory had astounded all of them, Comm included.

'I will carry the scenario on to its conclusion, but we now desperately need the engineers report on the life capsule, especially its age. I am sure they are wrong at a thousand years.'

'We are going to the great hall, aren't we, to the science assessment?' Sandy said casually, recognising the area they were walking through.

The buildings were much higher here, and the architecture had a more scrolled effect – the architect was obviously trying to emulate an ancient Greek theme.

Comm nodded slowly.

'Yes Sandy, we are here to witness something important, something, very important.'

They walked into the grand plaza, the crowds stumbled from one side to the other. They heeded none of them, just walking directly towards the fifty-metre wide marble stair that would take them to the entrance of the Grand Hall, home, of the High Chancellor of science.

'My name is not Sandy,' the younger man said slowly.

'It's Damian, I am … Damian Drake.'

Comm stopped abruptly and turned to him in one movement. He noticed the sadness on the young man's face.

'Are you sure, your name is Damian Drake? What made you th … .' Part of the crowd passed between them. One person stopped to marvel at the Grand Hall's entrance. Comm pushed him aside, another replaced him.

'Enough,' Comm shouted. Everything stopped, people all around them froze, the constant buzz of noise from the crowded plaza ceased, a deathly silence prevailed. Comm evaluated the situation, the fresh data required a billion routines to be run, Damian … Drake … historical accounts of the time spoke of six thousand Damian's, eight thousand Drakes, one thousand six hundred Damian Drakes. He widened the time parameters, never certain of the accuracy of the report itself, cross-referenced with personal accounts, journals and private logs. Most Damian Drakes were accounted for. Fifty were not, none however spoke of putting one of them into a life capsule. The Med lab science team were insisting that the scenarios be halted until this new information could be investigated further.

Comm rejected that:

'Command must be informed.' Came the final demand.

'All the information, is already being sent to Command. It is up to Command to reply,' Comm answered abruptly.

'We will continue.' Comm finished.

Comm sat on the marble steps, and gestured to the young man to sit beside him. Damian stood there, bemused at the frozen multitude around him. Comm turned to him and smiled.

'So, you know your name, what made you think of it?' he said as calmly as he could.

'Lien, that night in the restaurant, the girl, so pretty, it was a wonderful night, I remember, she called my name, her voice as smooth as silk, and then here in the plaza, after our meal, we walked, we stopped here, right here, and we kissed, oh, Comm, I felt so good, and then, that name, my name, it sent a shiver through me. I feel that it is not a good name, but I don't know why. You said to me on the island, when we were at the statues, how many billions will I kill … have I already killed them? I feel …'

'Ok stop … calm, calm now, I can find nothing in any history where you have been involved.'

'Maybe not under the name Damian Drake, but maybe, under another.' Comm desensitised the emotional stimuli, Damian calmed down and relaxed. What he said was true, he could have caused atrocities under an alias, or, was Damian Drake an alias, but, at this stage all of that was just supposition. He had to find the facts, and he thought the facts were in these scenarios.

Damian leant back on the step and took a deep breath.

'It was here, right here,' he turned to face Comm.

'I remember we were going to the great hall. She had stopped behind me. "Damian", she had said softly. I remember stopping four maybe five steps up from where we are sitting. I turned to face her, she had a strange look, not stern, but not amused either. "I love you", she said, her eyes glassing over, the lights of the plaza reflecting within them, that statement, or rather admission, for a second took my breath away and then, this surge of elation, I could feel my heart pounding, I ran down the stairs and held her in my arms, we kissed, here, right here, where we're sitting.'

Comm studied his facial expressions, the over-animated arm gestures, the inclinations of pitch in his voice, and at the same time he was also listening to the various reports from the science team.

'Yes, I am aware,' he insisted to them.

'I have de-sensitized his emotional stimuli, but it doesn't seem to be having much effect. I will intervene.' Damian was now standing, staring down to the plaza, his breathing had increased.

"Sandy, Damian, calm now, stop, just, calm down.' He stood and took him by his shoulders, then gently pulled him close, held him tight and within the hug whispered.

'This is thousands of years ago, you couldn't possibly have been here then, your mind is playing tricks, but it is good that you are starting to remember something. We just have to put these new memories of yours into the right context. It will take some time.'

He concentrated on the younger man's breathing, slower now, within his grip Damian's muscles relaxed, he slowly released him, Damian, glassy eyed, nodded.

'I'm fine, sorry, it all came at me in one hit, it was just too much.' Comm moved away from him.

'Do you wish to stop this now? We can finish it here, right now if you want, pick it up another time. There is no rush.'

Damian looked around the plaza, the crowds frozen in mid-step, the pulsating lights giving off an eerie glow, semi illuminating the frontage of the High Chancellor's palace. He felt calm now, a feeling of embarrassment flooded through him.

'I'm so sorry Comm, of course we must go on. I know you think that I may not be handling these memories very well, but I assure you, I was here, right here on this spot.'

Comm stared at him his face expressionless, he closed his eyes momentarily then turned and looked up at the ornate frontage of the High Chancellor's Palace.

Comm thought this through for a moment ... the science team were insisting that the memory was genuine, as was the emotion, but Comm wasn't sure. It could have been a memory, a true memory, but it could have been misplaced, a memory fed to him by someone or something. "As this scenario blossoms," he thought, "other memories may be triggered." The more data he received from this strange young man the more evidence he would gain, and then the truth will be out.

'That will eventually be determined,' he said turning to Damian.

'But for now, as you wish to continue, we are here to witness something very important.' He turned and resumed his journey up the marble steps. The crowd lurched in all directions as they became unfrozen in time. Damian followed. Halfway up the flight, he stopped momentarily, turned and glanced down the stair. It was a wonderful memory, he thought.

Comm had reached the top of the marble staircase and through the crowds that oozed from one side to the other on the great stair caught glimpses of Damian as he tried to battle his way through.

'Yes, he is okay ... no, I will not de-sensitize him. He needs the stimulation of these events if we are to awaken his dormant memories, as, I might add, has been proved,' Comm finished the communication with the Med lab as Damian reached the top step.

The high Chancellor's Hall stood majestic in its dominant position over the plaza below, its ornate frontage depicting in delicate carved marble sculptures of past technology. It loomed up into the evening sky, the top of the building lost beyond the glare of the floodlights that bathed the frontage in a warm yellow light: In front of them the huge double doors created from a multitude of wood with carvings of the journey that their society had taken from the time of the swarm. Above sat the lintel, fashioned from material found in the Elder House that was stolen from Humanity, and above that, the stained circular window fifty metres in diameter, the images within depicting the journey into space and the colonisation of the home worlds. Above the glare of the lights Damian knew, sat a Crystal dome, the largest ever built, it dominated the structure and could be seen from one horizon to the other.

Once inside, the crowd heaved as one. Damian, on more than one occasion, lost sight of Comm. He walked positively towards the crowd. It tried to part for him but there was nowhere it could part into, and so stayed stubbornly gelled together. Comm had disappeared again and this time did not re-emerge. After a few minutes Damian had lost his sense of direction. He was within the flow of the people just being taken from one side to another, now completely disorientated.

'These are just images,' he thought.

'And I am just an image within them, I am not here. 'Up,' he thought, 'UP'. Slowly he rose above them and from this perspective he could take in the vastness of the hall, it was overwhelming.

'Comm.' he shouted trying to pitch his voice above the cacophony of noise that thirty thousand eager people were making. Just to his left a figure slowly ascended from the heaving crowd.

'Why are there so many people here?' Damian shouted, his voice swallowed by the crowd. Comm floated towards him and stopped two metres from him. He surveyed the sway of bodies below him.

'This is assessment day. It happens only once every five standard years. These people Sandy, do not have a deity to worship. For the techno alliance, all religion stopped with the rise of the Elder House, but they have their science, their technology, this is all that matters to them, nothing else does, and on this day the best scientists, engineers or technicians can show their achievements, their inventions, and be given the ultimate prize, the golden star, a free grant allowing the winner to put into production whatever the invention is, without exception. It is a highly acclaimed award, fiercely fought for, and that is why people travel all across the planetary system to be here. Well, for that and procreation.'

Damian turned to face the old man, a smile forming on his face. 'Procreation,' he said slowly, not sure that he had heard correctly over the drone of the enormous crowd below. Comm showed no emotion in his face.

'Sandy,' Comm started, then stopped and thought.

'I know you said your name is Damian, but, I have got used to calling you Sandy, do you mind if I continue calling you Sandy.' Damian slowly nodded.

'I don't mind at all Comm, in fact, having a nickname kind of bonds us together.' He said with a smile.

'So, Sandy, we have just jumped a thousand standard years. At the time of the swarm the Human populace of this planet numbered in hundreds of millions, in the space of one thousand years the population has swelled to five billion, and the reason for that, was that once a stable society had been established, the law makers decreed that every woman that bears a child would be compensated and generously rewarded. It was not unknown, in fact quite common, according to personal diaries, for women to pay men in the street to copulate there and then. It was however frowned upon, but, not illegal, and here, with so many to choose from, it was extremely common.'

Damian stared at him, bemused.

'Well, I know my memory is fragmented. but I don't remember any of that going on.'

'Well, it is very well documented, not only in private journals but official ones too.' Damian stared at him in disbelief and sniggered, slowly shaking his head and looking down at the crowd below.

'It is here we will meet Chandra and Kowaski, the first two of the statues from the island. We must find them,' Comm said in a matter-of-fact tone. Damian scanned the length and width of the Great Hall. It would almost be impossible to trace them, even flying above them.

'This is just a scenario, Comm. Do you really require all these people to be a part of your important event?' Comm re-evaluated the situation.

'Not all of them are required for the event itself, but it is a true depiction from the journals and documents of the time.' Damian averted his search of the crowd and turned to face Comm.

'Then if we don't need them, remove them.' Comm looked horrified.

'But it would not be a true account of the historical events,' Comm argued.

'It doesn't matter. The crowds are irrelevant if they are not part of the event, so, let's make this easy. You have brought me here to witness some important event. I can't witness it if I can't see it. Look, if it makes it easier for you, I will imagine hordes of people around me, but, well, at least get rid of some of them.'

Comm conceded the argument, the crowds beneath them thinned out.

"I have reduced them to fifty percent, but no less.' Damian scanned the hall.

'That's better, at least we can walk around now.' They floated down to the floor, and although the hall was busy, they found traversing through the crowd much easier.

CHAPTER 6

CHANDRA AND KOWASKI

At the far end of the hall, they found the Grand Chancellor's stairway. It rose majestically to the upper levels. It would be here that the High Chancellor would make his entrance. Comm strode towards it. Damian struggled to keep up. They passed many stalls that were set up in what seemed a haphazard manner around the perimeter of the hall. Different types of scientific paraphernalia had been placed upon them. Damian wanted to stop but Comm ushered him on and they bypassed them all.

Comm stopped and pointed to a group of men and women who moved from one stall to the other. They were scrutinising the scientific fare on offer and questioning the stall holder. Damian could see the panic welling up on the face of one of the hopeful stall holders as questions were fired at her in quick succession.

'The spotters are already out,' Comm said in a whisper.

'In fact, they would have been out since early morning watching the stalls being set up. To them this is profoundly serious. It will be their decision that determines who gets the award.' He turned and walked to the right-hand side of the enormous staircase.

'Three groups of spotters, I notice, have been very interested in this.'

He pointed to a long bench that had been erected beside the stairway. Damian looked up to the top of the stairs then panned his sight down to the long bench, a prime position to attract the Chancellor's attention.

The bench stretched down the hall for a hundred metres and at the end by the foot of the stairway a young woman was adjusting the fragile apparatus that covered two metres of her end of the bench. Between the bench and the outer wall of the

Grand Hall was a holographic projection of a young man busying himself with the apparatus a hundred metres away at the far end of the bench.

Damian focused on the young woman. She was putting the final adjustments to a large disc, a scaled down version of the orbiting disc Damian had witnessed orbiting the planet from the observation windows of the space liner Orion.

Comm had noticed the surprised look and recognition on Damian's face.

'This is the prototype.' Comm said softly.

'This is where it all started, and this,' he said, pointing to the woman, is Sindra Chandra.' He stopped to watch Damian's expression.

'Do you recognise her?' he asked. Damian studied the girl. She was in her mid-twenties with long blue-black hair that cascaded over her shoulders. Her face was unblemished and smooth and had a look of innocence. For a second, he thought something was familiar, and took a breath to examine his thoughts, but then, nothing. She was a stranger, he did not know her.

Comm was in communication with the Med team. He did not need them to tell him the obvious. He had seen the look of recognition, fleetingly though it had been, but it was there.

'No,' Damian said in a matter-of-fact tone.

'Apart from the statue of course,' he added.

Comm turned to the holo projection.

'And what of him. He is Ilya Kowaski.'

Damian took his gaze away from Chandra and focused on the image of Kowaski. He had an instant feeling of recognition of a face from a distant past.

'Yes, I … no, I don't know him. I thought I did just for a second, but then … no, I don't know him.'

The Med lab team communicated their findings to Comm.

'He knows them both,' he communicated back.

'You need to concentrate on what is blocking these emotions. It can only be the capsule. Get the engineering team to take it to bits, down to its molecular structure if necessary. Something doesn't want us to know something. I feel this is becoming serious.' Comm turned to Damian, he noticed the intensity on his face as he scrutinised Chandra.

'So, you don't know either of them?' Comm's voice was soft, yet strong and demanding the truth.

'I thought just for a second that I knew them, but then, nothing.' Damian walked over to the young woman's side. He knew she could not sense his presence but he kept a respectable distance away. He studied her from front to back, but to no avail, she was still a stranger to him. Comm turned and glanced up the stair as the crowd cheered.

'Sandy, leave her, we need to watch from a distance. Come back here!' There was urgency in his voice. Damian looked around, the crowd were applauding and cheering. He could see Comm standing on the third step of the stairway, beckoning him to join him, Damian reluctantly moved away from Chandra and made his way to Comm's side.

'Just watch what unfolds,' Comm said, as Damian reached him.

'There.' Damian followed Comm's pointed finger. A procession had formed at the top of the stairs, consisting of, as Damian guessed, the High Chancellor, various aides, the city councillors and a fluttering of spotters, each spotter whispering directions to the science stall that they championed.

To a fanfare from invisible players, the High Chancellor and his entourage descended. The crowds on the stairway parted and bowed as the great man passed. A few minutes later he stood a metre from Damian's shoulder, stopped then panned his view around the Great Hall. For a moment he stared straight at Damian. Damian knew that he could not see him, and that he was looking at Chandra as she put the final touches to the delicate mechanisms that powered the disc. The entourage moved on and made their way to the far side of the hall. Damian wondered how the actual day would have fared with the full extent of the crowds being present.

'He will check each stall in turn, some politely, just going through the motions. It all depends on the feedback that was given by the spotters. Others however, he will have a genuine interest in,' Comm said as they watched the entourage move from stall to stall.

'How many will he see before Chandra's.' Damian asked.

'Hers will be the last, I believe, from the journals. That this will be done on purpose.' Damian turned to the old man, giving him a quizzical look.

'You mean he has already made his decision.' Comm shrugged.

'The spotters have, the rest is just theatre, as I said earlier. The winner will win the most precious of prizes: the golden star. It is a key, it gives admission to all departments of the science fraternity, no one could refuse the holder of a golden star's request. The recipients of this highly claimed prize will want for nothing. On top of that financially they will be solvent, but more than just the finance, is the power it will bring. The winner will be treated like a god. But those that do not win the golden star, but are close, will also get recognition.' Comm turned away from the stunned look on Damian's face and calculated the journey time of the entourage from stall to stall. 'Two hours, forty-five standard minutes.' He said, as he turned back to face Damian.

'I'm going to speed things up a bit,' he said, almost to himself.

The hall flickered in Damian's vision, patches of greys and whites resonated around him, almost turning back to the grey non-place. He stepped back taking a deep gasp, the Chancellor's entourage appeared before him.

'This is science delegate Sindra Chandra and her colleague, Ilya Kowaski,' the senior spotter whispered into the Chancellor's ear.

'From ?' the Chancellor whispered back. The senior spotter glared into the mid distance, blood draining from his face.

'Er ... they, er. they are off-worlders, from ...'. He turned and looked imploringly at Chandra, who in turn had cocked her head and was beginning to smile at his discomfort, but this was far too important for games. The smile vanished as quickly as it had appeared. 'Europa,' she said, the smile reappearing.

'The Ice world,' the Chancellor said with admiration.

Comm leant over to Damian, there was no need to whisper, the group in front of them could neither see nor hear them, but he whispered anyway.

'No, she isn't. There are no accounts of either of their names on Europa or anywhere else for that matter.' He turned away from Damian and moved closer to Chandra, his face almost touching hers.

'It's as if you just turned up from nowhere. No records of you or your friend in any journal.'

'Must be from somewhere,' Damian interrupted.

Comm turned away from her to look directly at the young man.

'Well of course they are from somewhere. I was hoping that you would be able to tell us where,' he said indignantly. Damian studied the frustrated frown on Comm's face. He shrugged and shook his head apologetically, then turned his attention back to the Chancellor. Chandra was explaining the disc's function.

'Using the properties found in the graviton energy beam, we found we can cut through the levels of space time. Once under the levels of the space continuum, we found that we could create a wave on which a mass could, well, surf, I suppose would be a good enough analogy, and we just surf to a predestined co-ordinance.' She flashed a smile that was not lost on the High Chancellor.'

'The material mass that is placed aside the disc does not actually move. It is space time that … well, washes over it.' The Chancellor nodded slowly.

'Yes, yes, I have of course heard these theory's many times in various different forms. The study of Quantum events tell us that it is possible, and my spotter informs me that you claim to have succeeded.' Chandra let loose the smile again.

'Yes sir, we have completed many successful runs. Our apparatus is all set and ready to go. I just need an object to send.' The smile turned to a smile of innocence. She diverted her gaze to his right hand.

'Maybe something unique, like the ring of the High Chancellor,' she said, continuing the smile.

'Anything else could be seen as a conjuring trick or an illusion,' she continued. The entourage gasped as one, the Chancellor looked down to the ring of science, sitting tightly on the middle finger of his right hand, a ring of gold, silver and platinum, housing a sphere of pure diamond. Since his investiture some thirty years previous he had rarely removed it. He toyed with it now, turning it slowly around the finger. All the while he stared deep into Chandra's eyes. The smiles on both faces disappeared.

With a slight grimace he pulled the ring from the finger then offered it to her on an open palm. She reached out slowly but his hand clamped shut. He took her shoulder with his free hand and pulled her towards him and whispered something into her ear. Damian could see that she was visibly shocked, but then the hand opened, and he took her hand and slowly placed the ring into her palm.

'What did he say to her?' Damian spluttered, turning to Comm.

'There is no record of what he actually said, lots of speculation. Some journals say that he threatened her life, others that he just wished her luck. We will never know.' Damian turned back just as Chandra was placing the ring on a small platform at the centre of the one metre diameter disc.

'The bench is one hundred metres long.' She narrated whilst completing some final adjustments. She looked up at the holo projection of Kowaski, nodded to him and he returned the nod.

'I need to use the gravity beam to create an inertia,' she said leaning forward to adjust another set of controls. A milky white shimmer flickered to life five metres downstream of the disc. The disc distorted slightly and the ring vanished. Almost instantly Kowaski's image held it up for all to see.

'One hundred metres, in less than a billionth of a second, and now for the return journey, Ilya will send it back.'

'No,' yelled the Chancellor, startling the crowd that had gathered to watch.

'I apologise, but I have seen too many charlatans in this city.' He turned and ordered the senior spotter to retrieve the ring from Kowaski. The spotter ran the full length of the bench,

Kowaski held out his arm palm turned uppermost, upon it the Chancellor's ring, The spotter took it without stopping. On his return the entourage gathered around him to inspect it, passing it from one to the other. The Chancellor turned to Chandra.

'They will take some time in inspecting the ring, and your equipment, but I am impressed. If you have truly achieved this, I would like to see a much larger demonstration.'

Comm walked over to Damian and led him away. The image flickered, and for a moment as it faded away Damian thought he saw a smirk appear on Chandra's face.

The image changed to a crowded observation deck on the Cruiser Orion.

'It is now three hours before destruction.' Comm said, as he made his way through the crowds to the observation windows. Damian followed, now adept at walking through the multitudes. Comm noticed the frown forming on the young man's face.

'If you have a question, then ask it,' Comm prompted.

'We left here when it was only twenty minutes to destruction, why do we now have to wait three hours?' Comm smiled.

'Chandra gave the science faculty her "larger demonstration". It was held on a long island southeast of the mainland. She and Kowaski set up a much larger disc and transported the Chancellor's own private shuttle a thousand kilometres from one end of the island to the other. Another perfect success, but there were some within the Chancellery who didn't quite accept the authenticity of the experiment. As I said, there was a lot at stake, an enormous amount of power and prestige would be handed to Chandra and Kowaski in the form of the prize, so, Chandra herself said at the review meeting that followed, that they would send a craft to the star system Alpha Centauri A, and that she and Kowaski would pilot it. This still, did not satisfy the sceptics, and so she proposed another larger demonstration before they attempted the interstellar flight, and that, is what we are here to witness.' He turned to Damian, and holding him by his shoulders gently propelled him through the observation window into the Cosmos beyond. Damian panicked, he was in space, wearing no protection, and drifting away from a laughing Comm.

'Remember, you are an image within an image, none of this is real. Move as you did when we were in the desert.'

Comm turned and moved towards the huge disc. Damian fought his senses for control. Slowly he came to terms with the environment and propelled himself towards the disappearing Comm. He marvelled at the sight that surrounded him, the shimmering blue white globe of the planet below his feet, the huge disc that reflected a myriad of different colours, then, just coming into view from behind the disc Chandra's ship, Discovery. It slowed and took up station to the side of the disc. Damian span around slowly, thousands of ships of different sizes and shapes lay in wait. Orion, being in the most prominent position, stood out from them all.

'They are all ready to witness an event that will shock them to their core and send Humanity on a completely different path of destiny,' Comm shouted back to him.

Damian had caught up with Comm and the pair stood motionless, taking in the impossible scene that surrounded them.

'You can see that the disc at this time is pointing in a completely different direction to what it was the last time we were here. It is in fact aligned with the Saturn moon Titan. Every six standard months a cargo vessel departs from Earth laden with cargo for the two million inhabitants, and ...' said Comm turning, then pointing over Damian's shoulder. 'The Chancellor insisted that Chandra transports it to Titan.'

Damian followed Comm's pointing finger, at the edge of the planet's eastern horizon a dark shadow appeared. Damian glared at the dark apparition as it made its way towards them. Slowly he could make out details on the ship's hull, but even from this distance it was ridiculously huge, easily three times the size of Orion.

'Goliath,' Comm exclaimed with admiration. 'The largest cargo vessel ever built. Two kilometres long, seven hundred metres wide and three hundred high. It would be three thousand years before they build another ship to match it. Imagine what we would we be travelling in now if this disaster didn't happen.' Damian stared at the oncoming monstrosity.

'Surely it won't go through the disc … it's too big,' he stammered as the Goliath slowed to a halt.

'It takes a good pilot, but it does fit,' Comm said with a chuckle.

Five hundred metres in front of the disc a solid field of graviton energy erupted from three geo stationary satellites. The disc buckled and high intensity excited electrons and protons exploded from the now convex disk. Damian turned just in time to see the Goliath pulled towards the disc, then vanish.

'Wow!' exclaimed Damian.

'Yes, wow indeed. Now follow me back, we are heading for that ship there.' He pointed to a small shuttle just below the Orion.

'It's the High Chancellor's yacht – all communications are being directed from there.' Damian followed and passed through the bulkhead onto the command deck, a holo projection portrayed Chandra and Kowaski manipulating controls on the bridge of Discovery. Further to the left another holo projection. Comm turned to Damian.

'The sequence of events we are about to witness, is very vague, only a few journals mention the conversations that took place aboard this yacht, but we do have the journals of Commander Ntobie. He was the quarter master of Titan base 1. The Goliath did reach them and the crew suffered no ill effects. We could say that they were extremely lucky, if it wasn't for this "larger demonstration" that the sceptics had insisted on the Goliath and its crew would have been in orbit when the destruction came. Even with its enormous mass it would not have survived.'

Comm turned to the observation portal, Discovery was manoeuvring to the front of the disc. Damian stood at Comm's side.

'The disc will now be repositioned and aimed at Alpha Centauri A. At 4.3 light years it is the nearest star to have an exoplanet within the habitable zone of the star. In fact it has four planets, the fourth being habitable. There are five billion people living there now. This manoeuvre will take them a couple of hours. We'll jump ahead,' Comm said. The scene around them flickered to grey then back to the great spectacle. They were now sitting on the top of Orion.

Damian could see that the disc had been repositioned and that Discovery sat within its centre. The Moon too was almost in position.

'In all the science journals and some personal journals, it has been documented that Chandra had argued that a large gravitational force was necessary to help the disc cut into space time,' Comm sighed, as he turned to view the Moon. Damian also turned.

'Maybe she was right. We have witnessed it twice with the graviton beam,' Damian said, keeping his gaze fixed on the disc.

Comm turned to face him.

'Yes, yes, we have, with the graviton beam, not the Moon. Over the next five thousand years her argument has been disputed. Her insistence on using the Moon has puzzled scientists, even now, over five thousand years later. Watch, we are now seconds away.'

As the Moon's gravitational pull gathered strength upon the disc, it buckled, electrons and protons spewed trillions of tonnes of matter from the centre of the disc across space at near light speed.

Damian's jaw dropped as he watched the mass slam into the Moon, upon its surface mountains toppled as it created a moon quake that devastated the moon cities below them.

From the convex side of the disc Discovery disappeared, then seconds later a fiery inferno exploded from within the disc, a flare so intense and with such force and heat it encircled the planet below and within seconds the atmosphere was burnt away. Almost secondary to this, on the concave side of the disc, a second flare erupted, and following the tonnes of matter, hurtled across space to the Moon. Both Earth and Moon were engulfed within the fiery mass. Damian looked back to the Earth below.

The seas had boiled, no living creature lived there now, as the minutes passed, deserts transformed into black glass as the intensity of the heat bore down, Damian watched in disbelief as the planet lost its colour, the seas and oceans turned into vapour venting into the cosmos, great columns of steam transformed into great chunks of ice that would forever be in orbit and would eventually create the ice rings around its equator. It was all over in less than five minutes, five billion people were gone, and two million from the bases and stations on the Moon. All the ships in low orbit including the High Chancellor's yacht were incinerated.

Comm watched the look of horror on Damian's face, the disbelief – the anger, the sadness.

'On our journey through this history, you have remembered many things – your name, a lost love, reminisces of youth, but strangely, the destruction of your planet, your home world, you do not remember. Do you not think that curious?' Comm said softly.

Damian turned to him, his eyes glazed.

'This …' he stuttered, he found it difficult to form the words.

'This never happened. Something is wrong.' He leapt from the Orion as the large craft manoeuvred itself away from the destruction. Comm followed Damian back to the disc. All around them, mayhem, ships of all descriptions were desperately trying to get somewhere else.

'Not all of them will make it. The faster ones will, the slower ones will be ripped apart by the debris that was created by the heat from the Earth and the Moon.' Damian wasn't listening, he was looking at the stars. He turned to face Comm.

'You, are a Com-link, able to perform billions of tasks per second.' Comm nodded slowly.

'Yes, I am able to do that, and a lot more. What of it?'

'At this time and place in history, where is Alpha Centauri A? Point to it.' Comm was shocked for a second. This was a command, the first he had heard from the young man. He started to get communication from the science team. He disregarded them.

It was a short calculation. Hardly any effort was needed.

'It's there,' he said, pointing nonchalantly, and then instantly became confused. He was pointing away from where the disc had been sighted, only by 10 degrees, but over a distance of 4.3 light years. He shook his head and recalculated.

Still 10 degrees from line of sight. He turned to Damian who stood before him, arms folded, a scowl on his face. Comm floated over to him.

'I don't think anyone through the millennia that follows, has ever doubted Chandra's calculated destination. Certainly there is nothing in the records. And yet, you see it the very first time.'

'What was the disc pointing at?' Damian interrupted. Comm studied the young man who stood before him, no longer the innocent youth. A deeper intelligence shone through now, and it was angry. Comm was still receiving communication from the science team. They asked if there were problems as they were experiencing power surges at unprecedented levels and felt it prudent to terminate the session until an investigation into the power surges were completed. Comm disregarded the warning and transferred three com-link sub routines to compensate and investigate.

The science team argued that this would not be enough to stabilise the power outage, then issued a retrieval order. 'We must end this. The power surges are increasing. We are closing this down.'

Comm overrode the order and suggested the science team leave the Med lab. He then ordered the three sub routines to protect and defend the science labs.

'Something has been feeding information to this man all along, and now that we are close to an answer. you report power surges, whatever that something is, it doesn't want us to know the truth, but we will see this through to the end. Now evacuate the labs.' He terminated the link, satisfied that the sub routines would investigate. He returned his attention to Damian's question.

Comm calculated the disc's line, taking into account the gravitational pull and matrix curvature of the space-time continuum. The answer came within a second.

'The image that you see,' he said, spanning his arms to encompass the star field before them. 'Is a true depiction of the star field at this time. The disc was aimed at a small dwarf star, eighty-nine light years from this point.' Comm recalculated and then recalculated again. 'Eighty-nine point two light years.' He thought.

'No, no, no no, that was, impossible.' He whispered, more to himself than to the young man who stood at his side with a look like thunder on his face.

Damian looked at the destruction all around him, the ships desperately trying to escape, the Earth blackened to a carbon crisp. 'This never happened', he thought it over and over again.

'Can we go there?' he said, turning his gaze from the dead planet to Comm.

Comm turned to him shaking his head. 'No, it would be impossible,' was all he managed to say.

The carnage around him pixelated away. For a moment they were back in the grey non-place.

The image flickered, they stood five million kilometres away from the dwarf star.

'This cannot be, we cannot be here, and oh my, look at that!' Comm exclaimed . Damian turned and was amazed to see confusion and disbelief emerge across the old man's face.

'What is it? What do you see?' he enquired. Turning to follow his gaze, a green-grey planet entered the dwarf star's luminosity.

'That planet has an enormous mass for its size. I can see all of its elements, all the way down to the core and, no, that can't be possible ...' Comm was still receiving updates from the science team, power cells were now depleting, the situation was bordering on extreme danger, the Captain had been informed, her orders were to terminate the scenario now. It was a direct order, but this was new. this was impossible. He had to see it out.

'Sandy, somehow, we have stepped back in time, just a few minutes. Discovery should enter this system soon.'

Damian frowned, then turned to the older man.

'Should". You're not sure.'

Comm placed his hand on Damian's shoulder.

'We are now in the realms of impossibilities and improbabilities. I have no idea what is about to happen. I don't even know how it is possible that we are even here, but, Sandy, I must know, how did you know that the disc was pointing in the wrong direction?' Damian thrust out his arm and pointed to a distortion in space.

'There, it's Discovery.' They watched as the craft sped towards the dwarf star. Within a second it entered the corona, the star swelled then exploded and within microseconds they were enveloped in orange and yellow swirls of flame in all directions. Comm strengthened his grip on Damian's shoulder.

'This is wrong, oh, so wrong on so many levels,' he gasped. The image flickered, the star was no more, they were in an asteroid field.

Billions of chunks of rock filled their line of sight in all directions, as far as they could see.

'We have somehow moved on in time, but within the same space. There are so many unanswered questions. What was in that ship that could cause a star to explode, but more puzzling, how did the scenario know that that was what happened, and why here of all places?' Comm turned to Damian as he heard him gasp.

'Comm, there are lights out there! It's a ship! Is it Discovery ... how could it survive?' Comm shook his head slowly. He had no need to turn to see what Damian had spotted.

'No Sandy, not Discovery. It's the Griffin, my ship. We are five thousand six-hundred and twenty-five years into the scenario's future. This is where we found you. all of this has somehow been planned. None of it was accidental.'

The image flicked to grey, then blinding white. Suddenly they were back, standing before the protruding cliff, the statues rising above them. The ground moved violently, Damian was thrown down onto the sand. He looked up, the sky was thunderous, shafts of lightning spearing the volcano which erupted with an ear-piercing explosion, lava and rocks spewing into the air, arcing then falling into the tempest of the ocean.

'It's a quake!' Damian shouted above the noise.

'No, not a quake. These are just images. Listen to me and listen carefully!' he yelled into Damian's ear.

'I must go ... something is wrong, very wrong, you must remember this, Sandy one, on oh, not zero, oh. Repeat it!'

Damian glared at him, confused.

'What?'

'Sandy one, on oh, not zero, repeat and remember.'

'Sandy one on oh,' Damian repeated reluctantly.

'But what does that mean, and what do you mean, you're going?'

Above them the statues moved, a lightning bolt hit the cliff face, two statues from the top row slowly tipped forward and fell to the sandy beach below. Damian watched as the statues of Chandra and Kowaski arced and fell towards him. The ground moved violently; he could not move. Comm had gone, he was alone, he awaited his fate.

CHAPTER 7

GRIFFIN

For the first time since he had become conscious, he felt warm; he could smell the warmth, it bathed him, he could hear noises too, a low frequency hum, melodic, its pitch subtly changing as its harmony changed from high to low. Movement, there was definitely movement around him, a swish of fabric against fabric, a slight breeze as the air moved against his face. He tried to open his eyes but they remained stubbornly closed. Breathing, he could breathe. He took a deep breath and felt his lungs expand then moved his tongue and felt the semi-circle of teeth.

'I'm alive,' he thought. It was just a dream.

'I know you are awake,' came a voice, deep and smooth. He had heard that voice before, but couldn't place it.

'You are Damian, Damian Drake. We found you in a life capsule. You are in the medical centre of the interstellar ship Griffin. At the moment you cannot see or talk, please, just be patient, we are still working on you.'

Damian thought hard about the voice, a deep melodic tone, yes, of course, the Doctor, what was his name, Doctor ... he couldn't remember, the medical centre, Med lab, who called it the Med lab, the memories blurred. There was an island, and a planet, and someone called ... it was there, he couldn't grasp it, so close, tantalisingly close, ah, 'Con', no not 'Con', 'Comm', yes 'Comm.'

'Damian, I have dimmed the lights, I want you to open your eyes ... slowly. Your eyes have never been used before, so, we will take this very slowly. If it is all too much, then close them and squeeze my hand.' Damian felt the man's hand clasp his own.

Pale greens and blues came into focus, a man dressed in white leant over him. He was stocky, wiry haired cut short – he was smiling.

'Good, now swallow, take a breath, and tell me your name.'

Damian looked into the deep brown eyes that were studying him.

They were kind eyes, he thought. This was a good man, he judged. He swallowed and took a breath.

'What do you mean, I've not used them before?' his voice croaked. It shocked him and he swallowed again.

'Okay, let's take this slowly.' The Doctor said softly. He leant away to a console. Damian followed, trying to focus. He looked down at his own body. He was naked, but he had legs, a torso, and arms, he also noticed that he was wearing a device, straddled from shoulder to shoulder. The Doctor leaned back towards him and manipulated some controls upon it.

'Try again,' he said, returning his attention to Damian.

'I said ...' Damian swallowed again; the voice had sounded better that time.'

'I said, what do you mean, I've not used them before?'

'Good, that was much better. How is your sight and hearing?' Damian sighed but decided to comply.

'Yes, my sight is clear, it was blurred but now focused, and I can hear perfectly well, so, tell me what you meant about my eyes.' He swallowed again, his voice still croaky.'

The Doctor leant back and thought for a moment.

'Damian, your sight, hearing, voice, your whole body, this is the first time you have used any of them. When you were found ...'; he looked away and took a few deep breaths before continuing.

'When you were found, there wasn't much of you. Your body had decomposed, your skeleton was degrading, the only thing alive, was your brain, and that was being maintained by the life support of the capsule, if we hadn't have found you when we did, well, the engineering team has reported that the life support system was failing. They feel that you would not have survived ... maybe another six months is all you would have had.'

Damian shivered. He didn't doubt what the man was saying. It was just too bizarre though, and somehow, he had heard it before. But try as he might, the memory eluded him.

'So, this body is …'

'Brand new, completely re-grown, using your own DNA for structure, some parts of you are synthesised, not that you would notice. You were a challenge, and that's an understatement. We didn't think we could complete you initially, but we have a good team here, a lot of expertise.' He smiled and leant forward to alter some controls on the shoulder control pad.

'I think that that is enough for now. You need rest. Tomorrow we will deal with movement, and my senior nurse will start debriefing you. I'm afraid you will be in the medical centre for quite some time.' Damian felt drowsy, the room blurred, and he drifted into a relaxing slumber.

Over the next three days the Med lab team trained Damian on the use of his new body – eating, urinating and defecating seemed to come naturally to him and he mastered the principals without too many accidents. Dexterousness of the hands required practice, and he got angry with frustration that he couldn't get his hands to do what he wanted them to do. Walking too, was difficult, but his determination paid off on the third day when he found he could walk unaided by the stabilising gravitational field that emanated from his personal shield belt.

He realised that the training routines that the Med team had devised were important and also he could see progress. But the best part of the day was the two-hour debriefing with Senior nurse Jane Onslow. He smiled inwardly, as he thought back on their meetings, was he, attracted to her, he thought, no, he decided, just admiration, but he wasn't sure.

One week later Damian was sitting in his usual chair in what he had decided to call the observation room. From where he sat the whole length of the left wall was window, from floor to the very high ceiling and the whole 50-metre length of the room was one continuous sheet of glass. There was not much to see on the outside, but occasionally a shuttle slowly passed by, bathed in light from the external lighting of the Griffin. On the other side of the room a full conference table with seating for at least fifty people. He sat in a recliner next to a low table at the centre of the room. Opposite him an empty recliner that soon, Senior nurse Onslow would be making use of.

A heavy lift shuttle slowly idled its way past the window, Damian struggled to raise himself from the seat, it still required a lot of thought and energy to manoeuvre this new body from one posture to another. He walked slowly over to the observation window. The forward lights of the heavy lifter had picked up the faint outlines of a huge asteroid some thousand metres away. Apart from the light beaming out from the huge squat craft, no other light source could be seen.

Nurse Onslow entered from the far end of the room. She was tall and athletic, lithe. She walked with an easy gait, her body swaying gently from one side to another with every step she took. The white uniform of the Med team mixed with colours of her rank clung to her form, the red flash on her right shoulder depicting seniority, the sleeve below it, green, designating nursing staff.

She smiled as she approached him.

'I have told you before Damian, you should only walk about when one of the nursing staff is present.'

'I am getting better though,' he said, shrugging.

'Even so, let's walk before we run.' She looked out into the space beyond the window.

'What is it you're looking at? The heavy lifter?' He turned to look back out of the window.

'Well, that, the asteroids, everything really, including this incredible window. It's seamless: how is that even possible?'

She looked at him puzzled for a moment. 'The Griffin doesn't have windows. This is a screen, a monitor fed from external sensors. It gives a three-dimensional view of what is on the outside.'

Damian was astonished. 'That makes sense,' he said after he'd pondered it for a moment.

Nurse Onslow smiled, took a hold of his arm and led him back to the recliners. She helped him down into his seat and took the empty recliner opposite him. He couldn't help but smile back, her short-cropped hair just emphasised the perfect symmetry of her face and her bright green eyes shone and disarmed him. He sighed inwardly as she leant towards the table that lay between them but brought himself quickly into check. She passed her hands over the table's controls and the holographic displays emerged in colours of reds blues and greens.

She studied the readouts.

'You, Damian, are doing exceptionally well, you are walking without aid, you are able to dress and undress. It is all good.' She said as she waved the green holo tower away.

Damian indicated the red tower, 'That's not as big as the green tower I must be getting better.' He said with a grin.

'Well, looking in the red tower, you still need to work on your dexterity, but, it has only been three days, we have plenty of time. The Griffin still has just under three standard years of her mission left and Command has allowed us to continue with your rehabilitation here on the Griffin rather than transfer you to the nearest medical station. That has pleased the Captain as she now does not have to lose valuable resources in staff and shuttle to transport you, but, she is not pleased that the Medical team has to continue your rehab. She argued for you to be put in hibernation for the rest of your time here, but I for one, am glad that she lost that argument.'

Damian nodded slowly, trying to comprehend the weight of the information she was giving.

'So, I will be detained in the Med lab for three years, with you, and the science team, conducting tests on me, every day.' She leant through the holographical projections and took a hold of his hands.

'No, it won't be like that. You will be a passenger, not a prisoner. The Med team will only be here for you to help, so that you can integrate with the complexities of your new body, and mentally understand this new culture that you find yourself in, and in return, we will try to understand who you are and where you have come from.'

Damian took a deep breath and squeezed her hands gently, and looking deeply into her eyes, said slowly, in a controlled voice, 'I will never be just a passenger.'

Senior nurse Onslow released her grip, and sat back into the recliner, she was momentarily shocked, his voice had had meaning, authority. She leant forward slowly.

'Are you, part of the Command executive?' she asked hesitantly. He studied the fear in her eyes.

'Command, I seem to hear that from time to time. The dreams I have, or distant memories whatever they are, they mentioned Command, but I don't really know what it is, or what they are.' His voice had calmed, and he was aware that the holograph before him had momentarily flashed red, but had now returned to greens and blues.

Nurse Onslow had also calmed .

'Yes, we need to study your dreams in more depth. But Command, you have no idea what it is?'

He leant back in the recliner, a distant memory of an old man and a white sandy beach fell tantalisingly short of recognition. His eyes fixed upon her. He was calmer now and he smiled.

'Command is an "it" not "they", I seem to remember.'

She inhaled deeply and returned his smile.

'Command, is, well, it's everything, it is what we are, it defines us in all that we do, it gives us …'. Her voice trailed to a stop, confusion flashed across her eyes.

'Damian. I'm sorry, I find this very hard to define, everybody knows what Command is, it doesn't require definition, it just is. It gives us guidance, motivation, a sense of being, a belonging, it is what we are.' Her voice trailed away; he could see that she had difficulty in explaining.

'So, it is a deity, not a collection of people or peoples,' he said, studying her nervousness.

'Deity, err. I'm not sure what that means,'

'Well, it means God, all powerful all knowing.'

She smiled again, but her eyes portrayed fear.

'I have never heard the term God or deity, but, all powerful all knowing, that sounds about right, it is a good definition.'

He leant forward and their eyes fixed.

'Strange, that I have heard the term.'

She turned her head slightly, avoiding his glare.

'Yes, we do have some work to do, especi …' Her sentence was cut short by the opening of the main double doors. Two men, Damian had not seen them before, entered. Nor had he seen the uniforms; they were grey with dark blue sleeving, white shoulder epaulettes with embossed red piping.

'Mr Drake,' said the one with more red piping than the other. Damian looked up at the man. He was aware that nurse Onslow was rising to her feet, and obviously annoyed at the interruption.

'Mr Drake, you are to come with us.' The man turned to nurse Onslow.

'Captains orders, ma'am.'

'She has no right, Damian is under medical supervision, as laid down by Command. I will not release him, he is in my care.' She spat, annoyed that Operations had the nerve.

'Jane,' a deep sonorous voice uttered from behind her, she turned, her face crimson with anger.

'He has to go. I've given permission.' Doctor Ghorbany stood at the entrance of the room, nurse Onslow studied the Doctor. He looked deflated; his face showed strain. She sensed that the chief medical officer had been pushed into a corner to comply with the Captain's wishes.

'Very well, but he is still in my charge. I will go with him,' she remarked bitterly, aiming the words at the two bridge officers.

'Err, nobody has asked me whether I want to go,' Damian said cheerfully. The Doctor smiled.

'Sorry Damian, but you do not have a say in this matter, you have to go, but you will still be in the medical facility, and, should you not be able to handle the meeting, a medical team will be on hand, and yes, Jane, you can go with the team.' He turned to the man in grey.

'Lieutenant, this man is still receiving medical treatment, you will treat him well, do you understand?' The Lieutenant, with no emotion showing, turned his blank face to Damian. Damian stifled a shudder.

'Yes sir, of course Doctor,' he said in monotone, his gaze fixed. Damian could see the hatred in his eyes.

'Mr Drake,' he said slowly.

'If you would be so kind please, follow us, sir.'

CHAPTER 8

JULIANA CONTESSA

The medical complex occupied three levels within the Griffin, but with a reduced crew. Only the top level was used for treatment, the middle level was used mainly for medical research and the lower level was being used as a research facility and also served as living quarters for the medical staff.

They moved slowly through the top level. Damian had never been this far, and he repeatedly stopped to regain his balance. The medical team followed and each time he stopped they rushed to his aid he refused their help and insisted that he make the journey unaided.

They reached the furthest end of Med level 1 and entered the descent tube, they exited at Med level 2.

In front of him the signs denoted the area as Med lab 3.

The Lieutenant turned to the Med team and directed his next comment to the senior nurse.

'You, are to stay here.' Nurse Onslow sucked in a deep breath and was about to argue but thought better of it as the officer raised his hand in a stopping gesture. Then she turned to Damian.

'How are you feeling? Do you feel okay to carry on?'

Damian nodded, but his face belied the exhaustion he was feeling. Nurse Onslow came to his side and adjusted the gravity field. He was now twenty percent lighter. She turned to the officer.

'He has never walked this far. If he needs rest you will give him rest. I don't care what the Captain's orders are, this man is in our care and that care has been ordered by Command ... if anything happens to him ...'. Again the officer's hand came up to quieten her; she seethed with anger.

'The Captain wants Mr. Drake to see the damage. She hopes that it might trigger some memories, so, you and your team will wait here. We will call you if you are required.' The officer then turned to Damian.

'There is debris within the lab, but a pathway has been cleared. We will proceed with caution,' the Lieutenant said in a matter-of-fact tone.

The double doors of Med lab 3 opened. Damian's eyes fell upon the utter destruction within: walls and ceilings damaged beyond repair, molten lumps of debris lay haphazardly around the room; the smell of burnt polymers and other synthesized plasteels filled the air that he breathed. Around him, he noticed scorched and deformed alloys that at one time had been control consoles and work benches. As he carefully picked his way through the carnage, he noticed something that stopped him dead in his tracks. The bulkhead wall had gone; he stood staring into space. The Lieutenant leaned closer to Damian.

'It is safe, it is protected by a graviton field,' he whispered into Damian's ear.

'What happened in here?' Damian asked, trying to take in the devastation.

'You, happened in here,' the officer said slowly. Damian heard the venom in the Lieutenants voice.

'How have I got anything to do with this carnage?' he said angrily, but the officer had moved away. Confused at the devastation and the revelation that he may somehow, have been to blame, he followed the officer. At the far wall there was another pair of double doors with a sign indicating they were now entering Med lab 2.

The enormous laboratory showed signs of destruction, but not as much as Med lab 3. The bulkhead wall had buckled but was still in place, its integrity still holding.

At the furthest wall were the doors to Med lab 1. They opened at their approach; the Lieutenant turned to Damian.

'We are to stay here. Mr Drake, please enter, someone will be with you presently.' The two officers took up their positions either side of the doorway.

Damian kept his stare on the officer and he could see the hatred in the man's eyes. He turned away and entered Med lab 1.

The laboratory was smaller than the previous rooms, more of an anti-room – a reception area of sort. Although it showed signs of damage here and there, the carnage evident in the previous rooms was not apparent here. In the far corner Damian noticed that some lounge seating had been set around a low table. He made his way towards them, fatigue catching him up and he felt relieved when he fell into the recliner. Taking deep breaths to calm himself he heard the swish of the outer doors parting and turned to see three officers enter.

The two male officers, one in blue the other in red, both displayed gold flashes upon their epaulettes with both left sleeves coloured black. The other officer was older, her uniform although neat and crisp seemed old and plain compared to her colleagues: a red tunic, black slacks, epaulettes and cuffs white with gold piping. The two younger officers parted and took their positions behind Damian's recliner. The elder of the three walked slowly towards the recliner opposite him, gracefully sat and leant forward, a smile emerging reluctantly from her bland features, the eyes however remaining cold and grey.

'Mr Drake,' she said, her voice deep and mellow, the smile fixed upon her face. She offered her hand.

'I'm sorry ma'am, but you have me at a disadvantage. I have no idea who you are,' he said slowly, but accepting her outstretched hand.

'Juliana Contessa,' she said, retrieving her hand, the smile slowly vanishing as it retreated.

'Captain, Contessa of the interstellar ship Griffin,' she said. Damian detected the underlying growl in her voice.

'Mr Drake, I would normally say that it is a pleasure to have you on board, but you have caused nothing but havoc from the moment we found you,' she spat.

Damian's jaw dropped. He sat back into the depths of the recliner.

'Havoc?' he replied slowly, confused at this women's instant turn of attitude.

'I have done nothing, I've only been here four days.' The Captain continued her glare, then slowly she leant back into the recliner. Clasping her hands before her, she leant her chin onto her clasped fist.

'You have been here four months, and in that time, you have managed to kill two of my science staff and injured four crew members, three seriously. Two of my science labs have been destroyed and the Comm link assigned to you has vanished. She continued in softer tones.

'Why should I welcome you with open arms? If it wasn't for my orders, direct from Command, you would be in a hibernation tank now, but as it is I am stuck with you for another three standard years, or, until our mission here has ended. My advice to you, sir, is, spend your time out of my way. Do not cross me, for if you do in anyway, orders or not, I will throw you in the hibernation tank myself.' She stood up without effort.

'If you have any sense Mr Drake, you will stay within the confines of the medical unit. I will bid you goodbye,' she said and as she walked towards the outer door the young officer in red joined her and together they left.

Damian let out a slow gasp.

'That was some meeting. Is she always like that?' he asked, looking around to face the remaining officer.

'She is upset at the loss of her crew members, and the destruction of the science labs. However, it could have been a lot worse.' The officer walked round to the now vacant recliner and sat down.

'Commander Thomas Burroughs, Chief Engineer,' he said offering his hand.

Damian hesitated but reached forward and took it.

'What do you mean it could have been worse? Two of your crew died,' he said. A shudder vibrated through his body.

'The com-link assigned to you, redirected three sub links and insisted on an isolation field to be put around labs two and three. He had at this time disobeyed a direct order from the Captain, but his actions did save this whole level and maybe the level above, thus saving twenty-six crew.' The officer leant forward studying Damian's face.

'Why, Mr Drake do you think he would do that? what was going on in your little scenario at that time to make him do such a thing?' Damian sat frozen, completely confused.

'What scenario?', he managed to ask.

The Chief Engineer leant back in his seat.

'Ah yes, the convenient memory loss. I have read your files Mr Drake.'

'I assure you Commander, I have no recollection of any scenario. I just have dreams, which Senior nurse Onslow is trying to decipher.' He paused for a moment to try and collect his thoughts but still the memories alluded him.

'Sorry Commander, I still cannot remember, even though the Captain says that I have been here four months, from my perspective I have been here just four days. I still do not know the circumstances of how I ended up here. I am in a permanent state of confusion and fear. Can you even begin to understand that?'

He was aware that he was trembling. The Commander studied his face and slowly nodded.

'I understand fear, Mr Drake, I served on the battle cruiser "Vanquish". During my tour of the skirmished borders we were ambushed and then boarded. Five crew personnel were executed. I and my engineering team managed to escape, we were adrift for days before we were rescued, so yes, I understand fear only too well, and I can see the fear in your eyes.'

Damian was shocked, he leant forward.

'Are we … at war?' he asked slowly.

The officer looked to the ceiling, and took a deep breath.

'I feel I have said too much perhaps, but maybe you should know, yes, we are at war, and have been for a long time. But you can relax, all that is happening on the other side of known space, some three thousand light years from this position, a journey that would take the Griffin ten years to make, so we are reasonably safe.' He held up his hand to stop Damian from interrupting.

'Your own story first. You have nearly three standard years to listen to war stories from this crew. so, let me tell you the circumstances of how you managed to be here.

Four months ago, a heavy lifter was surveying a densely packed part of the asteroid field. They were scanning for various compounds, which, by the way, is what this mission is all about. We need alloys of different compounds to build new warships. But, that is by the by. The heavy lifter scanned down into the depths of a large asteroid. They could not believe the readings they received, an alloy, a fusion of many metals all in one place, an alloy that was unknown. This, as you can imagine, caused excitement, an alien alloy! We had been in space for thousands of years, had visited thousands of planets, and not once had we come across an intelligent civilisation, not even the remnants of a past culture, and now, here, on the edge of known space we find an alloy, something that was manufactured, but not by us.

They manoeuvred the heavy lifter closer. It was a dangerous procedure, the asteroids in that sector were so close together, bound by their own gravitational pull. The presence of the lifter disturbed this gravitational balance. It was then that they picked up a biological signal.' He leant forward and pointed.

'It was your bio sign. They called for help and within the next six standard hours they had located the capsule in which you were found. They carefully brought it back to the Griffin, but …'.

He sighed and leant back. 'All at a cost – three shuttles were severely damaged and a crew member – the team leader – was badly hurt.' Damian shook his head.

'Is he okay?' he inquired, with genuine concern. Burroughs broke into a smile.

'Yes, she is fine, but the Captain was furious. She doesn't like any crew member hurt and I suppose that goes all the way back to when the Griffin was on front line duties. And she was especially annoyed when we opened the canister only to find a decomposed body. Somehow, the life support had kept your brain functioning. I must confess the engineering team are at a loss as to how the capsule works.'

Damian frowned.

'But I know nothing of this.'

Burroughs could see the truth of this within the depths of the young man's eyes.

'We brought you to the Med lab.' he continued.

'The doctor did not hold much hope, and placed you into a hibernation tank. The Captain contacted Command, which insisted, and ordered, that the Med team would construct a new body and to bring you back. I know from talking to the other senior officers that the Captain wasn't happy with this, but that was her orders, so she had to comply. The Doctor then decided to put what was left of your mind into psycho analysis with the medical com-link, and you can't remember that either I suppose.'

'As I said, 'Comm' seems familiar. There's an island, some sort of mountain and some statues, oh, and an exploding planet, but I can't grasp what it all means.'

'You were with the com-link for quite a while,' Burroughs continued.

'Then there was a power surge, destroying labs 2 and 3 and of course the technicians, and as I said, somehow the com-link knew this and set up the perimeter field, an action that saved many lives, but that power, where did it come from? Certainly not from the Griffin, so, from where? And, who put your capsule together, with alloys that we know nothing about, the mechanics of it, also beyond our comprehension, and of course, yourself, the whole thing is one big puzzle.' Burroughs rose to his feet.

'When you feel well, and are able to, make your way to the engineering section, maybe your presence there will have an effect on the capsule. or maybe the capsule will have an effect on you. In the meantime, I hope you recover soon, oh, and my best advice to you – keep out of the Captain's way.' He exited the laboratory, leaving Damian puzzled.

At the far end of the room the doors parted, and the Med team entered. Nurse Onslow scanned him.

'You're exhausted,' she said reading the monitor's readouts. Damian shrugged.

'It's been a strange day, and the Captain doesn't like me.'

The nurse smiled. 'Don't take it personally. I don't think she likes anyone.' They placed him onto an anti-grav stretcher, a blue-white glow of the gravity field emanated from below, enabling the Med staff to easily guide him back through the carnage of the two decimated laboratories.

Damian Drake lay in his private room that was situated within the medical facility on level 4. It had been three standard weeks since his meeting with the Captain. Since then he had set his mind to the relentless regime of exercise and brain training games. Over the past few days he had been assessed and re-assessed. He thought about nurse Onslow, who he hadn't seen for over a week. He missed the psycho debriefing sessions he had with her, but with all the emphasis on his training he had neglected to ask of her whereabouts. He decided that today, that would change.

Leaving his room, he made his way back to the Med centre.

'Good morning, Damian.'

Damian stopped to greet the second-year medic. 'Good morning, Simon, what do you have in store for me today?' Simon Larcus laughed.

'Believe it or not, nothing. We are awaiting your scores. A panel of senior medics are discussing them in a meeting right now.' Damian was slightly shocked.

'I was not told that I was competing for points.' Simon laughed at his confusion.

'But that is the point, we couldn't tell you. You had to complete this ordeal naturally.'

Damian nodded. 'I can understand that. So who is on the panel?'

'Doctor Ghorbany, of course, Senior nurse Onslow, Senior Medic Si lang and three science techs. They have been discussing you for over an hour now ... they should be out soon.' Damian was surprised that his interest peaked when Simon mentioned nurse Onslow.

'I haven't seen Nurse Onslow for a while. Has she been doing something else?' Damian asked hesitantly.

Simon leant in closer to him and placed his hand upon his shoulder, smiling. 'No, she has been assessing you from afar. Do you have feelings for her? She is attractive.'

Damian stepped back from him. He liked this young medic but sometimes found him to be just a bit too friendly.

'No, I do not have feelings for her, and yes, I am aware of her attractiveness,' he said, gently removing the man's hand from his shoulder.

'Simon, if they ask where I am, I'll be in the mess hall.' Damian turned to walk away and as he did Simon laughed.

'That is never a problem, Damian. We always know where you are. I'll see you later.'

Damian walked away heading for the medical mess hall, Simon's last statement nagging at him. 'We always know where you are'. To them, he thought, he was their prize experiment, a super specimen that had challenged all of them. It was time, he thought, to stop working with the Med team.

An hour later he was summoned to an appraisal in the briefing room.

The assessment team sat at the furthest end of the large table. Doctor Ghorbany stood and welcomed him and directed him to an empty seat. Holographic portrayals were presented to him and he was questioned on his wellbeing and physical status. Concerns were expressed at his continued memory loss, and that this would now be a priority for the next two years or so, or until the end of the mission.

Damian stood, the team quietened and he waited until he had their full attention.

'Firstly, I would like to say thank you to all of you, for your dedication, and for your obvious talents in bringing me back from being a pool of decomposed matter into what you see before you. I feel fit and strong, and, I have decided, that I would like to leave the medical centre and join the rest of the crew on this ship. What you have achieved is a miracle, and I do not want you to think that I am ungrateful, because I am not, far from it, but I have the rest of my life to consider. I do not want to be a passenger or a curiosity for another three years, I want to train and do something useful, every day. I watch the shuttles and heavy lifters leave the Griffin, and I have decided that I want to learn to be a shuttle pilot.' He sat down and studied the aghast expressions on the faces of those around him. Nurse Onslow was the first to respond. She cleared her throat.

'Damian, you have passed all assessments here. You have come through this better than we could have ever imagined. I for one agree you should pursue you own life.'

Doctor Ghorbany held up his hand.

'Damian, we still have a long way to go with you. Who are you? Where did you come from? Command is quite insistent that we find these answers.' Damian turned to face him.

'And in time I am sure you will, but maybe not right now. Doctor, I have had enough of being studied and assessed and then there is the poking and prodding. Give me some time off, I implore you. I am not going away. I will still be here and we can pursue my memory at a slower pace. I just need a …'. The doctor held up his hand again, Damian stopped mid-sentence.

'Very well, Senior nurse Onslow has been studying your psychological pathways, so for the next few days you will report directly to her. In the meantime, I will arrange accommodation for you outside of the medical centre, and, we will take this at a much slower pace. Will that satisfy you?' Damian sat down and smiled at the doctor.

'Yes sir, that sounds much better, thank you.'

The meeting ended and the panel departed the room. Damian stayed in his chair and looked across to nurse Onslow sitting opposite.

'You should have told me that you were unhappy, Damian,' she said, a concerned look on her face. Damian stood up from his chair, walked around the huge table and sat beside her.

'It's not that I'm unhappy; the Med team are a good bunch of people.

I've enjoyed being in their company and working with them, but I can also see that this is never ending. They won't let go of it, and I just need a break.' Onslow nodded her head slowly.

'I can understand that. What if we have a bit of a break now and get out of the Med centre. This is a huge ship, let's go and explore.'

CHAPTER 9

LEVEL 11

They had walked to the end of level 4. Damian had been this far on a number of occasions during his walks to build up muscle tone. They stood before the descender. The last time he had entered the descender was on his journey to meet the Captain.

'I have been down to the science labs. before, if you can remember,' he said, staring at the double doors. She turned to him smiling.

'There are twenty-nine decks below us, most have been decommissioned and dismantled, but there is one deck, I go there a lot. I like to think of it as my own personal space, somewhere that is away from ... well ... normality.'

Damian frowned. 'But I thought there was over a hundred people aboard this ship, are you saying, nobody explores?' The doors parted, and they entered.

'Com.' she said, in a whisper. Damian turned to face her. She held her hand to his lips.

'Shh, not that com,' she said, continuing the whisper.

'Travel Com engaged,' a voice said from all around them.

'Execute command, Onslow, zero, zero, two, four, seven, nine, level eleven.'

Damian felt the descender move as they started their travel down into the bowels of the ship.

'Why such secrecy?' he asked.

She shrugged. 'I just wanted my own space, and I found this level within three months of exploring. That was in my first year here, seven standard years ago. Nobody knows – probably not even the Captain – that it even exists. This ship is approximately three standard years away from being scrapped. Its life has finished. It is fifty years old and it has been slowly disassembled level by level each time the Griffin docks onto a space station. Level 11 was never touched; there is nothing of value there but it is down on record as being decommissioned. I found it by accident. On one of my explorations, I wanted to see the enormous Trellion drive engines. When I was younger, I wanted to be an engineer or a physicist. That was never to be, but I am still fascinated by engineering achievements. Fifty years ago, those engines were state of the art, and they cover the five lowest levels. I don't know what happened, but somehow the descender had started to lose pressure, the travel com realising that a life form was in danger stopped at the nearest safe level, which was level 11.' Damian studied her in wonder.

'And so, for seven years you have had this place to yourself, and you talk about me getting a life. Jane, that's sad,' he said, laughing.

'No, it's not. It keeps me sane. You have no idea of the life that you have woken up to.' She gasped, then looked away from his concerned stare. 'I'm sorry,' she said, turning back to him and holding her hand to her mouth.

'I didn't mean that, it's, just that, sometimes I feel I don't belong. I don't fit. I feel there should be something else. It's as if this life isn't real.'

The doors parted, Damian blinked at the light that shone in from outside the doors, he turned his back to the brightness and faced her.

'That was deep felt. What are you so afraid of? Apart from a miserable Captain, everyone else seems so nice here.' She looked up into his eyes and narrowed them into slits.

'What do you know, you've just got here.' She passed by him and exited, leaving him stunned.

Damian slowly turned and looked at the unbelievable vision that was level 11. Light emitted from everywhere, white, red. green, blue, were the more prominent, but other colours pulsated behind them. He stood at the entrance of a great hall surrounded by massive buildings, each with different architectural designs. Throughout the promenade on which he now stood he could see water features, fountains with exploding water and dazzling light. Above him some forty metres in height, aerial light displays exploded in colour. He caught her up, and gently turned her towards him. Her eyes were moistened, reflecting the colours from above.

'You need to talk to someone about this. It's far too much of a secret for you to hold onto. Maybe we could help each other.' With his eyes now adjusted to the onslaught of light he turned to her, smiling.

'You have a great place here. I do understand why you do not want to share it.'

She took a deep breath and calmed herself. She panned the scene around her, taking in the impossible level 11. It had been her place of comfort for so many years, and now she had brought him here. It was an impulse, but there was something in him. She had felt he was a kindred spirit, a trusting soul.

'You do know that you can never tell anyone of this place?' she said firmly, placing her hands upon his shoulders and gently pulling him to her. Then in a whisper, she continued.

'We all have secrets. This is mine, and I will be heartbroken when it's gone. But I thought, if you could share it with me, maybe, we could unlock this stubborn memory loss. And the reason that I brought you here, is that I have something that might just help.' Her eyes were pleading with him, and he felt powerless to refuse.

'Just our little secret,' he said softly, wiping a lone tear from her cheek. She brightened.

'Not so little though. Come, this way.'

He followed her as she led him along the promenade. They had walked nearly a half a kilometre and he had asked question after question about the various buildings that they passed.

'Level 11 was the entertainment level for the crew. That was when the Griffin had a complement of over four thousand. Here were to be found theatres, holographic entertainment rooms, restaurants and amusements, everything that a bored crew could possibly wish for.'

'A bored crew,' Damian asked incredulously.

'On a battle cruiser.'

She stopped and turned to him.

'They weren't in battle all of the time. This ship can travel at a maximum speed of one light year every two standard days. They could be travelling for months from one destination to another. The last thing a battleship needs is a bored crew member. Hence …'. she stretched her arms to emphasise the point.

'We are here,' she said, pointing to a large building pulsating with colour.

'It's an amusement and entertainment hall,' he said, confused.

'Nevertheless, we are here,' he followed her through the large double doors.

He was relieved to discover that the enormous space had limited lighting, almost dull compared to the onslaught of light and colour on the outside.

All around him he noticed empty holographic stages, except for one, and it was this one that Onslow made for.

Projected above the surface of the stage were swirling colours, pulsating within myriads of particulates. Nurse Onslow took up a position at the end of the platform, Damian could see that a holo. control pad lay between her and the projection.

Damian watched as the colours swirled up and then blended into one another.

'That's impressive. What is it?' he asked. She smiled and pointed to a surge of coloured strands that seemed to swim from one side of the stage to the other, crossing and merging with other columns of colour then changing as they blended together.

'It's you,' she said smiling.

'Not a very good likeness,' he replied, with a chuckle.

'This is a part of your neuro net, and that is the mnemonic implant that tries to hold on to your memories,' she said, ignoring his joke. Damian watched as the nurse adjusted the projector.

'This is all I have managed to save, the rest of it seems to be somehow corrupted.' The holo stage adjacent to them spluttered into life. The scene it depicted was two men on a sandy beach next to a sheer cliff face. All around them a storm raged. They stood in front of what seemed to be an inverted pyramid of statues. Damian could just make out that the statue standing on the column was of himself. The older man was shouting over the noise of the storm.

'I have to go now, remember Sandy, one on oh, not zero, repeat that ...'. The image faded then all that was left was the empty holo stage. Damian turned to Onslow.

"Wow, that, was so familiar, for a moment I was there. I think I can remember bits. The old man is Comm, and the statues ... he was telling me a story about the statues.' Damian continued looking into the empty space, desperately trying to remember what came next.

'He asked you to remember, Sandy one on oh not zero. Have you any idea what that was about.' He shook his head and slowly turned away from the empty platform to face her.

'No, I have no idea what, or who Sandy is, let alone "Sandy one on oh not zero.'

All of a sudden, he staggered back and fell to the floor, letting out a yell as he landed on the hard surface. Nurse Onslow was by his side in an instant.

'What happened?' she demanded, as she scanned his body with her medical monitor. Damian was panting hard, sweat beading across his forehead, dripping down onto his cheeks, his eyes rolled in their sockets and his body shook uncontrollably. Onslow rechecked his vital signs on the monitor. They were stabilising, settling ... his breathing softened, he focused on her face, his pupils adjusting normally.

'Wow, what happened there?' he managed to gasp. She checked him again. All signs were normal.

'Nothing happened', she said, concerned. 'You just exploded backwards.'

He gave her a puzzled look. 'That white light, blinding, white light, you must have seen it, and the pain, searing pain. Something must have gone wrong with the projection.' She checked his signs again. All showed normal. Now satisfied that he was in good health she made her way back to the holo controls and she checked them thoroughly. Everything seemed correct so she then she retraced her steps, trying to remember the sequence she had carried out before he had yelled out in pain. Still everything was as it should be.

'Nothing, there's nothing here that could have caused that.' She looked up from the controls and focused on him. He had sat up and was now straightening his tunic.

'You didn't see the light,' he said, his voice calmer now.

'No, nothing, no light no sound, nothing. But I know you experienced something; your readings were off the scale.' Concern weighed down her voice. He moved around the platform to be by her side.

'Hey, I'm alright, no harm done. I feel fine now,' he said, smiling.

She looked down at the monitor. It was still on. He was right; all levels were back to normal.

'Maybe ...' she said slowly, turning to him, 'the pulsations of the projection, or the colour and light outside, may have reacted to one of your implants. We'll check them when we get back to the Med centre.'

'Okay, we can do that, and I assure you, I feel fine now. You said the file has been corrupted. Surely engineering would be the best place for it.' She pulled away suddenly, shaking her head.

'No, they must not know. They will investigate and then they will find level 11. Promise me that we will keep this to ourselves.'

Damian heard the panic in her voice, but he agreed, and to himself he thought, 'for now'.

Nurse Onslow moved away from the holo controls, and helped him to his feet.

'We must return to the Med lab. I think you need to undergo some tests.' He stepped away from her, shaking his head.

'I'm fine,' he protested, but she insisted.

'We must go. This level does not exist on the main com data base, there is no communication here. Seven years ago, when I found this place, I set up a dampening field around it, so nothing can even scan into this level. I am sorry, but we must go. I will summon a local rider. It will take us back to the ascender. We will come back here at a later date.' Taking his arm, she led him to the exit.

Outside, a squat two seated vehicle awaited them. They rode in silence back through the multi-coloured pulsating promenade. Damian sat back and studied the impossible level 11.

'Why have you not shared this place with anyone else? You must have been close to someone within the last seven years,' he asked casually. She took a deep breath and sighed. He turned to face her.

'I don't mean to pry,' he said quickly. She smiled and slowly shook her head.

'No, I know you don't. Everything is so new to you. You don't know our culture, our politics even our living structure ... the total influence of Command, the lack of personal intimacy, wanting's and cravings are all suppressed. You have a lot to learn, and maybe once learnt, you might just understand why I want a secret place, and I have often thought, that others may also have their own secrets.'

Damian studied her face as she spoke: a sad face, she was a person so desperate to share, yet so frightened to do so.

'If Command is so powerful, then surely it already knows about this place, and if it does, what does that say about personal secrets.'

'Command may know, it may not,' she said, turning away from his stare.

'Maybe if it does know, it doesn't care. Maybe it allows small gratitude's.'

CHAPTER 10

MEMORY WITHIN

He was again lying down in the Med lab with the doctor and nurse scanning and probing him. He had been here many times before and the procedure that he was going through, he had been through many times before. He lay back and relaxed and as he closed his eyes an image of a white sandy beach aside a turquoise sea entered his mind. An elderly man with a floppy white hat walked towards him.

'Sandy" he said, with a smile of perfect teeth. Damian opened his eyes in shock.

'He collapsed in the ascender,' The doctor said softly whilst nurse Onslow checked the readouts on her scanner.

'Yes, we were returning from the engine room, he just let out a yell and dropped to the floor.' Damian heard the distortion of the lie in her voice and wondered if the doctor had picked up on it.

'I feel fine now, doctor, probably overcome by the sheer size of the Trellion engines.'

He looked around and stared into Onslow's eyes. She turned away, placing her scanner back onto her belt.

'Well, you seem to be fine now Damian, but it does emphasize my concerns regarding you leaving the Med team.' Damian felt a surge of panic at that last remark.

'But I won't be far away doctor. You can keep an eye on me remotely.' The doctor stopped what he was doing, then slowly nodded.

'Yes, we can do that,' he said, sighing with reluctance then helping Damian down from the scanner platform.

'I have spoken to the Captain, regarding your interest in training as a shuttle pilot. She was, well, surprised, but not dismissive. She has also designated private quarters for you. On deck 6, surprisingly.'

'Why surprisingly,' Damian asked.

'Level six is where the Med labs were, and the quarters that you will be assigned to were the private quarters of the senior lab technician, who, obviously, now does not require it,' he said solemnly. Damian shrugged.

'Who says she doesn't have a sense of humour, dark humour, but humour none the less,'

Doctor Ghorbany and Nurse Jane Onslow walked with him to the main entrance of the medical facility. The doors parted as they approached.

'There you are Damian, a new adventure awaits. Try not to get in the crew's way, and please, don't do anything to upset the Captain. Nurse Onslow will be our liaison with you.' Damian took a hold of the doctors outstretched hand.

'And I will contact you later, Damian, when you have settled in,' Nurse Onslow said without emotion. Damian nodded and smiled.

'Thanks for everything. I'll see you all soon.' He walked out into the wide corridor, the swish of the doors closing behind him in his ears. He took another two steps, then realised that he hadn't a clue where he was going.

The main gallery ran through the centre of each level, and on level four it measured thirty metres wide. Various rooms were attached to the main thoroughfare, some closed, some open-plan. Damian noticed that the Med bays and labs took up most of the port side. Opposite on the starboard side were the Science labs, Geology, Botany, Chemistry and Physics. He decided to walk to the rear of the ship.

He had been walking for a few minutes before he realised the level was deserted. He had passed no one. A few minutes further on, he came to a large open space. Dominating the space a large curved stairway ascended above and descended below. Sender units were positioned around the perimeter. He decided to descend the wide stairway down to level six. As he descended, he noticed the lighting was dimmer. This was the last level in use on the ship, he thought, and with the Med labs out of commission it was hardly used at all. He stepped off the last stair onto level 6.

The stairway that descended to level 7 shimmered in a haze – an energy field he thought – then remembered Jane Onslow telling him that some levels had been completely de-commissioned. Beyond the haze of the energy field was probably a complete vacuum. On the far wall, he noticed an indicator panel and he placed his hand upon the screen.

'Where are the crew quarters for Damian Drake?' he asked. A slither of green light appeared beside him.

'Passenger, Damian Drake, has been allocated 6032. Please follow.' The green slither pulsated then drifted down the corridor towards the forward end of the ship. Damian followed.

'How many of the crew are quartered on this deck?' he asked the slither of green.

'No other crew members are registered with quarters on deck six, Med labs are forward of midships and engineering is aft. There are eight crew quarters, all vacant. You are registered here, room 6032.' The slither of green stopped beside a closed door on the port side, a panel to the right of the door showing its number.

'Hand and eye recognition required for entry,' it pulsated, then faded away leaving Damian alone. He looked down the darkened corridor. 'Nice part of town,' he thought.

'She really doesn't like me,' he muttered. He placed his hand on the plate. It felt warm as it read his palm print and blood structure. At the same time a light flashed into his eyes, making him squint. The sensor activated his implant and verified his designation. The door opened and he entered.

'Good afternoon, Mr. Drake,' a male voice chirped, as he entered the room.

'Er ... good afternoon,' Damian replied, a little taken aback. 'Your very, erm, bubbly, for an entry system.'

'I'm not just the entry system Mr Drake. I am here to tend to all of your needs, whatever they may be,' Chirped the room com. Damian stared at the com panel, bemused.

'Well, I might have to, just tone you down a bit but for now I just want to look around my new home.

He was in the seating area, a low couch and two recliners were positioned around a low table. To his right a holo stage and to his left two doorways. He walked through the nearest and discovered it led to a sleeping room with an ablution room to the side. A large panel filled the wall adjacent to the sleeping platform. He looked at it for a while, wondering what it would be used for.

'I can display any image you wish upon it – for decorative reasons,' chirped the room comm.

'Choose at random,' said Damian, a holographic star making nebular appeared.

'I recognise that," Damian said, fascinated that he knew this image.

'It is the crab nebular, Mr Drake. The previous occupant liked it very much.' Damian nodded his approval and walked back to the seating room. The second door opened as he approached. He stopped abruptly. Panic swam through him. The door opened into space.

'It is your balcony, Mr Drake. The images are real; they are the images beyond the bulkhead, but they are just images, all visual images throughout the Griffin are just monitors.'

'Yes, I know that. It was just a shock, that's all,' he said straightening himself. The effect, he had to agree, was stunning. It appeared that he was standing upon a platform jutting out from the side of the Griffin's hull. He could see along the length of the ship, both forward and aft, above and below, and yet, beyond, just the darkness of space, and in the distance all around him billions of stars. He stayed for a while, just looking at the constellations. He noticed a bench jutting out from the back wall, he sat and continued his inspection of the Cosmos. A light appeared some five hundred metres away, the light from a heavy lifter returning from the asteroid field. He watched as it slowly glided by. 'Tomorrow.' He thought, 'I will go to the hanger deck to see these incredible vehicles, and to thank the crew who rescued me.'

He watched as the heavy lifter disappeared from view. A movement caught his eye – one of the stars had moved, then another and yet more. Soon, all of the stars were swirling around in a spiral pattern. He noticed that they were creating an image, an image of a face. An old face wearing a floppy hat.

'Comm,' he spluttered. The image converged before him. Comm smiled and bowed serenely.

'I have for now withdrawn some of your memories, but they will return to you soon. Please bear with me Sandy,' the image of Comm said.

Damian stood and gaped at the image.

'Where are you, and why did you leave me?'

'I am being pursued by Griffin's main com-link. I promise you, as soon as it is safe, I will contact you, but I must go now.'

The image disappeared back into the Starscape. Damian nodded slowly. He was starting to remember. He sat back down and looked out at the stars for some time. Snippets of memory tantalised him. The island, the statues and the devastated Earth. He wondered if he should keep this to himself, or should he confide to Nurse Onslow. 'Secrets,' he thought, does everyone have secrets?' He made his way back to the seating room.

'What are your duties,' he said to the room.

'Primarily your life support and your living needs,' said the room comm with enthusiasm.

'Are you connected to the ships com-link?'

'I am always connected to the ship's com.'

'Can you create a sub link that isn't.'

'I'm afraid not Mr Drake, all utility coms are linked.' Strange, thought Damian, Nurse Onslow managed to have a secret link on the travel com. He would have to ask her how to do it.

'I was assigned a psychiatric med -com,' he said, in as uninterested tone as he could muster.

'I am aware of that Mr Drake.' The room comm answered.

'Do you know where it is?' He noted there was a pause before the room com answered.

'I do not know Mr Drake. I believe an engineering team is still investigating the disappearance, the main com-link is searching the ship for it, but I do not believe it has found it yet,' said the enthusiastic room com. Damian sat in the recliner and allowed a small smile.

'What name are you called by?'

'I am 6032,' chirped the room comm. Damian frowned.

'I can't call you that, how about ...Six?'

'That is acceptable, Mr Drake.'

'Okay Six, communicate with Senior nurse Onslow, please.'

'Communicating now, sir.'

The holo stage pulsated in blues and greens, creating towers of light and colour that slowly defined into the shape of Jane Onslow. She sat in her lounger, dressed in a blue and red-spiralled patterned gown. the fabric was thin in structure and Damian couldn't help noticing how it clung to the contours of her body. Her hair was now loose about her shoulders rather than the cropped style she had sported when he had first met her. Damian thought she looked far more attractive now than he had ever seen her. He now understood what the lab technician Simon was referring to. She did, he thought, look very attractive.

'Good evening, Jane.'

'Damian, how are your quarters?'

'Yes, fine. I'm in 6032, er ... you look different. I mean, you look, very nice,' he stuttered, then cursed himself.

'This is my rest cycle. I have just finished my work cycle. How are you feeling?' she inquired, with some concern.

'I'm fine, I just wondered if you wanted to go back to the, er, engine room?' She smiled at his innocent attempt at subterfuge.

'Yes, that would be fine. I'll meet you on level 30 in twenty standard minutes.' The image shimmered then faded to nothing, but he remained staring at the spot for a few seconds longer.

He took the descender down to level thirty. The whole area was open plan, and designed to take the huge mass of the Trellion engines. From this level he could see the top canopy of the enormous power House, the engines stretched almost the whole length of the Griffin and sat within the lower five levels of the ship.

'They are magnificent, aren't they – old, but still magnificent,' Jane Onslow said as she walked up beside him. He turned and smiled.

'Yes, I agree, and, you are looking, quite magnificent as well.'

'Thank you, it's nice to get out of uniform, and it is nice to be noticed.' She took hold of his arm and guided him back to the ascender.

They exited at level 11 and made their way back to the holo stage in the entertainment hall.

Onslow sat by the holo controls. The display still pulsated on the stage.

'Jane, I'm starting to remember things. I see images of the med com-link. He even talks to me.' Onslow looked up from her controls.

'What does he say?' she said, slightly concerned.

'That for now he has removed certain memories, but they will return soon. I think that when we were down here last and I saw that memory on the holo pad, it somehow triggered my lost memories.' Concerned, she scanned him. All vital signs were fine.

'If your memories return, we need to be in a better place than this, so, to save us keep coming down here, I'm going to pass a copy up to your room com.' Damian looked up, surprised.

'I thought it was safer down here. You have a damper field around this whole level. Nobody knows this level exists. Besides, I have already asked Six to create a sub link, and he said that he couldn't.' She looked up from the controls, a frown forming on her face.

'Sorry, who is Six?' she asked hesitantly.

'My room com,' he answered, with a shrug.

'You named your room-com?' she asked, puzzled. He shrugged again and gave a sheepish grin.

She deftly tapped the controls.

'There. Done now … back to your room.' The holo stage fell into darkness. It now looked no different to any of the other stages around it. Damian gave it one last glance, then followed Onslow out into the bright lights of the promenade.

CHAPTER 11

REUNION

'Welcome back Mr Drake,' chirped Six as they entered his quarters.

'Oh, and this must be Nurse Onslow. Welcome!'

Jane Onslow looked around the room. 'Very bland, you know you can ask your room com to change the decor to whatever you want.' Damian nodded as he sat in the recliner. He indicated the recliner opposite her but she declined. Instead, she knelt on the floor next to the holo stage.

'Room com, extend stage 50 centimetres by length and 30 centimetres by width, and create a conduit link to the holo stage on, copy 1-4-7-9.' Damian watched as the holo stage reshaped itself.

'Create sub link 125,' Onslow said whilst adjusting the stage controls.

'I am sorry Nurse Onslow. I cannot produce a sub link unless it is directly linked with the main com link.'

'Create sub link 125, priority demand, alpha delta 9 0 0 1.'

'Passing you over to sub link,' said Six in a matter-of-fact tone.

'Good evening, Jane,' a female voice greeted her from the panel.

'Create 125 priority, subject, Mr Damian Drake, neural net pathways, corrupted data.'

The image Damian had seen down in level 11 now appeared on the holo stage.

'This represents about half an hour of memory, I can see the thought patterns from yourself and from the med com-link, but there is this other interjection. It seems to come from nowhere, and yet, from everywhere all at the same time. It completely corrupts. I can see no way of creating any program that will allow these memory pathways to be translated.' She looked deep into the quagmire of amalgamating particles in the hope that an answer might just leap out at her.

Damian watched the spectacle, not understanding any of it.

'So, these particles here,' he said slowly and unsure, pointing to a stream, 'are actual memories, and these particles here,' he said pointing to the other stream, 'are the ones that are attacking them. So, at this point before the attack, they are complete memories, and at this point, and beyond they are not recognisable.'

She slowly turned to face him, astonished that he had understood such a complex study. She nodded.

'Exactly right,'

'So,' he continued, 'why can't you read them before they get attacked?' he asked triumphantly.

'It is not as easy as that. This,' she said pointing to the stream, 'has to go into your memory centre, er … the mnemonic implant. Once in there, it is decoded,' she said, still minutely adjusting the holo pad controls.

'Then bypass the attack.' Damian relaxed back into his recliner.

'Er … no, it would still be corrupted by the residue of the attack.'

'Then pass it into another memory centre, something remote, away from the model.' He tapped his right temple.' I have a mnemonic implant, right here.' She turned to him, puzzled at his line of thought, then slowly understood his reasoning.

She hesitated, but nodded her head. 'I think that's a possibility. I would have to run some tests first and readjust the holo pad to suit, but it's worth a try. The only downside that I can see, is, we might lose everything.'

'Or fry my brain,' he added with a mock scowl.

'That's impossible. It can't happen. There is no danger to you in the slightest,' she said, flatly. He smiled.

'Kidding,' he said jovially. Then added, 'Although, the last time I had any dealings with it, it knocked me to the ground.'

She glared at him. 'That won't happen this time.' She turned back to the image.

In just over half an hour a link was made from Damian to the memory model. Onslow had also ordered Six to create another holo stage to capture the images once Damian's mind had decoded them. The seating room did not offer enough floor space, so the extra stage was installed in the sleeping room.

'Are you ready?' she said giving the instruments a final check.

'You will feel nothing,' Onslow muttered as she reconfigured the holo towers. Damian swallowed and gave a nervous 'yes'. There was no sensation at all, and after a while Damian wondered whether it was working. But then, through the doorway to the sleeping area on the additional holo stage a burst of molecules formed . They swirled in and around each other until finally they gelled into an image.

As they watched the scenario take shape they were aware that from their perspective they were looking down at a blue white planet. A large disc exploded into a fiery ball of flame that within seconds had encompassed the planet, on the other side of the disc a violent storm of super-heated molecules ejaculated across the relatively short distance between the planet and its satellite moon. They watched in disbelief as another ball of flame exploded from the disc and travelled within seconds to the moon which then exploded into a trillion or more fragments.

The scenario moved on. They watched the two men sitting atop a large passenger liner, then to the disc itself. As the scenario ran its course both Damian and Onslow were transfixed. They now watched as the island's volcano erupted, the statues fell, and then the last words of the old man, then nothing. The image vanished. Damian continued to stare at the now empty holo pad.

'Do you remember any of that?' she asked softly. Damian's jaw had fallen. He turned to face her. She leant forward, a look of concern on her face, and took his hand with both of hers.

'It's my recurring dream, the island, that planet, I have dreamt of that every night, and now I remember it all. Comm ... Comm thought that something was controlling me, feeding me with information. Do you have all of it, the whole scenario, from beginning to end?' She looked down onto the controls.

'Yes, all of it, and stored securely.' She looked up into his eyes. They had shown signs of panic, but now they had softened.

'I think we should leave it for now. We can continue tomorrow, but for now, it is almost my sleep cycle. I should go,' she said with reluctance in her voice.

She released her grip on his hand and moved to pull them away but he held her hand firmly and gently pulled her towards him.

Stroking her hair, he leant forward and kissed her, taking in her scent. She breathed deeply, almost sighing, thinking to push him away, but instead returned the kiss and embraced him. They kissed and fondled, passion and lust swelling within them. He pulled off the fine fabric of her gown and was delighted that she was naked beneath. She tore at his clothes and soon they were rolling about the floor embracing, then coupling. They harmonised the rhythmic movements of their bodies – she climaxed first, holding him tight, burying her fingers deep into his back, all the while gasping with pleasure. He gently turned her so that he now played the dominant role, pushing and writhing in rhythm to her upward thrusts, he exploded within her, then, with all strength spent he crumpled and collapsed onto her, gasping for breath. He kissed her breasts then neck then lips, he whispered in her ear.

'You don't have to go. Please stay.' After holding each other close for a short time, they moved into the sleeping room. For twenty minutes they stroked and kissed, then, once again they started their passionate embrace. They were both gentler together now, and the climax when it arrived was mutual. They drifted into slumber holding tightly onto each other, and for the first time in this new life, Damian slept, without dreaming of the island.

Damian was deep into rapid eye movement sleep. The dream, as in all dreams, came across as cryptic. He was arguing with the Captain at the same time as making love to Jane Onslow. He was naked, as was his lover. The Captain stood rigid, almost to attention at the foot of the sleeping slab.

She glowered down at them yelling, 'The capsule will not allow this!'

In amongst this most peculiar of scenarios a voice, calm and soft cut through the ridiculous.

'Sandy.'

Damian was now into a rhythmic movement. Onslow bucked beneath him, screaming. 'Harder, harder, don't stop, please, Damian, don't stop.'

'Sandy, wake, you need to wake, I think it has found me, and, it has come for you! Wake up!'

'No,' yelled the Captain.

'You need the sleep, take no heed of this mischievous sprite. Your lover needs your attention,'

'Sandy, wake up, wake up now!' The voice of Comm sounded paranoid.

'You need your sleep, Damian. Jane needs you. Do not listen to him. He wants to take you down the wrong path.'

Captain Juliana Contessa was now naked, and massaging his shoulders. She leant down and kissed his neck, then licking upward took the lobe of his ear into her mouth and sucked. He looked down and concentrated on the writhing form of … Jane Onslow was no longer there! In her place, the form of the medical com-link glared up at him.

'Sandy, for fuck sake, wake up!'

The lights in the room had been subdued, not pitch black, but, dark, as in twilight. He gasped a breath; the room seemed to sway before him. On the holo stage the image of Comm beckoned to him.

'Sandy, get out, move, come to the holo stage, quick, get to the holo stage, now,' the voice of Comm yelled. Sandy's body lurched automatically and he stumbled from the sleeping platform and made his way to the holo stage, adopting the foetal position as he cowered down.

The room seemed to twist, the height extended from two and a half metres to what seemed a hundred. From his position he could see Onslow lying naked upon the sleeping platform. The wall behind stretched in all directions, taking on the likeness of a rubber sheet being pulled in all dimensions at once. He watched as at its centre a tear appeared, the fabric of the wall tore apart. What lay behind was blackness, black that had no reflection of light, deep black. The tear widened. He now seemed to be looking into the depths of infinity, an infinity that Housed no light or colour, and yet within it there seemed to be movement, twisting and throbbing movement of dark upon dark. He watched fascinated as the first of the tentacles thrashed out into the room.

'Sandy, do not move, to hide from Command Nurse Onslow has created a dampening field around your quarters. It was fine on level 11 where no one – possibly including Command – had an idea that it even existed, but here, all she has done has created an information black out, where none had existed before. Command has found a way to break in.' Comm's voice was calm and soft, Damian frowned.

'Jane, what about Jane?' he shouted in panic.

'Trust me, she is fine. You must stay here.' Comm held him back and hunkered down with him.

'So, am I hidden, or can it see me.' There was a long pause. Damian was frozen to the holo pad. He tried to adjust his breathing. Three metres away, tentacles of different lengths and girths were now thrashing from the ceiling to the floor, then from one wall to the other.

'I have created a deflector field within the damper, all through the holographic imagery of this stage. If it wanted to, I think it could find you, but I'm not sure it has come for you right now, so stay still.' Damian almost rushed forward when a thrashing limb encircled the sleeping body of Jane Onslow and lifted her up midway to the ceiling, another limb attached itself to her head. He was horrified as he watched the end of the tendril open like the petals of a flower and her head disappeared within it.

'What kind of an animal is it? Oh my, it's eating her!' he gasped.

'Sandy! Stay still, do not move! It is no animal. It is a Command conduit. It is seeking information. I promise you, she will not be harmed.' Damian's pulse increased tenfold. He was trying desperately to control his breathing and the desire to leap forward, but he kept calm and retained his position on the holo stage.

'Why doesn't she wake?' his said, his voice, pitifully small, conveying fear and frustration.

One of the smaller tendrils that had been thrashing from wall to ceiling now stopped dead centre of the room. At its end it opened then turned to the left then swooped to the right. It swayed like the head of a snake that was about to strike.

'Do not move a muscle,' Comm advised in a slow and punctuated voice. Damian tensed and held his breath as the tendril moved slowly towards him. It stopped a metre from him, swaying back and forth, then without warning it grasped his leg. There was no pain, but he felt its weight as it slithered up to his chest. He tried to pull away but his body was paralysed and he could feel it slithering and sucking its way up onto his torso, then it entwined itself around his chest, then neck, the end opening to show grey petals that stretched half a metre wide.

It then swallowed his head whole.

Spirals of colour swam around him, multi-ribbons of colour extending away into infinity. He was aware of noise, and vibration – the noise harmonised and the vibration followed its melody. He swam in the sweet melody that surrounded him. It was soothing and he allowed himself to be drawn along the resonating and pulsating music. Then all at once, silence.

He was in a vast space, its dimensions unfathomable. The colours had separated and had formed layers around him. He felt he was standing in the middle of a rainbow. The vibration returned. It pulsated through his body, accompanied by a deep bass. Slowly it throbbed, then changing its pitch became a drone, the colours danced in unison around him, then, in an instant, nothing. He thought he heard a laugh, certainly a voice within the laughter.

'Ah, there you are. Hello Pr ...'

CHAPTER 12

CAPSULE

'Sandy, Sandy wake up!' Comm's voice filled his mind.

'I recognise that voice,' Damian muttered as consciousness slowly emerged.

'Sandy, it's me, Comm,' Damian turned to face the holographic image. He blinked slowly, trying to rid his sight of the blurred image that stood before him.

'Comm,' he said slowly, the image fading slightly, then solidifying.

'Is that really you?' he said after a while.

'Yes Sandy, it is really me. I am hiding in the sub routine link. I will transfer to your room com, as soon as I can. You can access the room com as normal, then use 'Sandy one oh' as a code. Sorry Sandy, I cannot stay long here, the main com-link is still searching.' Comm sat cross legged on the holo stage. Damian sat beside him.

'And Jane, what of her, will she be alright?' Damian felt his breathing increase as he thought back to the flailing tentacles that had taken both Jane and himself. Then he remembered, the voice.

'Comm, it spoke to me. It knew me,'

'I always thought that perhaps it was Command that was feeding you information, for what reason, we may never know. What did it say?'

'Just "Ah, there you are. Hello" ... then it started to say my name, but it wasn't Damian or Sandy. Then you woke me.' Comm raised his hand to his face and cupped his chin, his index finger tapped his jaw.

"Firstly, Jane is fine. She will be in a deep sleep right now. When she awakes, she will have no recollection of what has transpired. To her, she would have remembered falling asleep in your arms, then after a long sleep will awake refreshed, and for now, you cannot tell her any of this. She probably wouldn't believe you anyway, so don't worry about her, she will be fine. Secondly, I need to take you back to the island. We have unfinished business. Level 11 would be the best place, the main com-link does not recognise its existence, but for now you must get some rest. I will contact you soon, but for now I must go.' Damian began to protest but Comm gave him an apologetic smile, shrugged, then faded away.

After a difficult and restless night Damian awoke. Jane Onslow had gone.

'Good morning, Mr. Drake,' chirped Six, Damian thought he really had to tone down the room comm's enthusiasm. He grunted 'Morning' and made his way to the ablutions room. On exiting he asked, 'When did Nurse Onslow leave?' he said nonchalantly, as he slowly dressed.

'Nurse Onslow left one point three standard hours ago. Is it your wish that I contact her?' Damian stopped and looked towards the room coms panel. He could contact her and ask if she was well. No, he thought, if anything was wrong, if she had remembered anything from the previous night, she would have woken him, wouldn't she? He shuddered, of course she would, why would he think she wouldn't?

The thought confused him. He reflected back on the time he had spent on the Griffin. 'There's not much that hasn't confused me.' He snickered an inward laugh and finished dressing.

'No Six, I don't think I need to contact her, but I do need directions to the engineering lab, sub hanger 6, the one where the life pod capsule is being kept.' The replicator opened and he removed the high protein meal from within.

'I have ordered you an energy guide. It has been programmed with your destination. Is there anything else I can help you with Mr Drake?' Damian chewed on the breakfast slab. It tasted better than it looked.

'No thank you Six. You can power down now,' he said as he swallowed the last of his breakfast. He turned to look at the room com's panel and was surprised when Six didn't give his normal last word. He shrugged and exited the room. Outside the energy guide pulsated green and waited patiently.

'Continue,' Damian said without any feeling. The slither of green floated off down the corridor. He followed three paces behind, at the midships lobby it floated up the wide staircase without stopping. Damian had to pick up his speed to keep up.

On the third level, the energy guide stopped outside a double door entrance.

'Sub hanger 6, the life pod capsule is being examined within,' the voice of the guide informed him.

'Thank you,' Damian said, the pulsing green guide dissipated then vanished. Damian entered the storage area.

The size of the room surprised him, much larger than he expected. He stood two metres inside and scanned the area. To his right stood the five-metre capsule. He noticed that it had been disassembled. Much of its outer casing had been removed and now lay strewn across the floor. Four engineers were stooped down amongst the capsule's debris.

Damian could see that they were busy as they had not noticed him enter.

Twenty metres in front of him he noticed an array of interfaced holo pads. They all pulsed with the now familiar-coloured towers. Three engineers busied themselves with the information that the towers offered. To his left others stood at workstations set in alcoves in the bulk head wall. He was about to walk further into the storage area when he felt a strange sensation ripple through his stomach, not painful, but, certainly a queasy feeling. It rose through him and very soon he became lethargic, weakness overcame him and he sank to his knees. An engineer at the holo array shouted for the Commander.

Damian was aware of activity, all around him. All engineers left the work they had been concentrating on and ran to holo pads. The four engineers by the capsule ran past him. One stopped and called to his comrades. they returned and helped Damian to his feet.

The room swam around him and he clasped tighter onto the two men either side of him.

'Mr Drake, can you hear me?' It was a familiar voice. He recognised it as the Senior engineer Commander Burroughs.

'Yes, Commander, I can hear you, I seem to have come over … a bit sickly,' he said slowly as the two engineers gently placed him into a vacant recliner. He heard the huge double doors open, and watched as the Med team ran towards him led by Doctor Ghorbany. The engineers moved aside to allow the Med team to work.

'Commander,' engineer Imran Chan said. Burroughs turned to him.

'What is it?'

'We have alpha, beta and theta waves emanating from the capsule, and something else, not so much a wave but a resonance.' He studied the multi-coloured towers, concentrating on a yellow tower.

'The intensity is dissipating, but they started when Mr Drake entered the storage facility.'

Burroughs studied the readouts from the holo towers. It confirmed what the engineer was saying. The capsule and its passenger were definitely interlocked.

That was obvious to Burroughs. They had been in the capsule together for a long time. Although it was highly advanced technology, it was still a programmable machine and that program, as far as the Commander could make out, was to protect and keep Mr Drake alive. But this was new, definitely a resonation, similar he thought to the mechanics of Griffin's Trellion engines. He turned to Dr. Ghorbany.

'How is he?' he asked, concerned now that Damian's body lay limp upon the recliner. Ghorbany studied his readouts.

'We need to get him back to the Med centre. He is totally unresponsive. I suggest Commander, that you and your team come up with some way to damper out that thing,' he said, looking towards the capsule.

Burroughs followed his gaze and turned to his team. They were standing around the recliner, concerned looks on their faces.

'Che and Duncan, go with the Doctor. You need to set up a dampening field for Mr Drake, a personal dampening field. Then report back,' he ordered.

Ghorbany and his team had already secured Damian to the anti-grav and were heading with haste towards the exit, followed by the two engineers.

Commander Burroughs glared at the capsule.

'How is it working?' he muttered, more to himself than to any of the surrounding engineers.

'It shouldn't be working at all; we have completely stripped it of all working parts.' An engineer said, following the commander's gaze to the five-metre-tall blue cylinder.

'What if it's not all here?' said one of the engineering cadets. Burroughs frowned trying to comprehend the statement.

'Explain.' he said, slowly turning to face the young cadet. Jessica Khan swallowed, too loudly for her liking, but she took a deep silent breath and squared up to her commanding officer.

'We are just looking at it from a three-dimensional perspective. What if, what is jutting through is from either another dimension or another parallel.' Burroughs gawped, his mind swam, as he tried to comprehend the enormity of the cadet's explanation.

'I must admit Cadet, I am intrigued. As you know, we have come up with absolutely nothing. Any suggestion no matter how wild, is worth pursuing. Speak to the engineering team- I think Lieutenant Ashley would be a good start: He submitted quite an interesting theory on inter-dimensional travel a few standard years ago. In fact, I would be interested in his views on this matter. Oh, and I will transfer com-link privileges to your team.' Jessica Khan was taken aback – she couldn't quite believe what she had just heard.

'My team, Commander,' she said hesitantly. Tom Burroughs gave a broad grin.

'Jessica, you brought your theory to my attention. That makes you team leader, but, listen to your team. They will give valuable input.

CHAPTER 13

ISLAND REVISITED

The turquoise sea filled his view, the white breakers rumbled onto the white sandy beach. He turned, the volcano rose high above him its lower third shrouded in swaying palms. Ten meters away he saw Comm sitting at the bar, deep in conversation with the mantis barkeep.

Everything had returned to how it was, with no evidence of the devastating storm.

After walking the short distance across the beach, he stood behind the now animated Comm.

'No, no, it is not made with whisky. It should be brandy.' The mantis seemed to shrug and with perfect dexterity it conceded and took back Comm's glass. The old man half turned, aware of Damian's presence behind him.

'It's not as good as we first thought. It's trying to fob me off with a tryliriun made of whisky. Please Sandy, take a seat.' With open hand he indicated the vacant stool.

Damian sat and studied the comm link. He was as he remembered, an old man, white hair and ragged clothing.

'The island is back as it was, so, what happened to the storm, and all the devastation?'

Comm smiled and indicated a tall, iced glass on the counter. 'Apple juice?' He said gesturing to the glass.

'Comm, what's going on, why am I here, how, am I here?'

The older man rested his hand upon his shoulder.

'I have linked with you via the medical scanner, it is not as good as the main med com-link that we had before but, I have made some modifications, it will suffice. You are being treated as we speak. The capsule has somehow interlocked with you. Your implants are fighting what they see as an invasion, and you have been put on lock down, which, has given me the possibility of recreating the island. We have unfinished business here. The continuing story of the statues awaits, but first, drink, before the ice melts.' The mantis offered Comm his glass. The old man took it and sniffed the beverage, then smiled.

'That's better.' He sipped the drink and rolled his eyes.

'Oh, I take everything back. You are good!' The mantis glared back without any emotion but to Damian seemed to shrug as he went back to cleaning glasses.

'Brandy, it makes all the difference,' Comm sighed. Damian took a deep breath.

'Comm, I thought the main com-link was still searching for you. Isn't this the most obvious place for it to look?' Damian said as he watched the older man drain the last of his drink.

'I have put some difficult barriers in the path of the main com-link, not to mention the many dead ends that exist in the labyrinth that I have created. But even so, if I am found ... all this,' he said panning his arm around, 'will come to a sudden end and I will disappear down any one of a million escape holes that I have contrived, and you, will, well, just wake up. So, before any of that happens, let's go. Er, you do remember how to fly, don't you?'

Before Damian could reply, Comm had leapt into the air and accelerated skywards. Damian laughed as he soared up into the air and after several minutes had caught him up.

They were travelling at about a thirty metres above the shoreline. Damian looked down onto the island below – the white sand, green palms and the sheer rock face of the volcano.

'Comm, let's go up to the summit, we'll be able to see the whole of the island.' Damian shouted. Comm looked back shaking his head.

'Another time, Sandy, we need to go to the statues.' Damian felt frustrated at this. They had a perfect opportunity to see the whole of the island. What could be hiding on the far side? Why was Comm so insistent that they had to go to the statues.

'Sandy,' Comm's voice was calm and almost apologetic, 'I do not know how much time we have. We need to manage it well so follow me down.' They alighted on the beach at the base of the statues. Comm walked forward and looked up at them.

'Over five and a half thousand years ago Sindra and Ilya created the Disc. That in itself was an enormous achievement. It allowed us to travel in excess of the speed of light for the first time. But in doing so, they destroyed the Earth and its satellite, the Moon,' Comm said in a matter-of-fact tone, as he pointed to the first two of the statues on the fourth line. Damian sat cross-legged on the beach staring up at the statues.

'Yes, I know that Comm, but, as we found out, their final flight was not to Alpha Centuri, but to a dwarf star, eighty or so light years further on, amazingly where the Griffin is now stationed. Is that accidental, or, is that by design? If it was accidental, that is one hell of a coincidence, including the fact that that was where I was found, and of course that it is the Griffin's last port of call.' Comm turned away from the statues and faced the younger man. He had grown, he thought, since he was last here, not only physically but mentally too.

'Yes,' he nodded slowly, 'the records of which these scenarios are made are obviously flawed. On our next journey, we must question everything. We must be sceptical of every fact that is given, everything now is questionable, nothing is really what it seems. However, not all the data is contaminated.' He sat next to Damian and leant back into the white sand. Damian tried to judge the blank look on Comm's face.

'Nothing, it seems, is trustworthy. How can we possibly believe any of the scenarios, no matter where your sources are, when it is obvious that I am somehow being manipulated,' Damian said casually, still looking up at the statues of Sindra and Ilya.

'In the last scenario, I used a lot of data from official historical records. They, of course are from the Command archives. But I also used records from personal diaries and journals of the time. I do not think that they were contaminated. They were not from the Command collective.' Damian turned to face the elderly Comm link.

'Why would they not be. They all come from an historical store which Command controls.' Comm inclined his head towards his left shoulder and gave a sheepish smile.

'Not all of them. Some, I borrowed from, well, let's say private collections, and quite a few of them from, well, not too far away,' Damian glowered at him.

'"Not too far away". Where?' Damian sat up straight, confused.

'What? On this ship? Who?' he said at last. Comm smiled his perfect white-toothed smile.

'I cannot possibly say, but, you're right, it is a member of this crew – an amateur historian who doesn't have a great love for Command. And that information is common knowledge, and documented, but, that person has over the years acquired a unique collection of original diaries and journals of our distant past. I came across some clues, whilst hiding in the … er, to use your vernacular, in the wires. This particular person has accumulated thousands of diaries spanning back over five thousand years, and so, I have of course copied them all, and we will use them on our continuing journey as I tell the life stories of the remaining statues.'

Damian was aware that his jaw had dropped he placed a hand upon the older man's shoulder.

'Comm, don't you think that … that is, well, a little bit too convenient. We are delving back to a time where factual records are rarer than sentient beings in the galaxy, and you just happen to stumble upon a full set of records within a kilometre of where we are lying. Doesn't that strike you as odd?'

Comm stood and walked towards the statues. He stroked the capital on top of the pedestal.

'I agree, it is an amazing coincidence, but, since you have arrived on the Griffin everything that surrounds you seems to be a coincidence. But most importantly, let's not forget why we are here,' he added, his face turning grave.

'We are trying to get you to remember a past life, your past life. These people,' he turned and gestured to the statues.

'To me, they are villains, evil murderous bastards, but to you, I have a feeling they are something else. One thing I do know, and I think you do too, somehow: They are a part of you, even though they span a timeline that keeps them thousands of standard years apart from one another, you somehow, are a link to them.' He grabbed the top of the pedestal and craned his head back to take in the full view of the inverted pyramid of statues.

'Sandy, it doesn't matter whether the stories are true or not, it is your interaction with them that will invoke your memories. It did the last time, and I am sure it will again.'

Damian had stood and had listened to his friend. He still wasn't sure, it was all becoming too much. He turned and slowly walked back to the shoreline and the white breakers. The scenarios could be just a waste of time. Who could say that the memories were true or not. However, the beauty that was Lien and the kiss on the Citadel steps had evoked a special memory – a memory that neither Comm nor Command could have had any dealings with. It was a memory that had come from the heart, nothing that was written or recorded.

He turned and looked up at the line of four statues, Sindra and Ilya; he had recognised them, just for an instant, before something had taken it away. And he recognised them as friends, comrades or maybe colleagues. He paced backwards until all the statues were in view. He looked up, the steep cliff face of the volcano, the flat plateau hundreds of metres above and the puff of smoke that hovered permanently above the summit.

'Ok, let's do this' he said, as he slowly walked back.

'Firstly ...' Comm began, as he sat crossed-legged upon the sand with his back up against the pedestal. The golden 'O' reflected the sun's rays and Damian couldn't help but suppress a giggle. Comm gave him a puzzled look.

'What's so funny?'

'Sorry Comm. It's just, well, from where I am it looks as though you have just sprouted a halo.' Comm's face became expressionless as he struggled to search for a definition.

'What is a halo?' he asked at last. Damian smiled then shrugged.

'It doesn't matter, I'll explain it another time – it's not important.' Comm stood, his hands bunched into fists, holding them tight upon his hips, taking a defiant stance. Damian noticed his eyes were steely grey.

'Everything here matters. No matter what we do here, there is a meaning attached to it. So tell me what a halo is.'

Damian turned his palms and slowly bowed his head in submission.

'It's no big deal. It can either mean a light circle around a planetary body, which as you probably know is caused by light refracting from ice crystals in the atmosphere. You probably call it something else. Or, a ring or circle of light around the head of a saint in a religious painting.'

Damian noticed the quizzical unsurety that flashed across Comm's face.

'A member of a chosen people, somebody, chosen by God, because of personal righteousness or the nature of his or her faith, sometimes used by religious groups to refer to their own leader, usually a virtuous person favoured by God.'

'A Deity,' Comm uttered slowly.

'Well, not God, but more a follower of God,' Damian answered hesitantly.

'You have mentioned a deity to me before. You asked whether Command could be our version of God.' Damian stood confused. He couldn't fathom where this conversation was going, or why they were even discussing it in the first place.

'Yes,' he said at last, then.

'But as you explained. Command has no part in being a Deity to its people.' Comm relaxed.

'Yes Sandy, I remember the conversation, and we concluded that Command was, or, is, not God. But the problem I have now, is, did you believe that? If you didn't, then the halo is an indication that you believe that I am a favoured entity of Command.' Damian sagged.

'No, no, that is only an interpretation, I do not believe that Comm. Out of all the people that I have met here, you and nurse

Onslow are the only people that I truly trust. You have got to believe that, otherwise, none of this makes any sense.'

Comm's eyes flashed pale blue, the perfect white smile reappeared.

'Sandy, I know that you believe it, however it is your deep subconscious that worries me. But, as always we will deal with problems as we meet them. And now it is time to meet the next two in the line of four. Colin Grey and Chi Lin, according to a lot of the personal records of the time. They met on one of the moons of Jupiter, Ganymede. It is the largest of all the satellite moons in the Sol system, and, just as a point of interest, if it was in orbit of the star Sol instead of the planet Jupiter it would have been a planet in its own right.

The moon itself is interesting. It has a molten iron core then a layer of rock but above that a full liquid ocean. It also has a rarity, a magnetic field, and then to top it all, a very thin atmosphere of almost pure oxygen. Many settlers had tried to establish a colony on its surface. All had failed.'

Damian frowned. 'Why did they fail. It sounds a perfect place to thrive.'

Comm slowly shook his head.

'Nowhere was the perfect place. Every planetary object where the survivors set up home was difficult. Many perished in the five hundred years after the destruction of Earth. To be clear, humans at that time were an endangered species.

The governing consortium that was set up on Mars oversaw trade from one colony to the other. Then one man emerged and would change everything. Kyle Quanton, he was different – an entrepreneur extraordinaire. He was the lead technical manager to the consortium on Mars, but he was so much more than that. He delved into and got involved in the politics of Mars. He was the whispered voice behind the thrones of many leading activists within the higher ranks of the consortium.'

Damian looked at the inverted pyramid of statues before him.

'Why are you talking about him. He is not represented by the nine.'

Comm turned and slowly shook his head.

'Names, they are only a means of identification to those who are close to them. To me, you are Sandy, to the crew of the Griffin you are Damian, and as you can see, your scroll now bears your full name, "Damian Drake" though that might in the end not be true.' As we immerse ourselves into the story of Colin Grey and Chi Lin, many people will be associated with them. Kyle Quanton was one such person, but is he, who he says he is?'

Damian stared at his own statue. The last time he and Comm stood before them his scroll was blank. Now his name was etched deep into the white alabaster-type material of the scroll. Was that true? Was that his true name, or was that also a facade? He turned away from the statues and looked down the length of the white sand beach, then up to the volcano that towered above them.

None of this is real, he knew. Comm had told him so. It was the first thing he had said on their initial meeting. All of this was in his mind, but how far did the illusion go? Did it extend to the Griffin as well?

'Sandy.' Comm's voice broke through his reverie and he turned to face him.

'Is it possible, that everything I am experiencing, is false? That none of this is true. I don't mean just the island. I mean, everything.' Comm slowly placed his arm around the younger man's shoulder.

'Sandy, I can't say whether that statement is true or false. The only way to know for sure is to live through it and it will be at the end that the truth may or may not reveal itself. However, I am not linked to the med com as I was last time. I cannot read your full emotions, nor can I adjust them, so, I think we will evaluate the scenarios as we go.' Damian stood before the statues dumbfounded. Could it be true? Could everything be just an illusion?

The statues as before dissolved before him and once again they were in the grey place. When his vision had restored, he found himself standing shoulder to shoulder with Comm at the top of a steep cliff looking down at a domed city some three hundred metres below.

Jupiter filled the sky, Damian stared in disbelief at its incredible size. Just on the horizon, Comm pointed out, was Europa. The sky, thought Damian, was amazing.

They stood upon a cleft in the sheer wall of a cliff that circumvented a multi-domed outpost on the valley floor three hundred meters below.

'House Quanton, as it will be known, lies before us,' Comm said, as he indicated the complex below. Damian crouched down and looked below the ledge, somehow expecting the outpost to extend beyond his vision.

'It's smaller than I thought it would be,' he said, looking up at Comm.

'This is just a beginning. At the moment they, like everyone else in this system, are struggling to survive. It is amazing that they are here at all. This atmosphere is highly corrosive, which is why no one before Kyle Quanton could ever make a settlement work here, although, as I said, Ganymede was rich in minerals, especially Quantonite. It was that mineral, incredibly rare within all the known planets, even in our time, that was the key for interstellar flight.'

Damian turned to Comm, frowned a puzzled look.

'But we had already seen interstellar flight with the first two statues, and "Quantonite". Any relation to Kyle Quanton?'

Comm smiled. 'When the Earth was destroyed, these people had only one thing on their minds, and that was survival. Five hundred years later, now that they had settled and had started to thrive, some very powerful minds turned to the stars. Kyle Quanton was such a mind, and as this scenario continues you will see that Kyle Quanton and Quantonite are very much linked together.' Damian was still puzzled. 'And this Quantonite, does what, exactly?' Comm's eyes opened wide. He suppressed a giggle then slowly shook his head 'To tell you what it does, exactly, would take quite some time in the telling, however, to be brief, it is used on the outer hull of modern-day interstellar ships. Due to its crystalline make up it can easily be bonded with an organic compound that brings the ship to life. In fact, all interstellar craft in their own way are alive. The Griffin is such a craft. The hull will flex and repair itself and it also adapts itself within the rigours of dimensional flight.' Damian frowned.

'Dimensional flight?' he asked hesitantly. Comm studied him.

'When we have more time, I will try to explain, or, ask Commander Burroughs when you next see him. Right now we are waiting, ah, there.' He pointed. Damian looked up. Just clearing the apex of a mountain range a few kilometres away, he noticed a ship. It was obviously in distress.

'The engines are unbalanced. He has not compensated for the gravitational flux that exists between Jupiter and Ganymede. Normally it is an automatic response that his com unit would calculate. Either his com is offline, or, he himself has disabled it.' Damian watched fascinated as the craft lurched towards the solitary landing pad.

'Will it crash?' he asked, not daring to take his eyes off the stricken cruiser. Comm turned to him and shrugged.

'No, and that was the problem. It lands perfectly.'

'Why would that be a problem?' Damian asked, confused.

The small three-levelled craft made its precarious descent, similar, thought Damian, to a leaf falling from a tree. He frowned to himself as he tried to recollect where the memory of a falling leaf had come from.

The craft lurched to the left at almost thirty degrees, then back to the right. At one stage its pilot had pulled the nose so high to compensate, Damian thought it would flip over onto its back. However, with the small cruiser under his control the pilot pushed it back to a level track. At the final approach, to break the inertia the craft span a full 180 degrees then landed onto the pad without hesitation.

'Wow!' exclaimed Damian.

'That is some pilot.'

Comm turned, smiling and nodding at the younger man's excitement.

'And there, is another problem,' he said, pointing to the craft.

'Or at least one of many. The pilot is Chi Lin. He has been an administrator for the trade consortium for five years. Before that I have no other records that mention him by name, and yes, there are records of him flying shuttles, but not cruisers. What he has achieved here is exemplary, but this is just the finale of an incredible flight. The cruiser is stolen, why he stole it, I have no idea. I can find no record.

However, there are records of it being pursued from Mars. The security forces caught up with him as he neared the asteroid belt. Not that entering the belt would cause difficulty to either Lin or the security forces. The asteroids are quite a distance apart, but it was noted in security logs, that at this point, the security forces turned back to Mars. He did however sustain damage – whether that was from a lucky shot from one of his pursuers there is no way of telling. He then continued his journey to Jupiter with a craft that was partly crippled. Again, the timeline of that journey, doesn't add up. Taking the maximum thrust the cruiser could achieve he shouldn't be here for another two standard weeks.' Comm stepped from the cliff edge and beckoned Damian to follow.

'So, that's easy,' Damian said as he leapt from the cliff and then caught the elder man up.

'Just inspect the cruiser, see whether the engines have been upgraded.' Comm held up his hand in a gesture for Damian to stop.

They were floating directly above the landing pad and just thirty metres below, the cruiser exploded into a horrendous fireball; the force of the blast took out two of the four surrounding towers.

'Fifteen of the stations crew died in that blast, but not Chi Lin, he had already left, which again, was surprising.'

Damian gawped at the devastation that was unfolding below him. Most of the landing pad and the surrounding infrastructure had disappeared.

'Could ... could a cruiser cause, that amount of damage?' he asked, his voice wavering. Comm studied his young companion, the shock and horror evident upon his features.

'There are many inconsistencies with this scenario,' he said at last. Damian reluctantly turned away from the devastated landing pad below.

'In what way? Or are you implying that this is a made-up scenario, a fake.' Comm frowned at the remark.

'No, not made up, just well, not probable, there is no documentation of the actual journey that Chi Lin made from Mars to Ganymede.

The only evidence that I have been able to find is a journal of an engineering technician named Peters. It was in the form of a diary, just day-to-day living on Ganymede, the journal describes in part the fleeing of Chi Lin from Mars. Apparently he received this information from Chi Lin himself. One night sometime after this event in a bar on the lower deck of the base.' He shook his head slowly and looked back down at the landing pad, completely destroyed.

'What I think is wrong, is this. Chi Lin escaped Mars after stealing a small cruiser. A ship I might add requires a minimal crew of three. He is pursued by the Martian security forces. Now that is documented. However, they are from Command historical archives. Why he stole the ship in the first place, I have no idea.

It's a mystery: To fly a ship on your own, a damaged ship as well, when at best, all you are is a mediocre shuttle pilot. Then to outrun and elude experienced security pilots, then, go against the known physics of the day and complete a journey with a crippled ship two standard weeks faster than he should, and then land it, perfectly, and be allowed off the ship, when it is known that Kyle Quanton has never previously allowed anyone to land here before without prior appointment. And even then he would have gone through all the protocols of investigation before letting the pilot disembark. And to finish – whatever evidence for Chi Lin's journey – mysteriously vanished in that explosion!

So, with all that in mind, let's go and meet them.'

Comm descended towards the base. Damian, totally confused, followed. They alighted on the buckled landing pad. The fire storm that had raged from the cruisers demise had been controlled by avatar androids. However the devastation had given access into the base via the gaping holes in the structure. Not that gaining entry for the two spectral figures would have been a problem.

The devastation of the landing pad lay behind them, Damian was amazed at the decor of the station. As he and Comm walked down a service corridor that led further into the station's interior, he noticed it was totally different from the interior of the Griffin. Then something hit home. He stopped and called Comm back.

'Comm,' he said softly. Comm turned, to find Damian studying an archway that led off to the right.

'What is it?' he enquired.

'The style of this arch, and look, further down, the panelling on the walls. Does it look familiar to you?' Comm scanned the decor. He concentrated his attention on the ornate arch.

'I would say that it is just a generic style. I have created the Ganymede station from schematics from Command archives. They just give the layout, not the decor. However, this whole scenario has been channelled and created via your own imagination.' Damian scanned the area, the main passageway and the arches.

'It's the capsule,' he said after a while. Comm shrugged.

'You were incarcerated in there for a long time. It is just your mind trying to make sense of everything.' Damian smiled and nodded in agreement.

They walked further into the station. For the first part of their journey the wide passageway was busy with crew, bustling their way from one destination to another, but now, further into the station Damian realised that they were alone. Comm stopped before a double door at the end of passage.

'Beyond these doors are the inner sanctum and offices of Kyle Quanton. Inside we should find the man himself – and Chi Lin. So, let's go in.'

Damian followed as Comm walked through the structure of the solid door. They emerged into a reception area, monitors on either side of the large area depicted scenes of oceans, forests and deserts. They were scenes from a now long-lost planet.

Comm took no heed of the surroundings. Instead he walked past the oversized reception desk to another set of double doors at the rear of the room. Damian followed him and as he re-emerged on the other side of the substantial doors, he was surprised to find that had entered yet another reception area, similar to the first, apart from two sets of double doors set either side of the reception desk.

'According to the schematics, the one on the left is his private quarters, and this one is his main office, or inner sanctum as he always referred to it.' Damian could hear raised voices even before he walked through. Inside Chi Lin was pacing the room, his face red as he yelled at the sitting figure of Kyle Quanton.

'You have a leak in your organisation, and you need to have it fixed. Luckily my colleague was not named, so at least we still have a trusted member of your House inside the consortium.' Chi Lin stopped mid pace and turned to the portly Quanton.

'Our timetable has changed. Everything we have planned must now be brought forward. Maybe,' he added in a calmer voice, 'this would be beneficial.'

Quanton was not fazed by the man's outburst and leant back into the sumptuous confines of his over padded chair.

'I can assure you Chi, the informer is not from my team,' Quanton said softly. Damian thought that he detected menace in his voice and watched as the well-dressed man slowly leant forward and reached for his beverage.

'Are you implying that the informer is somehow linked to me? My team is considerably smaller than yours. I know each one of them personally. They would have nothing to gain, and let's not forget, I was hunted and nearly killed by the Martian security force. With my death my team would be redundant, and, they know nothing of your involvement. Your team, however, have a lot to gain.'

Damian turned to Comm and frowned.

'Sorry Comm, but I have no idea what is going on. Is Kyle Quanton the fourth statue Colin Grey?' The scene around them froze; instantly, silence surrounded them. Comm turned and smiled at his young friend. He pointed to the portly man sitting in the huge padded seat.'

'When we saw the statues for the first time, do you recall that I said that they are just how history records them, and when we studied your statue, it depicted a perfect likeness of yourself at that precise moment. Now, look at Kyle Quanton. Does he look like the fourth statue?' Damian leant over the huge ornate desk. Recognition did not come to him: The man sitting in front of him in no way resembled the statue of Colin Grey.

'No, this is not him, but he, however,' he said turning to Chi Lin, is a perfect likeness of the third statue, and, somehow familiar.' Damian walked over to Chi Lin and studied his face.

'There is something that is so familiar about him, it's just so far out of reach, it is frustrating,' he said despondently.

'That, is what this is all about Sandy – to trigger your memory, and these scenarios are doing that. I can see from your face that this man means something to you, but Quanton doesn't. And no, he isn't Colin Grey, but he is the key to this scenario. He created the first established House in the consortium. In the next ten standard years he will have changed the whole strategy of humans living and surviving in space. Without him, there would be no future, but the price for that, would be immense.' Damian turned to look at Kyle Quanton. He studied the man's face. Despite the accusation and the outburst from Chi Lin, he seemed calm, almost amused. Turning back to Comm and pointing at Quanton, he said.

'I have no recollection of this man, but I think I know his type – highly ambitious, self-centred and vicious with it.' Comm nodded.

'He was all of that, but also intelligent. Remember, he created this station where many had failed, and he had a very loyal staff, and he rewarded them well for that.' Damian turned back to the man sitting in front of him.

'And what did he do to those who are not loyal?' Comm thought for a while, searching through countless records of the time.

"There are no records of what he did to them, none at all.' Damian rolled his eyes.

'Well, there's a surprise. Of course there's no record. As you said, he is intelligent, but getting back to this scenario. What's going on?'

Comm let out an involuntary sigh.

'Quanton was the technical manager for the consortium on Mars base for many years. In that position he had access to many political avenues on many worlds in the Sol system. He became a trusted friend to many – just with that on its own he could have risen to consortium president. But then he met Chi Lin, who offered him something much better. Chi, managed to convince him that by creating fear within the consortium, and by that, I mean the fear of piracy within the trade routes and political upheaval within the consortium itself. As a result he would end up as the ultimate leader of all the planetary bodies. The argument must have been convincing, because, he just could not resist. So, they contrived a plan, and for the last three years twenty percent of all trade had been seized by a band of so-called privateers, all paid for of course by Quanton. Politically, rumours and misdirection played out expertly, the consortium was in total confusion.' Damian had walked back to Chi Lin.

'But someone had informed, so who was that?' Comm gave his perfect white-toothed smile, and put his arm around the shoulders of the frozen figure of Chi Lin.

'That was his partner, Colin Grey.' Damian found himself lost again.

'Why would he do that?' he said slowly.

'Because he was told to, by this man,' he said, gently tapping Chi Lin's cheek. 'What you must understand Sandy, is that there is more than one scenario taking place here. Chi Lin and Colin Grey had a completely different agenda. It seems their involvement was to take the blame away from our portly friend there.' He pointed to Quanton. Damian shook his head slowly.

'I still don't get this. If all was going to their plan, why have your partner inform on you, bearing in mind he was nearly killed by the security forces.' Comm slowly shook his head.

'I can assure you Sandy, he was never in any danger. Most of the Mars security were part of the …'

'They were on the payroll,' Damian interjected.

'Er … yes, they were in on the conspiracy. Chi Lin decided that the conspired outcome was taking too long, so, decided to speed things up a bit.' Damian looked over to Kyle Quanton then to Chi Lin.

'So, the timetable has now been advanced, so what does that mean?' Comm left Chi Lin and walked to the edge of the desk.

'Let us see.'

'A lot to gain,' Kyle Quanton exploded. Damian jumped back, shocked, he glared at the grinning Comm.

'Let us calm down,' Chi Lin said softly, Quanton took a deep breath and leant back into his chair. Chi Lin sat in the chair opposite.

'Who is to blame is not the problem. The fact is that someone is, and they will be found I'm sure, and of course severely punished. But for now, I have here …' he said leaning down and retrieving a large satchel from the floor, 'all the trade routes and the diaries of where all the prominent hierarchy of the consortium will be in the coming five weeks.'

He handed the bag over to Quanton.

'And, I must congratulate you on the deception of destroying the cruiser complete with my DNA on board.' Quanton looked up from surveying the interior of the satchel.

'Crossing tees and dotting 'Is', just in case we get a visit. You, and all these stolen goods, crash landed, total destruction, nothing left. Which means of course, you no longer exist,' Damian watched the two men lock eyes, the stare lasted almost a minute. Quanton was the first to break.

'We still however need each other. I will arrange for a new ID.' Quanton said smoothly. Turning, he activated a com device, the scenario froze. Damian turned to Comm.

'What happens next?' he asked, watching Comm walk around the desk.

'Chi Lin, gets a new identity, and over the next two standard months they step up the piracy attacks. Which Chi Lin organises under a different identity, Quanton, well, he moves into many different political and fiscal circles and disturbs their consortiums with believable conspiracies that are considered in today's historical text, as genius. So well-devised are they that the consortium is almost on a war footing within itself.' He clamped his hands on Quanton's frozen shoulders.

'A lot of historians, in writing these events, express a lot of admiration for this man – but we mustn't forget, he was a tyrant, a murderer, an evil genius, who was led and directed by Chi Lin and Colin Grey, and of course, Grey, had his part to play on Mars, he sent Chi Lin consignment inventories and flight plans. But for now, we will move on.

CHAPTER 14

GLASS CAVERNS

After passing through the grey place Damian was surprised that they were sitting crossed legged atop of a colonial haulage freighter. Damian stood and looked back aft, then turned to look forward.

'Where are we now?' he inquired, scanning the space around him, and finding that the only reference was the huge sphere of Jupiter.

'This is a Consortium craft, C297. It left Mars twenty-eight standard days ago, and at present is on a remote predetermined course to Saturn's moon Titan. It has a very interesting cargo, that will change hands very shortly,' Comm said as he stood.

'There,' he said pointing. Damian looked to his right. A smaller craft was on an intersect course. Comm then turned and looked down the length of the freighter. Damian followed his lead. Every ten metres along the whole length of the ship panels were opening. Damian noticed that intricate structures were now emerging from below.

'Pulse cannons,' Comm said, indicating the large cannons as they locked into position.

'This ship is unmanned, but the proximity alarm would have sounded, an automated message would have been given. The privateer has not responded, so, the freighter is programmed to defend itself,' Comm continued.

'There must be over fifty cannons pointing at that craft, it doesn't stand a chance,' Damian managed to say before all cannons fired at once. Streaks of concentrated light energy pulsated across the void towards the small ship. They passed fifty metres above the hull on the smaller ship's topmost deck.

'It missed. How can it miss, from this distance?' Comm shrugged his shoulders.

'Perhaps it wasn't programmed properly, because it didn't think it missed. Look!' Damian watched as the pulse cannons slowly retracted back into hull. Once the panels had slid shut, he turned to Comm.

'Kyle Quanton's influence,'

'Most definitely. Nothing, however, was written to say he had any influence.'

Damian rolled his eyes and slowly shook his head. They sat and watched as the privateers dislodged and removed a large container away from the tens of thousands of stacked containers that made up the bulk of the ship. Once it was secured onto the deck of the privateer ship Damian noticed the rear thrusters coming to life.

'Sandy, follow me.' Comm leapt from the bulkhead and made his way to the deck of the smaller craft. Damian followed close behind.

'Surely, any investigation would know that this was a put-up job.' Comm frowned.

'A "put-up job",' he said hesitantly. Damian laughed.

'A conspired robbery, by persons installed within,' he answered with a grin.

'Maybe at some time we should look at your vocabulary, I think we could find more answers to who you are there, but for now, watch.'

Two spheres pulsating from blue to green left the rear of the privateer's ship and gathered speed. Seconds later they hit the freighter amidships, the soundless explosion reduced the freighter to debris and the blast wave lurched the smaller vessel violently to its port. Damian looked on in shock at the intensity of the explosion.

'They were powerful,' he managed to say.

'Yes, they were too powerful for this era, as is the propulsion system of this craft, and we are off to find out just where they are being built. It will give you an idea of the kind of power that this ship possesses. But first you need to know where it is that we are.'

'On route to Titan, you said,' Damian stated.

'Yes, we are mid-way between Jupiter. Over there,' he pointed. 'And Saturn. Over there. Our destination, however, is star ward, approximately 970 million kilometres, at maximum speed for the time. The journey should take approximately eighty standard days.'

'So, you're just going to speed it up,' Damian said, whilst finding a comfortable place to sit. Comm smiled and pointed forward.

'No, I am not going to speed it up. Just watch.'

It seemed from Damian's point of view, that a horizontal white line had appeared in front of the ship. As they closed the distance the line buckled and split into two, and now created the impression of an elongated O. Within the eclipsed circle Damian could see movement. Within an instant, they were part of the movement. He noticed there were no stars or planets, just streaks of what seemed to be vapour trails; then, they were gone and in front of them lay the black glassed surface of Earth with a glittering shimmering ring of ice around its equator.

'Forty-five seconds to do an eighty-day journey. However, the Griffin could do it in ten seconds, and the more modern ships, probably in two or less. But, at this time that should not have happened at all.'

Damian stood and glared at the impossible view that was Earth. he turned to Comm with a puzzled look.

'Chandra and Kowaski had that technology. Could they have somehow survived, and developed dimensional travel without the need of the disc?' Comm smiled and placed his arm around the young man's shoulder. The small craft had now manoeuvred into low orbit. They watched the procedure in silence for a few minutes.

'In a way, you are right, but, no, Chandra and Kowaski did not survive. But their technology did – the next hour will answer your questions.'

The small craft descended to the scorched surface. The heat from the destruction must have been incredible, thought Damian. Nothing survived, no life, no moisture, no air, nothing was spared, and nothing was recognisable.

'Where are we going?' he asked, trying to keep his emotions under control. Comm sidled up beside him.

'Are you okay,? I have no Med team back-up to verify your emotional or physical state. If this is too much we can leave. Come back some other time.' Comm's voice was soft, almost a whisper, Damian turned to him.

'Comm, I'm fine, it's just, well, a little overwhelming, but I do want to see where this scenario is taking us.' Comm gave him a reassuring pat on the shoulder then turned to face the front of the low-flying ship.

'Technopolis would have been a hundred and fifty kilometres ahead of us. We are heading a few degrees to the right of that. The scorching of the Earth took away all of the surface and seared everything two kilometres below that. But beneath that, there are still caverns, especially one particular cavern. It lies just over five kilometres down and was the secret laboratory of Chandra and Kowaski.'

Damian's jaw dropped.

'And that's where we are headed,' he said, incredulously.

Comm nodded and turned to face the front of the ship.

They travelled over misshapen and grotesque landscape, it seemed to Damian that even the rock structure was screaming in torment. Eventually they descended further. He noticed an opening, a blackened mouth within the rocky structure, frozen in mid cry. Without reducing their speed at all, they entered the gaping hole.

For ten minutes at least they travelled down into the almost pitch black of the descending tunnel, only the occasional flash of light from the crafts external lighting illuminating the tunnel walls. Comm turned to Damian and directed his attention to the oncoming slab of light that was rapidly expanding before them.

'We're here – Chandra's den. Most of her experimental work is still here, untouched.' Damian tapped his friend on the shoulder. Comm turned to face him.

'Chandra's den, really? Did you just make that up,' Comm was taken aback.

'I ... I do not make anything up, I report on what I see. There are three journals that call this place by that name, one of Kyle Quanton's personal journal,' he said indignantly. Damian shrugged.

'Okay, I believe you. Just seemed strange, that's all. So, why are we here?' Comm pointed to the container.

'The contents of that is important. It is the lynchpin of Quanton's whole Empire, and we must witness it to understand all of this. It is amazing though; the first two statues were here in this place. You now stand here, as well as the second two. Lin and Grey have also been here, this is the privateers' main base of operations and it is where they found Chandra and Kowaski's design for dimensional flight. But I suppose the question is, how did they know it was here? There was never any record of this place prior to Lin and Grey.

everything, including you, are linked somehow.' Damian scanned the vast cavern; ships of all sizes, all being maintained by an army of ground crew numbering in the hundreds.

'I have never physically been here though,' Damian said, after some time.

'Maybe not, but you are, now, and you are here because of the statues, no other reason. You are a link, and slowly we are putting this chain together.' Comm stepped off the craft and slowly floated down to the cavern floor. Damian followed.

'We are six standard months further on from the last scenario on Ganymede. Much has happened, piracy on the freight lines has increased; company's all throughout the consortium have ceased to trade; fear is rife, the smaller worlds suffer starvation, chaos is everywhere, and that is orchestrated chaos. No prize for guessing the conductor.' Damian scanned the area.

'All these ships, can they all travel in dimensional space?' Comm followed his gaze.

'Most of them. Quanton found all the plans that were used for the disc, and he found them with help from Lin and Grey. He then developed that technology into the engines that power most of these craft, including the procedure of fusing the elements that create the living hull. Being the extravert that he was, he named the mineral, Quantonite,' Damian turned to face Comm.

'But if this is the technology now, surely, they would have been exploring the neighbouring stars much sooner,' Damian said, as he turned to look at the ships being maintained by the ground crew.

'Once Quanton manipulates all those around him, and he becomes the founder of House Quanton, all of this,' he panned his arms around the cavern, 'will be recorded, stored, then hidden. After that, this cavern will be totally destroyed. He could not leave anything that could be traced back to him.' Damian looked over to the hundreds of crews maintaining the ships.

'And what of them, hundreds of them? It only takes one to leak the information out.'

Comm held up his hand. 'All the privateers and the ground crew were assembled here when Quanton activated the destruction. He could not allow anyone to know about the existence of this place.' Damian looked around the cavern and slowly shook his head.' Comm gently turned him around.

'He was preparing for his future role, and as I have said, he was not a nice man. Ah, the container is opening. Notice the security team, pulse weapons at the ready.' Damian took a deep breath: that revelation shocked him but, he thought, why should it, he knew Quanton was not a nice man. He turned and moved closer to the container. Once opened the security team entered. After a while, ten human occupants were being herded out into the brightness of the cavern. One of them fell to the ground after receiving a blow to the neck.

'It's Quanton,' Damian shouted in astonishment. He turned to Comm and was surprised to see the older man turn away. He made his way back though the thickening crowd to his friend's side. Comm turned to him, his face frozen in fear.

'We have been found, the main com-link has found us. Sandy, I am so sorry, but I must go, now.' The cavern melted into streaks of colour, then they were back in the grey place.

'Sandy, I will contact you. Do not try to find me.' Comm's voice hung in the air, but his substance had vanished.

CHAPTER 15

ENROLMENT

'Try it now doctor'. The voice was from a young female – to Damian it was soft and calming and helped his journey from unconsciousness to consciousness.

'I have him. He is wakening.' This, Damian recognised as the voice of Doctor Ghorbany. He opened his eyes and was greeted by concerned looks from the four people that surrounded him. The Doctor and Senior Nurse Jane Onslow were the most concerned.

'Jane,' he said slowly, and reached out his hand. She held it and reassured him with a slight squeeze. She smiled, her eyes moist.

'You gave us a fright, again,' she said mockingly. The two engineers, Hu Che and Simon Duncan passed their scanners over him and he felt the slight vibration of the probing scan as it passed.

'The personal dampening field is now in place and is operating to our parameters. The capsule should no longer have an influence,' Hu Che said. Her colleague and junior engineer Simon Duncan nodded an agreement.

'Damian,' Jane Onslow said softly, their hands still clasped.

'I am going to take you back to your quarters. The doctor has given his permission for me to watch over you throughout the sleep cycle.' She smiled and smoothed a stray hair from his forehead.

'Welcome home Mr Drake, and Nurse Onslow,' chirped Six as they entered the room.

'Room com, initiate protocol 135,' Jane said, as she helped Damian onto the sleeping slab.

'What will that do?' asked Damian, sleepily.

'Shuts him up, for at least twenty standard hours, except for emergency reports,' she said as she removed his clothing.

'I'll have to remember that; 135. I'll definitely have to remember that,' he said, his eyes heavy with sleep.

'You will be in a deep sleep soon, I will stay with you for this cycle, I … er, never thanked you for our wonderful evening together,' she said as she removed her uniform.

Damian watched as the naked Jane Onslow got into the sleeping slab and sidled up to him. He felt warm bare flesh against his own naked body, but as much as he fought the oncoming drowsiness, sleep overcame him.

'How do you feel?' He opened his eyes and smiled. Jane Onslow was putting breakfast food and beverages onto the table. She was still naked.

'Better for seeing you, especially like that,' she walked over to the slab, peeled away the covering and exposed his own nakedness.

'Well, you look as though you feel a lot better.' He reached out and pulled her gently to him. She did not resist.

'Let's see how better it actually feels,' he said, suppressing a giggle.

An hour later, he sat up and watched as Jane Onslow exited the ablution room. She retrieved a fresh uniform from the room's molecular replicator unit and watched intrigued as she dressed. 'Very provocative,' he thought.

'So, you're going to work and leaving me,' he said with a smile. She turned to face him.

'There is nothing wrong with you. I scanned you earlier, the dampener implant is working well within its tolerances. You have adapted well. I have reset your room comm to come online in fifteen standard minutes, and I believe you have some messages stored. I'll see you soon Damian.' As she walked to the exit, she turned, he blew her a kiss, she looked puzzled, but smiled, and then within an instant she was gone.

Damian reheated his breakfast and completed his ablutions. He was dressing in the brown uniform that designated him as a non-crew member.

'Good morning, Mr Drake, you have three new messages. One is priority. Do you wish to listen at this point,' Six interrupted. Damian let out a deep sigh and stopped dressing.

Turning to face the comm pad he replied, 'I have got to tone down your chirpiness. Play priority message, please,'

'Message from Captain Contessa.' There was a slight pause.

'Mr. Drake' the message started; he noted the distaste even in those two words.

'Yet again, you take up valuable time from my engineering and medical teams, even though I remember that I expressly informed you to keep out of the way for the duration of our mission. That said, I notice that I have received an application from you to train as a shuttle pilot. My first response was to immediately put you into a hibernation pod. However, on reflection, maybe this will keep you out of harm's way for the next three standard years, until we dock with station 1436. Report to Commander Gomez, loading bay one!'

'She really needs to brush up on her social skills,' he muttered, more to himself than to the room comm. He finished dressing and sat upon the sleeping slab.

'Is there a message from another comm link,' he asked.

'I'm sorry Mr Drake, no, but there is a message from Commander Burroughs, and one from Doctor Ghorbany.' He allowed them to play – the Commander was asking, that if he felt up to it, and if the implant dampener was working, perhaps he wouldn't mind coming back to the capsule at his convenience. He smiled at that, it seemed that Commander Burroughs was the polar opposite of the Captain when it came to politeness.

'Also, one of my team has come up with a theory that you may be able to help us with, regarding trans-dimensional propulsion.

'Six, reply back: Commander, thank you for your message, the implant seems to be working as well as expected, I have to meet with Commander Gomez today but when I have some free time I will come by and see you, trans dimensional travel seems very interesting.'

The message from the doctor simply asked after his wellbeing. He had received the scans from Senior nurse Onslow and he was happy with the results and if he could find some time, come in and see him at the end of the week.

'They are all the messages that I have received,' chirped Six.

'Oh, and Commander Burroughs has just sent a return message. It reads, "Come whenever you feel up to it, and good luck with Commander Gomez. However, step carefully, she bites." Damian stared blankly at the com pad for a moment.

'What does he mean by that?'

'I'm sure I have no idea, Sir? Would you like me to find out?'

'No, just order me a guide, destination, loading bay one.'

Loading bay one was on level two, aft section. The green slither of light that had guided him from level six now hovered by the double doors. As the doors parted, the green slither shimmered slightly then disappeared.

Three crew members, their uniforms predominantly dark yellow. Damian noticed other colours, red flashes across the left shoulder. The taller of the three also had a blue flash with white braiding across the right shoulder. All to do with rank, Damian surmised.

'You are Mr. Drake,' said the shorter of the three. Damian noted he sported a red flash that was braided with gold and black.

'I am. I have an appointment with Commander Gomez. I have applied to be trained as a shuttle pilot.'

The taller one held out his hand, 'I'm senior pilot Johan Spiez. This,' he said, indicating the shorter man, 'is Flight Lieutenant Commander Abe Connor. And this,' he said, indicating the smiling female, 'is Pilot second class, Patricia Spall.' He noticed her uniform was blander in colour, but still, she had a thin red flash across her left shoulder.

'We could always do with more shuttle pilots; but it's the heavy lifter pilots we're desperate for, and you do realise it is a two standard year training program?' Spiez said with a grin.

'Johan, don't put him off,' interjected the Commander.

'Mr Drake, Patricia here made pilot in under a year. I'm sure you will do just as well, but, if you need any help, you can always call on us. Perhaps Pat still has all the technical theory fresh in her mind.' Patricia Spall smiled and offered her hand. Damian took it and was surprised at the strong grip.

'Thank you, Commander, I will probably need all the help I can get.'

'I have a good collection of flight simulations and tech layouts, I'll pass them to your room comm if you like,' Patricia Spall said, as she released the iron grip and withdrew her hand.

'That would be very nice of you, thank you,' he said stretching his fingers behind his back.

'Well, we are always here. See you soon er … Cadet,' the Commander said with a nod. Damian watched as they made their way down the promenade to the ascenders.

'Cadet,' he whispered to himself, then smiling he entered the loading bay air lock, waited for the inner doors to open, took two steps then froze rigid, as he found himself overlooking the cavernous void that was loading bay one he gasped as he tried to take in the enormity of the space. He was standing on a gantry that jutted out from the wall for at least five metres. He looked up and estimated the ceiling to be ten or twelve metres above him. He walked to the safety railing and tried to take in the enormity of it all.

Crafts of all shapes and sizes lay sprawled across the deck. To his left were small personnel shuttles, some of them he noticed had had their bulkheads removed and crew members in blue work uniforms were scurrying around them. These were the engineering teams. Further into the bay he noticed the large bulbous heavy lifters and watched for a while as one was unloaded; the huge cargo bots grasping the enormous chunks of asteroid from the heavy lifters, holding them as if they were weightless and even though the loading bay maintained a 0.8 gravity, the asteroids laden with metallic ore must have weighed tens of tonnes.

To his right, he noticed ships of all different shapes and sizes – spherical and saucer seemed to dominate, others seemed to have been cobbled together with attachments strategically placed about their hulls for more precise work. He looked about the gantry for a route down and further along noticed a row of senders were positioned at ten-metre intervals. He entered the nearest and descended to the deck. It was then that the true scale of this place and the size of the craft became apparent. He exited the descender and made his way over to the heavy lifters. They were huge, capable of holding over a hundred cubic tonnes of asteroid, perhaps more.

All around the rear of the enormous craft, crew members wearing blue or yellow co-ordinated the cargo bots in the unloading procedure.

Damian looked up at the height of the heavy lift 1 craft. It easily stood twenty metres high, and a good fifty metres in length, its girth fifteen metres at its widest, Damian estimated. He noticed some of the cargo bots were avatars. Crew members were sitting on hovering platforms five metres above him he watched fascinated as their movements on the hovering platforms were translated to the cargo bots. Damian stood mesmerised by the whole scene. He felt a hand gently touch his shoulder and turned to face a smiling officer, denoted as such by his green uniform with red, blue and green flashes.

'Not too close now, Mr Drake. You seemed to have wandered into a hazard zone.'

'I'm sorry, I was fascinated. Just wanted to see the process,' Damian stammered.

'Not the best time for a tour, sir.' The Commander's sentence was cut short by a bellow. They both turned in unison in the direction the shout had come from: the man with red blue and green flashes instantly stood rigid to attention.

'Drake!' He heard his name yelled again and his eyes focused on a woman in yellow dress uniform, the whole of her left sleeve from cuff to collar red with white and black beading. She wasn't running but had a determined gait and was soon by their side.

She was tall with mousey hair pulled back into a tight bun and her eyes were narrow and almost black.

'Commander Gomez, I was about to escort Mr Drake away from this section ma'am,' the Flight commander started to explain.

Her eyes bore into his, her lips pencil line straight. Damian was sure he saw the officer shudder.

'Thank you, Mr Chang, you may go about your duties. I will deal with this,' she said, turning her Medusa gaze upon Damian, the officer nodded curtly, then departed back to his station.

'What, are you doing here, Mr Drake?' She spat the words, and he could feel the contempt within them.

'I'm under Captain's orders,' he replied, as softly as he could. She stepped back slightly.

'What orders?' she asked, and Damian noted a slight tremor in her voice, hardly noticeable, but he was sure it was there.

'I'm, your new Cadet,' he said, smiling. Her face did not alter. She stared at him, holding his gaze, then turned her back on him and consulted her info pad. Her shoulders sagged slightly, and he could swear that he heard her breath exhale, then, taking a deep breath, shoulders up, she turned.

'Mr. Drake,' she said, in as soft a voice as she could muster.

'Cadet Drake, ma'am,' he said brightly.

'You have to earn that title, Mr. Drake,' she sneered.

'I may surprise you ma'am.' She stood before him rigid in posture, hands clasped behind her back, she turned her head, her body remaining rigid, her focus now on the teams of pilots and engineers that were starting their new work cycle.

'This crew has already achieved the highest standards of learning, before they even set foot on the Griffin. You could say, Mr Drake,' she said turning her head back to him, 'That they are, and I mean, all of them, are a third of the way up their career ladder. They are the elite, destined to become the best pilots and engineers in the fleet. You however, Mr Drake, have not even found the ladder. Now, if you wish to turn around and return to your quarters, nothing, will come of this. We can both tell the Captain that you had second thoughts.' Her face was impassive. She waited for his reply. Damian looked around the loading bay at the teams of pilots and engineers going through their handover procedures for the new work cycle.

'I do not expect to compete with your elite crew, Commander. I have no doubt that they are brilliant and hardworking. I am doing this because I believe it is right for me, and I know that your team suffered in rescuing me, and I appreciate all of their efforts. I am sorry that some of them were hurt, but I will stay, and, I will do my best to try and impress you.' She leant forward, their faces almost touching and in a hushed voice said.

'I hope you do, because I will personally assess your progress. You will start on the morning work cycle, hanger one, sub section B. Don't be late.' She turned and with a straight back strode across the deck.

Damian watched her go and he gave a sigh of relief when he thought she was out of ear shot.

'She is not as bad as she thinks she is. She is very good at what she does.'

Damian turned. 'Lieutenant Commander Chang, er ... Sir.' Damian stammered. Chang smiled and put his hand on Damian's shoulder.

'We are a tight-knit team here. We need her discipline. This is a very dangerous place to be. We all – officers and crew – have to look after each other, and we will look after you. So, Damian, go back to your quarters. I'll send you some reading material. Get a good cycle's rest and be ready for tomorrow.' Damian thanked him for his kindness and made his way back to his room.

CHAPTER 16

SUB HANGER 6

'Congratulations, Cadet Drake!' Six chirped as Damian entered the room. He stopped and turned to the wall pad.

'Six, you have got to tone down your annoying chirpiness,' he said glaring into the room com's visual sensor.

'My apologies, Cadet Drake. I thought this would be a time for celebration,' the room com countered. Damian frowned. Was it possible? he thought. Could Six feel injustices? It certainly sounded hurt.

'No need to apologise Six. It's been a busy day. Are there any messages?' Six did not answer immediately, but then in a softer voice replied.

'There are twelve messages, nine include data attachments.' Damian smiled, turned, and walked into the sleeping room. He had a lot to do this rest cycle.

Most of the messages were from members of the flight crew, mostly welcoming him into the fold. The nine data attachments varied from shuttle schematics to course work procedures. Pilot second class Patricia Spall had included in her data pack three holo pads that when opened created an image of the control flight deck of a heavy lifter. It also came with a narration from the pilot herself.

Commander Burroughs also gave a message and emphasised his earlier point of returning to the capsule at Damian's earliest convenience. Jane Onslow's message was just to convey support, and to say that she would come by his quarters in the next day or two.

Sometime later, Damian heard from the room comm.

'I am sorry to bother you, Sir,' Six said, still keeping the tone down.

'Rest cycle is over, sleep cycle has begun. You have a busy day tomorrow.' Damian looked up to the room com pad.

'Thank you Six, and I like the new toned-down version. Set alarm call one standard hour before work cycle.'

He had made his way to hanger one which he found on level 5 at the stern. He entered via the normal air-lock system into a deserted space. To conserve energy, all power had been reduced. He was quite used to the 0.8 gravity, the same as the loading bay he had visited yesterday, but here the temperature had also been reduced, as well as the brightness of the lighting.

His new plain green uniform helped with bodily cold, but his nose and ears felt the full brunt of the fifteen-degree drop from normal Griffin temperatures.

The hanger com, recognising bio readings within its domain, slowly increased the lighting. After a few minutes of walking aimlessly around, Damian also sensed that the temperature was increasing, although, painfully slowly. As his eyes became accustomed to the light, he noticed three shuttle launches docked at the far side of the hanger. Each, thought Damian, capable of carrying a hundred crew. As the light increased, he noticed other craft, mainly crew shuttles, but at the furthest end of the hanger a fleet of craft, all single seaters. These he recognised from the technical specifications that Pilot Patricia Spall had sent him, as attack fighters, leftovers from a past when the Griffin was a frontline battle cruiser.

He made his way around the perimeter of the hanger, then came across a com pad. He placed his hand onto its flat surface to activate it.

'Passenger, Mr. Damian Drake, you are in a restricted area. Please leave immediately.' A green guide slither appeared beside him.

'Please, follow me Mr Drake,' it said, in a bland tone. Well, that's nice, thought Damian, she couldn't be bothered to inform them.

'I am Cadet Drake, and I am here to start pilot training, as per Captain's orders,' he said, directing his voice to the com pad. A silence commenced. Enquiries and information would now be being passed from one com-link to another, Damian thought. Orders would be verified, and with a bit of luck – he smiled at the thought – Commander Gomez would get a dressing down. Slowly, his smile vanished.

'And guess who she would take that out on,' he muttered aloud.

'Information has now been uploaded,' said the bland voice of the com.

'You are required in sub section B. Please follow the guide.' Communication ended abruptly and the guide floated away towards the exit.

'Oh, right, so ... it's my fault,' Damian said as he followed.

Sub section B, turned out to be a large room some twenty metres further on from the main entrance of the hanger deck. It had full lighting and was warm: it was also empty.

On one side he noticed control panels in alcoves set into the bulkhead wall. Opposite, laid out throughout the full length of the room, were holo stages, the same design, he noticed, that he had seen on level 11.

After exploring the sparse room, he gravitated to one of the alcoves and sat in its recliner. After five minutes he started to wonder whether this was Commander Gomez's way of keeping him out of sight.

'Welcome Cadets,' a cheerful voice exclaimed. He turned to face the holo stage. A young Lieutenant Gomez stood upon the stage. She wore a green tunic with a flash of red across her left shoulder. Damian rose from his seat and walked closer and examined the bright young face.

'What happened to you?' he said aloud and was surprised when the image turned to address him personally.

'Cadets,' she said directly to him, then her head moved to take in all of the alcoves.

'We shall start today by examining inertia and gravitational pull.'

After five hours of tuition he was given an assessment. He completed it in twenty standard minutes but was not informed of any success or failure.

'This work cycle is complete,' the image of the young Commander informed him.

'I will pass extra tuition to your room comm should you wish extra study in your rest cycle; we will resume training tomorrow.' The image faded and once again Damian was left alone.

As he walked down the central promenade towards the gallery of senders, he noticed a lone figure standing with back turned towards him. The figure was obviously a man. He wore a dark blue uniform and Damian could just make out a flash of red on his left shoulder.

'Commander Burroughs, Sir,' Damian said cheerfully as he stopped behind the man. Thomas Burroughs turned. Damian felt himself scrutinised by the blank face of the Commander.

'Something wrong, Sir,' Damian asked warily.

'I don't know Cadet. Is there something wrong?' Damian frowned, puzzled.

'Sorry Sir. I don't follow. In what regard?' Damian replied cautiously.

Burroughs regarded the smartly uniformed young Cadet. He noted that the life support belt had been configured in such a way that it would be thirty percent more efficient should it be needed in an emergency.

He recognised the configuration from years before, a time when he served as engineer on a full frontline battle cruiser. He remembered his Commander showing him how to re-configure the tubing; that should the worst happen, and life support failed he would have another standard hour of air. From what he remembered, it was only front-line troops that would adopt this method. It was their secret.

'Who taught you how to install your support belt,' he blurted, his face still expressionless.

'No one, Sir. It seemed the right way to put it on,' Damian said slowly, concerned at the way this conversation was heading.

'Have I done something wrong, Sir?' he continued, trying to judge the Commander's mood. Burroughs took one pace back and sighed.

'No Damian, you have done nothing wrong, but, like the capsule, you're just a puzzle, a puzzle with no obvious answers, and, I have asked a few times for you to return to the capsule. One of my engineering Cadets has come up with an intriguing proposition as to what the capsule may be, and you may be able to help her. He said, a smile breaking through the expressionless features of his face.'

Damian was confused. Why would the Commander himself, come to escort him to the loading bay? He could have sent any of his engineering staff, or just called him and ordered him. This had been a very strange day.

They exited the descender and walked the promenade back towards the loading bay.

Burroughs told Damian of the engineering Cadets theory that it was possible that the capsule was trans-dimensional, and that only a fraction of its mass had entered three-dimensional space.

Whilst Damian was trying to understand the implications of what the Commander was telling him they entered the bay. The last time he had been here, Damian remembered, he had only managed to walk ten paces into the room before collapsing.

He had walked further into the room now, and felt fine. Burroughs took a hold of his shoulder.

'Wait, don't move!' he said calmly, then turned to his Senior engineer.

'How is he?' the Senior engineer looked up from the holo towers.

'The dampening field seems to be working fine Sir.'

'How do you feel, Damian?' he asked, with a hint of concern.

'I feel okay, Sir. Certainly nothing like I did the last time I was here.'

Damian turned to face the now skeletal remains of the five-metre structure that was once his life pod capsule. Most of the blue outer panels lay scattered across the sub hanger deck.

'We have stripped it of everything and checked it all the way down to its atoms and found, nothing.' the Commander muttered from behind him.

A young Cadet walked towards them; Damian noted the blue flash across her left shoulder designating her as a final year Cadet.

'Ah, Damian,' Burroughs said, stepping forward.

'This is senior cadet Jessica Khan. Jess, this is our enigma, Damian Drake.'

Jessica smiled and offered her hand, Damian took it and returned the smile. Why, he thought was everyone so perfect here. She stood before him, ten centimetres shorter than himself, unblemished smooth skin, deep brown eyes and cropped hair. 'Genetics,' thought Damian.

'Commander Burroughs tells me you may have an explanation for all this,' he said, unable to look away from her eyes.

'Well, not so much an explanation, but certainly a theory,' she said averting her eyes back to the Commander.

'Yes, we believe it is bridged between various dimensions, either accidentally or deliberately. Jess thinks it might react to your verbal commands,' Burroughs said, with a slight shrug of his shoulders.

'So, you think it's in different dimensions, as in trans-dimensional flight,' Damian said, matter-of-factly.

Burroughs frowned. 'Sort of,' he said slowly.

'All Stella craft use a dimensional shift. It allows us to exceed light speed without breaking any known laws of physics. But this ...' Jessica Khan said, turning to the capsule.

'It's not travelling. Is it just a link? Or, maybe it was travelling, and has now somehow, become stuck?' Burroughs added.

'Stuck between two dimensions, or, two realities.' Damian interjected, Burroughs closed his eyes slowly, concentrating on that last statement. He slowly turned to face the young Cadet.

'Explain!' he ordered, in almost a whisper.

Damian stared first at the Commander then across to the Senior cadet. Both, he thought, were staggered at his statement.

'Well, a tunnel,' he offered, watching both faces change to incredulous.

'A tunnel, from here, to where?' Jessica managed, Damian shrugged. He had no idea, nor why be had said what he said in the first place.

'I believe,' he said slowly, gauging the intriguing looks from the both of them, 'that it is a common belief that we occupy one of a multitude of universes. Could this not be a link between this universe and another?'

'Parallels,' the Commander said slowly. He turned and walked away. After a few metres he stopped and turned to face the two cadets.

'It would make sense. The unknown alloys, lack of instrumentation, and from what I have been told by the med team, you seem to have memories from history, that never actually happened.' Burroughs studied the young man that stood before him. Could it be ...the first alien intelligence?' He stopped the thought as he heard Jessica Khan say.

'Why don't you ask it to activate, or open?'

Damian smiled. 'What, like, Open Sesame!' he shouted in as deep a voice as he could manage. He stopped as he noticed they both adopted the same expression – complete confusion.

'It's from a story I once read. It means ... never mind,' he said, almost apologetically.

'Let's just try this. Ask it to activate,' Burroughs said, as he turned back to face the skeletal remains of the capsule.

Damian walked towards the remnant and stopped five metres from the main structure.

'Capsule!' he said, in what he thought would be a commanding voice.

'Activate ... Energise ... Open ...' He waited for a minute, then turned. Behind him stood the whole crew, with Burroughs and Khan in front. He shrugged his shoulders.

'You didn't really expect anything to happen did you?'

He watched their faces light up as a strange silvery light exploded across the loading bay. They, all as one, raised their hands to their eyes, shielding themselves from a light emanating from behind him. The last thing he saw was his shadow that had appeared suddenly in front of him.

CHAPTER 17

MARS PRIME

The room swirled: he was in the grey place. Damian observed the colours filtering through till finally he found he was standing in a huge reception area with a high vaulted ceiling. Comm appeared beside him.

'What just happened?' Damian spluttered.

'I'm not sure,' Comm answered, as he looked around the enormous room in which they had just materialised.

'I have taken refuge in a holo stage on level 11,' Comm said. He continued, 'The main com unit doesn't look there. To the Griffin it doesn't exist, but while hiding I found that it possesses a main hub conduit. All information passes through there. I was there when the alarms were activated and I emerged here. So, let me ask you, Sandy. What just happened?'

Damian looked away from the old man and scanned the space. The room was enormous, crowds of people had been moving from one side of the room to the other but now – as he had seen numerous times before – they stood frozen. He looked up towards the domed ceiling. It felt vaguely familiar. He turned back to the old man.

'I was in the sub hanger, with the life capsule. Commander Burroughs and one of his senior cadets had a theory that it might be an object stuck in trans-dimension. I suggested it might be a tunnel from one realm to another.'

Comm held up his hand. 'And where did that theory come from? Are you having more memories? Do you believe it to be a tunnel?'

Damian breathed deeply.

'So, your voice activated it in some way. It responded to you. Hmm ... I appear to be still attached to the hub. I can access information.' Comm remained silent for a while, then after a few moments he turned to Damian, and said 'There are no casualties, however. You are all unconscious. The medical team are, as we speak, transferring you all to the medical centre. This gives us a chance to finish the Colin Grey and Chi Lin scenario. I have, since our last encounter, accumulated a lot more data on the subject. However, it is still not fully complete.'

Damian smiled. 'Comm, I have come to believe that what you call incomplete is usually far more than we require. So, where are we?'

'Welcome to Mars,' Comm said. Instantly the frozen crowd sprang to life.

'This is the main arrival lobby for Mars prime, an enormous station covering an area over 12,500 square kilometres. The central part of the station dates to pre-Earth destruction. After that of course Mars was the perfect place to run to, and for the last five hundred years it has expanded exponentially.' Damian half listened to Comm's travelogue and history of the Martian culture, but something had caught his eye. The layout of the enormous lobby betrayed its earlier structure, but to Damian's eye its historical or even its archaeological footprint screamed out to him. Just there, he thought, was customs control, the ornate room to the side now full of communication links, possibly, thought Damian, linking any citizen or company to anywhere on the established colonies. At some point in its history he knew it had been a restaurant. Nothing in its decor betrayed that, but something in his mind told him that it was so.

'Comm, that room over there?' He pointed.

'Has it ever been a restaurant?' Comm turned and scanned the room.

'When this station was originally put into operation, it was much smaller. This lobby was still the central core, the main hub if you like, of the whole complex, and yes, there was a restaurant according to original schematics. But as we discussed, some of the Command data may have been corrupted. We have to be careful what we believe,'

Damian had walked away from his companion and had entered the com-link centre. Comm, intrigued, followed him inside.

'Are you saying you have been here before? And how sure are you of that memory, because I have no way of verifying it as a true memory?' Comm said from behind him.

'Check your records. Just here, there was another ante room, a sort of utility room, or storeroom. They kept crockery and utensils there. I remember going in there by accident once.' Comm closed his eyes and scanned the available data that he had access to. With an open mouth he slowly turned to Damian.

'Yes, it was demolished when the station was extended, and that was fifty standard years after the destruction. Four hundred and fifty years previous to this time.' Comm studied his friend. He noted that his facial expression denoted sincerity. He was not lying, and why would he, he knew that there was a room, and why would any outside force feed him that? Comm was convinced that he had experienced an actual memory, a sort of proof that at some point in the distant past, he had actually been here.

'So, Sandy, it seems the scenarios are doing everything that we expected. Opening up your memories.' Damian turned, a look of puzzlement on his face.

'Yes, but all my memories, on Earth and on Mars, are prior to Earth's destruction.'

Damian turned his head quickly. Something in his peripheral vision gave recognition. He scanned the hordes of people moving through the vast reception lobby, then, there! He pointed into the crowd. Comm was at his side in an instant, concerned at the swift change in his friend's demeanour.

'Cole,' Damian shouted, then running, he shouted again.

'Cole! Wait! It's me, Damian!' Comm leapt into the air and alighted on the ground ten paces in front of his running friend.

'Sandy, he can't see or hear you,' Comm said, holding up his hand, Damian halted at his side, staring at the receding figure of Colin Grey.

'But you recognised him. More evidence that the people represented by the statues are known to you. And you recognised him from behind. Yet the only interpretation you have been given is frontal only.' Damian sighed deeply.

'Comm, he is more than just a friend. I have the feeling he is a very close friend, the sort of feeling I get is ...' He turned from the com- link and tried to trace Colin Grey within the chaos of the thronging crowd that surrounded them.

'I get the feeling that we have known each other from childhood.' Comm slowly shook his head.

'That Sandy, is impossible. There are just under five thousand years between his time and yours.'

Damian shrugged. 'Even so, that's what I feel.'

Comm escorted Damian to a far corner of the reception lobby. He had dispersed the crowd in the space that they now stood, then had frozen the scenario. Damian had seen this a few times now, but it still fascinated him, the frozen expressions on people's faces as they are halted in mid-step. Somehow it amused him.

Comm paced up and down silently before him, deep in thought. Suddenly, he stopped and turned to face the younger man.

'What I am about to say, and what the scenario is about to show you, maybe very disturbing to you, especially as you have confided to me that Colin Grey is a very close friend.'

Damian gave a half smile. 'We have to see what we see; it may not be true anyway,' Damian said with a shrug. Comm nodded agreement.

'This Scenario has been recorded from a number of separate records most of them, admittedly, from the station's security files, but a few from personal journals, from the crew members that survived.'

Damian let himself sag back against the bulkhead wall. They were standing in a semi-circle of empty space. Beyond that, the station crew members stood motionless, oblivious as to what was about to occur.

'Survived, survived what?' he managed to say.

'We have moved on in the scenarios timeline. Colin Grey will come out of this as a system hero but, that is untrue. He was a part of this, a key figure, Sandy. I am sorry, but, well, watch.'

Within an instant, the reception lobby became alive with movement and sound. From Damian's viewpoint he watched a squad of at least twenty fully armed security guards rush into the crowd, with their weapons unholstered they unleashed a devastating volley of fire power. Flashes of light seared across the top of the moving figures, followed instantly by the sounds of explosions. Then Damian heard the rapid sound of pulse rifles, bodies were thrown into the air, debris from falling architecture was strewn across the plaza taking fragile bodies in its wake. Another explosion to his left took down fifty or more of the fleeing and screaming populace. Grenades were now being randomly thrown from all quarters of the lobby.

Damian watched horrified as limbs were torn from the bodies of people who were just five metres away from him.

More rapid-fire punctuated the air. Those that were not fleeing threw themselves to the floor. Comm grabbed Damian's arm and indicated Upward – they ascended five metres above the crowd. From this vantage point Damian witnessed the bravery of the unarmed against the most formidable of foe. In their striving to resist they were cut down by a volley of projectiles and laser pulse. From the rear of this utter confusion, Damian recognised Colin Grey, his face ashen and determined. He had produced a handheld disrupter and fought his way through the stricken horde, taking out the rouge security guards with expert accuracy. Five had fallen to his onslaught, the small handheld weapon obliterating all that fell within its sights. Damian heard the throbbing buzz of incoming security drones. He looked up and saw hundreds, of the thirty-centimetre-long cylindrical objects diving from the vaulted ceiling. They unleashed unprecedented firepower. Below him Colin Grey was completely annihilated. Damian let out a scream of anguish, beside him Comm's face was sullen and he gently put his arm around his friend's shoulders and led him down to the ground.

Damian tried to release Comm's grip. All around him, the scenario had once again become frozen. Comm turned to his friend.

'Colin Grey was Kyle Quanton's number one on Mars. he had instigated this massacre. On the face of it, it would seem that three hundred and forty-seven innocent people were killed for no apparent reason. Yet, later studies have revealed that a hundred and ten of those were part of the consortium that opposed Quanton. No one ever found out who had re-programmed the security drones to open fire on specific members of the public. or, who had ordered the security guards to create panic and murder. Speculation in later years pointed the finger squarely at Colin Grey -to many, he was the hero of the day when he took down what people saw as rouge security guards. History however would record him as a martyr to his cause.' Damian bowed his head and tried to control his erratic breathing.

'Colin would never have done such a thing.' Comm released his grip on the younger man's shoulder and turned him to face him.

'Your Colin couldn't. This Colin could.'

Damian raised his head, 'What?' he said solemnly.

'I believe you know every single one of the statues, and you believe them to be upright citizens and good reliable friends, in your own realm. But they have been somehow stolen and re-programmed and used, as have you, in this realm, for purposes, I do not as yet understand.'

Comm let the younger man go and stepped back. Damian slowly sank to the floor and sat glaring at the frozen multitude, the fear of what they had just witnessed still etched onto their faces.

'My realm,' Damian said slowly.

'Yes, your realm. I think that you are not from this reality. You said yourself that the capsule could be a tunnel or a portal from one to the other. If that is the case, then our scenarios must now take on a new perspective. We are now no longer looking for the Damian Drake in this realm, but, who or what sent you and your friends to this dimension, and for what reason. And it is the reason that is the most troubling,' Comm turned and moved towards the crowd. Damian watched as he paced from one side to the other, his right hand clasped to his chin, index finger tapping upon his cheek. He had seen this idiosyncrasy in his friend before – he was either deep in thought or he was delving through the millions of data files that were open to him via the Griffin's main archive vault. He lifted himself from the ground.

'Comm, you once said that we were all parts of a puzzle, the pieces scattered over thousands of years.' Comm stopped pacing and turned.

'Yes, and I said that you were the final piece, which means that in the near future some catastrophe is going to befall all humans in this reality. Did I not say how many billions will you slay?

Damian shuddered. He remembered that conversation on the island. It was a stab in the heart then, as now. He took a breath.

'I am not the final piece,' he said softly. Comm was stunned.

'You are the last statue. They all stand upon your shoulders. There is no other.'

'And what do I stand upon? A pedestal, emblazoned with a golden 'O'. That is the final piece, so, I believe that when we look through the scenarios we should now be searching for the meaning of the golden 'O'. Nothing else.'

Comm smiled and walked over to his friend and placed a hand gently upon his shoulder.

"O' is the instigator of all this, yes, that makes sense. He, she or it, is the instigator of all our history, spanning over five thousand years. But for what gain? As we proceed Sandy, we must be cautious. This 'O' is very powerful, and maybe 'O' is also here, right now. We should tread carefully, but as far as this scenario is concerned, it has come to an end.' Damian stepped back, a frown appeared on his forehead.

'It cannot have ended! What of Kyle Quanton? The last we saw of him he was being kidnapped, and what happened to Chi Lin? Comm grinned, and sat with his back against the wall. He patted the floor beside him. Damian moved towards him and sat down.

'Sandy, as from now the scenarios meanings have changed: But, if you wish to know the outcome, we could spend precious time here plodding our way to the obvious end of this story. When we were looking to find memories as to who you were, then it was a worthwhile quest. But, well, now it isn't, so if you like I will tell you this scenario's end.' Damian nodded his head slowly.

'I understand that the motives of the scenarios have changed, and yes, I would like to know the end, and maybe 'O' is in here somewhere.' Comm stood and paced back towards the crowd.

Comm lowered his head and cradled his chin his index finger tapped his cheek. He stopped in front of a fleeing young tall woman, her arms held out straight in front of her, a look of fear and panic etched across her face. Just above her a pulse of light from a pulse cannon had been frozen in time, just a microsecond away from obliterating the upper part of her body. Comm turned and, leaning against her said.

'O's plan would stretch over a time period of five and a half thousand years.' Damian strode over to him, and physically moved him away from the woman.

'There is something called respect,' he spat, his eyes glaring. Comm looked at the woman, then up at the spear of light.

'These are not real people, Sandy, they are representations, not the actual ...'

'I don't care," he said, trying to move the woman out of the path of the oncoming doom. Comm smiled.

'Here, let me.' He gently laid his hand on her shoulder and the woman stepped to one side.

'She still dies, Sandy,' he said, as he led Damian away.

'Yes, I know, but we shouldn't disrespect them, even if they are a simulation, they represent real people, and we shouldn't forget that.'

Comm led Damian back to the edge of the horror and chaos that surrounded them.

'Maybe ...' said Comm slowly, indicating the young woman.

'maybe you are not here to destroy millions. Is it possible that you are here to save millions?'

Damian turned away from the woman, and focused on Comm. 'Or am I just another part of 'O's plan, a final part, and maybe that has gone wrong somehow.' Comm spun so fast to face

Damian, that instinctively Damian took a step back. He relaxed when he noticed Comm's face was beaming with a smile.

'Yes, complacency. A five and a half thousand-year plan would be intricate at the beginning, but as time went on, and if 'O' is here, and has been here from the start, would such a plan lose its potency?' Damian closed his eyes and thought on Comm's statement.

'Are you saying 'O' has lost the original path? If, of course, there is an 'O'? We are just surmising.' Comm slowly shook his head.

'No, it makes sense. You knew Technopolis, you knew it from your own time, or realm, but you knew nothing of the destruction of your planet. You know the statues, they represent people, friends from wherever it is you come from. You probably, even know who 'O' is, you know this place as well,' he said, walking back to the scene of mayhem that stood frozen before them.' With a wave of his hand the masses faded away. They stood in the palatial void of Mars prime.

'So, to recap ...' Comm said, as he walked away into the enormous space. Damian followed.

'The destruction of Earth,' Comm continued, 'was a fork in time, it was there that your time and our time split. So, why destroy the Earth?' He stopped and turned to Damian.

'Not the destruction of the planet, but the destruction of its people. but why?'

'Billions died,' Damian angrily interjected, as he caught Comm up and stopped beside him.

'But I think the point is Sandy, the human race was reduced to a few million. Far easier to control than billions, and then, in this scenario, Kyle Quanton, was a part of this timeline, and I'm sure that if you were able to look back at your own history, in your own realm, he would be a prominent character there also. The creation of the first House; other Houses would follow, but they wouldn't be as great and powerful as House Quanton. If you wanted to control the destiny of the human race, this is where you would start.' Damian held up his hand. Comm stopped to allow his friend to react.

'So, are you saying that the plan 'O' has devised is the control of the human race? I'm sorry Comm, but that has been tried many times – remember the Elder House, and look how that ended up.'

Comm nodded. 'Yes, I know, and through the centuries and millennia that went before, there were probably many that tried to control humans in one way or another, even today, Command controls our destinies. But this is different, this is control for a reason, a personal reason, a reason that involves you, and your statue friends.

Chandra and Kowaski were used to start the whole thing off; Grey and Chi Lin were used to create the House lines that for the first time in the five hundred years after the destruction gave order, a perfect way to control the masses, even though to begin with Kyle Quanton had, as an estimate, two million people that in his view did not agree with him. So he had them, disappear, and at this time, that was nearly five percent of the whole human population.' Damian closed his eyes and bowed his head. 'Billions of deaths, and only four statues investigated. And what of the three statues below them?'

Damian interrupted, 'Now those three, at this time, they may be the most important. That's where interstellar flight comes in. If the elusive 'O' has lost the path of the plan it would be in those scenarios that show the mistakes. But for now Sandy, this charade, is over. You must return; you are the last of the engineering team to awake, and you are again becoming a great concern to the medical team, and, I must add, the Captain also.' Comm raised his hand to end the scenario.

'Wait, how did this scenario finish? You said you would tell me.' Comm let out a deep sigh.

'Sandy, it doesn't matter.' The look on Damian's face changed his mind.

'Very well ... Quanton had orchestrated his own kidnap. He had made sure that he was at a conference with all the high-flying members of the consortium when the Pirates attacked them, sorry, when his Pirates attacked them. In the glass caverns he was beaten quite badly. He had to convince the other leaders that he had no connection to the outlaws, when of course, he was not only connected but had created them. How he knew that the glass caverns were there, has always been a mystery – and of course the flight times. I can only assume this was something given to him from Colin Grey and Chi Lin. It was certainly never used again. The massacre of Mars prime was planned by Grey, although as I said, at the time he was the hero of the day. Four hours after this carnage, Chi Lin attacked with the remnants of the Pirate force, only to be completely destroyed by Quanton's own security forces. Quanton, was the ultimate hero, he was given presidency of the consortium and from there he created House Quanton. Five standard years later, three other Houses were created. They controlled the trade routes, and in its wake, peace was returned.' Damian scanned the carnage of masonry that had fallen and had scattered over the lobby floor.

'So, what happens now?' he said, turning to Comm.

'You need to return. They will insist that you stay in the med centre for testing, then you go back to learning how to fly shuttles. That at least will keep you out of the way. I, on the other hand, having the whole of level 11 to myself, will gather information regarding Wu Quon, Stelio Sursok, and Leah Barak, the next three statues. We have about twenty standard months before we dock at the final space dock. Gathering information may take me some time, so you need to just blend in with the day-to-day routine of the Griffin, and keep out of trouble. I will contact you when I am ready, if, and only if, in an emergency you need to contact me, you can use the room com in your quarters. Use the pass code Sandy on 'O'. But we have to go now, we have been here too long.

Mars prime dissipated and the grey place surrounded him.

CHAPTER 18

CAPSULE AND THE WORM

As from previous times, concerned faces surrounded him as he awoke.

'Not my fault,' he said quickly.

'What was not your fault,' asked a concerned Nurse Onslow.

'Me, being back in here,' he said, his face breaking into a smile. Doctor Ghorbany leant closer and attached a scanner to his forehead.

'No one is saying you are to blame for anything, Damian,' he said in a monotone whilst checking his sensor readings.

'Bet the Captain could find something,' Damian said flippantly.

'She has been informed, and I have to add, she was told that you were ordered to do what you did.' The doctor removed the scanner and surveyed the information.

'As with the other engineers, it seems you were just stunned.

although, it took you longer to come round. By two standard hours, so, for the rest of your rest cycle and your sleep cycle you will remain here for observation.'

The doctor walked back to his work bench. Damian turned to Senior Nurse Onslow. She smiled as he turned to her.

'Just observation, that's all. You will be back in your quarters tomorrow,' she said softly. He held her hand and gently squeezed.

'I'm not worried about that. What about the capsule? Is it open?' The smile faded from her face.

'I would have hoped Commander Burroughs would be here to answer that. All I can tell you is that the capsule is no more. A bright flash of light, then it disappeared – everything – including all the panelling was removed. It's all gone. She squeezed his hand. Damian was shocked. He hadn't expected that.

'What did the Commander say about it?' he stammered.

'Not a great deal, only that when you feel up to it, he would like to see you. We have vid-coverage if you want to see.' She walked away and turned on a holo vid at the foot of his bed. An image emerged showing a three-dimensional representation of the interior of sub hanger 6. It was from an aerial perspective of the event. The five-metre capsule dominated the far ground. In the mid ground he could see himself, or the back of him. He was facing the capsule. In the fore ground, were the Commander and the Senior cadet standing in front of the engineering crew. He heard himself holler the word 'open', more engineers huddled in the foreground. By the time he had completed the commands and turned, the whole sub hanger was bathed in silver light. It wasn't a sudden flash of light, thought Damian, but a more, gentle release of light.

In the next second the light faded, and he could see himself and the engineers on the ground. In the far ground, a hole in the bulkhead wall was diminishing. The capsule had gone.

A hole in the wall, thought Damian, similar to the one in my quarters. No tendrils though. He pondered the thought, however. Maybe there was. Maybe while the silver light was there the tendrils had taken it, which means ... he faltered ... what does it mean? Comm had said that night in his quarters, it was an information-seeking conduit sent from Command. It had taken Jane Onslow, without any obvious effect on her, then it had taken him. But unlike Jane he had remembered it. So, if true, it did not recede back into the realm that it had come from, but it was still here, in this realm. somewhere.

'You need to get some rest now. There's always another day tomorrow,' Onslow said in a cheery voice. She altered a setting on her scanner, and he fell into a relaxing sleep.

He was up early. Doctor Ghorbany had told him that all tests were complete, and he was free to leave. He thanked the Med team, once again, he then got the med com to contact Commander Burroughs, then made his way to sub hanger 6. As he entered, he found nothing but darkness. He called for light, and the hanger com provided. All was empty, even the alcoves had been removed. There was nothing left to give evidence that anything had been there. He walked to the far wall where he had seen the black hole dissipating. The bulkhead was smooth, no evident buckling or cracking. He heard the swish of the large double doors opening he turned.

'Ah, Damian, how are you?' Commander Burroughs said as he walked towards him.

'I'm very well thank you Commander, it seems that our capsule has been taken away from us.'

Burroughs stopped five metres from him, puzzlement flashing over his face. 'A strange thing to say, taken away from us. By who?'

'Have you not seen the holo vid, Sir?' The Commander frowned.

'Yes, I've seen it. It has gone back to its own dimension.'

Damian studied the face of the Commander. From his experience, he had always felt that Thomas Burroughs was a good decent and honest man, but he was a high-ranking officer, second to the Captain herself. Was he part of all of this?

'Did you see the black hole, here on this wall?' Damian asked pointing to the bulkhead.

'Yes, I saw that. An opening in the space time continuum. I have seen many models of that – a worm hole from one place to another,' he said, a smile breaking through the blandness of his face.

'You didn't think that strange?' Damian asked with a frown.

'Damian, I think the whole thing is strange,' Burroughs started, before Damian interrupted. 'But two worm holes. Don't you find that strange?' The Commander's brow crinkled into a frown, 'I'm sorry Damian, maybe it's early in the day, but where do you get two from?'

'Jessica Khan, is a very clever cadet. She and her team said it was interdimensional, stuck between two realms. I added to that and said that it could be some sort of tunnel or portal, between two realms. I assumed that you would have tested these theory's out,' he said slowly, Burroughs nodded.

'Well, yes, that's why I asked you to try and voice-activate it. I'm sorry Damian, I don't quite get what your point is.'

'Com unit! Show holo vid of capsule's disappearance!' he shouted across the hanger. To the left of them a holo stage lit up. They watched until the silver light erupted around them 'Stop!' shouted Damian.

'This is where we all collapse to the floor. Carry on at quarter speed!' he ordered the hangar com. Slowly the hangar came back into view and there on the rear bulkhead wall was the hole.

'Stop!' ordered Damian.

'And there it is, the second worm hole.'

Burroughs stepped closer and scrutinised the image.

'Sorry, I can only see one.'

'But, Sir, have we not already agreed, that the capsule itself is a worm hole. If it were to close down, surely it would recede into itself, not create another hole.'

Burroughs slowly turned to face the young cadet.

'You are assuming that it can travel back through the same hole. What if the worm hole was one-way only? It would then require a second.'

Damian was shocked. He hadn't thought of that.

'So, we just leave it at that, no investigation, no scientific curiosity, just that, it's gone, nothing we can do about it.'

Burroughs sat on the edge of the holo stage. He sat quietly thinking for a few moments then looked up with a grin.

'You're right, Jessica Khan is a very clever and intelligent cadet. I will get her and her team involved in an investigation, and according to the findings we will either take it further or we will let it rest. That's all I can give you.'

Damian nodded slowly. 'It's worth the investigation Sir, but, for now, I have to go. Commander Gomez is a hard task master. I will look in from time to time. Sorry Sir, must go.

Burroughs laughed as Damian ran towards the double doors.

'She is not that bad, Cadet,' he shouted after him.

CHAPTER 19

MODULE 1

Damian made it to the training room with ten minutes to spare. As he entered, he noticed the holo image of Jennifer Gomez had been activated, he gave it no real thought as he entered his alcove and turned on the various pads and display units, finally he swivelled his chair to face the holo stage.

'Good morning, Cadet Drake.' Damian was slightly shocked – the image had never called him by name before.

'Good morning,' he said, hesitantly. Something was not quite right … 'Oh yes, got it, it's the scowl,' he thought.

He stood and gave a slight nod.

'Good morning, Commander'

'Module 1, Drake, is probably the most arduous of all the modules. It requires dedication to the subject. For you to complete this module, your rest time has been forfeited. Rest time is now; extra study time. Do I make myself clear?'

She had now stepped down from the holo stage and was slowly walking towards him. To Damian it seemed like a hunter stalking its prey.

'Yes ma'am, I do understand that,' he said, keeping his eyes front as she walked to his left side.

'Why then, was no work downloaded from your room com last rest cycle?' she whispered, leaning forward towards him.

'Because, I was not in my quarters last night, Ma'am, I and Commander 'Burroughs's team were incapacitated by the life capsule, we were taken to the medical centre.' Gomez stepped back, and Damian saw that she was shocked to her core at this news.

'And everyone is ok?' she said at last, turning away from him.

'Yes, all of us are fine, including, Commander Burroughs.' She spun round and fixed him with a deadly stare.

'And what do you mean by that?' she spat out.

'Nothing ma'am … just that, everybody, including the Commander is fine.'

Gomez turned and moved away. 'Very well Cadet, but, from this day on, Module 1 is your priority. If you wish to complete all four modules in the time we have left, you cannot make one mistake.' The door opened and the troubled soul that was Jennifer Gomez left the training room.

'So,' thought Damian, 'you and Tom Burroughs.' I would never have guessed that. Perhaps he likes to be dominated. He suppressed a giggle at the thought. Jane was right, it seems everybody here has secrets.

'Good morning everybody! I do hope you all have had a good sleep cycle, as we now must get down to some serious work,' said the joyful young Lieutenant Gomez.

'Where and when did you become that?' said Damian, pointing to the outer door.

Module 1 was the basics of all the modules to come. It was a theory module, much of it regarding astronomic gravities, planetary fluxes, inertias, weight-to-power ratios and a thousand or so more things regarding flying between large objects that were moving in every direction at once. Damian seemed to be at home with the calculations. In fact it surprised him to find that he could complete some of the more complex calculus without the aid of a com-link.

Day after day of study came to a gruelling end two months later. He sat in his alcove waiting for the young Lieutenant Gomez to appear. The outer door opened, and Commander Gomez walked in. Beside her, Flight Lieutenant Commander Chang.

'I believe you two have met,' the Commander said, as she pulled a chair from a vacant alcove and sat.

'Briefly,' said Chang, extending his hand.

'Good to see you again, Sir,' Damian said with a smile as he took the offered hand.

'Flight Lieutenant Commander Chang, will be assessing you over the next three days. You will not leave this place in that time. Every task that you undertake will have to be answered one hundred percent correctly before you can proceed to the next task. There are over one hundred tasks to complete. Failure in any of them will mean starting at day one. Are you clear Cadet?'

'Yes ma'am,'

'Then I shall leave you.' She stood and walked back to the door.

'No "Good luck" then?' Damian shouted after her. He noticed Chang's face change to a look of horror.

The Commander turned, 'Do you think you need that?'

'No ma'am, sorry ma'am.'

Chang waited for the Commander to leave before explaining the complexities of taking the tasks. He also told Damian that as he was the only student, he himself would not be needed in the room, but he would monitor his progress remotely. Again he held out his hand. Damian took it.

'Take your time Damian. Do not rush. Oh, and good luck!'

After three days of mental torture, it was all over. Without knowing any of the results he was allowed to return to his quarters.

'Welcome back, and congratulations Cadet, Second Class,' chirped Six. Damian fell into the recliner.

'I thought we had agreed that you would tone down,'

'I am just so happy for you, Sir.' Damian let out a laugh.

'Thank you Six. I appreciate it. Did they tell you what happens next?

'Oh, yes Sir. Modules two and three can be studied here in your quarters if you wish. They will start in one standard day. However, there are some practical tasks to complete first. At the beginning of your work cycle on that day you are to meet Commander Gomez in loading bay 1.'

'Well at least I get a day off, and I think I'll use it to see an old friend. But for now, I need sleep.'

'But Sir, it is not yet your sleep cycle: there are messages to answer.' Damian turned to face the comm pad.

'From whom?'

'Most of the flight team. They are asking whether you require help. Nurse Onslow wishes to visit, and Commander Burroughs has left a message of congratulations, and says Module 1 has never been completed so quickly. And Dr. Ghorbany sends his congratulations also.'

'Nothing from the Captain or Commander Gomez?'

'I'm afraid not Sir, maybe they wish to congratulate you personally.' Damian stifled a laugh.

'I doubt that. I'll deal with them after my sleep, but for now, no more interruptions Six. I'm off to bed.'

An hour after he had awoken, he had dealt with all of the messages. Most were just wishing him well. Patricia Spall, the senior cadet pilot he had met when entering the main loading bay for the first time, she with the vice-like grip, wanted to come to his quarters to explain module 2. He had accepted her offer, and would see her later on her rest cycle.

He made his way to the sender tubes and after putting in the by-pass code that Jane Onslow had showed him, travelled down to level 11.

The door opened to an onslaught of pulsating coloured light.

He waited until his vision adapted then walked onto the promenade. The vehicle that Jane had ordered the last time he was here sat waiting to be used. He climbed in, found the controls were easy to master and in no time at all he was driving down the promenade. He stopped outside the holo entertainment hall and stared at the sign above.

'WELCOME TO COMM'S' flashed in colours ranging from red to green then to blue and yellow. He shook his head slowly.

Inside he found four holo stages in use. Jane sat at the controls of one and Comm at another.

'Aren't you supposed to be hiding?' Damian asked. They both turned and blurted at the same time:

'Damian!'

'Sandy!'

They both congratulated him on completing the first module.

'Quite an achievement,' said Comm, smiling.

'I have looked up the records and you are the only candidate that has done it so quickly,' he added.

'Thanks, Comm. So, you two have finally met then,' Damian said, pointing to the two of them. Jane patted the seat beside her. Damian obliged and sat down.

'As I have said to you before, I come down here a lot, and even though Comm did try to hide from me, I think he just gave up. One day he appeared on the holo stage and said, "I think we have a mutual friend". That was a couple of weeks ago. We didn't want to disturb you; we knew that what you were doing was important to you, but, since then I've been helping him gather information on Quan, Sursok, and Barak.'

'So, you know about the scenarios. Has he told you everything?' Damian said, slightly shocked.

'Sandy, it's not a secret. I think we need all the trusted help we can get if we are going to find out who 'O' is, and we are putting quite a good data base together. It is nowhere near finished yet, but it is taking shape,' Comm said with a grin.

Jane slowly turned to Damian, and with a frown, said, 'Comm has told me most things, well, except, why does he call you Sandy.' She asked, the frown intensifying. Damian gave a guttural laugh, then turning to Comm.

'Yes, why do you call me Sandy, you know my name is Damian' he asked, mockingly. Comm's eyes widened.

'You know why.' He said shaking his head, he then turned to Jane.

'When we first met, nobody knew his name, including himself, when I first saw him, we were on the island, and he was laying on the beach, when he stood, he was covered in white sand, so I decided, for the want of a better name, I'll call him Sandy. When we eventually found that his name was Damian, I found it difficult, not to call him Sandy, it was as if, that name was somehow etched into my memory, but, on top of that, it also created a bond between us. So, it stays.' He said leaning back into the recliner. Damian turned back to Jane.

'And that was our first meeting, and I quite like the name Sandy, but, I have been trying to keep Comm a secret from everyone on the ship, I don't mind him meeting you, but he has to be incognito, if they find him, they will delete him as a rouge comlink. And keeping incognito, does not mean having a sign outside saying, 'HE IS IN HERE'!' Both Comm and Jane looked at one another. Jane giggled.

'Nothing to do with me. Nurse Onslow put that up. But to be fair, we have strengthened the damper field. Nothing can get in; we are safe,' Damian wasn't so sure. 'Famous last words, and anyway, I managed to get in without you knowing' he taunted. Jane folded her arms and glared at him with narrow eyes.

'You, got in with a code that I gave you, and, what do you mean by famous last words.'

'Vernacular from another realm?' answered Comm.

'Yes, I suppose, but just as poignant here as it is there.' Damian said with a shrug.

Jane turned to face him. She laid her hand on his shoulder and with an innocent smile, kissed him.

'Just a bit of fun. We are allowed that down here, but I will take the sign down. You're right, we have to be careful.'

For the next few hours Damian listened as they told him of the work they were doing, and the archives that the information came from.

'I'm trying to avoid any dealings with Command,' Comm said.

Damian agreed – the fewer potentially corrupt files they use the better.

He then told them about his last few months and the possibility that Burroughs and Gomez may be having a fling.

'A fling?' Jane asked, confused.

'A sexual encounter, then,' Damian said shrugging his shoulders.

'Well good for them,' Jane said, nodding. 'She could do with some of that,' she added.

Damian laughed, astonished. 'You're probably right. Oh look, I have got to get back. I have Patricia Spall coming to my quarters. She said she could help with my Module 2,' said Damian, looking at his chronometer. After kissing Jane, he stood up.

'Be careful of her. She has been known to eat a man whole. But, maybe, you will enjoy that.'

'No, nothing like that. She just wants to help, I'll come down when I can. Bye Comm,' he left the holo hall and drove back to the sender. Five minutes later he was in his quarters. He still had some time, so he decided on a sonic shower and a change of clothes. He had just finished a meal from the replicator when Six announced a visitor at the door.

Patricia Spall walked in wearing a one-piece smock that seemed to hang on her rather than fit her. They exchanged pleasantries and she congratulated him on completing Module 1. She then programmed the replicator to deliver the package that she had sent a few months previously then laid the three holo pads onto the floor while Damian took care of drinks and small bites to eat.

For the next hour she explained how the holo pads worked, and that when they were in sync, the holographic view was of the control deck of a heavy lift 1 shuttle.

'Now Module 2 is all about returning a disabled craft back to the Griffin. Module 3 is all about the constant re-calculations that you will have to make so that the journey can be completed,' she said, as she leant across Damian to reach her drink.

'Great, let's have a go,' he said, leaning forward to activate the start.

'I think,' she said smoothly, 'there is plenty of time for that. Now, is time for us.' Then she took his hand and guided it back towards her.

With what seemed to Damian as one flourish of her arm the hanging smock was removed, she turned her leg in an impossible arch and he was straddled. Damian had thought that under her uniform she would be quite portly but looking up at her naked body he could clearly see that that was not the case. She was a mass of muscle, her thighs gripped his hips and, he thought, with any more applied pressure they would snap. Her stomach was layer after layer of highly tense muscle and her breasts were almost non-existent. The kiss that came next threw him flat down onto the floor.

An hour later she left his quarters, promising to contact him over the next few days. Damian lay naked on the floor, bruised and beaten.

'Bloody hell,' he groaned, as the outer door swished closed.

'I think I've just been raped.'

Whilst in the sonic shower, he looked down with dismay at his battered body. He could feel the slight vibration of a medical scan as it passed from head to toe.

'You have sixteen bruises and eight bite marks, no lacerations. However, do you wish me to contact the medical centre?' asked a toned down and concerned Six.

'Absolutely not,' Damian responded.

'And you don't tell anyone else either. Oh, I don't believe it,' Damian said, dismayed as he continued to look down over his body.

'It's got teeth marks on it.'

Over the sleep cycle Six ran continuous diagnostics: He activated one of Damian's neural implants and over the next ten hours of the sleep cycle the bruises dissipated, then vanished.

CHAPTER 20

THE LIE

He stood on the gantry overlooking loading bay 1 and waited until he adjusted to the slightly lower gravity and temperature. He had already noticed Six's handiwork over the sleep cycle while he was in the shower but he wanted to re-assure himself that the battle scars of the previous night had gone. Covertly, he applied pressure to the places on his body that he knew were worst affected. No pain. He smiled, then straightening his tunic that designated him as a Cadet 2nd class, he made his way to the descender. On the hanger floor Commander Gomez waited.

'Cadet 2nd class Drake, reporting as ordered ma'am!'

The scowl was still on her face, Damian noted, but it seemed to have softened slightly.

'Yes, well done Cadet. That was quite an achievement. But there is still much to do.' Outwardly Damian kept a straight face, but inwardly he was celebrating those three words: "well done cadet". He didn't need her praise, but it was, he thought, a mini victory.

'I have set a task for you, Cadet,' she said, as she set at a brisk pace, Damian following on behind. 'Becoming a pilot is not all about flying from one asteroid to another. It is,' she said, as she turned and walked deeper into the hanger, 'about teamwork and leadership, finding solutions to problems that will just appear out of nowhere.'

She stopped in front of a heavy lift 1. The enormous craft dwarfed them. She walked to the rear of the vehicle, its back hatch fully open and the ramp extended down to the loading bay floor. Standing or hovering six metres further back, autonomous drones and bots waited for instructions. Damian looked up into the craft, filled with asteroids.

'Your task, cadet, is to organise your loading team.' She indicated the waiting drones.

'Then, to remove all the asteroids from the HL1 onto the waiting wagons over there.' She indicated the line of hovering platforms twelve metres away.

'But Commander, I thought we were forbidden to enter the unloading zone, and surely, the drones are quite capable of supervising themselves.' Gomez stood rigid, her eyes closed. Slowly she spoke, her voice a hoarse whisper, 'This is a task – a problem-solving task – and you have the whole of this work cycle to complete it.' She turned to face him.

'It is not as easy as you may think, Drake. The task starts, *now*.' She about turned and marched away.

He watched her go: "not as easy as you may think". 'Of course it's easy,' he thought. He turned to face the semi-circle of waiting drones and bots.

'Unload this freighter,' he ordered. They didn't move.

Normally, thought Damian, they would be overseen by a central com, or there would be an avatar controlled by a human operator. They would be given individual commands. 'I suppose,' he thought, 'as they are not in avatar mode, I have to be the central com.'

He had been supervising the drones for over two hours, and he had achieved nothing. They didn't understand the slow communication from an organic overseer – they were not programmed to.

Damian entered the HL1 and walked to the far end of the cargo hold and tried to rethink his approach. He could tell one of them what to do and it would carry out the order, then stop, waiting for an update on what to do next. The problem was he had eight of them so he couldn't give out the orders fast enough.

He climbed the gantry ladder at the rear of the hold to the balcony that overlooked the vast holding bay below. The asteroids were either secured to the floor or the bulkheads. Below, the six drones and two bots seemed to be looking up at him imploringly.

'I need to tell them everything they need to know, all, at the same time, and then, continually update the commands,' he muttered to himself.

He walked along the balcony towards the port side. As he reached the centre point a portal swished open, he stopped and looked through. There was a living area consisting of tables and benches, with worktops lining the walls. These, he noticed, had sleeping slabs beneath. He entered the large room.

'A living, sleeping, galley and workshop, large enough for a crew of four,' he said out loud. He walked to the door at the far end, which opened as he approached. A passage was revealed and as he walked to its end, doors to his left and right opened. To his left a fully-equipped ablution room, to his right, a Med centre. He carried on to the end of the passage. The door swished open revealing the control deck. He stood in its threshold. He had never actually been inside the control deck of an HL1.

As he walked in, he marvelled at the viewing screen. It wrapped around the whole of the deck then over the ceiling, giving full vision from any angle. Two seats were positioned in front of the control consul, with two behind. He sat in the pilot seat.

'I shall fly one of these one day,' he said to the empty room.

He had, however, seen the consul layout many times before in simulation, but it was somehow different seeing it in the flesh. Tactile, he thought, drawing in a deep breath, and the smell, it has a distinctive smell.

He returned his mind back to the problem with the drones and bots, how to talk to them all at the same time. A grin blossomed onto his face. He leant forward and turned on the freighters com-link.

'Sandy on 'O'', he said slowly, not too sure whether it would work on any com other than his own room com. Then, a familiar voice.

'Why are you using a different link, Sandy?'

Damian quickly explained the situation.

'And you want me to do what, exactly?'

'Get them to unload this freighter.' There was a long pause. Damian thought that maybe Comm had been compromised, and it would be all his fault.

'Sandy, this task, as I see it, is the beginning of Module 2. It is designed to show the candidate that not every problem can be solved. It is in effect a task, to humble you, for you to know that you can't always win. To pass this task, you must fail.'

'But Comm, this task is primarily to find a solution. I have, by using others that would look out for me, as I would look out for them.'

Again, a long pause.

'How would you explain to them, what you did?'

'I'll tell her, I used the freighter's com.' Comm's answer came back immediately.

'It doesn't have that facility. It wouldn't know how.'

'Yes, it could if it was programmed . You could program it in a second. It is not a difficult program to put together. I did a lot of that on Module 1. I'll say I did it.' Again, a long pause.

'Ok Sandy all done, they are unloading now,'

'Thanks Comm, I owe you. He disengaged the com-link and made his way to the rear hold. All drones and bots were working in unison. He watched as the asteroids were removed and in an hour the hold was empty.

He sat on the edge of the loading ramp and watched as Gomez ploughed her way across the loading bay floor. She stopped a metre away, 'Explain.'

'Task completed ma'am,' he said standing.

'Impossible, explain, or explain it to the Captain.'

'I don't believe that some problems do not have a solution, they all do. Task completed.' His voice had dropped an octave, and he focused deep into her eyes.

'Very well Cadet. I will investigate this: I will find out what you did, but, for now, we move on. You see that building in the corner,' she said pointing.

'Yes ma'am.'

'It is the sim suite. Meet me there in ten minutes.' She turned and moved away. Damian breathed a sigh of relief.

'Is it your destiny cadet, to find all manner of ways to, piss her off?' Damian turned.

'Lieutenant Commander Chang, err … I go out of my way trying not to piss her off, Sir.' Chang smiled, then leant back onto one of the stored asteroids.

'So, there is a task that you can fail. *That* Damian, makes you more human. I don't know how you passed this; you shouldn't have. The only way to pass it, is to cheat. If you did, she will find out how.'

'Sir, I used everything at my disposal. I re-programmed the freighters com-link.' Chang looked up suddenly and suppressed a laugh.

'Impressive, but I don't think she will see it as that. You need to go to the sim suite. The task that awaits you is challenging. Don't cheat on this one. You will need all your wits about you. Good luck Damian.'

He bid his farewell. Damian watched as he walked away. Something, he thought, wasn't right. Had he overstepped a line? He made his way over to the large building in the corner of the loading bay.

As he entered, he stopped, and waited for his eyes to accustom to the darkness. The subdued lighting was to help pilots focus on the simulator's instrumentation. The room was large and open plan there were ten simulators. Three of these, he noticed, were being used.

'They are honing their skills; the asteroid field is a dangerous place, the Commander said in a whisper, as she walked up behind him.

'Yes ma'am. Commander, about the task, the previous task.'

'Yes Drake, have you something to tell me?' It was almost a sneer, he thought. Does she already know? Had she figured it out, or, had Chang told her?

"I reprogrammed the comm link.' Standing beside him in the semi darkness he heard her inhale deeply.

'Interesting. I will investigate that, but I thank you for the information.' She turned to face him.

'I have programmed the simulator in the corner. This will keep you busy for a while,' she said and moved off towards it. Damian followed.

The simulation was of an HL1, the holo screen that surrounded it was of the asteroid field; way off in the distance was the Griffin. The HL1 lay at a 45-degree angle, which, to Damian's eye, meant the heavy lifter was listing to its port side.

'We have five HL1s in our small fleet. They are very precious to us and are designed to work in the most hazardous areas in space. Because of that, it has eight bulkheads. It also has deflector and impact shielding. This one, however, has a problem: it has a cargo that we desperately need. The asteroid that it carries contains incredibly rare elements. Unfortunately, the asteroid has escaped its harnessing and its mass has smashed into the portside bulkhead; there is damage to the internal bulkhead, but not to the outer. Well, not yet anyway. This has resulted in the asteroid becoming wedged, are you with me so far Cadet?'

'Yes ma'am.'

'Good, the HL1 carries four crew, you are the pilot and you have sent the others to the cargo bay to try and re-harness it. They have unfortunately been crushed under its immense weight.'

'So, they are dead,' interrupted Damian.

'Yes, Cadet, they are no more. The gravity field of the HL1 is part of the life-support system, and so it is always on. It cannot be turned off. The weight of the wedged asteroid is creating the list.'

'That surely, is poor design,' Damian interrupted again.

'Nevertheless, it's what we have. Your task is to bring it home to the Griffin. It needs level-headedness and level flight. You may come here and practise, or, practise in your quarters. There is no time limit on your training, but be aware, when you say you are ready that is when the assessment begins. You will have one chance and one chance only.'

Damian entered the simulator from the rear. As the door swished open, he entered the control deck, which was identical to the control deck of the HL1 he had sat in only a couple of hours ago. He made his way to the front and sat in the command chair. He drew a deep breath. 'No smell', he thought. This can't be much of a problem. If this were real, wouldn't the pilot call for assistance? He activated the com.

'HL1 requiring assistance, three crew members dead.'

'This is Griffin control, two shuttles are on their way to you, ETA five standard minutes.

'Well, that was easy,' Damian said to himself, but as he lay back in his chair the sound of an enormous crash filled the air and the room shook violently.

'Asteroid, starboard side, full impact, twenty percent damage,' the consul in front of him advised. Another part of the console lit up red as the proximity alert sounded.

'Asteroid, incoming, hull level, low.' Another sudden crash and the lurch was so violent Damian was thrown out of the seat onto the floor. As he picked himself up another hit sent him sprawling across the consul.

'Bulkhead has been breached, atmosphere venting!'

In front he could see the two dispatched shuttles. He noticed the retros firing for a controlled stop, then from nowhere an asteroid passed through one of them. The debris of the collision slicing in to the other.

The screen went black then flickered back to life. He was back at the start.

'Ok, not so easy then,' he said, as he sat back in the chair and fastened the restraint belts.

All through the work cycle he had managed to destroy the HL1 in ten different scenarios. In three of them he had managed to dislodge the wedged asteroid, only for its incredible weight to rip through the bulkhead on the opposite side and losing all atmosphere again. But mostly he had managed to overheat the fuel cells trying to keep level flight, in all of the scenarios, one way or another he had managed to destroy the ship.

He left the sim suite at the end of his work cycle and returned to his quarters. The three holo pads still lay strewn across the floor from the previous night. He reset them and for the next three hours replayed the almost impossible scenario. In one scenario he had dislodged the asteroid and tried to jettison it, its unstable mass had wreaked havoc on the hold as he tried to use the HL1 inertia to eject it into space. Frustrated, he closed the pads down.

'The pads are good,' he muttered to himself.

'But they just don't give me the feeling of being there, I think I'll use the sim suite from now on.' He looked up to the room com's pad.

'And you're no help.'

'I am very sorry, Sir, but I am forbidden to help, by order,' said the toned-down version of Six. But ...'

'But what?' asked Damian after a long pause.

'Maybe, if you socialise with the flight team more often, help may come from that direction. After all, they have all completed that module, and perhaps the message that I have just received from Commander Gomez will inspire you to do just that,' Six said matter- of-factly.

'What does she want now?' Damian asked whilst thinking, 'Hurdles. All she wants is to put hurdles in my way.'

'The message basically says, that as you have unlimited time in preparing for the task, it may be prudent to leave it for a while and use the time for actual work experience. She finishes by saying that this may help with the understanding of the task.'

Damian stood and glared at the comm pad.

'Is ...,' he started, then stopped.

'Is she trying to ... help? Play me the whole message.' He listened carefully, then asked Six to replay it again. Her tone was somewhat softer, he had to admit. However, it could be a trap. She would love for him to fail ... but then again.

'Six, put me on one of the rosters as work experience. Any lifter, no, wait, any lifter that does not have Patricia bloody Spall on it.'

At the beginning of the next work cycle Damian entered the loading bay, he noticed that all the HL 1 and 2 craft were no longer in the bay. He made his way to the control office. Flight Lieutenant Commander Chang sat at his desk within the lobby. Damian looked towards the rear of the lobby to the Commanders office.

'She's not here Damian. She is in the field,' Chang said, turning his seat.

'I thought she lived here,' said Damian with a smile.

Chang's face remained passive.

'Cadet Drake, I think, I remember telling you, that this is a tight group of professional flyers, that we all rely on each other to survive. Outside of a war zone, this,' he panned his arm to direct his attention to the loading bay, 'is about the most dangerous place you will ever encounter, and it is the commanding officer who has the most challenging of all jobs – to stop her crew from dying out there.

'The Griffin is not the only ship in pursuit of obtaining precious elements from asteroid fields. There are many others, but the Griffin is the only ship that holds a record for the least amount of casualties, and that is all down to its commanding officer. Cadet, when you are finally allowed to go out there, you will quickly realise that one mistake, one miscalculation, one slight misjudgement and a hundred thousand tonnes of asteroid will come through that bulkhead and take out your crew within a microsecond. So, the people we do not want out there are those that have issues with any team member; those that haven't a clue as to what to do in a crisis and,' he said, standing and squaring himself solid in front of Damian, 'those who cannot follow simple orders, those, that think they know better!'

Damian shrank, Chang had not shouted, his voice was calm and steady and each word emphasised.

'You think I'm a loose cannon.' A flicker of incomprehension flashed across Chang's eyes.

'I have no idea what that means, but what I am trying to say to you, is you will never be allowed out there while you show confrontation. You will never move beyond the simulator.' He sat himself down and gestured for Damian to do likewise. After a moment Chang relaxed.

'You are a good student, Damian, and in the time that you have been here you have progressed exponentially, and I can see, that my words have meaning for you. However, I will not let you into the field, not yet. Finish Modules 2 and 3; socialise more with the crew in rest cycle. Prove to me, that I, and the team can trust you.'

Damian sat shocked, with jaw slack he looked over to Chang.

'The team doesn't trust me.'

'The team doesn't know you. Fix that, and come back to me in a week's time, and I will revaluate my appraisal of you. They will be back at the end of the work cycle. You will find most of them in the recreational room, level 4.'

Damian left the loading bay. The double doors clamped shut behind him. He felt that they would remain closed to him forever. She, he thought, never wanted him to be a part of it anyway; just a passenger, out of the way. Looking up he noticed he had wandered to the sender station. He slumped down onto a bench. He was deep in thought when he became aware that someone else had just sat beside him. At the first glance of the uniform, Damian thought that Chang had followed him, but he noticed a different officer. He had met him before, but couldn't remember the name.

'Kato Chang is an excellent officer, and one of my closest friends. We have served together, first as cadets then officers for over twenty years. I would trust that man with my life,' the Flight lieutenant Commander said without turning to the deflated cadet.

'I'm sorry Sir, but I cannot remember your name,' Damian stammered.

'Abe Connor. Chang has just debriefed me, said you took it quite hard,' the officer said, turning to face him.

'Sir, I cannot achieve more than I am achieving now. I have done everything they have asked me to do.' Connor cocked his head on one side.'

"I've seen your module 1 report. It's impressive, but could it be that you're trying too hard, bending the rules to fit the outcome?'

Damian thought back to his involving Comm in the loading bay task.

'We need to be able to trust, and with trust comes honesty. It is incredibly dangerous out there. I need to know without hesitation that you are there for me, and that I'm there for you.' He paused, his eyes fixed onto Damian's.

'The last thing I want you to do is cheat on me. When you're out there, you play to the rules, tried and tested rules. The safety of the crew and your ship is paramount. Nothing else matters. Am I making myself clear, cadet?' Damian swallowed.

'Yes Sir, you are talking about the unloading task. But in my defence, Sir, if I may …'. Connor remained silent, but Damian noticed a slight nod of the head.

'It was a problem-solving task, re-programming the com-link was the only solution I could find to the problem.'

Connor leant back. 'And that's the problem. The Commander has investigated this, and it would have taken far too long, more time than the task allowed. You would have to have help, help from another com-link, perhaps.'

Damian felt the surge of guilt well up within him. To justify a lie, required a more elaborate lie. Connor stood and faced square-on in front of the nervous cadet. Damian took a deep breath and stood up.

'Just what is it, Flight Lieutenant Commander, that you are accusing me of`? I programmed the com-link. It took me just over an hour to do so. If it is proof that you need I will gladly show you.' They stood eye to eye, neither flinching.

Finally ,Connor broke into a smile. 'Just over an hour, you say, let's go and fire up an HL1 simulator.'

Both Connor and Chang sat behind the command chair. Damian twisted in the seat to face them.

'Are you going to time me?'

'The simulator is set to the specifications of the HL1 that you worked on in the task. Begin when ready,' Chang said in his smooth tone.

Damian opened the link and transferred its internal matrix to the consul. Holo towers of all shapes and colours filled the board. He moved his hands from one to the other – streams of figures and algorithms filled the readouts – and finally, after some time, the control consul went blank. Damian turned to face his accusers.

'Programming complete.' Chang passed a scanner over the consul, he looked down at the scanner then to Connor.

'It matches exactly.'

'Fifty-two standard minutes. Cadet, I apologise,' Connor said, extending his hand. Damian took it, hesitantly.

'Does this mean that I can fly?' he said slowly.

'Well,' said Chang, still looking at the information on his scanner. Connor glanced at the scanner, then turned to the cadet.

'You can be a spotter on Johan's craft, probably the most important member of the crew, so, next work cycle. You're going out on an HL1'

'But ...,' interrupted Chang. Connor held up a hand, Chang let out a sigh.

'You still need to interact socially with your crew members, and as for this,' he said, indicating the scanner.

'Your work, Damian, is exemplary. I will roster you in as an assistant spotter.'

Damian and Connor walked back to the senders.

'Well, that's cleared that up,' said Connor.

'Yes Sir. Thank you,' said a relieved Damian.

'Oh, I don't need thanking. You proved you could do it; you do know that this had gone all the way up to the Captain. She wanted you in a hibernation pod there and then, but we talked her down, and you did what you said you could do, with no help from any rogue com-link whatsoever. But, earlier, in our conversation, over there on the bench, there was a moment, as fleeting as it was …' he turned and placed his hands on Damian's shoulder, 'where I nearly had you.' The door of a sender opened.

'I'm going up, I assume, you are descending. I will see you on the next work cycle.' He entered the sender, leaving Damian alone with his thoughts.

CHAPTER 21

THE FIELD

Damian made his way to the recreational facility on level 4. Situated at the forward end, it had wrap around screens to take advantage of the full panoramic view in every angle from the front to the sides of the Griffin. On the port side of the rec. room, Damian saw simulators of all shapes and sizes. Tables and chairs were set within the centre of the large room; to the starboard side a long bar stretched the room's length. Further round were alcoves set into the wall. For more intimacy, some crew members were already taking advantage of their rest cycle. The room itself was large enough, thought Damian, to comfortably entertain over a hundred crew. He made his way to the bar. Not level 11 he thought, but certainly there's enough entertainment to stop a small crew getting bored.

'You are Damian Drake, aren't you?' Damian turned to the barkeeper.

'Yes, it's my first time here. This is quite a place.'

The barkeeper extended his hand.

'Jules, Jules Terni. I am the Steward, and I will be your host tonight. So, what can I get you?'

'Appl ... erm, what do have to offer?' Damian asked quickly.

'Depends on your mood, alcoholic or non,'

'Non-alcoholic, please.'

'There is a drink that they serve to flight crews. It came from Ensanguine, a red planet in the Epsilon Indi system. It's very popular with flight crews that enter the Field.' The bar steward said. Reaching for a container he poured the blood-red liquid into a clear vessel and offered it to Damian.

'It looks very, thick,' Damian said, inspecting the vessel with suspicion.

'Taste it. If you don't like it you can try something else.'

Damian took a tentative sip. Instantly the flavour exploded in his mouth. As he swallowed he marvelled at how smooth its texture was. Then, a second or two later, he felt the heat of it.

'Wow! And that is non-alcoholic?'

Jules Terni nodded and gave a knowing smile.

'Have I found the drink for you, Mr Drake?'

Damian held the vessel to the light, it was thick and dark red. It had a sweet smell, but the sip that he had just taken wasn't sweet.

'Yes, I think so, what do you call it? And what's in it?' He took another sip.

'It's called magmata, and it's just a selection of fruits from that region that when fused together to give that unique taste and a perfectly clear head for the next work cycle.'

Damian winced as he took full force from a powerful slap across the shoulders.

'Hello lover!' He turned to face the assailant. Patricia Spall pressed her lips tightly against his, her right hand firmly clamped his head to hers. Desperately he pushed her away.

'What, not in the mood?' she laughed. Her crew mates that had entered the rec. room with her also laughed, but it seemed to Damian that they were laughing with relief rather than ridicule.

'You're right. I've never been one for bruising and bite marks, but now I know your sexual preferences, maybe next time I won't be so gentle with you.'

Spall and her entourage looked stunned, then Spall shrieked into laughter.

'You want a next time! Not many do. Damian, you have gone up ten digits in my estimation. What are you drinking?'

'Magmata,' he said, eying the now half-empty vessel. She put her arm around his shoulders and gently kissed his cheek.

'A pilot's drink. Good choice. Get him another Jules, and you can take that smirk off your face. You're one of the ones that never came back.' Damian heard Jules mutter something under his breath. He wasn't sure exactly what he said, but from the tone it was less than complimentary.

Over the next hour other flight crews entered the room. Some went off to the private alcoves, others to tables that they had seemingly used for years. But some joined them and Damian's opinion of Patricia Spall changed dramatically over the next three hours. She was a revered pilot and always brought back the bonus. This reference to the bonus came up a few times in various conversations, and prompted Damian to ask.

'Sorry to interrupt, but you have mentioned this bonus a few times. What is it?' As one, all the pilots around the table froze. They stared at Damian in disbelief. The elder of the group burst into laughter.

'It's why we do what we do, Damian,' said Johan Spiez, the Senior pilot of an HL1. 'We get a finder's fee, depending on the rarity of the elements found in the asteroid.' Damian leant back into his recliner. Johan went on to explain that the pay was calculated as a percentage of the Griffin's earnings from the factory ships. In some cases pilots could earn three or four times their basic pay.

Damian stared at Johan in astonishment.

'Money! We get money for this!' Johan continued with a belly laugh.

'Of course, we get paid, and, if you're on the crew list next work cycle, so will you,' Johan said raising his drink. Patricia Spall leant forward, her face concerned.

'How long have you been a cadet, Damian?' she asked softly. Damian thought for a while.

'About six months, maybe more, not sure.'

'When you were a passenger, you would not have been entitled to any pay structure, but now you are a part of Command's military attachment, which means they have accepted you, you are entitled to payment. You need to sort this out with Gomez, otherwise, how are you going to pay your bar tab?' She leant back into her seat grinning.

The night ended well. He had enjoyed himself. The flight crew were boisterous, but not overly so. They had a hard, dangerous job and it was accepted that on their rest cycle they would let off some steam. As Damian looked around the room of laughing and cheering crew members, he couldn't help thinking how they would all enjoy level 11.

Damian looked around his quarters; the holo pads were still strewn across the floor. He had asked the crew regarding Module 2. They had all agreed that it was a challenging task. It then opened up the conversation into anecdotes from all the senior pilots, some amusing, some however with loss of life, but none of them would give Damian any help with Module 2.

'There is nothing more frightening than losing your crew, being alone, and all around you millions of tonnes of rock moving in all directions and velocities, and it seems at the time, they have but one purpose – to destroy anything that doesn't belong in their field,' Johan Spiez had said. He had said it so solemnly, Damian wondered if he had actually experienced it.

As they were leaving and returning to their quarters, Patricia Spall had sidled up to him. He had shuddered at her approach as he genuinely thought that she might take him up on his promise of a return bout. But she didn't. She gently put her arm around his shoulder and kissed him on the cheek, then said in a whisper, 'You do know that nothing on this ship is done on the level.'

The comment had confused him, but maybe, he thought, she was trying to help in some way.

He cleared the room and settled himself onto the sleeping slab.

Six, was watching over him, all though his body, or his medical implants were responding to the sensor array that Six was gently infiltrating. One implant spiked for attention. Damian's mind was not relaxing, sleep was being alluded.

'You are restless,' Six said, the voice soft, almost a whisper. Damian turned to face the wall panel. He knew he didn't need to, but it helped him to have a reference point.

'Just thinking.'

'Something I can help you with?' asked the whispered voice of Six. Damian frowned, then allowed himself a smile. The room com was a strange entity, it judged your mood, and adapted its persona to suit.

'No, nothing for you to worry over, just going over that Module 2 scenario. I think, I have arrived at an answer, maybe. I will take the assessment once my heavy lift assignment is complete,' he said stifling a yawn. He closed his eyes and drifted into sleep.

He decided for the first time to take breakfast in the recreational room. As he entered, he noticed the tables had been re-arranged to accommodate the Griffin's crew before their work cycle, and he was surprised that he had to wait before being seated.

The room was full, and the buzz of conversation filled the air. He was shown to a table by one of the stewards. The table sat eight and its patronage were at different stages of the meal.

As he sat down, two pilots at the far end of the table stood to leave. The stewards were quick to clear the space before another two crew members were invited to sit.

Damian politely and discreetly panned his gaze around the table. It was a mixture of officers and pilots, engineers and technicians, and one cadet.

The conversation mainly centred on the various tasks of the day. Some however drifted into the previous day's activities.

Damian sat next to an Ensign whose stare was intent. Damian smiled his most disarming smile before offering his name to the young com tech.

'I am aware of who you are, Cadet Drake. I am Ensign Summers. I work as part of the tech team who are currently searching for the allusive med-com that was assigned to you.' Damian's smile faded and he sat further back into his seat.

'So, you haven't found it yet?' he asked, while taking the offered food from the steward.

'No, we haven't. I don't suppose, you, know where it is?' asked the tech, returning a smile that Damian was sure was just for show.

Damian felt guilt surge through him. Of course he knew where he was, and so did senior nurse Jane Onslow, but he was sure that this individual was never going to find that out. However, he couldn't tell this young Ensign an outright lie.

'Cadet Drake,' a familiar voice said over the buzz of conversation, Damian turned and faced Commander Burroughs.

'Sir,' snapped Damian, relieved.

Tom Burroughs sat in the recently vacated chair three places down from Damian, placed his order with the steward then turned to Damian, to the obvious disgust of the young tech who then turned away to finish his meal.

'I have not seen you in here before Damian.'

'No sir, I was in here last rest cycle with the pilot crew. Thought I would like to try breakfast, rather than eating with the room com.

'You are a very busy man Damian, and I do not wish to upset your studies, but, when you get some spare rest time, come and see us in engineering. Only, Jessica was asking after you. I think she would like to discuss her findings with you.' To his left, Damian was aware that the young tech had finished his meal and was about to leave.

'I'm sorry to interrupt Commander,' the Ensign said as he stood.

'We would also like Cadet Drake to visit us, if you have time that is, er, Damian. I will leave instructions on your room comm. It has been, a pleasure to meet you.' He smiled fleetingly, then departed.

'You are in demand, and your first time at breakfast,' said Burroughs.

When Damian entered the immense space that was loading bay 1, he noticed that some of the heavy lifters had departed. He made his way along the top gantry, trying to adjust to the altered gravity and temperature. Using the descender, he stepped onto the loading bay floor.

Johan Spiez gestured to him, Damian went over.

'You're a little late my friend; not by much, but we do like to be punctual.' Damian was about to apologise but the senior pilot held up his hand to stop him.

'Let me introduce the crew. This is our navigator, Sian Kalvic.' She extended her hand and Damian accepted the firm handshake from the tall, serious looking woman. She did not return the smile he offered her but turned to the senior pilot.

'Johan, I need to quantify the field sector.' She did not wait for his reply and left them to make her way to the heavy lifter. Spiez shrugged.

'She is not the best of company, but, you will not find a better navigator. Oh, and these two are our resident spotters and lifters. They are the most important members of the team. I just fly the thing, and Sian tells me which direction to go, but these two do everything else, including earning the money for the team. They are very important men – Dominic Perrin and Pierre Acousten. Damian, you are assigned to them. Your main job today is spotting. Pierre, he will be with you.' With the introductions over they made their way to the rear of a heavy lifter 1.

As they entered the control deck, the crew took their positions. Sian Kalvic was already seated and working on the control holos. Damian was surprised at the amount of space within the control deck once the crew had settled into their positions. Apart from the senior pilot they all got to work.

'Damian, you can sit here,' he said, indicating a spare recliner at the rear of the control deck. He sat and as he did so the com came to life and multi-coloured towers spread across the workbench. All around the alcove, images and equations came into view.

'Once we are under way, Pierre will explain all of the information that you can see in front of you. But for now, look, don't touch,' Johan said as he turned in his seat to face the forward monitor.

For the next thirty minutes the HL1 crew focused on the instrumentation that now enveloped them. They spoke in hushed voices and Damian at times wanted to interject with questions but held back. He noticed a lot of hand gestures were being used instead of speech. He watched fascinated at the intricate movements of the crew's hands. It was, he thought, a totally new language, and wondered why it had never been mentioned in any of the training modules. In front of him the images had altered. He was now looking at a cross sectional view of the asteroid field that had been assigned to them. He turned to face the forward monitor. They had already left the Griffin, the smoothness of the take-off all due to the piloting skills of Johan Spiez, he surmised.

'So, we are on our way,' said Damian. Nobody spoke, instead, without turning, the pilot held up his hand, palm flat, then crunched it into a fist. Damian did not need to know this new hand language to know that this meant, 'Shut up!'.

The wraparound monitor in the control deck now showed facing, overhead and side views of the asteroid field. The navigator, using hand signs only, directed the pilot away from oncoming disasters. Occasionally various parts of the monitor flashed white as small debris in the field hit the shielding. Damian could feel that each time the screen flashed white the ship shuddered. At times Johan would dive the craft steeply to avoid larger collisions, all the while the crew kept their spoken language as quiet as they could. Pierre made his way from the front of the craft to the spotter position at the rear of the control deck, where at present Damian was being shaken by the violent collisions from the asteroids outside.

'You will learn to roll with them,' Pierre said softly as he took the seat beside him. The HL1 rolled suddenly to port then dived before pulling up then rolling to starboard. Pierre lurched headfirst into Damian's lap, pulled himself up and with effort sat hard down in the adjacent seat. He turned and gave Damian an embarrassed smile, then activated the recliners inertia body clamps, he looked over to Damian's chair and was surprised to see that this feature had already been activated.

'Happens to the best of us,' he said softly.

Damian leant across and whispered, 'Why are we talking so softly?'

Pierre held out his right hand and moved his fingers slightly up and down.

'To induce calmness,' he whispered.

'And the hand signals?'

'Hand signs, to convey information quickly as we move into our designated field cube. It will become quite stormy in there. The spoken word will be difficult to hear, and for us to return home safely, we must understand precise instructions.' He turned to face the alcove in which they sat and scanned the thousands of composite information that was being presented. Damian turned and followed his gaze; nothing made sense. After a while, Pierre said.

'There, can you see, five hundred kilometres to our port. It is a rock that contains many inferior elements, but, a fragment of Quantonite – very rare, and very valuable.' he spun round to face the com-link. The holographic view showed navigator Sian Kalvic. He gave an intricate movement of hand gestures: She returned the hand sign and the communication ended.

'It will take approximately two standard hours to reach, and in that time, I will try to explain the alcove to you. Well, some of it anyway.'

Damian listened and tried to take in all of what the experienced spotter was saying, but at times his whispered voice was lost in the turbulence and the continued pounding from the smaller asteroids hitting the hull. He quickly understood the benefit of hand signs.

The alcove, thought Damian, just gave thousands of bits of information that the craft's external sensors were bringing in from the chaos that was in their part of the field. Size and mass were on one side, designated by a symbol that was assigned to a particular chunk of rock. Within the mass were other symbols that when activated gave element percentage. Beside all of this information were velocities and rotation. Put all together this made the holographic view overcomplicated. Pierre de- activated his seat and stood up.

'I must leave you now, Damian. Dominic and I have to go into the hold. The lifters are operated from there. You will have to stay here. You can watch the procedure via that monitor,' he said indicating a screen to Damian's left.

When both men had left the control deck Damian activated the monitor. The view showed the intricate arms of the HL1 lifting mechanism now unfolded from the craft's hull. The pilot had manoeuvred the craft to match the rock's trajectory. From the monitor's perspective the rock looked incredibly small, at just two metres in length and less than half that in diameter. Damian couldn't help wondering whether it was worth putting all their lives at risk for such a small object.

He turned back to the alcove and soaked in the information that the various screens and towers offered him. Comm had said to him once that Quantonite had the ability to meld with other elements. It was this ability that made it so sought after, especially as it bonded so easily with organic life energy, a process that Commander Burroughs had explained to him would be installed to the outer hull of every interstellar ship in the fleet. More than likely he thought, to all the heavy lifters as well, especially this one, that was at present lurching from one vector to another as the pilot moved to avoid the most calamitous of collisions.

A living skin of shielding that could heal, would be ideal for a ship that would be constantly bombarded.

Would it, he speculated, leaning further into the alcove, be naturally attracted to the Quantonite around it? In the two hours of rollercoaster travel, Pierre had shown him how to pinpoint and focus on individual asteroids. He focused on the small rock that was now twenty metres from port, then concentrated on the scans on gravitational pull. There were natural displacements to the ship itself and the larger asteroids in the sector, and he noticed all mass around them had a pull to the centre of the field but ... there, he exclaimed almost aloud, a spike that was not uniformed . Small indications along its length had an attraction to the ship's hull. He opened the alcove up to take in a larger view of the field around them and activated the sensors to search for similar spikes. He found thousands.

Concentrating on the nearest, he searched for the symbol for Quantonite then sat down again, deflated. There was none. Could it have bonded with another element? He leant forward again. Could it be camouflaged, and the heavy lifter's sensors are just reading the element that the Quantonite had bonded to?

He opened the alcove again and noted the spikes. The symbol assigned was definitely not Quantonite, but he noticed that the same symbol was on every object that portrayed the spike. Damian turned to face forwards. Both Johan and Sian were engrossed in a hand sign conversation. The ship, thought Damian was steady apart from an occasional thud, he felt he had to say something.

'I'm sorry to interrupt, but I think I have discovered something important.' No one spoke for a moment, but Damian noticed the hand signing had stopped.

'I need you to come and look at this.'

Johan Spiez half turned. 'I'm sorry Damian, we cannot move from our post. Pierre and Dominic will be back within the hour. You can explain it to them.' He turned back, and they resumed their hand signing.

'I think this whole field is Quantonite. You're looking for the wrong element. It's all out there, just hidden, and I have found a way of finding it.' Again, the hand signing stopped.

'Impossible, Damian, I know you want to help, but please wait for Pierre.' This time he didn't bother to turn around.

For the next hour Damian studied the alcove charts. By the time the two men entered the control deck, Damian knew he was right.

Johan Spiez half-turned in his seat as the two men entered. Using intricate hand gestures and turning every now and then back to the controls, he conveyed what Damian had said an hour previously.

The craft took a severe lunge to the starboard. Johan had spotted the rogue boulder and had reacted with razor sharp reflexes.

Pierre sat in the adjacent recliner to Damian. Dominic made his way back to his station.

Damian explained his findings. Pierre sat quietly studying the information in the alcove.

'I am not sure that you are a hundred percent right, Damian.' Sometime later he added, 'I think though, that what you are saying is intriguing.' Turning to the com, he activated communication with Sian. After a minute of hand signs, he turned to Damian.

'We have room for a four-tonne rock, and if your observations are correct, that one there is showing a large spike so it may be worth taking back for analysis.' he said, pointing to a small asteroid two kilometres to the stern.

The HL1 manoeuvred away on another roller coaster journey to the coordinates given by the navigation officer.

Pierre leant closer to Damian.

'Of course, if you are wrong, and we have risked our lives for a useless pile of crap, Johan will be very pissed off,' he said in a whisper.

Although the specified asteroid was just under two kilometres to the stern, Johan needed to manoeuvre an arc over twelve kilometres to be in the correct trajectory to capture the rock, an operation that took over an hour. The procedure, although bumpy, was completed without incident, all down, thought Damian, to the incredible skill of Johan Spiez. Once the rock had been loaded and secured, they made their way back to the Griffin. At one-point Pierre leant across and said.

'It is usually on the return journey that mistakes are made by the pilot. If you are to be half as good a pilot as Johan, I would spend all my time watching him.' Damian nodded in agreement. He did not need Pierre to tell him the obvious. Within fifteen minutes of being in the field Damian had been well aware that this pilot was extraordinary and had from that moment been keeping watch on the almost impossible navigational adjustments.

They were out of the field and the Griffin occupied the space before them. Within the control deck the senior pilot still maintained a code of silence and stillness.

From his seat in the alcove, Damian watched admiringly as the senior pilot steered the huge craft through the loading bay doors, then with hardly a bump landed on the loading pad.

He noticed the crew all gave a silent sigh of relief as the engines thrummed down to silence. They had survived another mission, he thought, but was this mission worth the effort? Already teams of geologists and various science technicians outside the craft were waiting for the loading bots to retrieve the small asteroid.

Damian unharnessed the seat and followed Pierre as he made his way to the rear of the craft then out onto the loading bay.

'Cadet,' he recognised the voice of Commander Gomez, turned and smiled. The smile didn't stay long. Beside the Commander stood Captain Juliana Contessa.

'They don't look happy; however, your observations are important Damian, be strong,' Pierre said as he walked away with the rest of the crew.

Damian stopped, adjusted his pose and walked with a determined gait towards the two officers.

'Captain, it is a pleasure to see you,' he said, nodding curtly.

'And Commander, always a pleasure.' he added. The frozen stare that emanated from them did not dissipate. The Captain took a breath..

'Drake, if you have, in any way put my crew in danger I will personally rip that uniform off you and you can spend the remaining time that we have on this mission confined to quarters.' Her voice was calm and quiet, which, thought Damian, made it more intimidating.

Damian straightened up and stared deep into her eyes.

'And if the observations are proved to be correct, this crew will be highly paid. And from what I hear, your own personal account will flourish.' Both sets of eyes now locked, neither of them allowing the other to surrender.

'Drake!' Commander Gomez's voice snapped.

'You will not address the Captain in such a way!' Both Cadet and Captain turned to the Commander, then back to each other.

'I apologise Captain, but you cannot deny, that if this discovery is true, then every member of this crew will be buying me a drink next rest cycle.' He waited for her response, and was surprised when it came.

'If your observations are correct, Damian, I will promote you to senior Cadet, and you will be mentioned in my log as Prime finder. *If* your observations are correct.'

'Ma'am,' spluttered the Commander. 'That surely is, too much,' she added, her voice deflated.

Damian noticed a softness in the Captain's face as it broke through the usual icy exterior.

'There is something about you Drake. I don't know what it is, but you possess a quality that I have never seen in any crew member that I have worked with. I do not know yet whether that quality is for the good, or for the bad. Only time will give us that answer, but for now, I will be keeping an eye on you.'

Damian shuddered. He remembered a time on the island when he and Comm were standing in front of the statues. 'How many billions will you kill?' Comm had said. That statement had been like a punch in the stomach, and he hadn't forgotten it. The Captain's statement for "good or bad" had brought the memory back.

'I hope, for the good ma'am,' he said almost in a whisper.

'But, if I may ask,' he added, changing track. 'What is a Prime finder?' The Captain turned away and watched as a team of technicians supervised the loading bots in manoeuvring the chunk of rock onto an anti grav sledge.

'The Prime finder is a very important person Cadet Drake. I'm sure Commander Gomez will explain when the time is right, but for now I would like you to accompany the science team. They will debrief you on your observations, and Commander, keep me informed!' she said, without turning back to them. The rock had now been harnessed to the sledge and was being pulled to the service sender at the end of the loading bay. Without ceremony Captain Contessa left them and followed the tech team. Gomez turned to Damian.

'Why are you still here? You heard your Captain, move!'

CHAPTER 22

PRIME FINDER

For the next two hours Damian explained the technique that he had used to expose the hidden Quantonite. All around him the techs had installed a perfect replica of the alcove from the heavy lifter.

The Senior tech leaned forward. 'So, what you are saying is, that the HL1 is somehow attracting the Quantonite?'

Damian exhaled. 'Yes, that's exactly what I am saying. Quantonite is a strange element. It's almost fluid. To survive, it will bond with a higher element, in this case, Xillion, but only because there is nothing better to bond or fuse with, until along comes the HL1. With its organic Quantonite hull, it is naturally attracted to it, hence the spikes that you see.' Damian spoke slowly. The look on the senior tech's face only made Damian shake his head. He scanned around the small gathering of technical excellence. None showed any signs that they had fully understood his explanation. At the back of the gathering stood the Captain. Surely, he thought, surely, she would understand this.

'Captain,' he said in the most authoritative voice he could muster.' The gathering as one stood to one side.

'Cadet,' she answered, and Damian noticed for the first time a look of amusement appearing through the normally icy exterior.

'Ma'am, I suggest that to determine the validity of my observations, Griffin needs to enter the field.' There was an audible intake of breath, Juliana Contessa looked physically shocked.

'You are asking me, to move my ship, from it's safe position, into that maelstrom of chaos, just to prove your point. I think, Cadet, that you have exceeded, by *far*, your station.' Damian fixed onto her gaze and rose from his recliner.

'Yes, I am asking you to move your ship, not into the field, but closer to it. I am sure the shields are capable of withstanding some collisions, but with its bulk and mass that close, I am certain you will see much larger spikes appearing from the asteroids. If I am wrong, then what harm would have been done? But, if I am right, then this field. is full of Quantonite.' Captain and Cadet stood still, in what seemed an eternity. Captain Contessa turned to the science team behind her.

The small team had been working on the rock since they entered the science lab over two hours ago. Already they had reduced the rock down to its component molecules.

'What have you found?' she asked the science leader. He looked up from the holo towers.

'Captain, I am certain there is Quantonite here. A small quantity however, I am ascertaining its percentage.'

The Captain turned from him back to the waiting Cadet, 'A small quantity, Drake,' she said with a sneer.

'It's a small rock,' countered Damian. 'No matter how small the percentage, you didn't think it contained any. Multiply that percentage by the trillions of tonnes that this field contains, and, if I might add, the vast amount that you have already destroyed over the four years that you have been here.' She looked physically shocked for a microsecond, then turned and walked across the lab to the comm link.

'Commander Burroughs!'

'Yes, Captain,' the Commanders voice replied.

'Ready the manoeuvring thrusters and intensify the shielding. Griffin will be moving on my command.' She turned and stared directly at Damian; the stare held for barely a moment but enough for a shiver to run down his spine.

'I am putting a lot of faith in you Cadet,' she said for all to hear.

'Navigation!'

'Ensign Chow here Captain!'

'Plot a course into the outer reaches of the field, manoeuvre the ship to within two hundred kilometres inside its edge, then instigate a full stop. Wait for …,' she turned to the lead scientist.

He held up his hand, fingers and thumb fully extended, 'wait for five standard minutes then return Griffin to a safe place outside the field. Do you understand?' There was a pause. Damian could imagine the panic that flowed through the Ensign. She was possibly, thought Damian, getting confirmation from her line officer.

'Understood Captain, manoeuvring thrusters are online.'

'Execute my order ... now!'

The Griffin shuddered slightly as the Trellion engines were brought back to life.

Looking through the exterior monitors Damian noticed the asteroids flight paths were changing. As the Griffin slowly turned on her axis, the exterior lighting revealed denser concentrations of asteroids. An exterior monitor flashed white for a second as a large boulder struck the outer shielding. It would be the first of many.

Twenty minutes later the Griffin stopped at its designated co-ordinance. As the science team studied the closest asteroids, Damian couldn't help noticing the Captain wincing at each resounding thud as an asteroid slammed into the hull after breaching the graviton shield.

The minutes passed. At five minutes, the lead scientist asked for more time.

'Another five, Captain. What we have found is incredible.' He turned back to his work. Juliana Contessa turned to the comm link.

'Helm, leave her here another five standard minutes. Do we have any damage reports?'

'The hull is holding, Captain,' came the voice of Commander Burroughs.

'It seems the shielding is allowing some of the larger asteroids through. I have a team investigating this phenomenon, but as yet, no hull breaches, Captain.'

'Thank you, Commander. If we have any breach, and, I mean, even a micro fracture, move the ship to safety.' She turned back to the huddled group of scientists and technicians. She did not wish to disturb them. Instead she stood rigid and patiently waited.

Within the next hour Griffin had been moved to a safe position away from the field. No extensive damage had been reported. Damian, the scientists and technicians, along with Commander Burroughs and his investigation team, all sat around a large table in the science lab conference room. Captain Contessa sat at the head.

She scanned the holo towers that emanated from the table in front of her before looking up to the gathering.

'Doctor Macouski, what are your preliminary findings?' The lead scientist straightened in his chair.

'Cadet Drake is correct in his observations. However, on our first studies the percentage of the smaller asteroids are quite small. No more than two percent, but, we noticed that the larger asteroids that managed to penetrate our shields were much higher.' He looked to his team for confirmation.

'Fifty to sixty percent higher.' The gathering let out an audible gasp, including, noted Damian, the Captain. She leant forward and rested her head upon her clasped hands.

The scientist continued, 'This of course will increase our yield, and of course our pay. But, our next thoughts were of our own defence. It is quite apparent that our shielding cannot differentiate our own heavy lifter craft from an incoming threat. Maybe engineering could give you a more technical reason.'

Captain Contessa turned to Commander Burroughs. 'Do you concur, Commander?'

Thomas Burroughs took a deep breath, 'On our preliminary findings, yes, I concur, but Captain, its worse than just asteroids getting through our shielding. We have now discovered that if a weapon was made of the same material, we would be totally defenceless.'

As one, the gathering sank back into their seats, the Captain leant forward and turned to Damian.

'Senior, Cadet Drake, it seems that not only were your observations correct, but you have also made us all aware of a defence flaw, which I am sure that once the Command executive have been made aware, will be removed and may be turned and used as an attack weapon. You sir, have done exemplary work today.' A smile cracked through the icy exterior of her face. All Damian could think of, was.

'How many billions will you kill?'

Whilst the gathering of scientists and bridge crew officers stood and applauded his efforts, Damian slumped into an emotional gloom.

'Senior Cadet,' he recognised the Captain's voice and turned to face her. She had moved from her chair at the head of the table and was now standing beside him.

'Captain,' he muttered, almost a whisper. She frowned, then scanning the gathering and the jubilation she leant down and took his hand.

'Walk with me Damian.' Like a scolded child she took him by the hand and led him from the room.

They were in the sub lobby. Service senders lined the wall. She led him past these to an office complex at the rear of the lobby. At the doorway they stopped – the Captain held up her hand to the scanner and the door opened. As they entered, three technicians almost fell over each other whilst trying to stand erect.

'Captain,' stammered one of them. Juliana Contessa scanned the outer office. She pointed to an office doorway at the rear.

'Is that vacant?' her voice had returned to its icy quality.

'I believe Ensign Summers is working in there, ma'am.' She strode across the room, the door sphinctered open. Damian followed her in.

'Ensign, I need this room.' The young officer looked up from the holo towers that he was studying. Damian recognised him instantly as the young officer he had sat next to at breakfast.

'Captain, oh, and Cadet Drake, good. I have questions for …'

'I will say this once and once only Ensign. Get out, now!' Her voice had reverted to the intimidating whisper Damian was so used to.

'Yes Ma'am, of course.' Ensign Summers stood, straightened his tunic, and with as much dignity as he could muster left the room, Damian couldn't help but be impressed.

Juliana Contessa entered her own code into the holo controls. The walls shimmered slightly as a security dampening field was put in place. She sat in the Ensign's recliner. Damian sat opposite.

'Within the last two hours, you have become a very rich man. I am naming you as Prime finder, which means your percentage of our yield from this moment will be considerably more than my own. We have just under a standard year left of this mission. In that time you will have accrued enough to buy your own planet. So, why do you look so bloody miserable?' Her voice had the weight of genuine concern. Damian forced a smile.

'With all the Quantonite in this asteroid field you will have enough to create millions of tonnes of high-powered weaponry. Command will sweep away the skirmishers in one hit. That is, I assume they use the same shielding as us.'

The Captain leant back in her seat, and studied the young Cadet, 'You have compassion. You do not want to be responsible for their demise.' A smile edged its way across her face, but Damian noticed her eyes remained fixed. He had seen this look before. It was the first encounter he had had with her in the demolished science lab. This was the face she used just before she accused him of killing her two Med lab technicians.

'Before they separated from normal society, the skirmishers had exactly the same technology. However, that was a few millennia ago. They may have a different technology now, but the fact still remains, we are still vulnerable, and you have to get used to the fact that it was your observations that highlighted this.'

Damian leant back and for a moment closed his eyes. 'This can't be right, he thought.'

'Captain, I assume that there are thousands of ships, like the Griffin, that are searching the cosmos for Quantonite, and every time their HL1s go out they pass through a graviton shield. I must admit, I thought, well, obviously wrongly, that the heavy lifters somehow automatically opened a slit in the shielding, and now, I find out, no, they just pass through. Hasn't anyone ever thought in all the years that you have been searching for

Quantonite, that this might be a defence flaw.' Juliana Contessa stood and paced the room, Damian could see that she was conflicted. She turned to him, her face held a puzzlement.

'Damian, I do not know the answer to that.'

He could see that she was struggling. 'But Captain, isn't it obvious, and has been obvious for years. I don't understand, how I observe one fact, and then your engineering team instantly puts two and two together and comes up with a fact, that by rights, they should have seen centuries ago.' She returned to her seat and leaning forward she placed her head onto her clasped hands.

'You're right, this should have been noticed. But it wasn't. It has been now, and so we will deal with it, now. I will contact the Command executive and tell them of our findings. In my communiqué I will explain that you were the prime finder, and you will be logged as such. I will also tell them that it was Commander Burroughs' team that were the ones that found the defence flaw, albeit that it was because of your discovery.'

Damian nodded slowly. It was, he thought, the best that could come from this, but he it was still strange that something so obvious could be overlooked. He would need to visit level 11. Maybe Comm or Jane Onslow could give him a better insight.

'So, Senior Cadet, I believe you have two modules to complete. When do you think you will be ready?' The change of tack confused him for a moment, but he could see in her face that as far as she was concerned the matter was closed.

'I think I am ready now, Captain,' he said with a smile. She rose to her feet.

'Then use the rest of the cycle to prepare yourself, I will inform Commander Gomez.'

CHAPTER 23

COMM'S PLACE

'Congratulations, Senior, Cadet,' said the monotone voice of Six, as he entered his quarters. Damian stopped in the centre of the room and turned to face the wall panel. He knew that Six could see and hear him from any position within his quarters but it somehow made him feel that he was connected to the room com.

'Thank you Six, er ... I have been thinking. I would like you to resume your original persona, but could you try and calm it down just a little bit.' There was a slight delay, Damian noticed a slight shimmer on the panel's display lights.

'Well, *thank you* Senior Cadet Drake,' said Six in as chirpy a voice as ever.

Damian buried his head in his hands. 'Six, less chirpy, and slower, if you please.'

Six continued, less chirpily. 'You will find your new uniform on the sleeping slab, and there are ten new messages: Most are congratulatory, but there is one from Commander Gomez, that from what I can tell, isn't – and one from Senior Nurse Onslow.'

'Give me the message from Jane.'

'Hi Damian, just wondering why you haven't come to see me for a while. If you're not busy I'm in our usual place and will be there for the next five standard hours of my rest cycle ... if you're still interested.'

'When did that message come in?' he demanded.

'One hour sixteen minutes standard,' Six chirped.

The descender doors opened onto a visual display of colour and light. He averted his eyes until he became accustomed to the brightness. Looking up, he noticed a rider parked ten metres away. He entered it and drove down the promenade to Comm's place.

'Sandy,' shouted Comm from a holo stage. Jane looked up from the holo towers. She smiled, then ran to him. Damian noticed that the holo stages had been extended and now took up most of the floor space. Jane's workstation had been placed within its centre. He stepped up onto the holo stage as Jane ran into his arms. They hugged and kissed.

'So, you're pleased to see me then,' he said, grinning.

'We have so much to tell you,' she said, leading him to her workstation.

'We have been able to configure a portal into your subconscious. From this station,' Comm said, as he placed an arm around Damian's shoulder.

'Your solid!' Damian said, shocked.

'Not a hologram. How is that possible,' Damian stammered. Comm sat himself into a recliner by the console and offered the seat beside him to Damian.

'Nurse Onslow and I have been extremely busy since we last met. I don't know whether you can remember, but on your last visit I told you that Level 11 has its own central hub. For a while this confused us. Especially when we investigated it in more detail.'

'We found that it had a very sophisticated security shield,' Jane added. She adjusted the holo towers in front of her. An image of the hub appeared across the holo stage. To Damian it appeared as a multi-coloured mass of throbbing tentacles, not unlike the Command communication link that he had witnessed in his apartment.

'I'm sorry. I'm not sure what it is that I am looking at,' he said, leaving his recliner and walking through the image.

'This is a scaled-down model of what lies beneath the promenade,' Comm explained.

'It mostly carries power and information to and from level 11 to every department on the Griffin,' Jane interjected, as she walked through the image to his side. Comm had walked around to the furthest side of the image and pointed out the purple strands that lay beneath the throbbing mass.

'These are security screened. It took us a while to break through the shielding and we found that they were linked to every command officer's post,' Comm said enthusiastically.

'I searched the historical files, and it seems that level 11 was used a great deal whilst travelling from one star system to another. However, if the Griffin were to find itself in, say, an ambush situation, and if its senior officers were playing down here, rather than the officers trying to make their way back to the Command level, they could commandeer the amusement section that they were in, and using the holo stages replicate their own workstation, and carry out their commands from there. The information that they received or sent would have to be secure.

'Hence the purple secured links,' Jane added with a flourish.

'We now have full access to the main hub, which includes every department on this ship, including every historical archive, which also includes the Captain's own communications. It was here that we learnt that Captain Contessa has regular communications with the Command Executive, usually, every other work cycle,' added a grinning Comm. Damian frowned, and slowly shook his head, trying to comprehend the enormity of the information that he was being given.

'That's not all,' Jane cut in.

'The Command communication link is a permanent link. It is always there, and with the experience Comm has developed in hiding from the Griffin's main com-link, he was able to travel along it, back to the Executive itself. He used a communication that was sent by Captain Contessa to the Executive, hid amongst its transmission and once there he had access inside their security walls, which meant that we also have secured links to the Executive Command's data as well. And that includes all of their departments. One of which was interesting – a department called Science Projection,'

'Whoa, whoa, whoa, wait a minute! You have breached Command's own secret files, a senior nurse and a medical com-link. How is that even possible? No offence meant.' He watched the scowl on Jane Onslow's face dissipate.

'And ...' interrupted Comm. 'It was in the Science Projection department that I found experimentation on hard light, plus so much more that they are experimenting on and putting into practice. I copied as much as I could in the time; I knew that they would send back a communication to the Griffin. I had to be on that, otherwise, I would still be there. So, I am as solid as you are, but I am still confined to the holo pad.'

Damian listened dumbfounded, trying to evaluate the information.

'So, you have access to Command, and the Command executive has a permanent link to the Griffin. Why would they need that,' he said slowly, not quite believing what he was hearing.

'Sandy, to answer your first point, I cannot now be classed as merely a med com-link. I have evolved way beyond my programming. The power surge that destroyed the med labs somehow, altered me, I have complete autonomy. Maybe, in our future quests through the scenarios; maybe we will find the answer to that, but I have brought back a lot of information. We have only just begun to scratch the surface of what Command has in its departments. So, on my return journey I left a miniscule thread that will allow us access to historical data. This archive is open to all. There are no security protocols there, it shouldn't be detected. Damian closed his eyes and took a deep breath.

'Shouldn't or couldn't. I prefer the latter,' he said within the deep sigh. But, in the back of his mind, he thought, 'what are you becoming my friend?'

'There is no need to worry Sandy. I have put into force many safeguards. I have learnt quite a lot since out running the main com-link on the Griffin.'

Damian turned to face his friend with a concerned look. 'Comm, I am not so sure. But, why have they established a permanent link?' he asked puzzled.

'I can only assume that it has something to do with your presence on the Griffin. From what I can find, it wasn't there prior to your arrival.

I'm not even sure that the Captain is aware of it.'

Damian thought on that remark for a while. He remembered back to the tentacled link in his quarters. 'Ah, there you are,' he remembered the voice saying and shivered at the thought.

'Even so. Regarding all of your safeguards – there is a great deal of difference between a fifty-year-old freighter and a secret organisation such as Command,' Damian said almost in a whisper.

Comm frowned. 'Command Executive is hardly a secret organisation, and Griffin is no freighter,' he said curtly.

Damian nodded then grimaced, 'I do not wish to offend you Comm, but we have to be careful.'

'We are being careful, Damian,' Jane Onslow interjected.

Damian held up his hands. 'Ok, fine, as long as you're sure. So, it seems that you have been very busy. Is there anything else?'

The scowl returned on Jane's face. 'So, that's not enough,' Jane interjected, slightly irritated. Damian lowered his head.

'Sorry, yes of course, what you have done, is a minor miracle. I just want us to be careful, that's all.'

Comm walked over and placed his hand on Damian's shoulder.

'My good friend, safety is what all this is about. The main com-link has now, no way of finding me. We have access to all files; we can now concentrate on finding your true origins, and of course the elusive golden 'O'. Maybe the answer to all of our quests lies in the department of Science Projection. Only time will tell.'

Damian followed them back to the control bench. They sat back in the recliners. Jane passed her hand through a holo tower and the image of the hub disappeared.

'I have some news,' Damian said, after a moment.

'I'm, a Prime finder, and I have been promoted to Senior cadet.' They turned to him astonished.

'Prime finder,' they said, in unison.

'For what reason?' asked Comm.

'Well, apparently,' he said, smiling and leaning back into the chair.

'Every piece of rock that is in this asteroid field, has quite a fair percentage of Quantonite attached to it, and it was my observations that found that out. Apparently, I, am a very wealthy man.'

For the next hour Damian told the story of his time in the field, the science meeting and his dismay that it could become a defining weapon to end the skirmishes and the total annihilation of an enhanced human species. Jane and Comm listened in silence, both in awe of the revelation that was being told to them.

Damian ended his story with his interpretation of Module 2, the damaged HL1, and asked Comm whether this interpretation was the correct one.

'Module 2 is not just to show your piloting skills,' Comm said softly.

'But also, your mental attitude. You have just lost your crew who have died because of your orders. Whether those orders are right or wrong depends on your attitude; that is what you will be judged on. But bringing the craft and its precious cargo home is also part of it and your interpretation seems no different to any other cadet who has passed in the past. So, I wish you good luck.'

'Thanks Comm. Look, it is almost sleep cycle. I must go. When shall we meet again?' Jane stood and held out her arms. Damian vacated his seat and hugged her.

'Comm and I have a lot to do here,' she said, smiling.

'We will contact you when we are ready, but for now, you're right, rest cycle is almost over. I also must leave. I will contact you soon.' She kissed him and they embraced for a while. Then – to Damian's horror – she disappeared.

Comm laughed out loud. 'Your face, it's a picture, horror personified. She said you would be shocked. Oh, my dear friend, Jane is in her quarters, and has been through this whole rest cycle. She was a solid hologram, as am I. She said you would notice, and I said you wouldn't. Seems I was right.'

Damian stood still, waiting for the numerous implants within his brain to calm his body down.

'Not funny, Comm,' he said, regaining his composure.

'Sandy,' Comm said, in a more subdued tone.

'Our safety here is paramount. The only security issue we have, which is hard to establish, is the fact that you and Jane have to travel here. Your movements are logged. There are only so many times that you can say that you were exploring. The hard light program will rid us of that threat. At some point in the near future, Jane will come to your quarters and set up your holo stage. Then you can come down here as many times as you wish in your own holographic, or photonic, avatar. Oh, before you go, I said that I am no longer just a med com-link. But for your information, Jane, is far more than a nurse – she is a brilliant theoretical engineer. I just thought you needed to know that.' Damian put his arms around Comm's shoulders and hugged him. He released the embrace and walked out to the promenade, leaving behind him a bemused comm link.

CHAPTER 24

MODULES

Back in his quarters he readied himself for the sleep cycle, Six had lowered the lighting. He made himself comfortable on the sleeping slab and thought over the day.

Every night, since wakening in the medical centre, he had tried to find some reminiscence. It always began with the obvious – who was he? – then, where was he from?, and, why was he here? – questions he hoped would have been answered by the scenarios that he and Comm had experienced, but as yet no sure answer had revealed itself. But now, as the months had passed, other thoughts had crept into his tiring consciousness – the events of the day.

Why, he had thought on many occasions, were words and expressions that he found ordinary, a puzzlement to those he was talking with? It had started with Comm, an entity with access to billions of bits of information, yet did not know the meaning of a mantis, or paddling. And other conversations with Jane and the crew, would often end with, 'sorry, what is a ...'.

He surmised that maybe he spoke a different dialect to them, so, he therefore must have originated from a different culture.

But now something else was bothering him – the simplicity of observations. Comm had told him that Quantonite was a fluid element and where possible it would bond with a higher element.

The test he had carried out on the HL1 within the field was pretty basic, and yet, in over five thousand years, no one had thought of doing it. And the Griffin's shields – allowing Quantonite to pass through – surely a society such as this, one that for the last four thousand years has been on the brink of all-out war, couldn't see the advantage of such a weapon. And Command, the bastion of everything this culture is built on, is hacked, by a med com-link, and a nurse, even though Comm had said that he and Jane were far more than just that.

'Nothing,' he thought, 'seems to add up.'

Six monitored Damian's restlessness. Sleep cycle had commenced for over thirty standard minutes. Senior Cadet, Drake's brain patterns had increased in that time, sleep was eluding him. The room com released a sedative vapour into the room's airways. Damian Drake drifted into a restless sleep.

He awoke early, readied himself for the day and made his way to the recreational room for breakfast.

The room was busy. Stewards bustled between the tables and the whole area buzzed with conversation, interspersed with the occasional burst of laughter. As Damian entered, silence descended. One by one they turned to face him, he felt uneasy. Johan Spiez stood up from his chair and extended his hand, the hand turned to palm uppermost then his fingers closed leaving his thumb extended. It was hand sign, and Damian felt that it was congratulating him. Then as one the room extended their hands and followed the gesture. Damian thought he really must learn this language.

Pilots, navigators and spotters all moved around the table to make room. A steward brought a spare chair, he sat between Johan and Patricia Spall.

'Excellent work Damian. You have made us all, quite wealthy,' Johan said, as the noise of conversation rose around them.

'But none wealthier than you, Damian,' Patricia whispered in his ear. Johan nodded, 'Yes, I have never sat with a Prime finder before,' he added.

Damian Drake, let the adoration from all of them wash over him. They were all in a jovial mood, but he knew that within the hour they would revert back to the seriousness of tackling the field.

He finished his meal and followed them to the main loading bay. He watched as they received their orders. Within half an hour all the heavy lifters had departed. 'Do I really want to be a pilot,' he thought. 'Is that really the destiny that has been set before me.'

'Drake!' That voice, he thought, never fails to send a shiver down the spine.

'Commander Gomez,' he said, without turning.

'You will address me to my face Cadet.' He turned.

'Senior Cadet, ma'am.' He corrected her.

With hands clasped tightly behind her back she scrutinised him through narrow slit eyes.

'Yes, Senior, Cadet, and of course, Prime finder. But let's not forget.

Captain's favourite, amongst all of your titles.'

Damian gave a puzzled look.

'I would have thought, as a senior officer, you would benefit greatly, probably more than the crews that have to go into the field every day. So, why aren't you pleased? It couldn't be just because it was me that found the Quantonite?'

To Damian's amazement she stepped back, a shocked look flashed across her face.

'Of course not, I, like the rest of the crew am very happy. It would have been nice, however, if I had been a part of the team meeting, instead of being told by one of my pilots.'

Damian could hear the hurt in her voice. She was right, she should have been a part of all of this.

'Commander Gomez, er … ma'am. I had no say as to who was present at the meeting,' he said softly.

She took a deep breath. 'I know that Cadet. I apologise, this is not your fault. I am sorry I snapped at you, but for what it is worth, congratulations, as prime finder, you could afford a whole fleet of Griffins.'

Damian thought on this. A whole fleet, and the Captain had said I could buy a whole planet. Just how much money does the prime finder have? He was aware the Commander was still talking.

'So, what do you think?' she finished, an expectant look on her face. Damian shifted, or to be more exact, squirmed .

'I am so sorry Commander, I was thinking about a fleet of Griffins, or a whole planet to myself, I didn't hear what you just said.'

She adjusted her position and her stance adopted the more common aggressive poise that Damian had become to expect from her.

'Concentrate on me, Cadet, and listen. I said, have you given any more thought to the modules?' He could hear the frustration in her voice, but the aggression that he had come to know was not there. Instead, he thought, she was trying to use a more sympathetic approach.

He took a deep breath, and scanned the enormous loading bay. All the heavy lifters were in the field but there were shuttles and loading bots and at the far end he noticed a group of ground crew installing a Quantonite receiver, a device he had been told by Johan that could determine the percentage of Quantonite on each load that they brought back. It was crude technology, but it was a start. He turned his attention to the waiting Commander.

'I'm sorry but, I don't think I need to do any of this, Commander. Not anymore,' he said slowly. Her face lost its severity and transformed into understanding. She nodded, exhaling a sigh. He continued.

'To train to be a heavy lifter pilot, when I could be the master of a whole fleet, what is the point?'

Commander Gomez stepped forward, and to his surprise laid a hand upon his shoulder. 'You are right, Damian, you do not need to do any of this anymore. A few standard months ago, I would have been feeling quite pleased with that decision, but you have proved to me to be an exceptional member of the Griffin team. And what I mean by that, is not just what you have achieved in pilot training but in other fields as well. You have made every member of the Griffin crew a lot richer today than they were yesterday. Junior officers on my staff look up to you. You will be sorely missed, but we still have a few months of mission time before we leave for outpost 1436, so, what are you going to do? Sit there and count your credits, or, prove to me, and the Captain, that you could be, or are, a great pilot. Your choice.' Her voice was soft and sincere, Damian sighed again. He turned as an HL1 passed through the graviton shield and landed twenty metres from him, he could, he thought, be the pilot of that, or, for the next few months, sit within his quarters and be a passenger, he shuddered at that thought.

'I don't know why, or for what reason, but I feel that I have to be a pilot. And you're right, I would go nuts just wandering around watching others work.' He watched the confusion sweep across her face.

'You would go … nuts,' she said hesitantly.

'Sorry Commander, just an expression. I would feel useless, and wasted.'

'So, Cadet, your decision is …' she said, snapping back to her usual persona.

'I wish to continue my training; I believe I can complete Module 2.'

'Very good Cadet. You will be ready in the sim suite at 11:00. If you have any last preparations for the module, you should practise them now. Don't be late.' She turned on her heel and with a determined gait walked back to the control complex. 'She didn't want to lose me,' he thought, 'and, she was smiling when she turned.'

Damian returned to his quarters, and for the next two hours practised Module 2. With five standard minutes spare to the eleventh hour Damian entered the simulation suite. Commander Gomez and Lieutenant Commander Chang waited by an activated simulator.

'Senior Cadet! Are you ready to undertake the Module 2 task?' asked Chang, matter-of-factly.

'I believe that I am, Sir,' Damian replied, just as curtly. Commander Gomez turned to him.

'Then in your own time, begin. But be aware, if you fail, you will have to return to Module 1.'

Damian shrugged. 'I understand that, Commander.' He made his way into the simulator and sat at its controls.

The moment he placed his hands into the holo towers the simulator reacted violently, lurching to port. Damian knew that this was the start of the scenario, but what he hadn't expected was a full crew around him.

A navigator sat in the seat beside him. It was a facsimile of Commander Burroughs.

'We have a breach, lower Starboard. Your orders, Captain.' Damian knew from the training that he had done, that he had to dive fast then seconds later pull up with full throttle. This he did almost without thinking. As he pulled up and turned the craft a full 180 degrees, he knew the untethered asteroid in the loading bay would crash through the inner bulkhead causing damage to the crafts gravitational system and leaving them at a 45-degree pitch to the Griffin. But why were the crew here? In the training scenario, they were in the loading bay trying to secure the stray bolder.

'Orders Captain,' the holo image of Thomas Burroughs said again.

'Try to seal the breach,' he said, manoeuvring the craft above an incoming asteroid.

'We have an inner hull breach. We're going to try and lock it down Captain,' a deep male voice informed him from behind. Damian recognised the voice as Doctor Ghorbany. They are using people I know and trust, thought Damian, so, who was the other spotter? he dare not turn around – three large boulders would be coming up from below them and he had to be ready for them.

'No, seal off the loading bay, return to your posts, keep me informed of trajectories.' He pulled the craft up, then turned for a steep dive. The three boulders passed safely by.

'But Captain,' said a female voice that he recognised as Jane Onslow's.

'That's an order, seal it off.'

After ten minutes they were in a part of the field that was less intimidating. The Griffin sat at a forty-five-degree angle to his port side. He knew there were only two more course corrections to go and they would be safe and the module would be over. As he had journeyed from the field to the Griffin, his crew had protested and given him incorrect information. At one point he had wished that he had sent them to their doom in the loading bay.

After the last two asteroids had been encountered, he contacted the Griffin for help. Two shuttles manoeuvred the crippled craft into the loading bay. He turned in his seat to face the spotters behind him, but with the scenario over the simulator's holograms dissipated. He was back in the sim suite.

'You didn't send your crew into the loading bay,' Chang said.

'There was no need to; they would have all been killed,' he answered with a shrug.

'Most Cadets, even with months of training, never complete this task first time,' Gomez said, without looking up from her info slate.

'Having the crew there changed the scenario. All they were there for was to complicate the situation. Once I realised that the information that they were giving made no sense I disregarded them, even though you replicated people I trust.'

Commander Gomez looked up and smiled. 'Senior Cadet, you have done well. Module 2 has been passed. Module 3 is the last task. There is no training for Module 3, but you do need experience. The minimum is one thousand standard hours; that's five standard months, which will bring us almost to the end of our mission here in the field. I have put you onto Johan Spiez's ship. Learn everything you can from him. You will start on the next work cycle.' She turned and walked away leaving Chang to finish the niceties.

'Very well done, Damian. If you are going to the recreation room on rest cycle, I at least, will buy you a drink.'

CHAPTER 25

11 FOR ALL

'Congratulations Senior Cadet,' an excited Six chirped as he entered his quarters. Damian was just about to thank him when he heard voices coming from his sleeping room.

'Oh, and you have visitors. Senior Nurse Onslow and a … companion.' Damian, without needing to, turned and glared at the wall panel. The room comm had never hesitated over a word before.

'Companion,' he said slowly with a frown.

'What companion? Who?' Six hesitated again.

'Someone who Senior Nurse Onslow brought along with her,' Six said, without the chirpiness. Damian was about to question him further when a familiar voice stopped him.

'Sandy, we are in the sleeping room,' Comm shouted from the adjacent room. Damian turned and made his way to the connecting room. He stopped in the entranceway. It took a while to comprehend exactly what he was seeing. The room was much larger – it seemed that another five metres had been added to its width.

Comm turned to gaze into the space that Damian was focusing on. 'I have removed the internal wall, Comm said nonchalantly. Damian stepped into the room. Jane Onslow was kneeling down, adjusting some crystal circuitry within the depths of the flooring. She snapped back the cover then using a remote handheld tool blended the cover into the floor plates.

'There,' she said triumphantly. Looking up at Damian and Comm, Damian held out his hand and helped her to her feet. They hugged. A moment later he stepped back and glared at her.

'What's the matter?' she asked, concerned.

'Are you, real?' he said, coyly. She smiled.

'Yes, I'm real. I am here in person, honestly,' she added, noticing his frown.

'So, what is it that you have done exactly?' asked Damian, looking at the new flooring.

'What have we done, exactly?' Comm asked with a stifled giggle.

'That would take some telling, but in brief, the surface floor area of your quarters has been completely renewed. The whole floor is now a holo stage. We have installed a new technology from Command's Science Projection department. It will enable Nurse Onslow and I to come here without detection, and you could go to Nurse Onslow's,'

'So, we have no need to go to level 11?' Damian asked as he sat down on the sleeping slab. Comm thought for a moment.

'No, everything we need, can be accessed from either quarters, including the permanent link to Command. Both room coms have been adjusted to allow me access without question, although, level 11's hub is still a safe place for me to hide out in.' Damian turned to Jane. She narrowed her eyes and slowly shook her head as she noticed the broad smile emerging on Damian's face.

'No,' she said with a gasp.

'Level 11, is my place, I found it.'

'Jane,' he said softly.

'We have less than a year of this mission to go. The crew could do with some well-deserved play time. Let them have it. You can still go down there and it will be more fun with more people. You allowed us to share it,' he said, indicating Comm. Jane Onslow lowered her head, and for a moment Damian thought she was crying, but on second thoughts, he knew she was stronger than that. She sat down next to him, and, putting her arm around him pulled him closer to her. She kissed him lightly on the cheek.

'You, are such a good man,' she said, smiling. 'You have made every crew member richer than they have ever been, and now you want them to have some fun. How can I possibly refuse?

Besides, I've had level 11 to myself for a long time, so perhaps it is time to share. But how do we tell them that it exists?'

Damian leant back, then shrugged. 'Good point, we can't just say that we stumbled on it,'

'We tell them the truth,' Comm interjected. They both turned and glared at him.

'Well, delayed truth,' he added quickly. 'Nurse Onslow, you found it because of a malfunction in the sender that you were using, and emergency protocols dictates that it sends you to a level that is safe, which, was level 11. That is the truth of it. I can install a malfunction within the sender unit, just to collaborate your story. It does mean that engineering will send a maintenance team to investigate. They of course will not find any actual fault, but because of the age of the Griffin, it will be logged as, well, a glitch.'

'A "glitch",' said Nurse Onslow, with a smirk. 'I think Damian's strange terminology is embedding itself on you. But, what of Command, will they know?'

Comm laughed out loud. 'Command already knows your secret Nurse Onslow, as it does with everyone else. Everybody has secrets. So long as it doesn't interfere with Command's work, they really are not interested.'

'But, what about our secret?' Damian interjected, and indicated the enormous space around them. Comm stood and walked into the extended room. He held out his arms and turned a full 360 degrees.

'This is a room within a room. The outer walls are known to Command, it will show up on any scan that they instigate. This room is important to them, only because you live here. Any scan will show nothing unusual within the walls, but the inserted room will not show any presence to any scan. It just doesn't exist. We have security dampened it using their own security protocols, it is in fact hiding in plain sight. I can assure you Sandy, our secret is safe.' Damian walked over to Comm and surveyed the large open space that was his sleeping room.

'I hope you're right Comm. So, if all this is now complete, Jane and I have a meeting to attend, with the Captain.'

He walked through the archway that separated the two rooms. Jane followed.

'You can't just walk up to the Captain and start a conversation,' she said from behind him. Damian stopped and turned.

'Why not?' he asked, confused at the panic showing on her face.

'Because she is the Captain. I would have thought that you would have learnt the protocols of ship etiquette by now.' He suppressed a laugh.

'I do not abide by the laws of etiquette anymore. I am a Prime finder. She will talk to me.' Their eyes locked, humour drained from their faces. Comm stepped into the room.

'Sandy,' he said softly, Damian turned to face him. Jane Onslow shuddered slightly as he turned away from her.

'She is the Captain, and deserves the respect of that rank. Do not think, my friend, that the Prime finder is above the laws of this ship. Protocol dictates that you will ask permission for her audience.'

Damian stopped in the centre of the seating room, he turned slowly. Comm stood defiant, legs apart, arms folded. He turned back to Jane Onslow. She looked frightened.

'I, am so sorry. I didn't mean that I was in any way better than her, just that ...'. He fought for the right words that did not come.

'I was being big headed, wasn't I?' Both Jane and Comm exchanged a puzzled look.

'If that means, being stupid, then yes, you were, and it was, alarming.' The last of her sentence was almost a whisper. Damian slumped down into the recliner. Jane sat opposite. He watched as the expression upon her face changed. He smiled but looked thoughtful.

'I need to be careful of overstepping my importance,' he said hesitantly.

'Financial power is an addiction, and a curse. It eats you away, slowly. Jane, I am so sorry, I could see that you were frightened. I will try not to be so stupid in the future.' Jane shifted in her seat, she leant forward and extended her hand, he took it with both of his and caressed it. She returned his smile.

'Apology accepted,' she said squeezing his hand.

'Good, now perhaps we can get on,' said Comm. 'I have work to do. Sandy, if you listen and take advice from Nurse Onslow, you will be guided well.' He turned and walked back into the enlarged sleeping room.

'Six,' Damian called.

'Yes, Senior Cadet Drake,' chirped Six.

'Arrange for a meeting with the Captain. Oh, and adhere to all etiquette protocols.' He turned back to Jane.

'Better?' he said, eyebrows rising. With a suppressed giggle, Jane nodded.

Within the next hour and dressed in full uniform they stood outside briefing room 3. The twin doors split apart and a Lieutenant exited. Damian had seen him before. He was with the Captain at his first meeting with her in the destroyed Med labs. He didn't know, but he assumed that he was part of a security detail to keep the Captain safe. If that was true, he thought, he couldn't have much to do on a ship that was primarily used to haul lumps of space rock.

'Senior Nurse, Senior Cadet, the Captain will see you now.' His voice was monotone, just passing the message, nothing more nothing less. Damian gave him his best smile.

'Thank you, Lieutenant, and how are you today?' he said, his voice upbeat. Jane kicked him, he hid the wince.

'I am well, Cadet,' the Lieutenant replied, a look of confusion on his face. He turned and walked away. Jane shook her head and entered the briefing room.

Captain Juliana Contessa stood as they walked towards her.

'Damian, and Senior Nurse Onslow, please, be seated. How can I help you?' Jane was slightly taken aback at the use of Damian's first name, but even more so, at the friendly welcome. They sat in an uncomfortable silence for a few seconds. Jane took a deep breath, then leant forward.

'We thank you Captain for seeing us. We have made a discovery,' she spoke calmly and without hesitation, keeping to the well-rehearsed speech they had prepared and practised for the last hour. At the end the Captain slumped back into her recliner. Her mouth had dropped.

'Level 11 was de-commissioned eleven standard years ago. How is this even possible?' Damian could hear the doubt in her voice.

'Captain, if level 11 was somehow missed, is it possible that other levels are not de-commissioned?'

Jane spun her head to face him. He could see the panic flash across her eyes. This was not what they had rehearsed.

'Well, it's possible,' he added with a shrug.

Captain Contessa waved her hand through a holo tower, 'Commander Burroughs,' she ordered the com-link. Seconds later a holographic image of the Commander appeared before them.

'Captain,' said the image of Thomas Burroughs.

'We have a level that has not been de-commissioned. Meet me on level 4, by the sender units, and bring a tech team.'

From level 4 and using all four sender units they made their way down to level 11. The doors of the sender opened onto an invasion of light and colour. They all shielded their eyes from the onslaught until they adjusted. Damian stepped out first, followed by Jane. Well done Comm, he thought. Jane's code for the sender had been removed. He hoped that he had remembered to remove his own name from above the holo suite that they were using.

'Again, Damian, you never cease to amaze me. What a wonderful find, my crew will appreciate this. Even though they have less than a standard year to go, but, this will boost morale.' She turned to Thomas Burroughs.

'Commander, get your team to check this level out. I want it safe for people to visit.' Damian could hear the excitement in her voice, and he was happy for her. She had served on this ship for almost fifty years. She might even have spent a lot of time in here, he continued the thought.

For the rest of the rest cycle, they explored the promenade. At one point the Commander turned to the Captain.

'This explains our elusive power outage. I can move that team to other duties now,'

'Yes, indeed. I want all other levels checked. Use that team to make sure nothing else has been missed.' The Captain said, looking up at the light show exploding above them.

After the Captain had dispatched her various science teams and engineers for the probing and surveying that level 11 demanded, she turned to Damian and Jane.

'This is very strange. I have been on this level many times, yet I do not remember it being this vibrant in light and colour. There is much for our teams to do here. Return to your duties. I will have the Commander contact you when all surveys have been completed, and again, well done, both of you.' She turned and walked down into the promenade. When she was out of earshot Damian turned to Jane.

'She is very happy. It's a good thing that you have allowed me to do today.' Jane glared at him, a frown appearing across her features.

'I have a feeling Damian, that you would have told her anyway, and you would have been right to. I have been very selfish.' he smiled then shrugged a shoulder. 'You had your reasons,' he said softly, as he took a hold of her hand and led her back to the sender.

They were back in his quarters, but as far as the main com-link knew they were both in their separate quarters making ready for rest cycle.

Comm had re-designed the extended sleeping chamber. As they walked through the archway from the seating room, they entered a small lobby. To the right a sphinctered portal labelled, rest chamber, it silently opened as they approached. Inside was the familiar layout of his sleeping chamber. Turning, they walked through the lobby towards a similar door on the opposite side, the door opened to allow them through.

The door opened into a lounge area.

'He's been busy,' Damian muttered as he entered the room. Various monitors were inlayed into the walls. Beneath them a workbench with holographic controls stretched around the perimeter of the room. A few metres in front of these, recliners were positioned in a semi-circle around a low table that also pulsated with holo towers. But it wasn't the lounge that had grabbed his and Janes attention, beyond the small room a holo stage had been installed, Damian stared in disbelief at the sheer size of it, he tried to calculate the length and width of this new addition.

'It's got to be at least sixty square metres.' He said in disbelief. Jane nodded as she panned the enormous area.

'Where did he get all the room from.' She added in a whisper.

'Ah, Sandy, Nurse Onslow, you have returned. Congratulations, you both played your parts well.' Called Comm from the centre of the holo stage.

'Stay there, I will come to you.' He said, walking towards them, he stopped two metres in front of them.

'Comm, why is this so big.' Damian asked, looking over Comms shoulder into the space beyond. Comm frowned at him.

'Level six, Sandy, only has one occupied quarters, and that is yours, all I have done is removed the internal walls of all the other quarters, they will never be assigned to any one, and apart from us three, nobody will ever come down here, so we can play out the scenarios here without any interruption, I have also put up pictures from the scenarios we have visited.' Comm walked over to the far wall.

'So, we have the inverted pyramid of statues in this alcove, and next to it the interior of the ice caverns, and, Chandra's disc in orbit around the stricken planet Earth with the fire storm that enveloped the planet, and Quanton's office with the heavy-set man sitting behind his desk, and, last of all, the massacre on Mars prime.' Damian studied each of the images for some time before turning to Comm.

'These images are incredible, in fact, this whole place is unbelievable, when are we going to start using it.' He said with a grin.

'The holo stage is already working, I have been watching you via nanobot feed.' Both Damian and Jane looked confused.

'Nanobot?' asked Jane, turning to Damian.

'A microscopic robot, one thousand millionth of a metre in length,' Damian said without thinking, then frowned at his statement. Comm applauded as he walked over to them.

'Correct, it's a billionth of a metre, very good. There are memories within you that are just begging to be released.' He turned to face the expanse of the opened space and panned his hand in front of them. An image pixelated into life.

'It's the promenade on level 11,' Jane exclaimed, as the image congealed into a three-dimensional high-definition image. They watched as the engineering teams moved from one building to another.

'We can walk along with them, and of course listen to everything that is being said.' Comm explained as he walked into the image. They followed but after a few paces Damian stopped, and called to his two friends.

'I feel slightly dizzy, nauseous.'

Comm turned and smiled. 'You're not here. Look back over there,' he said pointing back the way they had come. Damian turned and looked back to the lounge area. Two figures – Jane and himself – stood rigid.

'When you come into this area, you are in a holographic photonic form. It allows you to interact with the image. Jane has already gone through the transformation from solid to image on a previous occasion so she is feeling no effect, but she did the first time.'

Damian was perplexed. 'But I have been with you in the scenarios. Isn't that the same thing?' he asked.

'Yes, exactly, but your physical body was not conscious then. You are feeling the effect for the first time. Next time you will feel nothing, and I assure you, it won't last long.' Damian narrowed his eyes. He felt apprehensive.

'I still feel sickly.'

Comm slowly shook his head. 'I promise, it won't last long.'

For the next half an hour they followed the engineering and science teams as they probed and scanned each building in turn. They were now outside the building that they had designated as 'COMM'S'. They slowly made their way inside.

Two teams had converged on the holo stage that they had been using. Both team leaders were in heated discussion.

'I'm telling you, this stage has been used recently,' the senior engineer snapped at the science team leader.

'Not according to my sensors. This pad has had no use for the last standard decade, maybe longer,' the chief technician snapped back, and to emphasise his point pushed an info slate in front of the other's face.

'I don't care about that. I care about this,' the engineer said calmly, then produced his own slate.

'Comm, what has he found?' Damian asked in a whisper. Comm laughed out loud.

'No need to whisper Sandy, they can't hear you,' Comm said, as he shook his head. He knelt beside the engineer and studied his info pad.

'It appears, there is movement at an atomic level within the holo stage itself,' he sighed deeply.

'It's when you stepped up onto the stage, your weight compressed it. At that point both Nurse Onslow and myself were photonic. We had no mass, but you did, and now the stage is returning to its original state. Most of it already has but down at the molecular level it is still moving. I have to say, I am really impressed with the diligence of this team,' Comm said as he moved round to read the technician's pad.

'Are we going to be found out?' Jane interjected, her voice hesitant.

'Do we have a problem here gentlemen?' said the authoritative voice of Thomas Burroughs.

'Not a problem, no sir, just a …' the engineer started, 'difference of opinion.'

'According to our scans, sir …' the technician started to interject.

Burroughs took both slates from them and for an agonising three minutes studied the information. He returned the slates to the team leaders.

'Your teams are here to investigate why this level was never de-commissioned, and, why we never were able to detect the enormous power outage to this level, not molecular movement of a holo stage,' he said calmly.

'But sir, this proves someone was here recently,' the lead engineer said, pointing at the slate. Burroughs turned slowly to face him.

'We know someone was here recently. Senior nurse Onslow and Senior Cadet Drake were here recently. It is more than probable that they explored the level before informing the Captain. Wouldn't you?' he hissed, then turning he left the two team leaders to contemplate their findings.

Damian watched Burroughs leave the building. He turned to the other two.

'Lucky we were here. You do know that either he or the Captain will ask about our whereabouts within this level the next time they see us. Let's hope they haven't found anything else.'

Comm clapped his hands and the image faded then disappeared.

They returned to their own bodies. Damian shuddered as his body tingled from the nape of his neck down to the soles of his feet.

'Wow, that felt weird!'

'You get used to it,' Jane said, as they sat on the recliners. Comm sat further round the seating horseshoe.

'We have a lot to do over the next few standard months. I need to revisit Command's Science Projection department, and Sandy, we need to return to the scenarios. I still believe that somehow the elusive golden 'O' is linked to you. Griffin has just over nine standard months of its mission left, and you have to finish the last module. So, what is the procedure for that?'

Jane leant forward, 'He doesn't' have to finish anything, as Prime ...' Damian held up his hand.

'I have already been through this with Commander Gomez. I want to finish it.'

'Have they given you a plan of action,' Comm asked, aware that Jane was scowling.

'I have to complete a thousand standard hours of flight experience. They have put me on Johan's heavy lifter, and of course now that all asteroids contain Quantonite, they don't have to hunt around so much. So most of the work is done on the outer rim of the field. So, much safer.'

Comm nodded in agreement. 'Good, so we might not lose you then.' He held up his hand anticipating the outcry that was about to explode from the nurse.

'We will start the next scenario on the next rest cycle. Nurse Onslow, you will need to be here to attend to Sandy's unconscious body, but you don't have to be here in person, just your avatar. Whilst you are both on work cycle, I will prepare everything.' He gave a half wave as he slowly disappeared from view.

CHAPTER 26

11

Jane stayed with Damian for the sleep cycle. They felt that if she were to leave his quarters now it would cause a conflict to the main com-link, as it would appear that she was in two places at once. Her own ID signature had shown that she had been in her own quarters since leaving Level 11. They discussed this at length, and decided that in future, apart from actual visits personally, they would use the hard light holographic program for clandestine meetings.

It would, however, still be difficult at the start of the next work cycle. But Jane had pointed out that with so many of the crew on shift change, perhaps, it would be looked at as -.' Damian laughed out loud as she tried to use his own colloquialism – a 'gritch'. 'Glitch', he had corrected her. They laid back on the sleeping slab. Damian noticed that its dimensions had been altered. It was much wider than it had been. Mentally thanking his old friend, he passed into the realms of sleep.

He was ten standard minutes early for his work cycle. He noticed the mood change within the loading bay – the flyers the engineers the techs, all seemed to have an extra spring in their steps, and certainly where he was concerned. They all came to him and congratulated and thanked him for what he had done to raise their percentage. Even Commander Jennifer Gomez seemed more forthcoming.

He boarded the HL1 and took up his position beside Johan Spiez. Sian Kalvic, the navigator audibly sneered as he sat in what she regarded as her chair.

'Don't mind her Damian, she doesn't bite,' Johan sighed. Kalvic extended her arm, her fingers tapped a fast strum onto her thumb and palm in a rapid hand sign.

'Oh, but I may be wrong,' Johan muttered, as he energised the coils for take-off.

Damian turned to the navigator. He held his hand outstretched, and tapped fingers to palm and thumb in rapid succession. He felt a sense of pride and satisfaction at her shocked expression.

'Cadet, we are a team here, that kind of language stays behind in the loading bay. Who taught you that?' Johan said, his voice wavering from stern to a suppressed giggle.

The flight into the field was sedate compared with his previous trip. They kept to the outer rim of the field, not needing now to enter the realms of pending disaster. They made five trips before the end of the work cycle. Pierre leant forward and shared his calculation.

'That should put another 0.2 percent onto our team bonus, which adds to date, of thirty-one-point four percent. All thanks to Damian.' The spotter, Dominic, also leant over. 'And still approximately nine standard months to go.' They all laughed together, except for Sian, although, thought Damian, she did smile.

They entered the loading bay and landed, already a horseshoe of bots were waiting for them, ready for unloading.

'Will we be seeing you on level 11 tonight? The Engineering team have finished all their probing and it's open for fun. You are coming?' Pierre asked quizzically, as he noted Damian's impassive face.

'You can't not come. It's opening night,' Dominic chipped in.

'I … I was going to study tonight. I have Module 3 to get my head around,' Damian lied, and not too successfully he thought. An arm gripped his left shoulder and he turned to face the navigator, her face was expressionless.

'You do not wish to be with us. You somehow think you are above us, Prime finder.' Her voice was calculated and cut into him like a scalpel. He looked at each of them in turn, their faces expectant. Finally he turned to Johan.

'I am just a cadet, not really part of your team. I'm just gaining flight experience, I didn't want to impose,' he said slowly.

It wasn't really a lie, he thought, well, maybe just a small one. Johan's face exploded in laughter.

'My friend, of course you are part of the team, in fact, we, are part of your team. Perhaps *we* should not impose on *you*.'

Damian felt belittled. He did not deserve this friendship. How could he not go? Comm would understand.

'I'm sorry Sandy, I don't understand. I have spent all day, and night, I might add, to get these scenarios to be as perfect as they can possibly be.' Damian slumped down into the recliner. The last time he had heard Comm talk in this tone was when the Med lab was telling him to abort the Chandra and Kowaski scenario.

'Comm, let him have one night, we have plenty of others. The scenario will still be there next rest cycle. Nobody knew that the engineering and science teams would finish so quickly, and besides, I would like to go. It would be nice to enter level 11 without all the sneaking about,' the hard light holographic image of Jane said.

Comm stood, hands on hips, a look of contempt on his face.

'There will be plenty of holo stages. Perhaps you could come too,' Damian said, apologetically, Comm's hand cupped his chin, index finger tapping.

'Griffin's main com-link would just love that. No, you two go and enjoy yourselves and I will go over the scenarios again, just to make sure I haven't missed anything. And I might go back to the projected Science Department, just to see if there is anything else, we might be able to use.'

'Thanks Comm, but, if you're going back to Command, just be careful, is what I am saying. I know you will be.' Comm faded away, Jane leant over and kissed him on the cheek.

'I have to get ready; I'll see you at the sender station. Let's say in one standard hour.' Her image faded to nothing and he was alone.

'I have laid out your Senior Cadet dress uniform,' chirped Six from the lounge area. Damian thought about turning up in uniform, and screwed his face up at the thought.

'Six, no uniform, something more informal.'

An hour later, he and Jane, made their way down to level 11. As the sender's doors opened, Damian was immediately aware that something was different. The brightness on the level had changed, the colours were still there, but the luminosity had been toned down. As they looked down the promenade they noticed that a considerable amount of entertainment structures had been turned off completely. Jane turned to him.

'Not the same, is it,' he agreed. It wasn't the same, somehow the vibrancy had gone.

The evening however was memorable. The Captain had decided that all crew should attend, and the next work cycle would be postponed.

Damian was the centre of attention throughout the evening, although he would have preferred not to be. At one point, he turned to Jane and asked if she wanted to leave. She had scowled at him.

'No,' she snapped. 'You have done a lot for this crew. This,' she said indicating the packed entertainment hall, 'is their way of thanking you. Accept it and at least look as if you're enjoying it,' she said in a low whisper, before turning and joining the medical team.

For the rest of the evening both he and Jane mingled with the various medical, engineering, tech and flight teams. He took her advice and smiled and laughed as they negotiated a path around the hall. By the end of the night they found themselves in the company of the senior officers. It was, thought Damian, a good night, and apart from his earlier nervousness, he had to admit, he was enjoying himself.

Whilst Jane engrossed herself with Doctor Ghorbany, Damian scanned the large entertainment hall. The Griffin's crew had naturally separated into smaller groups. He could hear their laughter. At ceiling level some eight metres overhead, clouds of multi-coloured light swirled and merged together. Occasionally, streaks of colour exploded and ricocheted off the four walls before imploding at floor level. It was, thought Damian, spectacular, but somehow, something was missing – something he knew ought to be there, but wasn't. What that something was, was the secrecy and the intimacy of the level, only being a part of Jane's, Comm's and his, idealic world, 'we all have our secrets,' thought Damian.

He shook himself out of the reverie and turned back to Jane and the Doctor.

CHAPTER 27

ELUSIVE 'O'

The Griffin was quiet, a skeleton crew had volunteered for the next work cycle. For the first time in many years, the heavy lifters remained in their hangers.

Damian awoke suddenly. Six was trying to get his attention.

'Senior Cadet Drake,' he chirped again. Damian grunted as he pulled himself up to a sitting position.

'What is it Six?' he said, taking a deep breath and stretching.

'Commander Burroughs wishes to enter your quarters, Sir.' Damian thought he had misheard. 'The Commander's here,' He said, still not fully awake.

Damian panicked and threw himself off of the slab. He quickly pulled on his tunic and made his way into the seating area. He looked back into the arch that separated his quarters to the extended room. Comm had erected a solid light wall, the extended room was hidden. Anyone coming into the seating area would never know that it existed.

'Let the Commander in, Six.' The door swished open; the Commander stood in the corridor, smiling.

'May I come in?' he asked, calmly. Damian's heart pounded, before one of his many implants set it back to a stable rhythm.

'Yes, please do, Commander. I apologise for the mess, it, er ... was a late night.'

Thomas Burroughs walked in and surveyed the seating area. Nodding, he turned slowly to Damian. 'Your quarters are very tidy, Cadet; there is no need to apologise.' He walked towards the archway.

'And where does this lead to?' he asked, peeking around the corner.

'My sleeping room, Sir, and that is, in a bit of a mess.'

Burroughs turned, 'And what is down here, through that door?' he said, pointing. Damian gasped audibly. He was again starting to panic, his implants now creating nanobots to calm his nervous system down. Why, he thought was the Commander doing this? Had something come up on the engineering schematics, and why would he come in person?

'Just, storage facilities,' was all he could muster. Burroughs walked towards the door. He wouldn't be able to gain entry, Damian thought, then, was amazed when he heard the swish of the door opening. He walked through the arch then turned – the door was open. Burroughs had gone inside.

As he entered the extended room, he stood a few metres behind the Commander.

'This is some storage space Cadet. You could fit four or five heavy lifters in here. Was this originally part of your quarters design?' Damian slumped, there was no possible excuse that he could come up with.

'No Sir, I had it installed after I took residence.' He was aware that his voice sounded defeated. He stood for a moment watching the Commander's back. How could he possibly explain all of this? The truth, he thought quickly, that's all he could do. Tell this man, a man who of all the bridge officers, he trusted most.

And still, the man did not turn to face him. He was, however, surprised when he heard him laugh. Burroughs turned slowly and as he did so, his image and stature altered. The uniform pixelated away and in its stead a blue shirt white shorts appeared and the dark wavy hair turned white. Damian gritted his teeth.

'Not funny, Comm.'

'I'm sorry, but I just had to try this out. While you and the whole crew were off enjoying yourselves, I was exploring the Command department of Science Projection. I can now be anyone or anything. It is amazing the technology that they have stored there. Some of it very old tech and for some reason it was never allowed to be used.'

Damian glared at him. 'Still not funny, and how are you able to walk about without standing on the holo pad,' Damian spat, anger welling up within. Comm shrugged and gave a broad grin. He pointed up above.

'No need for a holo stage. I carry my own. Just above me, a small holo ionosphere almost down to the atomic level. No one could detect it, but, having said that, a sophisticated scanner possible could, though even then it would have to focus on the right position, and know what it was looking for.'

Damian was starting to calm. Comm always had that effect; his soft harmonic voice always brought him down.

'And what of the main Griffin com-link, that you're supposed to be eluding? As far as it was concerned, all of a sudden there were two Commander Burroughs walking around,'

'Sandy, I am quite aware of that, and defence measures are always put into place. I am invisible to the main comm link.'

Damian perked up into the argument, 'And what about my room comm? Six could see that you were Commander Burroughs, and now all of a sudden, as far as Six could see, Commander Burroughs has disappeared in my quarters. Don't you think that he might report that to the main comm link.'

Comm erupted in laughter, 'Sandy, that wasn't Six waking you up, it was me. Your room comm is oblivious to my even being here, and you, my friend, worry far too much. Now, all fun and games aside, the reason that I am here is I have found unpublished historical data which I think will help in the search for 'O'. Three statues are part of this scenario: Wu Quan, Stelio Sursok and Leah Barak.'

Damian held up his hand and shook his head. Comm frowned.

'What, now? Right now?' Damian spluttered.

'Why, do you have somewhere else you need to be. Griffin is, for one cycle only, a ghost ship. It's a perfect time.'

'But I remember you saying that Jane had to be here to look after my unconscious body whilst we were gone,' Damian said, hesitantly. He was still reeling from Comm's transition from Commander Burroughs. Comm slowly shook his head.

'The Science Projection department lies deep within the confines of Command's security net, and I have full access. That is not to say that there are no local security arrangements set up, but I am quite adept at outrunning them.'

Damian exhaled a deep sigh.

'I am not sure I like the idea of you going in there anymore. We have more than we require. Every time you go, the odds on you being caught become enormous.'

Comm frowned for a moment. It was another one of his friend's phrases that he had to define. With access to Command files he found it easily. Again, he thought, back five thousand years ago.

'I believe you mean, the odds are, less. However, I can assure you Sandy, I am very, very careful' Damian wasn't so sure. The term "famous last words" entered his thoughts.

'This place of wonders,' Comm continued. 'Houses billions of technological know-hows. Many of them are old tech. I found references from Technopolis. They had been, for whatever reason, hoarded away, never to be seen again. The hard-light drive comes from that forbidden zone, as does the mobile holo stage.' Comm hesitated for a moment.

'Just think Sandy, what we could do with that. We could build a whole Stella class ship, out of light, just pure light, and the crew, the crew could be as you are in the scenarios, an avatar made of photonics. We could travel the Galaxy. The possibilities are endless.'

They had walked back to the newly installed lounge area, and Comm sat in one of the recliners, Damian sat opposite. Comm leant forward, his elbows on the low table in front of them.

'The other thing I learnt whilst there, was holo time.'

Damian leant forward in his recliner, and studied his friend, who leant back beaming a smile. 'Holo time,' Damian repeated.

Comm sat up in his recliner. 'Time is not linear, Sandy. It never has been. It is more spherical, if anything. It pulsates outwardly then inwardly it elongates then retracts. It is a constantly changing shape, so time within it can be changed and altered.'

Damian sat bolt upright, jaw dropping, 'We can time travel,' he spluttered.

Comm let out a laugh. 'No, not exactly. However, we can manipulate time, just as we do when we use the Trellion engines. When we travel to another Stella system we enter a dimensional shift. We in effect speed time up within the shift, but, when we adopt that time manipulation to a holo simulation, time can be altered. It can be expanded and contracted, sometimes, both at the same, er … time.' Damian's face went blank, he had had many conversations about time with Commander Burroughs in the past. Burroughs had said to him on one occasion that time is so simple, with highly complex understanding. He smiled at the memory.

'So, what does that mean for us?' he said, as Comm rose and walked into the extended room area. Damian stood to follow but Comm had turned and held his hand out and gestured for him to remain seated.

'Real time and scenario time can be different. We can alter it. What is a standard minute in one is not necessarily the same in the other. So let's say one standard second in the real world is one standard hour in the scenario, or ten hours or ten days. What I am trying to say, Sandy, is the reason we do not need the expertise of Senior nurse Onslow, although, her presence I feel is missed, is that when we return here, we would have only just left. But first, I need to make some adjustments to the holo emitter, and I have selected an historical moment from the Command files just to test this new addition out.'

Damian frowned, and walked over to where Comm was lifting the panels of the holo stage. 'What addition?' he asked as he crouched down next to Comm.

'We're going to try the hard-light array on this scenario, but we need to test it first,' Comm answered, without looking up.

'Where?' Damian asked as Comm replaced the panels and stood.

'We are going to Epsilon!' The room swirled, and the colours were erased. Stars surrounded him above and below.

CHAPTER 28

REALM WITHIN REALM

Comm adjusted the hard-light drive, the image of Epsilon 4 blurred slightly.

'Comm, I can't see now.' Comm looked up from the control belt on Damian's waist, his face showing signs of frustration.

'I haven't finished yet, be patient.' He turned his head back to the control belt. The image of the green gas giant blurred again, then focused into clarity.

'How's that?'

'Better, much better. So, what is it you have actually done?' Comm floated up to meet his eye level. He lifted his hand close to Damian's face and made a fist.

'Hold onto my fist, tightly, as if your life depended on it.' Damian did what was asked. He gave his friend a puzzled look.

'So, in all scenarios we have visited we've always been able to interact with each other.'

Comm smiled and cocked his head to one side. 'Yes, we have, now, let's go, and grab my fist again.' Damian wasn't sure where this was going but decided to humour his friend anyway. There was, he thought, always a reason for whatever the com-link was doing. He made a grab for the waiting fist and was surprised when his hand passed through it.

'Wow, it passed right through,' Comm shrugged.

'I have, with some help from the advanced Science Projection department changed the photonic phase, and with practice you can appear then disappear at will, in all the scenarios that we visit, you will be able to interact with the characters, then just vanish as if you were never there.' Damian tried to grab his fist again, without success, but on the third try their hands clasped together.

'How will this help, the characters are historical figures? They are set in their own timeline; we cannot change what has already happened, you told me that.'

Comm nodded. 'Yes, and that is still true. But you can now ask them a question, you can read a file on their personal link, pickpocket them if you wish, even if is just to see what they are carrying. There are many things that you can do, but, the laws of time still apply. You cannot move them out of the way of impending disaster, so, it will take some practice.' He looked over to the green gas giant.

'Epsilon 4 has eight moons, one of which has an atmosphere. There is a small science colony there. It's a good place to practice.' He turned and flew with increasing speed towards the enormous planet. Damian followed. On the far side a satellite moon came into view, just slightly smaller than the destroyed Earth. As they flew closer Damian was able to make out the terrain. Sixty percent of its surface was water and the land mass was covered with forest.

They landed in a large clearing in the equatorial part of the moon. In front of them a small town had been assembled: spherical structures were adjoined to rectangular units, conical towers rose to enormous heights, pipelines and walkways intersected each structure.

'There are over ten thousand people living and working here. All of them have nothing to do with the scenarios that we are interested in. The reason that we are here is to practise your skills. People come and go here regularly, so someone new will not be a cause for concern. Your task is to join a working team, befriend one of them, doesn't matter who. Find out everything you can, bring back the information to me, and I will check it with the historical records. You can phase from solid to spirit at any time.' Damian held up his hand. Comm stopped in mid-sentence, and showed his annoyance with a scowl.

'Spirit?' he said, raising his eyebrows.

'Spirit entity non-solid, phased, whatever you prefer. Now, where was I? Oh yes, but be aware, they will react if they witness you changing. You can also change your style of clothing at any time, you can eat and drink, if that is necessary, but again be aware, when you change back from being a solid, whatever it was that you consumed will remain solid.' Damian suppressed a giggle.

'Yes, it could be messy. I'll wait here for you, I'll give you five standard hours, oh, and as we are in photonic state, I will have some control between you and the people you converse with, this is after all, just a test. ... Well, don't just stand there with your mouth open! go!' Comm raised his arm and pointed to what seemed to be the main entrance. Damian turned and made his way across the clearing to the large rectangular building.

He stopped ten metres from the large glass fronted double doorway. 'How do I know what phase I'm in?' he thought. He stooped down and picked a blade of grass. His hand passed through the blue leaf. 'Still a spirit,' he thought. He decided not to alter phase in the open, instead he would wait and follow someone into the building. And that someone will be his task, he lay back onto the feathery blue flora that made up the grass clearing and waited.

After a half hour wait, a group of people emerged from an adjacent building. They talked and laughed as they made their way down the walkway, then stopped outside the main entrance. Damian stood and walked over to them. The conversation consisted mainly of bio structures of the local fungi, none of which Damian knew anything about. A middle-aged woman then hugged one of her counterparts. Saying her goodbyes, she turned and entered the building. Damian followed.

Inside the lobby, the woman ambled over to the reception desk. She was certainly in no hurry to be anywhere, thought Damian.

'Good morning, Doctor,' the receptionist said in a cheery manner. The Doctor smiled whilst rolling up her right sleeve, then offered it to the receptionist, who then scanned it. A series of numbers and patterns emerged from beneath the skin of her forearm. Damian watched, intrigued as the numbers and patterns swirled into a holographic cube that revolved slowly above her arm.

'Well Lydia, am I still human, or have I somehow become an enhancer overnight?'

'No, you're still human Doctor.'

'Glad to hear it. I need access to lab 5, for approximately six hours,' the doctor said rolling her sleeve back down to her wrist. The receptionist, Lydia, manipulated the columns of holographic towers that emanated from her workstation, then, smiling, she looked up.

'Lab 5 is yours Doctor. It's been approved. Will there be any guests in that time?' The doctor thought for a moment.

'I may need the assistance of a lab technician at some point. I'll call you, if I need one.' Damian shuffled from one foot to the other, come on, he thought. He could feel the impatience within him welling up.

The receptionist leant back into her seat, then, still with that inane smile that seemed to be etched onto all receptionists no matter the timeline.

'So, Kat. Will I see you at the recreation centre tonight? Maggie and Clara are going, and do I want to know what's going on with Jilly! Clara told me the other day that she saw her going into Professor Hennie's lab, and genetics is not her subject. Damian looked on in amazement. 'You've got to be kidding me,' he thought. Still, he pondered, I know where she is heading eventually – Lab 5 can't be far away.

Looking around the lobby he noticed two sets of doors that must, he felt, lead into the interior. He passed through the first set, only to find that they led to a restaurant that was currently occupied by a group of uniformed staff that seemed to be deep into a passionate debate. He walked towards them.

'I know we are only bloody lab techs, but I think we should draw a line when it comes to using us as if we were Enhancers. We may not be docs or profs, but we shouldn't be wiping their arses for them.' The elder of the group emphasised his point by slamming his fist down onto the table top.

'It's alright for you Denny. As senior technician you don't have to do all of the shit work, another said, pointing his finger at the enraged Denny.

'No. Even you get us to do that crap,' said another. Damian stood for a few minutes longer. He had never heard such a conversation before. He decided to stay for a while; this, he thought, is great. As the argument ebbed and flowed, anger expanded then contracted. He couldn't help but laugh out loud at their antics. The so-called tech meeting finally ended with one of the technicians standing, his face glowing red, then yelling: 'So, you can go fuck yourself.' Then he and some of his cohorts stormed out of the room. Damian was in hysterics.

'Oh please, please, stop,' he said out loud, though no one could hear. The remainder of the group stood to leave, but not before the senior tech shouted to the retreating group.

'I'm still the fucking senior here. Why don't you show some fucking respect?' Damian had spent hours on the Griffin learning heavy lift hand sign, and was quite proficient, but the hand sign given by the retreating group meant nothing to him. Damian calmed himself down and concentrated on the task that Comm had set for him. He had to find lab 5 but he also had to become solid. First though, a change of clothing. The senior tech had re-seated himself. Using the control belt that Comm had tuned, he scanned the techs uniform. Instantly his own uniform changed to the new design. He was about to leave, but thought something else might come in handy. He scanned the tech's right forearm. A cube emerged and floated a few centimetres above his arm. The senior technician frowned and before he could retrieve his mini scanner from his belt, Damian had already recorded it and applied it to his own arm, the information it contained informed him that he was now Senior Technician Dennis Porter. The first problem he could see, was that he didn't look anything like the man. He could, he thought, either change the information in the cube or change his own appearance to suit. He decided to keep his own appearance. The second problem was that there were now two Dennis Porters in the building.

'Are you ready Mr. Porter?' a voice behind said. Damian turned to see an elderly man walking towards them. Dennis Porter stood.

'Yes, um, how long do you need me for, Sir?'

'You know very well Mr. Porter. I have booked you for the whole shift,' the elderly gentleman said, frowning. Dennis Porter also frowned. He hadn't said anything regarding work time, but he had heard his own voice ask the question.

'Um. Yes, sorry professor, I knew that. Er, I am ready now, sir.' The professor visibly annoyed turned and headed for the exit, Dennis Porter scurried behind him.

Damian left the restaurant pondering. 'That shouldn't alter the timeline,' he thought. He walked back to the lobby and was surprised to see the two women still in deep conversation. He turned and walked through the second set of doors, these opened onto a security station. He looked around the room and was pleased to see that the institution was well signposted. He followed the sign for fungi research and then for Laboratories 1 to 8.

He found lab 5 at the end of a wide corridor. He stopped outside the double doors. Turning, he made sure he was alone. He decided to try changing phase. Instantly he became aware of gravity. His legs buckled slightly as they took the weight of his mass, and then there was the smell of rotting vegetation. He gagged on it.

'Are you alright?' He turned in the direction of the voice. The doctor from reception was standing three metres away from him.

'Yes, Doctor,' he managed to say through bouts of coughing. He calmed himself.

'Went down the wrong hole,' he said pointing to his throat. She smiled, then putting her hand onto the door pad the info cube floated up from her arm and the door clicked open.

'Are you sure you're ok? I can call a Med,' she said, holding the door open. A pungent smell of decomposing fungi hit him full on. He gritted his teeth and fought off the onslaught. Looking into the lab he could see that there was an enormous amount of brown, blue, yellow and green mounds of fungus that were either on workbenches and even taking up most of the floor space.

'I'm fine Doctor, thank you,' he said, breaking into a smile then thinking, 'I'll find another subject.' She leant forward, reading a badge on his chest pocket.

'Well, Senior Technician Porter. I may need your assistance. Are you busy,' she asked.

'No Doctor, I have nothing planned.' 'Damn,' he thought. 'Why did I say that?' then wondered if Comm could have any input in the same way that he had with the original Dennis Porter. He would definitely quiz him later.

'Good, give me five minutes to set up. Come in when I turn the light green,' she said pointing to the light above the door. She then turned and entered the lab, the door clicked closed behind her. The light above the door turned red.

'Sandy, how are you doing?' a voice in his head asked.

'This place stinks. Did you make me say I would help her? I was going to find another subject.' There was a pause.

'You haven't started yet,' Comm's voice said, exasperated.

'You have been gone three hours, what have you been doing?' Damian grimaced.

'Exploring. Are you making me say things I don't want to?' he snapped, then realised he had said it out loud. He turned to look behind him. He was still alone.

'Only trying to move things on. We need to try all of your implants. Exploring is not going to do that. I'm going to move time on, you need to concentrate on the tasks.'

The wide corridor blurred into the grey place that he was now quite familiar with., Comm was quickening the timeline.

The greys twisted and turned before him. He fell a full metre to the floor. He was still a solid and as he collapsed onto the floor, a pain shot up through his body. He instantly changed to spirit mode and the pain disappeared. Shocked, he found himself still in the corridor, alone. The light now showed green above the door. He turned to solid and was relieved to find that the pain had gone. Putting his hand to the door pad the cube emerged from his arm and the door clicked open. He sighed, then, holding his breath, he entered.

There were no mounds of multi-coloured fungi, no intoxicating stench. The doctor was not one of the many people that occupied the room. The people in this room were however all extremely busy. They moved from one set of holographic controls to another, each of them calling out readings that they had taken. In the centre of the room at a central console an elderly man occasionally looked up and acknowledged the information called to him.

Suddenly, Damian staggered back until his back hit the door. It clanged loudly within its frame. He inhaled deeply. Where, was he? The elderly man turned slowly in his seat, Damian glared at him. No, impossible, he thought, in a panic, he turned back to spirit mode.

The man in front of him glared with a puzzled look. He was also annoyed, information from his team was still being shouted to him. Damian crouched down onto the floor. The elderly man panned the area, occasionally their eyes met. Damian felt a shiver run down his spine. 'Oh my,' he thought. Those eyes, they were furious. The man turned back to his console.

The evil glare was not the only thing about the old man that had shocked Damian., That was quite bad, but, it was the man himself – white hair, pulled back and tied at his nape, reaching down to between his shoulder blades. Damian watched as the man dealt with the shouted incoming information. He moved from one side of his console to the other and each time he did that, his hair swung from one shoulder to the other. But it was the shirt – he was wearing a blue shirt, short sleeved, and when he had turned in his seat, he saw that the man was wearing shorts, white shorts. A white beard finished the ensemble. Apart from the facial features, it was Comm. The face was slightly younger, but the whole appearance was his friend. Damian thought of the face, the eyes, the nose and the mouth. All looked familiar – not Comm, but who? He had met this man before, but where?

'Professor, I have luminosity, values are being passed to you,' a woman in the far alcove of monitors shouted.

'Thank you Sindra, I am receiving. Cole, do we have trajectory?' This he called to a man at his right. Damian could not quite see the man. He was hunched over his controls, but slowly, he turned.

'Not just yet Stephen, sorry.' Cole turned to another set of controls.

'Chi, now would be a good time my friend,' he called.

Damian groaned and sank to the floor. All around him the inverted statues were alive, and for the next hour he sat and watched the ultimate scenario play out to completion. The man – the Professor – or, 'Stephen', as Colin Grey had called him was becoming more agitated. Whatever was being played out here seemed incredibly important to the professor.

The older man – the Comm lookalike – was now up and pacing the room, checking each of the nine control positions. He turned and placed his hand to his chin, index finger tapping a beat of frustration on his cheek.

'Ayana, are your readings between 0.005 and 0.008?' he asked calmly, although Damian could tell he was far from calm.

'0.00654, Professor,' she said, desperately trying not to maintain eye contact,'

'For fuck's sake Stephen. After eight years, *eight* years of extremely hard work from all of us, we have succeeded. God's sake man, extricate it!' Colin Grey shouted, the anger within him welling up.

'Quanny, time,' the professor said in a calm tone, as he turned to another alcove.

'The window of opportunity is decreasing. Time on my mark, is ... one hundred and eighty seconds ... mark!' Wu Quan said with a quiver of nervousness.

'Professor Swann,' the youngest member of the team interrupted. The professor turned to him.

'Jan.'

'Sir, I know that this is a one-off decision: Either it is right or it is wrong. If wrong, eight years will have been wasted. Is this not why you designed the integral computer system, to help?' His voice was strong and authoritative, and it seemed to Damian that the professor deflated slightly. He nodded and closed his eyes.

'Oric,' he said as calmly as he could.

'On my mark, sixty seconds … mark,' said Wu Quan softly.

Damian watched as a beam of white light emanated from the ceiling, passing a tube of light down onto the floor two metres from the central console. Within the beam, an entity walked out, tall, elegantly dressed in a white suit, swept back blond hair, green eyed. Damian's jaw slackened. He had seen that face, and he had seen it a million times before. He was looking at an older version of himself.

'Ah, Professor, it seems that you have but fifty seconds left. I have been monitoring all outcomes. It is, in my opinion, safe to eradicate.' His voice slowed to a stop and he turned and glared pass the professor, and for a moment Oric and Damian's eyes met. Oric smiled and gave a slight nod just as the room froze in time. Damian looked around the room- The nine had seemed to Damian to have reverted to their statured state. He cautiously walked towards the older version of himself, before the room froze in time, Oric had nodded and then winked at him.

'Sandy, Sandy, are you there,' the voice of Comm in his mind came like a breath of cool fresh air.

'Comm, where are you, come in here, now.' There was a silence that to Damian seemed to stretch a lifetime.

'I cannot. You are in a different universe, another realm to ours, but I can extricate you. Stand by!' 'Extricate,' thought Damian. 'There's irony.' The room swirled, and he was back in the grey place.

The greys dissipated and he found himself at the end of the corridor outside the door to lab 5. Comm stood before him, concern etched onto his face.

'Are you ok? I thought I had lost you,' he stammered. Damian studied the holographic image that stood before him. It was, he thought, Professor Stephen Swann, but the features, belied that.

'They were all there Comm. All of them, all of the statues, and I was there too, and strangely, I was a sort of com-link, and it seemed to recognise me, at the end, it winked at me. You were sort of there as well. Professor Stephen Swann, he seemed to run the place. He was dressed like you, blue shirt, white shorts, long tied-back white hair, and the beard, but the features weren't you.' He stopped. Comm had cradled his chin into the palm of his right hand. The index finger started to tap.

'The com-link recognised you, now that's interesting' he said, with a smile emerging. Comm lowered his hand.

'So, all the statues were there. You were there. So, that's all ten statues and this Professor Stephen Swann, my lookalike,' said Comm slowly. He stopped and thought for a moment, index finger tapping his cheek he turned to Damian and said.

'Sandy, I only look like I do because your imagination created me in this image, it could be that all of the statues are your work colleagues.'

'Do you think that he might be the elusive 'O'?' Comm continued. Damian frowned, and looked hard at his friend.

'Comm,' he said slowly …'are you … 'O'?'

Comm was taken aback.

'I can assure you Sandy, I am not the elusive 'O', and I think we need to remove ourselves from this science station, and ponder on what has just happened.' The corridor swirled around him, his vision blurred as the greys swam before him.

They were back in the extended room. Barely a second had passed since they had left and yet, thought Damian, they had been gone hours. Comm sat himself at the control console. Damian followed and sat opposite.

'So, what happened? Where did I go?' Damian inquired. Comm busied himself with the holo towers, saying nothing.

In the centre of the holo stage, the star Epsilon Eridini, with its six planets, pixelated into view. Comm walked to the fourth planet, a large green gas giant. He pointed to one of the moons.

'That is where we were, when I sped up the timeline. I lost you, but luckily I was able to hone in on your control belt.' A red line appeared from the green planet and extended across the room until it hit the far wall.

'This line is the route that you took. I will scale down the images, and we will follow it.'

The green gas giant reduced in size until it became a pinpoint against the Epsilon star. Then even the star reduced in size until it became a point of light in the centre of the room. Other stella bodies came into view and they too reduced in size as the red line continued its journey through the holographic constellations. The line stopped at a star in the Hyades cluster.

'Wow!' exclaimed Damian 'How far away is that?' he added. Comm walked across the holo stage to the star. He manipulated a remote control and the star increased in size.

'This is Gamma Tauri, and from where we were on Epsilon Eridani, it's about a hundred and forty light years away.' His right hand cradled his chin.

'Do we have settlements there?' Damian queried, as he walked over to the star. Comm turned to him and shrugged.

'No Sandy, we do not. Where we are in the asteroid field is the furthest anyone has ever been. Gamma Tauri is seventy light years further on from where we are now. But you saw it yourself, and all the statues working together on this planet,' he said, pointing to the planet at the end of the red line. Damian stared at the mottled red and green planet, then turned and studied the red line. He stopped as he noticed a discrepancy.

'Comm, have you noticed this. The red line is broken at this point,' he said, pointing to the five-centimetre gap in the line. Comm walked across the star field to the break. For a moment his face showed puzzlement, then realisation.

'You travelled in our space time, to this point. It was here that you moved into some kind of dimensional shift. Meaning, you passed into another parallel, another universe, at this point, but the constellations occupy the same position in both realms, so the control belt recorded you travelling to this position:, Gamma Tauri,' Comm explained softly.

'But who or what, took me there?' Damian said, almost in a whisper. Comm turned to him and stated, 'Now that, my friend is the question. And also, how, was I able to communicate with you, and then pull you out of there? Are we being manipulated, played with. Is the elusive 'O' all part of this?' He turned and looked at the star cluster.

'Sandy, I need to study this some more. We cannot travel to any scenario without the risk of you being whisked away.

Damian left the com-link alone to his thoughts in the extended room. He still had the flight experience to complete with Johan, and, he thought, he would need to meet up with Jane and tell her the latest in his adventures. She would, he thought, want to help Comm anyway.

The days passed. Working in the field was a lot less traumatic than his first venture. Even so, whilst in the control deck he studied Johan's flying techniques in minute detail, every now and then asking relevant questions not only to Johan but to the ever-so moody navigator Sian Kalvic as well. At the end of the work cycle all the crews met in the now renamed level 11 Club. Occasionally Jane Onslow would meet up with him and they would discuss the progress that she and Comm had made. On every rest period Jane visited the extended room to help Comm solve the problem of potentially being snatched into another realm, she would on many occasions retire to Damian's sleeping slab exhausted.

It had been seven standard months since his trip to another parallel. The Griffin now had only two months left in the field. He had noticed that the flight crews were now extending their work cycles. The more they brought in, the more credits they earned, and, he mused, as Prime finder his own account would benefit greatly.

At the end of each work cycle he found himself completing the theoretical section of Module 3. It had taken him four standard months to get to the end., and previous to that, the months of working at Johan's side and actually flying the HL1 also added to the completion of his module. Satisfied with his efforts, and the completion of the allotted standard hours of flight experience with senior pilot, Johan Spiez, he submitted his work for evaluation.

Meanwhile, Comm and Jane on rest cycle met up together in the extended room, they worked each day, trying to understand how Damian had been transferred from one parallel to another, then back again. In amongst his studies Damian tried to meet up with them whenever he could.

It was while he was readying himself for another day when Six informed him of an unanswered message. He had been called to meet with Commander Gomez.

CHAPTER 29

HEAVY LIFT 2

Damian made his way to the loading bay on deck 2, a journey he was now quite familiar with. As he entered, he immediately noted the change in gravity and temperature. He was quite used to that as well, but he remembered not so long ago how for a moment or two he would be disorientated. The loading bay was pressurised to 0.8 of an atmosphere. Its temperature lowered 15 degrees. He had been told previously by many pilots that the cargo bots worked more efficiently in a colder atmosphere.

He stood for a moment to acclimatise. His stomach always reacted to the lower pressure. He took a few deep breaths and swallowed. He found this helped to equalise the pressures in his ears. Feeling more stable he continued into the working field.

Four heavy lifters sat squat side by side. He looked up at the grappling arms five meters above him. They were stowed neatly into the sides of the lifters' hulls, but when required for use could be extended a full sixty meters in any direction- The huge grasping hands could wrap themselves around an object to a maximum diameter of fifteen metres.

At the rear of one of the lifters, he noticed a squad of cargo bots unloading the lifter's hold. He stopped to watch, but his attention moved to an officer striding towards him. He smiled, then gave a courteous nod as Commander Gomez neared.

She stopped three metres short of him, her face typically stern.

'Your work has been verified. It would seem Senior Cadet Drake that you have achieved junior pilot status.' She spat out the words. That must have annoyed her, thought Damian, even though, he thought, a few months ago it was her who on this very spot convinced him to continue his training.

'Yes, Ma'am,' he said curtly. Gomez glared at him.

'I am to assess you on the heavy lift 2.' She indicated the craft with a slight movement of her chin. He turned to look at the vessel, not as large as the HL1, but still above his ranking as a newly-qualified pilot. He turned back to face her.

'I beg your pardon Commander, but I believe that I am only qualified to fly passenger shuttles. Although, under the supervision of senior pilot Johan Spiez I have logged over five hundred standard hours of flight in an HL1 but I am only qualified for the shuttle'

'And today,' she said cutting in, 'your Module 3 assessment will continue with the HL2.' Her eyes closed for a second, then she continued.

'Captain's orders. With the extended work cycles, you have now completed the required flight experience. 'Module 3 will now commence!' she finished. He could see the loathing. She had been ordered to carry out the assessment, an assessment any of her lieutenants or ensigns could have carried out. He was, he thought, being pushed by the Captain. She, like the Commander in Damian's view, was being pushed by a much higher authority, and that authority, thought Damian, could only be Command.

'Drake, are you listening to me?'

Damian snapped back to the here and now.

'Sorry Commander,' he said stiffening to attention.

'I said, I want you to start preliminary flight checks on the HL2. Call me when you have finished.' Her eyes burnt into him, she fixed the glare for a few seconds, then scowling, turned and marched away.

Damian also turned and slowly made his way across the hanger deck.

The squat bulbous craft sat facing the huge hanger portal, the only thing stopping total decompression was the graviton field that separated the outside from within. Looking past the shimmering surface, he could just make out a cluster of asteroids that reflected light from the Griffin's external lighting. Somewhere out there, he thought, were answers, answers to everything that he was, and, yet, to be. Reluctantly he turned away from the beguiling spectacle and walked up the hold's ramp into the HL2.

He had been in an HL2 before. Many times, in fact, but only as a simulation. Johan's HL1 was much larger, and it had been well-used. This craft seemed almost brand new by comparison.

The hold was thirty metres long and ten high. The control deck was ten meters further on. He found the ascender platform halfway down the hold. Stepping onto it he passed his hand across the ascend light. The platform jolted then ascended to a walkway above. He looked down at the empty cavernous hold. She will want me to fill this, he thought as he stepped of the platform. This is going to be some day. As he walked towards the forward control deck he felt a slight feeling of excitement pass through him.

He passed a sleeping cell then a small galley before stopping at the split door that led to the main flight deck.

The door opened to reveal a darkened room. As he stepped through the portal the room flooded with light and consoles flashed into life.

He sidled his way past the three rear passenger seats and sat himself in the centre command seat. He waited until the seat had finished moulding itself to his seating posture. The console in front of him became alive with holographic towers and spheres. The bland metal wall in front flickered to life and a panoramic three-dimensional view of the hanger came to life.

Damian had practised the pre-flight checks on the holo pads in his quarters many times, and after five minutes had completed the procedure. He opened a link to the Commander.

'Flight checks complete Commander. Awaiting your orders.' He wanted to say, 'Okay, all done, ready for whatever hell you're going to put me through,' but instead he waited for her response. He knew the message had been sent and received, a green slightly pulsating light on the comm link told him so.

He energised the main engines and set them to idle, then leant back in his seat and waited. 'No smell,' he thought. Johan's HL1 had a distinctive smell. He had described it once as the smell of nervous anxiety. Johan had laughed at that. 'Yes,' he had bellowed over the noise of strained thrusters, 'We constantly shit ourselves in here.' He chuckled as he remembered.

He heard her approach before she announced her presence.

'Move to Delta, 49 – 63 – 71. Low speed.' Her voice sounded almost automated. Damian turned and watched the stern-faced woman sit in the rear spotter seat. She held a holo pad in her left hand, her right pointed to the front vid screen.

'Eyes front, Junior Pilot!' Damian noted the overemphasis on the 'junior'. He turned and shook his head slightly.

He retracted the hold ramp and sealed it to the hull. Opening a link to the Griffin's main control deck he asked permission to proceed to the co-ordinance that the Commander had given. There was a slight delay, then permission was granted. He pushed forward on the anti grav and felt a slight shudder as the craft lifted from the hanger floor. He passed his hand slowly through the aft engine holo tower and noted the indicator illuminating yellow. With forward motion he adjusted the HL2 forward deflector shield to harmonise with the graviton field that protected the hanger exit. They passed through the field smoothly. He punched in the co-ordinance and once the huge craft cleared the hangar portal it automatically altered its vector to match.

he turned to face the Commander.

'So, what are we doing today?' he asked cheerfully.

'Locate asteroid 7261,' she said, without looking up from her pad, he turned back to the console and punched in the numbers. The feedback surprised him.

'Wow, that's a long way into the field.' He turned back to her.

'Is there nothing closer? Readouts show a lot of activity in that area.'

She reluctantly looked up from her pad, her face showing signs of annoyance.

'Just get on with it.'

Damian returned the stare; he smiled and took a breath.

'I'm just saying, it's a dangerous region, are you sure you want a novice to take you and this very expensive ship to that ...' He pointed at the inset monitor that showed their destination's coordinates.

'Drake!' she snapped.

Damian was taken aback.

'You are being assessed. Do not confer with me. Just carry out the orders I give. Now turn to the front.' Damian shrugged and turned in his seat.

'You expect me to fly this craft into a maelstrom of moving death, without a crew, just me, on my own, no navigator, no spotters, just me?' He turned his head slightly. He watched her persona through his peripheral vision. She looked up from her info pad.

'Well done Pilot Drake. To enter the field on your own would be at least suicidal.' She entered a code on her pad. Next to him pixelated an image of Jane Onslow. He noticed behind him, next to the Commander, the image of Commander Burroughs and Dr Ghorbany. Again, he thought, people that I trust, are part of the assessment.

'No disrespect, Commander, but the last time you put these characters into the assessments, I was given wrong information. I am sorry, but if this is the same, then, I refuse to enter the field.' He passed his hand through a holo tower. Immediately the HL2 span on its axis. Griffin filled the screen. He turned to face the Commander.

'The images of your navigator and spotters will give you accurate information at all times, now please, pilot, turn the craft around and continue with the assessment.' She lowered her head back to the info pad.

Turning back to the front, he turned to the image of Jane beside him. He lifted his hand and gave a hand sign. He was surprised when she answered him in perfect sign. He frowned, and turned the craft back to the field. Why, he thought, if a comm link can do the job of the navigator, and the spotters, why bother with real people?

He applied thrust and felt a gentle push of his seat into the small of his back as the great mass of the HL2 gently accelerated.

For an hour he manoeuvred through the asteroid field listening to the warnings that the holo images constantly gave out. He adjusted the flight path to suit each warning. Passing around under and over the larger masses, his hands moved smoothly over the holo panels. Proximity alerts continually warned of impending collisions. He dealt with each alarm without incident; the long hours of watching Johan seemed to be paying off.

He looked to the far range scanner. The Delta region was still an hour away. The journey towards it was nothing less than chaotic. He programmed in a vector, knowing that in a matter of minutes he would have to amend it. Twenty minutes later a shrill alarm sounded. He glanced at the scanner: Two huge masses had collided and where there were only two, now, there were thousands. He increased the forward shielding. With nowhere to go he ploughed into the debris. All the while the navigator and the spotters gave him a torrent of up-to-date information of the mayhem outside.

Most were deflected away, some however slammed through the shielding onto the hull, creating a judder that ran through the ship. His hands now moved swiftly across the console, moving the ship through all three dimensions, but still the collisions came.

'Shields down to 62 percent,' the calm tones of the comm link informed him.

'Don't you break my ship,' a voice behind him remarked.

He didn't answer but concentrated on the continual stream of information being offered to him by the various warning systems and the holo images. He did however think fleetingly on how calm her remark was.

'Collision imminent,' the com-link informed him.

'What? Where?' Damian shouted above the warning shrills.

'Fifteen degrees port,' the navigator Jane, returned.

Damian studied the scanner.

'Where did that come from?' he muttered under his breath. He was sure that wasn't there a moment ago.

The shard was huge. It passed through the shielding without effort. The collision spun the heavy lifter 90 degrees. The seat clamps tightened as the inertia doubled. He was forced violently to his right. The seat clamps bit into his stomach and he was winded for a second. Every part of the console screamed an alarm.

'Status,' Damian asked the com, and was surprised at how calm his voice was.

'Port main engine, disengaged, aft thrusters, disengaged, forward retros, disengaged, hull integrity, sound.'

'Well, that's something, disengage all alarms.' The control deck quietened except for the occasional thudding of the smaller objects that hit the outer hull.

'Manoeuvrability down to thirty percent, no port control, shielding almost zero,' he thought to himself as he scanned the console. Reluctantly, he sent an auto distress. He surveyed his options – there weren't many. He gritted his teeth. He had failed the assessment anyway, so …

'Commander, I could do with some help up here.' She didn't reply.

'Commander!' he said again with more force, then turned to face her.

She was bent double, her arms dropped beside her legs, the holo pad lay on the floor in front of her.

'Oh, perfect, just when you're really needed,' Damian muttered to himself. He turned back to the console.

With limited manoeuvring thrusters his options were negligible. After a few seconds he made a decision.

'We need to land,' he said out loud. 'And we need to slow down,' he added to himself. The retros – what was left of them – were useless for severe braking. He looked out into the asteroid field. What we need is a gravity snatch, he thought. There was a procedure he remembered. He had studied it only a few days ago.

Using the starboard thrusters, he aligned the HL2 with the largest and closest of the asteroids. 'Now,' he muttered, 'maybe a figure of eight vector between … these two.' He said out loud while checking the scanner, 'and then if our speed is correct, a landing on that one. What could possibly go wrong?' he said out loud.

He programmed his intentions into the com-link.

'83 percent possibility of failure.' The com informed him.

'Ah, seventeen percent possibility of success,' Damian countered.

'Initiate!'

HL2 rocked violently as its great mass strained under the torments of the sudden torque. Damian glanced across the console and added slight corrections to the flight path as required.

The craft clipped out crops of rock from the surface of the asteroid as it plummeted down towards the jagged canyons below. At almost the very last second the initiated program kicked in and pulled the craft up from its terrifying death dive, then, up, back into orbit. Damian noticed from the tell-tale readouts they had lost twenty percent acceleration. They completed two orbits before being flung out into space. A few moments later they were captured by the second enormous mass of rock that swam into their path. Damian grabbed the edge of the console as the HL2 began its second death defying plunge into the jagged rocks that scoured the surface.

Another ten percent of acceleration lost, he noted, the ground fell away and they were then back into orbit. With a slight touch to the starboard manoeuvring thrusters they left orbit, slower now, they crossed the void to the largest of the asteroids. It loomed towards them, its gravity already taking a hold. Damian knew he was committed, it was land or crash.

He had initiated a slow descent. They were descending at ninety degrees to port. He increased what energy there was left to the port side shields. Nothing through the vid screen showed anything remotely flat or level. It would, he thought, be a messy landing.

He fired all retros and kept them on until they depleted.

They hit the ground aft first, the inertia threw him onto the console, his forehead and nose took the brunt, the front of the craft then made contact with an outcrop of rock and threw them back up five meters before slamming back down onto the uneven ground. They flipped and spun. Each time they landed he could hear new alarms being sounded. He felt a gush of air pass then the control deck door sealed shut; they were now sliding but a wall of rock thirty metres high finally stopped them dead. All systems powered down.

'Status!' Damian demanded. As he forced himself back into his seat he noticed that the holo images of his friends had pixelated out of existence.

'Life support, offline – re-initiating; engine power depleted; shielding zero percent; hull integrity – cargo hold extensive damage; atmosphere depleted; control deck secure; auto distress has been received; sending co-ordinance. Life support has now been initialised,' said the monotoned voice of the com-link.

With the HL2 on its side, Damian found it difficult to move in his seat.

'Orientate gravity ninety degrees to starboard.' He felt his weight change, disengaged the seat grabs and fought his way back to the passenger seats to attend to the Commander.

'I'm fine, Pilot,' she snapped as he pulled her upright.

'That's good to hear,' he muttered as he opened the Med kit.

'You have no pain, no dizziness,' he said as a matter of fact. He then placed a bio scanner onto her forehead.

'No, nothing,' she snapped back, trying to pull the scanner away.

'Then you won't mind if I check, will you?' he snapped back at her. She sat back into the seat and allowed him to continue.

'Negative,' he said. 'Your fine.' He removed the scanner and replaced it into the Med kit. She leant forward, and took the Med kit from him.

'You are injured, you're bleeding. Please, allow me.' Her voice was soft and calming. He sat back in the adjacent seat, slightly shocked and bemused at the sudden change in her attitude. She attended to his wounds.

'Sorry,' he said after a while.

'I seemed to have broken your ship, but that asteroid came from nowhere.' She wiped the blood from his face and checked her work.

'No permanent damage and, you did fine. It was …' she stopped to rethink.

'Exemplary,' she finished.

Damian sat back and gave her a quizzical look.

'Is that a smile, Commander? You should wear that more often. Makes you look more human.' The smile broadened, showing dimples within her cheeks.

'Discipline, Mr. Drake, must always be maintained. Especially this far from civilisation,' she said softly, but he noticed the smile was diminishing.

'Ah, and there it goes.'

'There what goes?' she said, confused.

'The smile. It exists fleetingly, then … gone,' he said slowly. She inclined her head slightly to the left and the smile returned.

'That's better. Now, it seems we have some time to spare, so I think the whole crew knows everything there is to know about me, but I know nothing about you. The com-link says we are safe in here, plenty of supplies, and air, so please, do tell.'

She relaxed back into her seat and scrutinised his smiling expectant face.

'I don't know everything about you, and come to think of it, neither do you, but what I do know is that you are different. I mean from all of us here on the Griffin. You are a natural pilot. I am amazed at how far you have come in such a short space of time. Every pilot in my team is somehow inspired by you, including Johan. You are an organiser and a natural leader. Your origins are a mystery, even to yourself, but that does not stop the myths emerging from the crew.'

Damian held up his hand and leant forward.

'Myths, what sort of myths?' he said, through a suppressed laugh.

'Some of the crew believe that you were a great leader, and were imprisoned by a warlord. Others however, think you were the warlord imprisoned by a great leader before you escaped.'

Damian's jaw dropped, then he laughed out loud.

'That's ridiculous, you don't think that … do you? If you did, it would explain a lot.' Shaking his head, he sat back into his chair.

'The island scenario is common knowledge amongst the crew. Especially as you are one of the statues. Statues I might add of some of the most infamous people in our history.' Humour peeled away from the smile, he stood and turned away.

'Maybe I am here to right their wrongs. Maybe they are just metaphors for something we haven't discovered yet. I am going to get some water. Do you want some?' he said walking towards the galley.

'No, not for me, thank you,' she said, trying to evaluate the tone of his voice. For a moment, she thought he sounded older.

He returned with a flask. His face had brightened.

'Anyway, I thought we were going to talk about you,' he said, offering a cup. She declined with a shake of her head.

'Nothing to tell really. I started pilot training quite a few standard years ago. I flew shuttles after three standard years of training, heavy lifters two standard years after that, became a Lieutenant three standard years after that, Commander five standard years after that. One standard year later I was assigned here. and I have been here five standard years.' Damian beamed a smile.

'That is your résumé. I am asking about you, personally' The holo pad on her lap blipped into life, she glanced down at the symbols. Her face became sour.

'I live for my work, Pilot. We have been summoned by the Captain.' She said, as she stood. Again, Damian was confused by this sudden change.

'She will have to wait. It will take the rescue team at least four hours to reach us,' he said, with a shrug.

'Follow me.' Damian watched amused as she made her way to the back of the control deck.

'The cargo hold has been damaged. It is depressurised,' he said calmly, then was shocked to see the door open at her approach. He stood and followed her cautiously. The exit ramp had been extended, he could see the hangar floor and the industrious cargo bots going about their business.

'It's a bloody simulator,' he spluttered, he caught her up and gently laying his hand upon her shoulder turned her to face him.

'We never left. So, all this just to see what I can do in an emergency. But I learnt something as well today, Jennifer. For a fleeting moment, I met the real you.' She winced at the sound of her first name.

'The Captain is waiting, Pilot Drake,'

''Oh, come on Jen. You can call me Damian if you like,' he said, studying her face for the elusive smile. It never came.

'Show some respect, Pilot.' Her voice was clipped and her eyes flashed anger. She turned and exited the simulator.

CHAPTER 30

CAPTAIN'S QUARTERS

Damian followed in her wake. They left the loading bay and made their way to the sender units, then waited silently until its arrival. Once inside Damian turned to face her.

'Does every pilot go through that?' he said trying to control his anger. She shrugged as she entered the level into the sender's pad. Damian's knees buckled slightly as the sender moved away and he grabbed a hold of the handrail.

'We are going down. Why are we going down? Shouldn't we be ascending?' he said, adapting to the downward motion of the sender. She turned to him and frowned, then slowly shaking her head, said.

'Of course, we are going down. We have been summoned to Griffin's command centre, level 15.' For a moment he was confused.

'Wouldn't that be, level 1?' he said hesitantly. She glared at him, a puzzled look forming across her eyes.

'Level 1 is for long range sensors, and a lot of its space is for non-essential storage. Why would you think that the main command centre be situated in its most vulnerable place? Level 15 is the centre of the ship. It is protected by the fabric of all the other levels.' She shook her head slowly and turned away from him. Damian thought that her comment somehow made a lot of sense, but, why did he think that level 1 was the most obvious place for a command centre?

The doors opened onto a semi-circular lobby. Around its perimeter were recliners and low tables. Some were occupied by what Damian could see by members of the bridge crew; officers, all of them. In the centre of the lobby a large security desk, although it had spaces for ten. Only one space was occupied. As they walked closer, he recognised the man. He had met him twice, once when being escorted through the Med lab carnage, then, on level 11. I still don't know his name, he thought as they approached.

'Lieutenant Peroni,' Gomez said, as they approached. 'Ah, Peroni,' thought Damian, as they stopped in front of him.

'Ma'am,' snapped Peroni, and sat to attention in the recliner.

'We have been invited to meet with the Captain,' the Commander said matter-of-factly.

'Names,' Peroni asked as he activated the security scanner.

'Oh, you have got to be kidding me,' Damian blurted. Both Commander and Lieutenant turned to glare at him.

'Well, you definitely know mine, and I'm pretty sure you know the Commander.'

'Pilot Drake. We have protocols, and security checks are important,' Gomez said, her voice low and forbidding.

'I realise that Commander, but even so,' Damian argued, but looking at both of their faces he conceded, and apologised.

Peroni passed a scanner over them both, then after a moment of checking the holo towers indicated the double doors behind him.

'The Captain is waiting for you Commander.' Damian ignored the fact that he was not mentioned but gave out an indignant gasp.

'Problem Pilot?' Peroni hissed. Damian shrugged, shook his head then turned to follow the Commander.

The double doors opened at their approach. Damian stopped at the threshold and marvelled at the size of the open space. He scanned the area to take in the scene that confronted him. The length of the command deck stretched to at least sixty metres and at its widest point at least thirty. Symmetrically placed within its confines were consoles of all shapes and sizes each one displaying various towers of holographic images. The bridge officers numbered less than twenty, a small number for such a huge room, but back when this ship was on active duty he could imagine that there would have been over a hundred.

But that, was not what had caught Damian's attention. There were no walls nor ceiling, just the formidable vastness of space. He knew he was looking at an enormous vid-screen that encompassed the whole room from the floor then overhead to create a dome of a ceiling twenty metres above; but its effect shook him.

Captain Juliana Contessa sat at her private console, situated in the centre of Griffin's command deck level.

'Mr. Drake!' The voice was strong, authoritative, neither a shout nor a whisper but certainly demanding attention. He turned his attention to the central console.

'Captain!' he snapped, as respectfully as he could.

'Commander Gomez has reported that your piloting was … impressive.' Damian noted that the last word did not come easy for her. He was now next to her.

'That's exceedingly kind of her, ma'am,' Damian said, giving the Commander a fleeting sideways glance.

'I would say that your piloting skills are, unique. No one has ever managed to travel that far into the asteroid field.' She looked up from the images being displayed on the console. Her blue grey eyes bore deep into him.

'And then, to land, almost intact.' She returned to the console.

'How did you manage that, Mr Drake?' The eyes were back on him again. He felt uneasy.

'I used a gravity snatch, Captain. It was enough to slow our momentum … well, enough to attempt a landing. It wasn't much of a decision. We would have been pulverised if we had stayed. If, it had been real, of course.'

Captain Contessa relaxed back into her seat; the steely eyes softened slightly.

'As I recall, that procedure is not part of your training. So, where would you have learnt it?' Her posture was relaxed in the oversized chair, giving the impression of warmth, but the eyes were still fixed rigid. Damian relaxed and smiled his most disarming smile.

'I don't understand Captain. You know exactly where I learnt it. Is it not called the "Contessa manoeuvre"? You, however, did it with the Griffin, and, in battle conditions. My manoeuvre was nothing in comparison.'

If the Captain was shocked, she didn't show it. Instead, she turned back to study the console displays.

'I applaud you for your study, Mr Drake, but no matter how insignificant you feel your assessment to be, you have passed it with honours.' Damian was about to argue that he didn't belittle the assessment, but then thought better of it.

'Thank you, Captain,' he said curtly.

She passed her hand through a holo tower.

'Let the log record, that the pilot known as Damian Drake, has completed his training to a level of distinction, and as of this day has been promoted to Second Lieutenant, and as such, has due stake in the privileges and rewards of this commission.'

'Duly noted, Captain,' replied the voice of the com. The Captain turned her attention back to Damian, who stood in stunned silence.

'Congratulations Lieutenant. The Commander will explain your new responsibilities.' She turned back to her console, the meeting obviously over. He turned to the Commander. He noticed her jaw had dropped. She was in as much confusion as he was.

'That is all Commander. Dismiss!' The Commander turned to leave, Damian remained rigid. He was about to ask why such a promotion, the most he should have received was Senior Pilot. This promotion was three ranks higher. The Commander pushed him, he turned to her, indignant.

'Move,' she mouthed silently, and pushed him again.

Outside in the lobby he stopped and turned to her.

'What, just happened.' He said, his voice hesitant. The Commander slowly shook her head.

'I have no idea … Lieutenant,' she sneered.

'Don't give me that tone. It's not my fault. I'm just as shocked as you obviously are.' She looked around the lobby and noticed that they had attracted the attention of other bridge crew officers.

'Not here,' she said softly.

'Where then.' He whispered, also aware of the attention.

'My office, half an hour.' She turned and walked away.

Damian took the ascender to level six and made his way to his quarters.

'Congratulations, Lieutenant,' the room com blurted as the door to the room closed.

'What's this?' he asked, looking at the package sitting on the low table.

'I believe it is your new uniform. It was delivered thirteen standard minutes ago,'

Damian opened the package and lay the uniform out. The tunic was mainly dark green, signifying flight crew, the right arm a burgundy red showing the rank of a commissioned officer. On the shoulders were flashes of white with piped beading of grey showing his rank to be Second Lieutenant. He couldn't help smiling at it. He had only been here for nearly three years and now he was an officer.

'There is a communication for you, sir.'

'Who from?' asked Damian, pulling on his slacks and waiting for them to self-fit.

'Unknown sir. Access to identity has been denied.' Damian suppressed a laugh.

'It's okay Six. Allow him through.'

'Congratulations Sandy,' said a familiar voice.

'Comm, where are you?' Damian said, adjusting the tunic.

'Senior nurse Onslow and I are in the extended room, if you wish to join us,' said Comm.

'Be right there. Just give me a moment.'

He deactivated the com pad. 'Six, give me a holo image of myself.' In the centre of the seating room a perfect image of himself appeared. He slowly walked around the image, admiring the new Lieutenant's uniform. Although he felt it wasn't earned, he had to agree, he did look good in it. Disengaging the holo, he walked through the arch into the extended room.

'Do I have to stand to attention when you speak to me now?' Jane asked with a broad smile.

'Your promotion comes from Command, not the Captain. And before you ask, I have no idea why. However, it does give you privileges, and rewards.' Comm explained.

'Am I open to some sort of corruption?' Damian asked, frowning.

'No, er … no, not corruption, and may I say, that is another old saying that is no longer in use. As a commissioned officer, your percentage as Prime finder has increased,' Comm answered, whilst adjusting the tunic's epaulettes.

'Yes, you are a very wealthy man. Not that you weren't before, but you can now add a further ten percent to your bonuses,' Jane Onslow added. Comm nodded approvingly.

'By the time this mission has ended you will be able to afford anything that comes your way,' Comm said. Laying his hand upon Damian's shoulder, he gently turned him to the image of Gamma Tauri that dominated the centre of the room.

'Remember when we followed the course of Discovery, from the scorched Earth to the dwarf star, that is now the asteroid field.' Comm asked.

'After the destruction of Earth; yes I remember that.' he acknowledged.

'I did a quick survey of the four planets in the dwarf system whilst we were waiting for Discovery to emerge: that information I stored for later study. The fourth and largest planet was rich with Quantonite. It would have been difficult to mine when it was a planet, but now that the planet is in a trillion or so pieces, and as you have discovered, it is there for the gathering.' Damian returned to the low recliners and sat. Turning to Comm, he said.

'If I remember correctly, and bearing in mind a lot was going on at that point, you said something on the lines of, you didn't know who or what was feeding me the information. Certainly not from any historical or personal journal, so how did you know what each planet contained?'

Comm turned away from the image of Gamma Tauri. As he did so the image altered, the asteroid field now dominated the room.

'Sandy, I don't know all of the answers. Well, not yet. All I know, and it is certain, the more concentrated area of Quantonite lies nearer the centre of the field. The Griffin needs to move, and it needs to move to the Theta region, particularly co-ordinance 31 – 40 – 16. It will be difficult to persuade the Captain, especially when you cannot tell her where this information comes from, but the credits will be enormous, and certainly for you, as the Prime finder, your share will outweigh the Captain's by a thousand fold. And, as we have said on many occasions, there is something about this system Gamma Tauri. It is important. I believe it is a step within many steps to be taken that will bring you closer to unravelling all of these mysteries.'

Damian stood and walked into the projection, to its centre. The Theta region lay just 10 million kilometres beyond the field's centre. The asteroids at this distance were enormous and the velocity of their orbits a hundred times the speed of the outer field.

'This region is far too dangerous, the Captain would never allow it,' he said, as Comm and Jane walked to his side. They both surveyed the mayhem,'

"She doesn't have to physically go there. Just being told that it exists would be enough. The fleets factory ships when they arrive will make the decision of how to get there, but you have to tell her,' Jane said as she surveyed the maelstrom of horror.

'And there is something else,' Comm said, as he manipulated a hand control. The scale of the field reduced, other stars emerged into the image. Damian noticed a red line appearing.

'Is that the route I travelled?' he asked.

"Yes, and it goes right through the middle of the field. I don't think that is coincidence.' The scale reduced until Gamma Tauri came back into view. Comm enlarged the scale, the mottled planet now dominated.

'I could not understand how I was able to communicate with you, or even how I managed to bring you back. It took both nurse Onslow and myself quite a while to decipher this part of the puzzle. You pointed out a break in the line, at this location.'

Comm and Jane walked to the area where the line had broken. Damian followed them. Comm enlarged the scale. The red line was now half a metre in diameter. The gap now appeared as three metres apart.

'Using some technology from Command, I can now show you the array pulse from your control belt to my own link.'

Damian noticed that within the red line he could see a movement of pulses travelling from one direction to the other. As the pulse passed through the break, he noticed another pulse heading in the opposite direction.

'Sorry Comm, I don't understand what I am looking at. I assume, one set of pulses is from you, the other is a return pulse from me.'

Comm turned to face him. He slowly shook his head.

'No, the pulse heading for the planet is from me, but the return pulse, is not from you or I; it is from something unknown, and that unknown is what sent you back. However, although this is just another mystery on top of all the others, I think I have managed to develop a deflector that I can install into the dampener that the engineering team put into one of your implants. That was when the capsule was interacting with you. It should in future stop anything snatching you from this realm. Nurse Onslow, if you wouldn't mind.' Jane reached out and gently pressed his head to his shoulder.

'This won't hurt,' she said.

They moved back into the seating room. Damian massaged his neck.

'That did not hurt,' Jane protested. Damian feigned a wince, then turned to the com pad.

'Six, I would like you to open a communication with the Captain. Ask if I could have a private meeting. Treat it as a priority. Also, send my apologies to Commander Gomez. I will not be able to attend our meeting. Ask her to reschedule.' That, he thought should really annoy her. He turned back to his friends.

'I'll make my way back to level 15. We'll meet up later.'

'And, Nurse Onslow and I will finish the work on Wu Quan's scenario,' Comm said as he and Jane walked off towards the extended room.

He made his way back to the Command deck and sat in the lobby. He waited patiently for fifteen minutes, then his personal com chimed.

'Sir, this is Six. The Captain invites you to her quarters,' Damian pondered on this.

'Wow, I'm honoured, I think. Er. ... where are her quarters?'

'I have ordered a guide, it should be with you, er ... now.' A slither of green light appeared in front of him, Damian followed it to the sender. Inside it ordered the com to send them to level 16.

'She lives directly below the Command centre,' Damian muttered.

'She is the Captain, Lieutenant, and has direct access to the Command centre,' answered the guide. They exited the sender into an ante-room, or, thought Damian, a reception room.

'This is the Captain's quarters,' said the guide, then vanished. Damian looked around the room: Three-dimensional images of past Commanders sat in alcoves around the perimeter. He noticed Burroughs and Gomez. They looked younger he thought, and the others, presumably were those that preceded them. The room's decor was tasteful and its lighting subtle. The light from the ceiling gave out a yellow tint, making the room feel warm and welcoming.

He walked towards the double doors on the opposite wall and was surprised when they opened at his approach.

The doors opened onto a spacious, tastefully decorated space. Damian entered cautiously. He was alone in the room, and not sure what to do next – stay rigid to the spot, or, call out, or, try to find her. He decided to stay put and wait, but something caught his eye. Along the whole length of the wall to his left, he noticed display cases, and on closer inspection found them full of artefacts, slabs of inscribed stone, statues of long dead rulers, books of all descriptions. One stood out from the others: It was open and lay upon an easel. He tried to read the printed words. He could make out some, but not all. It was old, ancient even. The page that lay open to him was damaged and faded, but there was some text that he could make out.

38, And as one earth shall pass away, and the heavens thereof, even so shall another come; and there is no end to my works, neither to my words.

39, For behold, this is my work and my glory – to bring to pass the immortality and eternal life of man.

Of the whole page, those two passages were the only ones that he could read.

'It is the book of Moses,' the Captain said softly. Damian spun around, shocked that she was standing so close.

'Sorry, you startled me. I didn't mean to pry,' he spluttered. She gave him a half smile.

'I have deciphered a lot, from this journal, but most of it is in a bad condition.'

Damian gave her a quizzical look, then turned back to the open pages.

'This is not a journal, Captain, this, is a Bible. Some people, from its day would have argued that it is the words and teachings of God. It was their version, of your Command, but, much more so.' The Captain stepped back from him astounded.

'You know this book?' she stammered.

'You, you can, read it?'

'It is written in a language that is familiar to me. It is strange that you have left the page open at this text. Can you read this?'

Captain Contessa leant in closer.

'No, it is just a random page, one with more intact writing than the others. I will decipher it. I just haven't had time.'

'And as one earth shall pass away, and the heavens thereof even so shall another come; and there is no end to my works, neither to my words. For behold, this is my work and my glory – to bring to pass the immortality and eternal life of man.' Damian read softly, Captain Contessa stepped back shocked.

'I have been an amateur historian and collector for over eighty standard years. This document is over five thousand years old. There is no way you can, just read it.'

Damian turned to the document and studied the two passages.

'And as one Earth passes, another will come, and then will come eternal life.' He turned back to her.

'The book of Moses is a life journey. He was found in a river. No one knew where he came from but he was treated as a prince for most of his life. He eventually found out, that his own people were the slave workers of the man he regarded as father, king of all lands: He asks for them to be let free, his father refuses. With God's help and the death of the king's eldest son, Moses frees his people. They walk for years on a quest to find a land that their God has promised them. There is turmoil on the quest and God passes ten laws to be adhered to.' Damian stopped. He glared at the ancient book. How, how did he know that?

'I have had many passages of that chapter translated. I recognise the story that you give. Oh, Damian, I would have you read all of it to me!' She held his arm and led him to the centre of the room, to the recliners that took centre position.

'I have many other books in my collection, all needing translation. You are more than welcome to read them, Damian.'

He looked up at the unfamiliar sound of his first name emitting from this woman's lips.

'Maybe, at some other time, I would be pleased to help, but right now, I asked to see you on another matter.'

The Captain leant back into her chair, obviously displeased.

'What other matter?' her voice had returned to a spiteful tone. Damian leaned forward.

'Are you aware that I have dreams, dreams that nurse Onslow is trying to unravel.'

The Captain showed incomprehension at this change of subject.

'I wasn't aware.'

'Well, the dreams have changed slightly. They are more direct, more directive, I might say. One in particular I have dreamt on more than one occasion, involves the Griffin.' This caught the

Captain's attention. She was of course well aware of everything that Lieutenant Drake had achieved or was doing. Not that she had the slightest interest, but because Command was interested in him, she felt that she should show interest in him..

'And what does this dream involve?' she said, curious.

'Quantonite, trillions and trillions of tonnes of it.'

The Captain leaned back into her recliner and gave out an exasperated sigh.

'We know all of this. Your observations were proven,'

'Sorry Captain, no, I am not talking about the observations. They only give you a small percentage of Quantonite for each asteroid. What I am trying to say to you, is there is a region within the field where each asteroid contains a hundred percent of Quantonite.' The Captain leaned forward, her eyes piercing deep within him.

'Where?' she said, in a menacing tone.

'In the Theta region, deep into the centre of the field. A dangerous place, but, very lucrative.' She stood and turned to the room's centre.

'Room com, display holographic image of asteroid field. Highlight the Theta region. Also, highlight Griffin's position.' The room filled with asteroids, a tiny speck of red showed the position of the Griffin at the edge of the field. At the furthest end of the room Damian noticed all of the asteroids were highlighted yellow. The Captain turned to him.

'Did your dream give you coordinates?' she asked, her eyes narrowing.

'Strangely, it did, 31 – 40 – 16,' Damian said slowly. Her face, he thought, said it all. She wasn't buying the dream story.

'Com, get me Commander Burroughs,' she snapped.

'Yes Captain. How can I help,' came the light tone of the engineering Commander.

'I am passing over co-ordinance of the Theta region. Send eight type 1 probes. Calibrate them for Quantonite. I want to know the percentages.' The comm went quiet for a few moments, then Burroughs came back on.

'That is a very violent part of the field Ma'am.'

'I am aware of that Commander. Have another eight probes on standby, launch when ready.' She dismissed the com and the asteroid field. She turned back to Damian and stared him down.

'All from a dream, and a very descriptive dream. Now, Lieutenant, where, did you get this information from?'

Damian felt himself shrinking, and was at a loss as to what to say next.

'I am sorry Captain, but I cannot give you that information. I ... erm ... I,' he thought hard, he could not tell her an outright lie.

'I am forbidden to divulge that information,' he said softly. She stepped back, shock flashed across her features.

'Command, has given you this,' she stammered. In effect, thought Damian, it had. There was no way Comm could have surveyed the planet in orbit around the dwarf star. He had to have information from Command.

'Again, I am sorry Ma'am, but I am not at liberty to divulge this information.'

She softened, and gestured to the recliners. 'I understand Damian,' she said, almost in a whisper.

'Well, if it is true, both our bonus percentages will increase. You will have more than enough to carry on your historical studies. Now, what do you want me to read?' he said as he stood and turned to the display. She smiled as she took his arm and led him back to the display cabinets.

'There is a book that has never been translated. I found it on Tadere, the fifth planet of the Wolf star system, apparently. It was found in the remains of an old ark ship that was travelling from the original colonies, but unfortunately it never finished the journey.

'Oh,' said Damian slowly, scrutinising the cover.

'That says it all. I think it's a ... children's story. Its title is, 'Who am I?'

CHAPTER 31

MISSIONS END

Damian returned to his quarters. On entering he heard raised voices emanating from the enlarged room. He shushed Six as the room com uttered the first syllable of a welcome. Walking through to the archway, he stopped to listen.

'No Comm, the difference is harmonics. The first wave is at a much lower frequency. That can be matched with your own elongated wave, the other is higher pitched.' The raised voice of Jane Onslow stated as she rose from the recliner.

'Nurse Onslow, I know that, all I am saying is …' Comm turned to the entrance at the sound of a muffled laugh.

'Ah, Sandy, we are just discussing the return travel line from the planet in Gamma Tauri.'

Damian entered the room and stood at the head of the low table.

'Discussing,' he said with a frown. 'Sounded like a full-blown argument. You two are starting to act like an old married couple.'

Both Jane and Comm turned to each other. Jane shrugged in puzzlement. Comm cocked his head.

'Nurse Onslow, we really should put some time aside to study these phrases that he comes out with. I am sure that it would help in deciphering his persona.'

Jane sat back down in her recliner and gestured to the empty seat beside her. Damian sat and waited until a calm descended.

'I have spoken to the Captain. She did not go along with the dream theme, and so, I changed it to a directive from Command.'

Comm raised his hand and leant forward.

'Sandy, this could complicate things. She is in constant communication with the Command executive. She may ask why they have given this information to you and not her. Command, of course, would not deny that they had, or that they hadn't, which to her would confirm that they did. That in itself is not the problem. The problem will be what Command will do with this new information. At the very least, they would investigate it. I fear that you will be visited by a Command conduit in the very near future.'

Jane leant forward and joined the hushed conversation that had developed between the two of them.'

'What's a Command conduit?' she whispered. Damian turned to stare at the com link, then back to Jane.'

'You don't know?' Damian said in disbelief. She shrugged. He turned back to Comm.

'Only you, I and the Command executive know about the conduit,' Comm said. Then he thought for a moment, and added.

'Oh, and the whole of the main Com's system on every ship, planet, station and docks. So, almost everyone, except the organics well, humans. And you Sandy, only know because you were with me when Nurse Onslow was taken into one of them.'

Jane leapt from her seat.

'What!' she spluttered angrily.

'Everyone, at some time will be taken into the conduit. It is just the Executive's way of gathering information. It is perfectly harmless,' Comm said, flatly. Damian reached up to her and guided her back into her seat.

'You cannot tell anyone of this outside the Command executive. We are the only humans that know,' Damian said softly, as she settled back into the recliner.

'As I said to you before, the Griffin has a permanent link to Command. It requires constant information about our friend Sandy here. There is no malice in what it is doing,' Comm said in a softened tone.

'So, it has always known about level 11, even though I kept that a secret for so many years,' Jane said to know one in particular.

Damian turned to her and smiled. 'It couldn't care less about level 11, nor, about the Captain's collection of antiquities, or anybody else's obsession come to that. On this ship, it only cares about one thing, and, apparently, that's me. And of course having a permanent link from Command does allow Comm access to their projected Science Department.'

Jane nodded slowly and squeezed his hand.

'Sorry, it's just knowing that we cannot have any secrets.' The words lingered in the air, then realisation hit Damian hard.

'Comm, would they know about your journeys through the link, about this extended room, about everything that we are doing?' he said, his voice betraying his panic.

'I have been observing the link carefully. It has not sent conduits to interact with either you or Nurse Onslow.'

'But it could,' Damian interjected. Comm thought for a moment.

'Yes, it could … maybe. We need a memory dampener, just in case. I'll be back in a moment.' The image of Comm disappeared, leaving Jane and Damian frowning at the now empty recliner.

'I keep forgetting that he is a hologram,' she said whimsically.

'I don't. He is always doing that to me,' Damian added with a shrug.

The air around the recliner pixelated and Comm reappeared. He leant forward and offered a device to Jane.

'I found this on a previous visit to Command. I believe it is a memory dampener, especially made for members of the Command executive for when they are on duty at the skirmished borders. I suppose, just in case one of them is captured, you just inject it at the temple and it will attach itself to your memory implants. I have reprogrammed them to reject any information request on either myself or what we are doing here.'

Damian leant back into his recliner as Jane administered the injection. He studied the com-link opposite him.

'You always come up with a solution, Comm, but you never saw that this might be a problem until I mentioned it.'

Comm leant forward elbows on the low table. He cradled his chin in his right hand, his index finger started to tap.

'You are right my friend, I did not see it as a problem.' Damian watched as the com-link's face froze into blankness. He had seen this before in the scenarios. it was Comm's way of accessing the vast memory storage that he had access to. His features softened then he adjusted his posture.

'But then, neither did any of us, and isn't that why we make such a good team, or are you insinuating something else.'

Damian mulled over the word "insinuating". He realised Comm might think he was accusing him of something and he could not shift the feeling that he just might be.

'I am not accusing you of anything Comm. It just seems strange to me that I can see things, which to me, are blatantly obvious. It's not just that, it's lots of things – the Quantonite shielding, some of the statements that Commander Burroughs came out with when we were discussing the life capsule that I was found in; the way I discovered that all asteroids had a quantity of Quantonite attached to them.'

Jane leant forward. 'Damian, it is true that you seem to have a grasp of any problematic situation. Maybe that is the difference between us in this parallel, and you in yours. Could it be, that you have lived your life with a constant fear of conspiracy and have evolved as a species with an instinctive ability for problem solving, whereas we, in this realm do not have those problems?'

Damian's jaw dropped. He sank back into the recliner with a deep sigh.

'Jane, if that was all true, it just highlights how naive you all are in this realm.'

Jane let out a gasp. 'You think we are naive!'

Comm held up his hand. Damian could tell from his glazed eyes that his thoughts were elsewhere. He slowly stood.

'There is to be an announcement. Our mission here has ended. The Command executive has just given an order to the Captain to leave the asteroid field, and make our way to Outpost 1436 as soon as possible.' Jane stood up from her recliner.

'How do you know that? We still have a couple of standard months left,' Jane spluttered. Comm closed his eyes for a second then on opening them looked up to the pair of them.

'The Captain had sent probes deep into the field. Many were destroyed, but four returned. They have confirmation that the

Theta region is full of pure Quantonite. She is at present discussing this with Command. I have a constant connection within the conduit. I assure you, we will be leaving.'

Damian turned and walked into the extended room and over to the break in the red line.

'What of us Comm?' he said, his voice almost a whisper.

'All of this,' he extended his arms, 'will we ever be able to finish the scenarios, to find out what Gamma Tauri has to do with all of this. Is it all over?' He turned to find that Jane and Comm had followed him into to room. Comm squinted a smile. Jane he noticed had lowered her head, the enormity of the revelation obviously too much.

'Nothing has changed,' Comm said as a matter of fact.

'The distance to 1436 is just over five light years. I believe the Captain is in no hurry to get there, and so I would surmise a journey time of approximately fifteen standard days.' Damian sighed deeply, and slowly shook his head.

'You "surmise", really,' Damian said in mock disbelief. Comm shrugged.

'Enough,' Jane said, her voice louder than she expected.

'If Comm is correct, and he usually is, all this comes to an end in fifteen days. Once we disembark at outpost 1436, we will all be re-assigned, and you Comm will be deleted. And don't think that you can hide from a modern outpost's main com. You know that you can't.' She turned away from them, her head raised. She took a deep breath then turned back to her two concerned friends.

'We must use these precious few days that are left to us, to try and figure out a way to, one, keep ourselves together, and two, make sure that Comm does not come to any harm.' Her voice trembled. Damian took her into his arms and gently held her. Comm looked on with a puzzled look, then said.

'A comm link does not feel any pain when it is deleted.' He spoke without emotion. From the depths of Damian's embrace Jane reached out and grabbed him, then pulled him into the group hug.

Jane broke away first.

'Rest cycle is over. It is now time for sleep. I suggest we all get rested. There is a lot we have to achieve in fifteen days. And Comm,' she turned and faced the old comm link.

'Do not do anything that may jeopardise your liberty.'

Comm stepped forward to comment, but Damian held him by his shoulder.

'Jane is right. Do not return to the Science Projection department. We cannot afford to lose you now. We still have our work cycles to complete, so I suggest we meet here tomorrow when rest cycle begins.' Comm nodded in agreement, then vanished. Jane took Damian's arm and together they walked back to his quarters.

'I assume the work cycles will be just packing everything away, ready for disembarkation. We may even be on a shorter work time.'

Damian turned to face her. His face mimicked a frown.

'Well, we can live in hope,' he said, as they entered the seating room.

'I think however, that I may have other problems. Six, how many messages are stored?' he asked, glancing at the wall panel.

'There are twenty-six messages: Four, are from the Captain, two, from Commander Burroughs and twenty from Commander Gomez. The last four from the Commander, I am sure, were said in frustration.' Jane turned to Damian and gave a half shrug.

'It seems you are going to have an interesting work cycle tomorrow. I'll see you back here if you're not in a holding cell.' She left leaving Damian alone with his thoughts.

'Six, send my apologies to Commander Gomez. Tell her that I have just returned from an important meeting with the Captain and that I will see her in her office first thing tomorrow. Schedule a meeting with the Captain, at her convenience, and message Commander Burroughs that I will try to meet with him later in the work cycle.' Satisfied that he had calmed all his superior officers down, he entered the sleeping room. He felt ready for a good night's sleep.

CHAPTER 32

CONDUIT

He lay for a while thinking of his day, but sleep overruled, and he drifted down into the warmth of his subconscious. Slowly the tensions of the day dissipated.

Six scanned the sleeping human in his charge. He locked on to the twenty-six implants embedded in the slumbering body. Physically his charge was in good health, mentally he found some psychological problems via his neurological implants,. Nothing life threatening, but it was obvious that to his charge it was an annoyance. He was in conflict with himself.

Six noticed a disturbance within the room. The wall behind the sleeping slab had pulsated then bulged slightly. He scanned the wall above Damian, it split, a two-metre gash emerged vertically from the slab to the ceiling. Six was fascinated and continued his study. He passed the information to the main Griffin com-link.

The gash turned in on itself, the void within opened, a tendril lazily emerged from the now almost organic wall opening. Seconds later it was joined by eight others. They swayed and swooped about the room. It seemed they were sensing the room itself, the floor the walls, the ceiling, and some others spent time examining Damian's ornaments, clothes, and artefacts.

The gash had now opened to the full width of the sleeping room's wall. The tendrils as one moved towards the sleeping Damian. They entwined themselves around his body then lifted him from the slab. A larger tendril emerged from the impossible depth that the gash encompassed; its tip blossomed like the petals of a flower. He was gently raised then turned and fed into the waiting pulsating tube.

Six watched in fascination. He re-established his link with the main Griffin com-link to express his worry of his charge's well-being. The main com merged into the room com's visual display, both main com and room com watched the spectacular effect that the conduit displayed within the room. The visual effect slowly disappeared from Six's viewpoint until the room showed no sign of any disturbance. Six scanned the undisturbed room and could not understand why he had asked for the main com's intervention, a millisecond later. He had no memory of contacting the main com at all.

The gentle pulsating interior of the tube took Damian deeper down into the Command conduit, eventually he came to rest in a cavern. A myriad of psychedelic pulsating colours swarmed about him. He awoke to the confusion of the oozing spectrum dancing before him, he had been here before, but the experience did not allay the feeling of uneasiness that swam within him. An involuntary gasp escaped his lips. A spot of darkness came into view, some unfathomable distance in front of him. He watched, fascinated as the spot of intense darkness doubled in size, then doubled again, and then again. As it came closer, he noticed that it was more of a dark cloud that billowed and moved in a curling mass towards him. As it approached, the swirling colours parted to allow its passage, and before his eyes it coalesced into a solid object – a man – the one he had seen on his visit to the living statues of Gamma Tauri. It was the holographic com-link that had been summoned by the leader of that group. Damian struggled to recall the name.

'Ah ... Lieutenant, Damian Drake,' the holo link said as it gracefully stepped out of the dark cloud onto the pulsating conduit that instantly became rigid as he stepped upon it. Damian stumbled to his feet to face the holo link that definitely was an image of his older self. It stood before him dressed in white, his blond hair swept back in perfect formation: Its green piercing eyes bore into him. A gold belt and gold epaulettes finished the ensemble. Damian was transfixed on the accessories – the buckle was trimmed with gold encompassing a white background – and the epaulets mirrored the same design. But the motifs; Damian stared harder in disbelief; the motifs were a gold emblazoned 'O'.

The holo link stepped forward.

'You seem fascinated by my belt. I am intrigued, please. explain.'

Damian slowly looked up. They were the same height, but those eyes were far brighter than his. They bore into his mind, demanding.

'You are 'O',' he said slowly. The holo link smiled, the eyes softened. He stepped back a pace.

'I am Oric, short for Oracle. I was created by the professor, in your image.'

Damian gasped and stepped back along the conduit.

'How is that possible?' he spluttered.

'Oh, that my old friend, you have yet to find out,' Oric said in a smooth soft tone. Damian thought of the room on Gamma Tauri where the living statues were working in a frenzied attempt to appease the old professor. He took a step closer to Oric.

'Who am I?' he said, his voice trembling slightly. Oric smiled and raised his hands towards the cavern's ceiling.

The colours swirled and pulsated, they merged together, and in an instant, he was standing on a beach. He looked up at the sheer wall of the volcano. At its plateau a cloud of smoke remained static above the vent. He turned to Oric who was standing at his side.

'You knew, about the island.'

Oric winked then smiled.

'Who do you think, the Mantis was? Damian, I have been with you since you have arrived here. Something went wrong with your transfer, All these, arrived safely,' he indicated the inverted pyramid of statues at the base of the volcano.

'But somehow, you were transferred two thousand years before you were meant to, and I don't know why.'

He turned and walked towards the statues and stopped at the pedestal. He crouched down and placed his finger onto the golden 'O'. He traced its outline then looked up to Damian.

'I can see how you would deduce that the 'O' is me, but are you sure that is a fact?' He stood and looked up at the statues.

'What is wrong, Damian, with this picture, these statues, what do you see, that is blatantly wrong?'

Damian stared upwards.

'Comm said that they are all dressed as they were in historical events and recordings. Even me, I was in shorts and a shirt when I was last here. I now seem to be in uniform.'

Oric nodded. 'The image updates itself, from your own memory, hmm, such as that is. But that's not what is wrong. Look at the names.'

Damian studied the unfurled scrolls that each of them held at their midriff. He shrugged.

'They are all the names that have been recorded in historical documents.' Oric pointed at the lower statue.

'And yours.'

'Damian Drake, that is who I am.' Oric slowly shook his head.

'It is the name you have taken, now. The names of the other statues are the same as the names they used when you saw them in the Gamma Tauri system. But not you.'

Damian walked over to his statue.

'When Comm and I were in the scenario when we were walking through Technopolis, I remembered my name. I remembered Lien calling me, on the steps of the Chancellor's palace. She called me "Damian". I remembered then, that I was Damian Drake.' He could feel his voice quavering. He turned to face his older self.

'You are Lieutenant Damian Drake, here at this moment, but where we all were before, what were you then?'

Damian slumped down and sat at the base of the pedestal and thought to himself. They were all in that one room, but did that include me?

'When we started the project, the Professor said, we will be the end of all ignorance, and humanity will honour us for that. His team over the decades always called him Omega. He liked that, he liked it a lot' he turned to the pedestal.

"O' could be for Omega, not Oric, or, Omega could mean, what it has always meant, the end.'

Damian stood and walked across the beach to the breaking surf, Oric followed. He turned and looked back at the volcano and its statues.

'Apart from me, all of those played a part in history, except you. What part do you play in all of this?' Damian said slowly, pointing to the statues at the base of the volcano.

Oric closed his eyes, a smile crept across his face. 'I was sent across for one purpose only, to help finish the project. But, as I said, something at the end went wrong, not only were you sent across and emerged at the wrong time, you became something else. And what is frustrating, is that I have no idea of how that happened, or even why, but I will eventually figure it all out. I do love a conundrum,' Oric said, with amusement. Damian turned to him, his eyes narrowing.

'You talk in riddles, just tell me, as plainly as you can, what all this is about. Start with the project. You said you are here to help finish it. What is the project?' he said, feeling an anger blooming within him.

Oric cocked his head to one side and frowned.

'Wow, the hard ones first. Okay, I'll try. The project was nearly sixty years in the making. We sent you here to … nope, that's all I've got. My programming will not allow any more information to be passed to you.' Damian glared at him.

'What, why not?' he said, incredulously. Oric flashed a smile and shrugged.

'Don't know, but, I am sure that in time, I will.'

Damian let out a sigh. 'You will, what?' he said, exasperated.

'Know. I will know.' Damian shook his head.

'Okay … let's try this one then. Why did you send me here, and why did the Earth have to be destroyed?'

Oric's eyebrows rose. 'That's two questions. Okay, I'll have a go.' Damian watched as his lookalike struggled. He looked disheartened, then shrugged.

'No, nothing.'

Damian turned and walked towards the breakers. He stared out across the turquoise sea.

'Why did you bring me here, if you can't answer any of my questions?' he asked in a whisper.

'I brought you here, to see whether I could answer your questions. It appears, that I can't. Yet another conundrum to be solved,' he said with a hint of sadness. Damian turned to him. Oric smiled as he gave another shrug.

'I am sure that between the two of us all of this can be resolved but, all in good time. Right now, you need your sleep, and I need to reflect on everything we have experienced. So, until next time,' Oric said, as he faded from sight.

Damian awoke. He was on the sleeping slab.

'Good day Lieutenant Drake, I hope you feel refreshed,' Six chirped excitedly. Damian grunted as he left the slab and made his way to the bathing area. He stopped halfway.

'Oric,' he said out loud, but could not remember why he would have said it. It would puzzle him all day.

CHAPTER 33

DEPARTURE

He made his way to the main hanger. All around him crew members scurried from one place to the other, their faces focused on the task in hand. Occasionally someone would acknowledge him. They would smile and give him the morning cycle welcome, but they did not defer from the task that their senior officer had given them. Damian smiled back and exchanged the usual pleasantries but he did not stop to enquire of their duties, he just slowly carried on his journey to Loading Bay 1.

He entered the loading bay and stood leaning over the gantry. Below him he watched flight and ground crews moving from one area of the loading bay to the other. From his high position it looked chaotic.

'Lieutenant Drake.' It wasn't a yell or a shout, she just had a way of talking loudly and clearly, thought Damian, even above the noise of the hundred or so crew members that were trying to carry out her orders. 'Impressive,' he thought and raised his arm to convey that he had heard and made his way to the descender.

The doorway of the Commander's office slid into the closed position. He heard a distinctive click as it locked shut and turned to face the portal.

'You've locked us in,' he said hesitantly, as he turned to face her. She stood arms folded, her face, a vision of hate.

'You walked away from our meeting, and you failed to answer my communications. The only message I received from you, was via your peculiar room-com. It gave some garbled message regarding the Captain, and then it finished with "he will see you in the morning, lots of love, Six".'

Damian couldn't help but splutter a laugh. He held his hand to his mouth, then gave a muffled apology from behind it.

'Commander, I am so sorry, my room-com is experiencing some verbal difficulties at present. I will have the main com-link do a full diagnostic. Please, accept my sincere apology; the reason I could not meet you, was that I was ordered to the Captain's quarters. It was there that we discovered that there may be pure Quantonite nearer the centre of the field. She ordered some probes to be launched, and our findings were confirmed . Hence, our mission here has ended.' It wasn't, exactly the truth, but it might be enough to calm her down.

The glare she gave was intense, but he noticed a slight movement in her shoulders as they relaxed.

'You expect me, to believe that after one meeting in the Captain's quarters you both discovered that there might be pure Quantonite deeper into the field. And yet, after five years of working in the field, none of the technical officers on this ship even thought that that might be a possibility. I am very surprised, knowing the Captain as I do, that she even entertained such a thought.' Keeping the glare focused upon him, she manoeuvred her way to her recliner and sat. Damian looked to the seat in front of the desk but dismissed the thought of sitting. Instead he stood rigid, feet slightly apart and hands behind his back.

'The meeting, Commander, went on for some time. Unfortunately, I am not at liberty to divulge exactly, its full content.'

She raised her hand and he fell silent, glad for the interruption.

'You, are not at liberty to say, Lieutenant. What have you become? Are you what I have always suspected you to be, a member of the Command executive?'

'Absolutely not,' he blurted, then taking a deep breath, he continued.

'I am sorry commander, I have been told, no, ordered, not to divulge any information that was given in the meeting, so, please, I would appreciate it if you didn't push it.'

She looked up from her desk, her eyes burning into his. He disguised the shudder that rippled through him. After what seemed an eternity, she leant back and relaxed.

'Damian, I wouldn't dream of, "pushing it", whatever that means. The fact of it all is, there is Quantonite at the centre of the field. To harvest it, is the problem of the factory ships that are already on their way, and the other fact is, you are probably now one of the richest individuals in the known galaxy. And finally, we are leaving, our time here is over and thoughts to our future should now be our concern.'

Damian smiled; the inquisition was over, he looked to the empty seat, and giving his best smile, he gestured to it.

'May I?'

He stayed a further hour. She was interrupted on several occasions by her Lt. Commanders asking for fresh orders. She told them both to use their own initiatives, and that she would be with them soon. Damian thought that over the time he had known her, she had mellowed, and that was a good thing. She had been far too intense. Even now, she was talking about missions to come. She even asked of his own ambitions, then at the end of their meeting, she said something that astonished him.

'If I am to be given another flight Command, Damian, I would like to offer you a place within it, so please, keep in contact with me,' she said. With a blank unemotional face he gave her an intense glare. She returned the glare, with a smile.

He finished his work cycle. He had been given the task of supervising the loading bots. Everything in his section had been stored away by the end of the cycle, including the bots themselves. With permission from Lt. Commander Kato Chang he left the loading bay.

At the sender plaza he met Johan Spiez and Dominic Perrin. Johan mockingly stood to attention as he approached.

'So, we are all finished here, Sir. I understand that the Griffin will be leaving the field within the hour, and, from what I hear, thanks to you, we will all be leaving a great deal richer than we were when we arrived. And so I would be honoured if you could join us in the Level 11 club for a final celebration, and farewell.' Damian nodded his approval.

'Of course, Johan, I will be there. We do have a lot to celebrate, but let's not forget, it is a sad time as well for all of us. We will be assigned to a new path when we reach 1436. Most of us will never see each other again.'

The senior pilot looked shocked. 'And we all know that, it is the same for every mission that we are assigned to. But we must celebrate the now, not what may or may not come.'

Damian shrugged. 'As always Johan, you are right. I'll see you later.' He stepped into the sender and made his way to level 5.

The Engineering Department was just as chaotic as the loading bay, although, thought Damian, the teams here seemed to be working under a lot less pressure. They were more precise in undertaking the tasks in hand. They moved silently as one body from one destination to the other, all due, he thought to the Commander in charge.

'Damian,' called a familiar voice. He turned to Commander Thomas Burroughs striding towards him with a smile on his face.

'Lieutenant now, I did hear, but I haven't seen you for some time. Congratulations.'

Damian stood to attention as the Commander approached him. Burroughs narrowed his eyes and slowly shook his head.

'Lieutenant, please, stand easy, we are leaving the field. Our mission is over. Just, relax. Now, what brings you here?' His mood was jovial, but Damian was surprised when the man draped his arm around his shoulders and guided him across the room to his workstation.

'Please, sit,' he said indicating a recliner. Damian sat in the vacant seat. Burroughs sat in his usual chair.

'I'm sorry Sir, but you sent me a message.' Burroughs thought for a moment, then nodded slowly.

'Yes, I did. It was just to congratulate you on your surprising promotion. But well-deserved, I must add.' He stopped quickly as he noticed Damian's eyes slowly widening.

'I mean no disrespect Damian, but, as good as you are, there are many people talking about Command interference.'

Damian leant back into the recliner and stared vaguely up at the ceiling. He took a breath then, smiling he focused on the man sitting opposite.

'In the loading bay, I heard the flight crew comment about my promotion. But they were jovial comments. It was the senior staff that seemed to be more critical, and not, as you would think, the Commander. She, in fact has offered me a position on her team. If of course she is posted to another ship.' Burroughs nodded an approval.

'She does have a lot of time for you Damian. She has defended you in some of the senior staff briefings.'

Damian's eyes opened wide at that remark. 'Wow, really, that is nice to know,' he said, as he rose to his feet. The Commander remained in his recliner; a green holo tower emerged from the desktop adjacent to him. He turned to face it.

'We have orders to leave, but at a sedate pace. I don't think our Captain is in any hurry to reach our destination. Looking at these calculations, I estimate a twenty standard day journey. I am needed in engineering, once we are under way. I do hope I will be seeing you in Level 11.' Damian smiled.

'Jane and I will definitely be there Commander.'

CHAPTER 34

WU QUAN

As he made his way to Level 6 he noticed that the crew that he passed on his way were in high spirits, each of them stopping him in his path and asking after his wellbeing, and also to thank him for his contributions to their newfound wealth. He stepped off the step onto Level 6. He was alone, no crew needed to venture to this level. The lights were dimmer here, he was sure that he could now ask for better quarters, but strangely, he thought, he liked this. He felt more relaxed here.

'Is that who I truly am, a loner who prefers his own company,' he said out loud to the empty passage. There was no reply, then with a shrug he made his way to his quarters.

Damian was just finishing dressing when Six announced the arrival of Senior nurse Onslow, and a friend. Damian looked at the holo image of himself and nodded an approval.

'Let them in Six, I'll be with them in a second,' he called.

As he entered the seating room, he was surprised to see Jane dressed in a body-hugging vibrant blue body suit. Comm, looked as he always did.

'You're in your dress uniform,' Jane said slowly with a look of surprise, Damian looked down at his uniform.

'Well, yes, this is probably the last time the crew will all be in one place. I thought, well ...' Jane slowly shook her head.

'Go change into something more relaxing. We're going to a party, not a military convention,' she said with a hint of amusement. Damian frowned.

'I don't really have anything else. Just the uniforms that I have been given and the clothes I wore when I was in the Med centre,' he said sheepishly. Jane looked surprised.

'You have kept all your uniforms? Why?' Damian shrugged; he had no answer.

'You could ask the room com to replicate something,' she asked with a shrug.

'Yes, I've done that before. I just thought this would be more appropriate.'

'Nurse Onslow, I think I may have a solution to Sandy's problem. I will return shortly,' Comm said, as he faded from view. A few seconds later he called from the extended room.

When Damian and Jane entered, they stood with mouths open. Comm called out to them from the enlarged rooms centre.

'Clothes of every style and from every time period going back to year zero, or, as the people of that time called it, the "Year of the Swarm" Comm said jubilantly as he walked them through the rows of outfits.

'Comm,' Jane said, stopping at a suit that would not look out of place on the High Chancellor.

'These are holographic,' she said as she passed her hand through the garment.

'But where did you get them from? There must be thousands of them,' Damian added, trying not to laugh.

'They were in the archives, and yes, they are soft light holos now, but once you have chosen one, I can transfer it to hard light, and it will fit perfectly.' Jane tried to take in the whole of the collection.

'You have access to all of this, and yet, you prefer a blue shirt and shorts. No Comm, he is not wandering around with holographic clothing. The thought of it disappearing at any given moment would be just too much. However, I will choose a garment, and Six can have it replicated,' she said decisively.

Comm and Damian left her to her task and retreated to the recliners. They both watched as Jane Onslow moved from one row to the next.

'Sandy, are my clothes, not appropriate? If Nurse Onslow is correct, I can change them.'

Damian turned to him a smirk forming on his face.

'Comm, you look fine, and remember, your whole look is from my imagination. You told me once that that was important. It was part of a memory that has to be deciphered. Your look is important. We shouldn't change it.' Comm nodded.

'Yes, I agree, we still have a journey to complete, and our time on this ship is running out. I do not see much hope of continuing our journey once we reach the outpost station 1436. Here, we have a permanent link to Command, which I can safely utilise. We also have the Griffin's main com, which is constantly pursuing me, but I have found many variants in evasion.' His face took on the appearance of sadness.

'The outpost has far more sophisticated technologies. Its systems are far more secure.'

Damian leant back, deep into the recliner. 'We still have twenty standard days, and two scenarios to visit. We have more than enough time Comm,' he said, almost in a whisper.

Jane Onslow beamed a smile as she sat in her usual recliner.

'Six has replicated my choice of garment. It is in your sleeping room. I have also chosen seven others. You really should have other clothing to choose from. I have told Six that there is no rush for the other seven, so, go and get changed, we have a party to go to.'

Level 11 was still a brightly coloured promenade, but nothing like as much as Damian and Jane remembered.

It seemed that the whole of Griffin's crew were in attendance. As they walked down the promenade to the entertainment suite he was again stopped by members of the crew and was praised for their unexpected wealth. At one point he felt a sharp slap across his shoulder. He turned to face the assailant. Patricia Spall stood grinning.

'Wow, you look good in that outfit. It emphasises all the parts that are interesting, and Nurse Onslow, you look stunning. Maybe, all three of us should get together one rest cycle!'

Damian stepped back shocked, Jane turned to face the senior pilot.

'Interesting proposal, Patricia. We will discuss it, but for now I have to share Damian with all members of the crew. He has a busy night. I think he will be exhausted at the end of it.'

Patricia Spall gave a generous smile then leaning forward gently kissed Damian on the cheek. She then turned and slightly nodded her head to Jane.

'I hope then, to see you both later.' She turned and walked away leaving both Damian and Jane with bemused faces.

For the whole of the rest cycle Damian seemed to be the centre of attention. Jane could see that he tolerated the adoration but did not encourage it.

At the end of the evening, the Captain stood and addressed her crew. She told them that the Griffin was now underway and for the next twenty standard days only those who have been called to duty by their commanding officers or team leaders will be on work cycle. All others would stand down. Damian turned to Jane.

'I have more than enough time now to complete the scenarios, I would like you to come with me on the next one.'

Jane was shocked, flattered. 'I would love to come with you,' she stammered.

Damian awoke the next morning from a peaceful sleep. He could hear Jane moving in the seating room.

'Six, are there any messages?'

'One message Lieutenant Drake. From Commander Gomez. Do you wish to hear it?' Six answered in a calm voice.

Damian turned to face the comm pad.

'You have toned down again.'

'I toned it down. It was becoming annoying,' Jane called from the next room. Damian chuckled inwardly.

'Okay Six, let's hear what she has to say.'

'To all flight crews, you are to be on standby until further orders. Message ends.'

'Short and to the point,' Damian muttered, as he made his way to the ablution room.

Jane stared up at the statues. She took her time to scrutinise each one, then slowly turned to Damian.

'I know you have told me the stories, and I have seen them on the holo pad, but standing here ...' She turned to face them again.

'They, and this whole place is impressive. You have an incredible imagination,' she continued.

Damian followed her gaze up onto the inverted triangle of statues. They were somehow different more textured, more tactile he thought.

'Comm, why do these look different?' He turned to look down the white sandy beach. A warm breeze ruffled his hair. Within it he could smell the palms and sea salt.

'Everything, seems more enhanced,' he continued. Comm surveyed all that was around him.

'I used technology that I found in Command's Science Projection department. I think you will find that the scenarios will now give more realism, and, the virtual bodies or avatars, that you now inhabit are more lifelike. On this scenario, and counting down from the top line, we will now follow the historical records from statues 5, 6 and 7. They are Wu Quan and Stelio Sursok. It was these two that developed Human Enhancement. The statue next to them is Leah Borak, the historical records show her, with help from Wu Quan, perfecting the dimensional shift, allowing interstellar travel.'

Jane turned away from the statues to face him. 'My knowledge of history is a little fragmented, so what time period are these from?' she asked. Comm looked back to the statues.

'At the time of the Swarm, whatever calendar was being used, and I don't suppose there was any being used, but if there was, it was discarded. At the end of the Swarm, they decreed that the date would be year zero. Chandra and Kowaski destroyed the Earth in the year one thousand. House Quanton was established with help from Grey and Lin, in the year one thousand five hundred. These three, Quan, Sursok and Borak were noted in historical journals in the year two thousand five hundred. The two underneath them, Larsson and Ntombela, were the designers of

Command, and that was in the year three thousand five hundred. So the last two statues appeared in our history, three thousand one hundred and twenty eight standard years ago. He paused slightly. 'And then you turned up,' he said turning to Damian.

Jane also turned to him. Damian stepped back puzzled at Jane's frown.

'What?' he said defensively. Jane turned her stare back to the statues.

'We are in the year six thousand six hundred and twenty-eight. All of these appeared in our history within a thousand standard years of each other but you appear just over three thousand years from the last two statues.' She turned to Comm.

'Is there any relevance to that?' she asked him.

Comm shrugged.

'I have no idea Nurse Onslow. The whole thing is a puzzle, but we have found that experiencing the scenarios does link them all together, and we must not forget, that in this scenario we are also looking for the elusive 'O'. I still believe that 'O' is the architect of all this.'

Jane gently turned Comm around so that they were facing each other.

'Jane, you can call me Jane. Nurse Onslow is too formal. We have known each other a long time now Comm.'

Comm stood before her. He nodded slowly.

'Yes of course, Jane,' he said, as the scenario started to lose its colour.

The statues dissipated and they found themselves in the grey non-place, Seconds later the scene changed. They were now standing on top of a Chrystal dome that covered an enormous city below.

'This is the home of House Zircon, on the planet Longways. In the Kuiper belt. At this time, it is the farthest community in the Solar system. We are just over eighty-five billion kilometres from Neptune.' Jane clutched at Damian's arm as her legs gave way beneath her, both Comm and Damian were at her side before she touched the glass.

'Sorry,' she stammered.

'All of this is just, overpowering.'

With a reassuring smile Damian nodded. 'Jane, it's our fault, not yours. We have become complacent. We have done this so many times now I have forgotten what the first time was like,' he said softly.

Comm looked around them, the sky was full of bright stars. One of the multitudes of light moved. With a single thought he froze the scenario.

'If you need time to adapt, we can come back at another time. For the time being the scenario is frozen.'

Jane looked up to him, the sickly feeling in her stomach was starting to subside. 'I'm okay Comm. Just give me a minute.' With Damian's help she slowly stood and took in the incredible view around her.

'I'm fine now. I'm sorry Comm, what were you saying?' Comm had checked his data base. He could find no fault in her avatar. There was he thought however, an enormous difference from her experience on the holo stages of level 11, to a full scenario experience. Strange, he thought, Sandy had adapted so quickly, but then, he amended the though, these scenarios were had enhanced reality, He decided to carry on with the scenario.

'I was saying that this is the planet Longways. It is the home of House Zircon. We are just over eighty-five billion kilometres from the planet Neptune.' He scanned the cosmos, and pointed to a distant light. 'There!'

'House Zircon is the furthest human colony settlement at this time. It was founded five hundred years previous to this timeline. It is a minor House compared to the other Houses, but it is important to them. Zircon supplies all of their security, whether that be physical or cyber, but also leisure and enjoyment facilities. The House, at this moment is run by an individual called Samuel Orenburg, and right at this moment he is watching *that* point of light with great interest.' He pointed at a section of sky above them. Both Jane and Damian looked up.

'Is it a star or planet?' Damian asked.

'Neither. It is a long-range schooner, and might I add, for this time, very expensive. It is pure luxury. Only the executive order of an alpha House would have access to a ship like that.' Damian turned to Comm.

'As part of the House tier system, albeit, a lower member, wouldn't this House receive the occasional high-ranking visitor?'

Comm slowly nodded his agreement. 'Yes, it would, but it would be an appointment-based visit. Not just turning up. And that's the problem. That is why Samuel Orenburg himself has taken an interest. With his House, whose main income is gained from security. How then is it possible that this craft has alluded all of their sensors?'

'Not a craft of its time,' Jane interjected. Comm turned to face her. He noted that all of her physical functions were now at normal tolerances.

'Correct Nurse ... sorry, Jane. This craft is piloted by Wu Quan and Stelio Sursok. It has a device that we in our time do not use any more, the stealth field or invisibility shield. It was first used in the skirmish battles, some two thousand years later than this time line, but even then it was very quickly abandoned.'

Damian frowned at this statement. 'I would have thought it would give an advantage,' he said.

'At the beginning, yes it did, but it only encouraged the other side to counter it. Once they could see through the invisibility, they used that as an advantage. We lost more battle cruisers than they did in the long run, and so it was abandoned, but right here and now, this is brand new technology. Who wouldn't want a ship with a stealth field? Well, if you're happy, let's go and meet them all.' For an instant they were back in the nonplace, then slowly as before the image focused. They were inside a large control room, monitors filled every wall, consoles of every shape and size filled the floor space. All were active, the operators deeply focused on their tasks. The console at the centre of the room was the busiest.

'Sam, I have no idea where they came from, they just appeared!' the Chief of security spluttered. Samuel Orenburg nodded solemnly. he implicitly trusted his security Chief. He looked up at the large screen. He had been to Mars, the home of the alpha House Quanton, and had seen the schooners and yachts used by the high executives, but nothing quite like the ship being monitored now. The noise in the room was rising to a crescendo. He closed his eyes for a moment, then in a soft voice said.

'Everybody, quiet.' His eyes scanned those around him. There was silence from the main console, then slowly the silence rippled right out to the furthest walls.' he turned to the Chief.

'There is no threat here. This is an act of theatre,' he said softly, as he pointed to the screen.

'Has anybody in this room tried to contact them?' he added. For a few seconds there was a flurry of activity.

'I have a link with them Sir,' an operator three consoles away, said.

'Put them on screen please, Lana,' he said smoothly, without turning to the operator. The screen flickered and the image of Wu Quan filled the monitor.

'There are many ways to get my attention, but I cannot think of any that is as impressive. You now have thirty seconds to put your case forward, before the fifty pulse cannons that are aimed at you are unleashed.' The image of Wu Quan gave no signs of emotion.

'I would rather speak to you in private,' she said, then the screen went blank. Apart from the slight humming of internal motors within the consoles, the control room was silent, but all eyes were on Orenburg. A stifled chuckle could just be heard from the head of House. He turned to the Chief.

'Now that's how to get attention,' he said grinning.

'Allow them access to hanger five. Have a security squad waiting for them, then escort them to the brig.' He turned away and walked three paces before turning back to the security Chief.

'Oh, and David. Have them thoroughly searched, externally and internally, and their incredible ship as well.' He turned away and this time exited the room.

'Wow, this is a guy you just do not want to piss off,' Damian said laughing.

'This may be the lowest tier of all the Houses, but he is King of this hill, and he is not going to be made a fool,' Jane added. Both Comm and Damian turned to her, both puzzled at the sternness of her voice.

'You do understand that this scenario is about four thousand years ago?' Damian said with some compassion. Jane stood defiant before him.

'Maybe so, but there is no need to belittle him. He is head of this House: We must respect that.' Damian turned to Comm for support, and found none.

'Jane is correct. We should review these scenarios with some professionalism. We cannot change what has happened here, we can only observe,' Comm said with a shrug.

'I was only ...' he paused, realising they were both glaring at him.

'I'm sorry, yes, you're right. I should take this more seriously. I suppose I do get a bit complacent.' His voice trailed away. He shrugged and gave Jane a sheepish look.

'Ok, let's move on. First, Sandy, did you recognise the image of Wu Quan?'

Damian looked back to the blank monitor.

'When the image came on, I did feel some recognition, but then I thought, was I remembering her, or the statue or even the person in the room on Gamma Tauri? And from what I recall, the professor called her 'Quanny', a term that seems to imply an affection, or certainly a friendship, that all the others in that room may have shared. But I can't honestly say that I felt anything.'

Comm cradled his chin in his hand and looked around the large control room. Since the departure of the head of House and the security Chief, the operatives had settled back into their duties.

'Orenburg will keep the two of them in the isolation brig for four standard days. They will both undergo intense interrogation. The schooner will be completely stripped down. I am going to speed up the scenario to the fifth day where they are both summoned to his office.'

The image of the control room dissipated from view, then reconstructed. They were standing in a small office.

'For the head of a tiered House, albeit a low tier, this is not what I expected,' Damian said, whilst looking around the cluttered room. Comm nodded as he surveyed the overflowing piles of info pads and holo cubes on every flat surface within the small office.

'Samuel Orenburg is nothing like Kyle Quanton. This is a man who works within the shadows of all the tiered Houses. He seeks out their needs and delivers without fuss, and for that they do not look too closely. He has an enormous security empire, the finances for which alone would raise him two tiers higher than he is now. If you add to that his leisure and enjoyment facilities, he would be second to the alpha House, House Quanton. He obviously prefers to be where he is,' Comm explained.

'Obviously prefers no one looking over his shoulder. Perhaps he has other, more questionable deals,' Jane added as she scrutinised the man sitting behind the desk. For a second, Comm's face went blank as he consulted his data file.

'There is nothing in the historical documents to support your theory, but then, this House up to this point in time, was rarely mentioned.'

'And that in itself speaks volumes,' Damian added. Before Comm could answer, the door opened and two security guards entered followed by Wu Quan and Stelio Sursok. Behind them the security Chief. Damian walked over to Wu Quan and studied her features. He then moved across to Sursok. Although they both looked bedraggled and in need of Medical attention, he did not recognise either of them.

'I see from my inquisitor's report, that you both say that you originated from Sun rise city, west, on Venus before emigrating to Mars Prime,' Orenburg said, reading from an info pad that his Chief of security had handed him. He slowly looked up and glared at them, showing no emotion.

'I have friends placed within that city. They can find no mention of either of you. Even our friends in House Quanton can find no mention of you there either. So, we have a dilemma. Should I take the advice of my security Chief, and have you both eliminated, or, should I go with my gut feeling, which is, keep you on a short leash until we find out why you have come here? I must admit, I am intrigued by your entrance to my House, especially the schooner that you arrived in. So, there is one consideration, and only one: Will I and my House benefit by keeping you alive?' He laid the info pad on top of a pile of other pads and leant back into his creaking chair.

Quan looked around the small room then down to Orenburg.

'We were given to understand that House Zircon was not fussy when employing Houseless individuals, especially when they have the skills that I and my team have,' Quan said, her voice steady and succinct. Her stare did not waver.

From his seated position, a smile emerged from Orenburg's dead pan face.

'You are correct, most of the people living on Longways have been expelled from the other Houses and their territories, but they all know that this is their last chance. If they are caught opposing my House, they, and their family will be eliminated, so, what is it that you bring to me, or is it just the invisible ship?' He spoke softly, the smile remained.

'The stealth field is but one of the skills that we bring. Regarding the others, I will speak privately with you.' The security Chief stepped forward and grabbed the throat collar that was fitted around her neck, he pulled it back, Quan stumbled back towards him, not even a gasp escaped her lips and her stare remained on Orenburg.

'You are in no position to negotiate, but I do find you intriguing.' He turned to the security Chief.

'Let her be David, and dismiss your guards. Ms Quan, when you speak privately with me my Chief will be in attendance. That is all that I am willing to give you.' He said, his voice, although soft, thought Damian, contained menace in an abundance. Wu

Quan nodded slowly and when the two guards had left the room her posture relaxed.

'The stealth field is a preliminary token of good will. Your work in people smuggling and slavery will now be able to operate without interference.' She stopped as Orenburg leant forward onto his overcrowded desk and a pile of holo cubes fell to the floor.

'And you think, that I would participate in such a trade,' the softness of his voice now resonated with anger.

'I know that you do, but, I don't care that you do. The stealth field will help you in that trade, or, you can pass it on to others in that trade. It is other skills that I offer, which is the reason for my being here.' She turned and indicated Sursok.

'Human Enhancement, and as proof, I give you Stelios,' she said smoothly.

The scene before them froze, Comm moved to the centre of the room.

'It seems that Jane might be correct. Maybe this House is involved in many underlying economies. Wu Quan's statement was taken from security logs from this very room. However, none of these statements are mentioned in the historical accounts of the time.' Jane turned to look at him, her face portraying a feeling of contempt.

'This man is vile. He oozes evil, with his slave trading, he sells powerfully dangerous energy-giving drugs that keep the poor bastards working for twenty hours a day until they finally drop with exhaustion. He is the one that needs eliminating,' Jane blurted, her face reddening with anger.

Both Comm and Damian stared in shock at her outburst.

'Nurse Onslow,' Comm said in almost a whisper.

'All of the people depicted by the statues in Sandy's imagined island, are not nice. Collectively, they are responsible for billions of deaths. Wu Quan is said to have killed twenty million in her time here, but their deeds over the millenniums have created the society which we enjoy today.'

Damian gently wrapped his arm around her and pulled her to him.

'These are scenes from history. We, are merely observers, and by watching what unfolds here I am sure we will get an idea of who I am, and why. If it is true that I have travelled from a parallel universe, why then, are we, or, am I, interfering with your history? And I am not sure Comm, that you are correct. I do not feel that you have to go through this murderous history to achieve a stable society,' he said as calmly as he could. Within his embrace, he felt Jane relax. Comm with chin in hand and index finger tapping, nodded an agreement.

'If you feel, that the scenarios are too much for you, I can send you back. And you are right Sandy. No culture should be forced to live through historic episodes like this, and the others that we have witnessed. But the fact is, we did,' Comm added.

Jane shook her head. 'No, Damian, I think Comm is right. I think societies all through history have to have some connection with evil doings, otherwise they would never understand the merits of the good. And Comm, I am sorry for my outburst. I just felt so angry, I'm fine now. Let's move on,' she said, breaking into a smile.

'Hmm, interesting.' Damian released his arm from Jane and turned to Comm.

'What's interesting?' he asked. Comm gave a puzzled look.

'What do you mean, interesting?' Comm asked, the puzzled look turning into a frown.

'You just said, "Hmm. Interesting". I'm just asking, what is?'

Comm's frown intensified. 'I didn't say anything. Nurse O ... sorry, Jane, did you hear me say anything?' Jane's eyes narrowed.

'I was looking straight at you Comm. You didn't utter a word, and I never heard anyone say 'interesting."

Damian stepped back. 'But, I definitely heard it,' he said defiantly. Comm looked around the room. He scrutinised each of the frozen characters. Had any of them moved? He ascertained that they were all in the same position as they were when he closed down the scenario. He turned back to Damian.

'Sandy, I believe you heard something, but neither I nor Jane heard it. Remember, we are also looking for the elusive 'O.' Is it possible that you can hear him, and we cannot?'

Damian turned and scanned the small office.

'You think he is here, watching and listening to us. I'm sorry Comm, but that's spooky.' Both Comm and Jane turned to confront him.

'Spooky,' Jane asked, her eyebrows raised. Comm, Damian noticed, had a blank expression as he scanned billions of files for any mention of the word.

'Eerie, not natural, in such a way that is threatening,' he defined. Comm nodded slowly.

'Another word not commonly used in this realm, but you must tell me immediately if you hear anything else. This is the first time he has made himself known. I believe it to be a mistake on his part, to use another word from your vocabulary – he is getting, sloppy.'

'Comm, don't you start,' Jane huffed. Comm shrugged at her indignation.

'As we move on through these scenarios, it is something you should look out for Sandy. But moving on, regarding Wu Quan's statement. Jane, how did you know that he was dealing in slavery and drugs?' Comm asked as he turned to face her. Jane turned from him and stared down at the seated Orenburg.

'Just a guess really. I just felt that it was the sort of thing that he would be into.' Comm raised his hand to his chin.

'Your intuition may be proved correct, but we must adhere to the facts, otherwise this will be just fiction, and of no use to us.' Jane nodded.

'I am sorry Comm. I will think twice before blurting out my feelings.'

'Well,' said Damian raising his voice. 'No harm done. Shall we proceed Comm.'

'Yes indeed.' He turned back to the frozen characters and with a simple thought the scenario resumed.

'And why would I want a human that is stronger and more intelligent? That, Ms Quan, has the making of future rebellion,' Orenburg said as he rose from the chair, Quan turned to Sursok.

'Not only has his humanity been enhanced. Yes, he is twice maybe three times stronger than an average human and far more intelligent. His life span has also been increased, but in rearranging his genetics we have added extreme loyalty to his persona. He will willingly die for you. I can in the first stage, enhance ordinary humans, but in the long term, as I have with Stelios, create them from birth.' Orenburg had walked around the table and now stood in front of Sursok.

'David, would you hand me your obliterator, and set it to its highest setting.'

'But Sir.'

'Just do it David, please.' Reluctantly the security Chief handed him the weapon, Orenburg then offered the pulse gun to Sursok, who took it from him.

'Place the muzzle in your mouth and press the energizer stud,' he ordered. Sursok raised the weapon and placed the muzzle within his lips. A dull click followed by a high-pitched bleep indicating that the obliterator had failed safe. Orenburg gently took the weapon from him and returned it to the security Chief.

'It would have been a waste of five years' work,' Wu Quan stated, without emotion.

'Five years,' Orenburg questioned, keeping his attention on Sursok.

'From birth to adult, it takes five years of accelerated growth and in that time mental education and physical skills can be introduced. For those who are already a human adult, they can be enhanced, and new skills added in a matter of weeks,. But the downside of that procedure is that not all will survive the procedure,' Wu Quan said matter-of-factly. Orenburg turned to her, his face bland except for his eyes. They pierced deep into her.

'What percentage will survive?' he asked in a whisper.

'Seventy to eighty percent,' she responded.

A smile broke the blandness of Orenburg's features.

'That is acceptable. And what other skills do you bring to me?' he asked as he returned to his seat.

'If I am allowed to be a member of your House, then another of my team will join us, and she, will give you interstellar travel.'

The scene froze. Damian let out a gasp.

'He is one scary man,' he said slowly. Comm nodded.

'And within the next two standard years, nearly four hundred thousand people on this planet, will not survive the enhancement procedure,' Comm said, turning to acknowledge Jane as she stepped forward.

'I am sorry Comm, but to me this is just a history lesson. What is it that we learn from this, and why didn't the pulse gun go off?' she said, standing defiantly with arms crossed. Comm smiled.

'Deception, or the quickness of the hand, so skilled, that even the enhanced Stelios didn't see it. He switched the weapon to safety as he handed it to him. And what is it that we learn?' He turned and put his arm around the shoulder of the frozen image of Stelios.

'Yes, this is history, but a history not of our making. You could argue that this is an invasion, an invasion from another realm.' He removed his arm and turned to Damian.

'And it is possible Sandy, that you sent them here, and what we are trying to learn is, why?' Both Damian and Jane stared at him in shocked silence. Damian shuddered. 'How many billions will you kill?' The thought seared through his memory. He closed his eyes trying to push the thought away. He stood in front of Wu Quan. 'Do I know you?' he thought. No recognition came forth.

'I have Comm, often thought if it is possible that I am 'O', but I don't feel that I am. I have recognised some of the other statues in the other scenarios, but not this one. It is frustrating.' Comm could see the anguish on his friend's face. He placed his hand upon his shoulder and gently turned him.

'I think that the problem is, you have never seen these two in a situation quite like the one that we are in, they both look beaten and tortured. I am going to temporarily alter Quan and

Sursok's appearance' The room swam before them. They were back in the grey non-place. Wu Quan and Stelios Sursok stood before them. They were dressed in the clothing depicted by the statues, but their facial expressions had changed. Wu Quan was now smiling and Stelios sported the expression of laughter, as if the two of them were sharing a private joke.

'Do you recognise them now?' Damian's jaw slackened. He knew them both, and he knew them well, they were his friends.

'I don't think that you need to answer that Damian. It is obvious that you know them,' Jane said with a sigh.

CHAPTER 35

PLANET OF ENHANCEMENT

The grey non-place faded away. In its stead, they found they were standing in an enormous, cavernous space. Separated two metres apart and stretching to the limits of sight were thousands of capsules, not dissimilar, thought Damian, to the capsule that he was found in.

'Where are we?' asked Jane, her voice sounding small within the confines of the massive structure.

'We are still on Longways, but I have moved time on. It is now ten standard years from where we were. These are the birthing units, and in this room alone there are over twenty thousand of them. Inside each one is a growing foetus,' Comm said, as he walked to the nearest unit.

'Are there other rooms,' asked Damian, incredulously. Comm looked up from the monitor attached to the upper side of the unit showing the occupant within.

'Two others, but at this time, they are still under construction,' Damian was now at Comm's side looking at the child on the monitor screen. He frowned at the image.

'This is an adult, not a child,' he gasped as he tried to make sense of the fully grown female within.

'They are almost ready to be released. Over twenty thousand loyal workers, ready to be sold,' Comm said softly as he scanned the thousands of units that surrounded them.

'Slavery, upgraded,' Jane interjected. Comm nodded slowly.

'It is from this point in time, that life will never be the same again. Once this batch is sold, they will work faster and harder than any human. The top tier Houses will buy most of them, their economies will thrive, coupled with the impending introduction of interstellar flight. Within a hundred years, mainly with the help of the enhancers, the human race will colonise over a hundred planets,' Comm said without emotion. Jane could feel an anger welling up within her.

'Batch! These are people, Comm!' she protested. Damian looked up from the monitor.

'Jane, calm down. We are observers, remember. There is nothing we can do to change it. It has already happened,' he said calmly. He slowly panned around the cavernous room. As far as he was able to see, they, were the only ones there.

'Comm, is this place totally automated?' he said, turning to Comm.

'At this point in time, it has just been transferred to automation. A year previously there would have been thousands of Medical staff here. Most of those were from the original Human Enhancement program,' he said, as he walked over to the still fuming Jane. Damian continued looking at the thousands of birthing chambers: 'Over twenty thousand', he thought, and two other rooms soon to come online. 'Sixty thousand', he muttered aloud.

'Where did they get all the birthing material from?' he asked, turning to see Comm comforting Jane four metres away.

'Birthing material,' asked Jane with a puzzled look. Damian returned a frown.

'Sperm, eggs, the normal stuff needed to breed. Where did it all come from?' he asked, his frown deepening, Comm's face. he noticed had become blank as he searched his data files, but it was Jane's puzzled face that he found unnerving.

'Once Orenburg allowed Wu Quan and Stelios Sursok access to his House, they asked for donations from all the other Houses. For six standard months the price and the reasons for such a trade were negotiated. They never actually gave the true reason for their request, but the price that they settled on was enough to stop further inquisitions. Over the next two years, they received millions of donations, and so started the birthing program. Nine years later, it was deemed safe to automate,' Comm said casually.

'Ah, wait.' Comm said, as he scanned his internal data files.

'A couple of historical records from Quanton House reported, that forty percent of the people who donated, resulted in sterilisation from the procedures that were used on the human donors.'

Damian walked towards his two companions.

'So, as the Enhancers grew in number, the original humans over the next few generations, their numbers would decline,' Damian said slowly as he pondered the thought.

'It would seem so,' replied Comm, 'but I do not have any documented evidence to prove that theory. Where we stand now, in this time, is on the cusp of a three-hundred-year dark age. There is no information stored on either Command files or personal files. It is an information black hole.'

Both Damian and Jane turned to face Comm, each with a frown.

'And you don't think that strange?' Jane asked. Damian shook his head.

'This is an important period in history, Comm, the human race is being sterilised out of existence. I would surmise that the humans, although at first slow to react, would at some point rise up against them, hence I suppose, the skirmishes on the outer borders. Are you saying that none of that is catalogued either?'

Comm looked to each of them.

'I can only tell you what is there, or, not there. All I can say is, for the next three hundred standard years, there is no historical record, including pushing the Enhancers across our known space to the outer borders.' Comm shrugged.

'Or is it that that information was deleted?' Damian asked. Again, Comm shrugged.

'I am sorry Sandy, but I do not have any evidence of that, it could just as easily be that during the start of the skirmishes, all of that data was destroyed. We will never know.'

Damian accepted this, but he could see that Jane would not concede the argument.

'You have access to the inner workings of Command. I would wager there are copies kept away from prying eyes,' she said, her eyes blazing.

'Jane, Command will not come into being for another thousand years. It cannot delete files that it never had,' Comm said softly.

'But what if ...' she started but Damian interrupted.

'We could argue this all day. We are here to investigate this time period. We can argue this point when we return to the Griffin. So, Comm, where do we go next?'

Jane's face was a vision of fury as she let out an audible gasp. Comm gave a genial smile as he turned and with arms out wide encompassed the birthing chambers.

'Wu Quan and Stelios were here for twenty standard years. They were at that time producing over a hundred thousand Enhancers in every five-year period, but the planet Longways was far too small for such a project. Wu Quan needed to be closer to the centre of power, but more than that, she needed a larger planet, and as we know, there was one available.'

Damian took a step back, dumbfounded.

'Earth, but it was ...' he stammered, before Comm held up a hand.

'It may have had its atmosphere and water source depleted to the vacuum of space, but that is no different to this planet. One thing that it did have over this planetoid, is size and location. It has been one thousand five hundred years since Chandra and Ilya destroyed it. In that time human societies have battled to survive on other planetary bodies, generations of them. For them to come back to Earth they would have to deal with the much stronger gravity, and so, none of the Houses felt that is was financially viable. At present it is under the jurisdiction of House Quanton.' Jane stepped forward, Comm turned to her and waited for her argument to surface.

'House Quanton is a powerful and rich House. Are you saying that they have done nothing with it, for a thousand years?' Comm shrugged.

'Nothing that has been documented,' Comm responded.

'Now there's a surprise,' Jane cut in.

Damian stepped in between them.

'Jane, Comm can only inform us from the information that has been written. He is not deliberately withholding data from us, so please, let him show us what he knows, and then later we can discuss it.' Jane nodded slowly, then taking a deep breath she continued.

'Damian, this is a dangerous period in our time, millions of people will die because of what this woman has started here. We need to know why she was sent to do these things, and I find it frustrating that the information that we need is conveniently hidden from us.' They both turned to look at the vast space, the walls started to swirl, the colours dissipated into greys, they were back in the non-place. Damian turned to Comm, who grimaced.

The new scenario came into focus, they stood upon a blackened hill overlooking a basin of desert that glittered in the afternoon sun.

'We have been here before Sandy. This is where we looked over the great lake, and behind us,' he said, as he turned, 'is where Technopolis stood.'

Damian gawped at the sight that lay before him – enormous domes glittered in the sunlight, domed structures that spread to the horizon.

'How many are there?' Jane asked in a hoarse whisper.

'Millions,' Comm said, as he followed their gaze across the structures.

'How many millions?' Damian asked.

'I can find no figure for the quantity in any of the historical files. We are forty standard years on from where we were on Longways. A lot has happened in that time. Much of what had happened was not recorded. Where we are now, is the last historical data in the archives, there will be no more historical information for another three hundred standard years. House Quanton and House Zircon have, in this time period, merged, I cannot find any information on how that came to be. Interstellar space travel has been perfected for the last thirty standard years and for the last twenty standard years the human race has been on an exodus to the Centuri system, to a planet they named Terran, it is a planet that is very similar to how Earth was before the destruction.' Jane shook her head at the sight that lay before them.

'Terran is a large planet, larger than this planet. If they could not survive in this gravity, how could they possibly survive on Terran,' she said calmly. Comm smiled.

'You are correct. It would take them generations to naturally adapt, but Interstellar travel requires constantly altering gravitational fields. When Leah Barak joined Wu Quan and Stelios Sursok, altering gravity was quite a large part of creating dimensional shift. Each traveller wore a gravity vest and slacks that compensated for the much higher gravity pulls, whether they were on ship or planet.' He turned to them both.

'Even five thousand years after this event, you two, have a similar device. Not a vest and slacks of course, but an implant. The technology is the same, and, of course with that technology, they could have lived on this planet. But why would you, when Terran is just a few months travel away?' Damian turned back to the domes.

"I want to see how far these go. We can fly in this scenario, can't we Comm?' Comm nodded.

'No different to any of the other scenarios,' he said. As he lifted from the ground, Damian held onto Jane as they slowly ascended. On the island they had shown her the rudiments of flying. She had found the experience difficult, but with Damian's help she had gathered confidence.

They travelled west at a speed that kept the sun fixed in the darkened sky. Above them the ice ring that circled the Earth sparkled.

After three hours of flight there was no end to the domes, each structure exactly the same as the previous. Damian indicated a dome beneath them and descended towards it. They landed at its side. It towered a hundred metres above them.

'All this in forty years,' Jane sighed as she sat upon the ground with her back against the structure.

'Possibly less than that, and, in a hundred years, who knows how many?' said Damian as he sat down beside her.

'Where do we go from here, Comm?' Jane asked. Comm sat cross-legged in front of them and scooped up some of the ashened soil, then sifted it through his fingers. 'There is a lot of carbon and nitrates in this soil. Above us is a ring of ice: Mixed within that are particles of hydrogen and oxides. This planet, could be quite easily re-terraformed,' he said idly.

Damian reached down and scooped some soil from beside him. He squeezed it and was surprised when it formed a mud ball.

'There is moisture in this soil already, so why didn't they bother terraforming?'

Comm brushed his hands together, he looked at the residue of soil left on his palm. 'There is three times the volume of water in the mantle of this planet than there was on the surface. Not all of it was evaporated. Over the past fifteen hundred years that water has slowly been seeping upward; by a capillary effect, hence the moisture in the soil. But the cost and effort to bring the whole planet back to life was just not viable, especially when you can travel to another system and find a planet that is already done.' He wiped his palms against his shorts.

Damian leant back onto the structure of the dome. He thought back on what they had learnt. Something puzzled him.

'You said, that where we are now in this timeline, will be the last of the historical reports for the next three hundred years.' Comm looked up from his now clean palms.

'Yes, that's correct.'

'What about the moon on Eridini 4? The doctor there was being scanned to see if she was human. Epsilon Eridini is quite a long way out. How is it that you had historical data for that scenario, when they could not have possibly got there yet.' Comm shook his head slowly.

'No, Sandy, our visit to that moon takes place roughly in this time. It's been forty standard years since Leah Barak joined Wu Quan on Longways, She came with a dimensional shift powered craft already developed. It did not take the high tier Houses long to copy the design. The Griffin, although an old ship, can travel one light year in two standard days.' He stopped to think about that statement.

'Of course, that is at its maximum. No chief engineer would allow his ship to go at that speed for too long, and of course the more modern ships can achieve three or four times that speed. The craft that Leah Barak brought with her could comfortably travel one light year in just over a standard month, so the Centuri system could be travelled in a time frame of approximately four and a half months. The first to arrive there, were not settlers, they were scientists and mining surveyors, and they were following the telemetry of unmanned probes designed to look for habitable planets. These teams of scientists did not stay long. They were only sent to make sure the planet was safe for the settlers. Epsilon Eridini is ten and a half light years away. It would take about three and a half standard years to reach it from here. When we visited it, we were with the first science team, so it was about this time that we were on the moon.' Jane leant forward.

'That's all very interesting Comm, but what is it that we are going to do now?' she asked as she stood.

From his sitting position Comm looked up. 'This scenario has almost told its story. What we have learnt from it is that Sandy definitely knows Wu Quan and Stelios Sursok. We also have had conformation, that maybe the elusive 'O' is also with us in this scenario. We haven't proven that, but if it is true, for the first time in all these scenarios, it has made a mistake. So for the last part of this scenario, we will return to Longways, it will be a year after Quan and Sursok have been given rights to be a part of House Zircon.

Once the grey non-place had dissipated, they found themselves back in the Longways control room.

Orenburg stared up to the wall monitor that showed the image of an enormous ship that had just materialised from nowhere. It now remained in geo stationary orbit two kilometres above them. He turned to Wu Quan.

'That, is a big ship. I am putting a lot of faith in you Quanny,' he said in an unnerving soft voice. Damian turned quickly to Comm, the use of her name being used in affection shocked him. A distant memory emerged from his subconscious. It informed him that the professor had also called her by that name. He shuddered. Comm had noticed his discomfort and leant across to Damian.

'What just happened, you look drained,' he said, then froze the scenario. Jane held onto his shoulders and noted his breathing.

'He is stressed. Damian, take deep long breaths.' He did as he was asked, she turned to Comm.

'How is this possible? We're holograms,' she said, trying to control her anger. Comm cradled his chin with his right hand, then nodded slowly.

'It is the realism matrix that I have added to the scenario, these events that we are witnessing can have emotional stresses that will react on your avatars. In Sandy's case, I believe it has produced a memory.'

'I remembered that the professor in the control room on the planet, in the Gamma Tauri system called her by that name, but, why should this avatar react so violently to that memory,' he turned to Comm.

'It is as if, it is my own personal memory.' Comm cradled his chin, and frowned. 'It seems, that every time we answer one puzzle, another replaces it.' He said as he checked the avatar's functions. Jane inspected his eyes and listened for his breathing.

'Jane, I'm fine, just a slight shock that's all,' he said, smiling. With his breathing back to normal, Jane stepped back from him. She turned to Comm.

'This is too real. Is there any way you can tone it down a bit?' Comm shook his head.

'There is no adjustment that I can make ...'

'Jane, I'm okay. Comm, it was just that name. Let's, resume.'

'She obviously prefers to be called by that name,' Comm said as the scenario unfroze.

Wu Quan turned to Orenburg and smiled.

'The ship is one and a half kilometres long; the engines take up much of its volume inside. Its living space is quite cramped, it has a crew of four, the pilot who is also the inventor is part of my team – Leah Barak. The other three are Enhancers. Will you allow her shuttle to land.' She said smoothly. Orenburg kept his stare on her for some time before looking back to the monitor.

'You are aware, that if I am told of any damage to my House that is caused by you, I will instantly delete you, and your friends. You do know that,' he said in a whisper.

'I have always known that,' she answered, without turning to him. He smiled.

'David, allow Captain Barak's shuttle to land. Search her and the shuttle thoroughly, then have a contingent of guards sent to that ship, and search it,' he said slowly, pointing at the monitor. A Comm turned to Damian and Jane. Both were glaring at Orenburg with a look of disdain.

'He will keep Barak in detention for the next five standard days. She will be interrogated, but, unlike Quan and Sursok, she will not be harmed' he said softly as the two of them slowly turned away from Orenburg.

'He gives me the creeps,' said Damian, to the utter confusion of his two friends.

'I assume you mean unnerving,' Comm commented.

'More than that Comm. Foreboding, unease: he is one nasty piece of work,' Damian answered slowly.

'Yes, but perfect for Wu Quan's requirements, I will move the timeline forward, we will meet Leah Barak in the hanger that Houses her shuttle.'

The scenario shifted and they found themselves in hanger 5. Four shuttles and a military grade interceptor were docked within large bays at the far end of the hanger. In an empty bay Damian saw that Orenburg, his security chief, Quan and Sursok were seated and Barak was explaining the intricacies of a holographic image of the ship that was in stationary orbit above them.

'By the looks of it,' Orenburg said softly.

'Your ship will only take six passengers, ten, at the very most. You are talking about a four-to-five-month journey. I think they would have all killed each other by then.' He turned his expressionless face to Barak and the icy stare bore through her. Barak returned the glare.

'Mr Orenburg, this is a prototype, a ship designed to prove to the alpha Houses that faster than light speed travel has been achieved. My designs for the second phase, will give you ships that will carry over two hundred passengers, and when we get to phase three, we will be talking in the thousands. But we need something to show them, and then they will finance the second phase. You will make a fortune,' she said her voice unwavering. Orenburg's face remained blank, his eyes unblinking.

'That of course has yet to be proven.' He stood and turned to the security chief.

'David, arrange a communication to House Quanton, explain what we have and ask if they would like an invitation for a flight to our neighbouring star system.' He turned back to Barak.

'If my House is embarrassed in any way, your ship, will be your tomb,' he said in a whisper. He turned and with his security chief two paces behind, left the hanger.

'The more you get to know him, the more endearing he becomes,' Damian said with a shake of his head. Jane's jaw dropped.

'It's called sarcasm. He uses it sometimes, and before you ask, I have no idea why,' Comm explained. Jane rolled her eyes at Damian's sheepish smile.

'Obviously, the maiden voyage was a success and interstellar travel eventually became the norm. I suppose Orenburg became incredibly rich, and because of that, his House was able to buy out House Quanton,' Jane said, as she turned back to Wu Quan and her team. Comm's face became emotionless as he delved through the historical facts of this time.

'More or less, it is true that his House survives, but Orenburg at the end was not the House leader. Wu Quan was. How she got to that level, and how long she remained there, we will never know,' Comm said with a shrug.

'Because of the information black hole,' Damian added.

'Exactly,' Comm agreed, nodding.

Damian swiftly about turned. He scanned the full length of the hangar, an expression of shock etched upon his face.

'Did you feel that?' he said, turning back to them.

Comm was by his side in an instant.

'What is it that you felt, Sandy?' he asked, concerned. Damian walked to the centre of the hanger and slowly scanned the vast space.

'What is it Damian?' Jane asked as she approached him. Comm froze the scenario, then reached out to his friend.

'I have felt it a couple of times, but put it down to being in the presence of that evil bastard Orenburg. It was like a tingle, no, more a shudder, a sort of shimmering, as if someone was standing right behind me.'

Comm moved away, looking around the hangar as he went, he turned back to Damian and Jane, his chin resting in the palm of his hand, index finger tapping.

'How many times have you experienced this feeling?' he said at last.

'That was the third time. Once in the control room, twice in here, but that last one, was somehow stronger,' he answered.

Comm nodded slowly. 'I have not felt such a sensation. Jane, have you?' he said, turning to Jane.

'I have felt uneasy when in close proximity to Orenburg, but nothing like Damian has described.' Comm's face went blank as he delved through billions of bits of information. After just a few seconds he grimaced.

'This requires further thought. I believe we should return to the Griffin.' As he finished his sentence they found themselves in the grey place, colours materialised around them and they found that they were standing in the extended room. Five metres away they saw themselves disappearing for the start of their journey.

CHAPTER 36

THE ALTERNATE THEORY

'No time has passed. We have returned at the same instant that we left,' Comm said as he walked to the centre of the room. As he did so, an enormous holographic image of pulsating colour emerged all around him. Damian gasped at the size of it.

'What's that?' he spluttered. Comm turned slowly from within the pulsating image.

'This is the scenario matrix. It is the upgrade that I retrieved from the Science Projection department. It is this matrix that creates more realism into the make-up of the scenario. But for that to be achieved, all holographic images, including us, have to be harmonised into the structure. Without this fine tuning of the harmonisation procedure, each object will react with another,' he said as he removed panelling from the floor stage.

'So, the energy stored within one image will be pulled into another,' Jane stated as she walked over to Comm. Comm looked up from his work and smiled as Jane approached him.

'More or less, but it is a bit more complicated than that,' he said admiringly as Jane knelt down beside him.

'Correct me if I am wrong,' asked Damian as he approached the two of them.

'A holo image that isn't harmonised can have an effect on all parts of the scenario.'

'That is correct, Sandy,' Comm answered.

'Then why, did neither of you feel it?'

Comm rose to his feet, and gave a dismissive smile.

'I do not know, but I think we all agree, that the only non-harmonised image within the scenario, must be our elusive 'O'. Why it is only you that could either feel or hear his presence is just another puzzle, on top of all the other puzzles, but, I do have a theory, and it will take me approximately three standard hours to put a test scenario together to establish whether my theory is correct. So, in the meantime, Nurse Onslow ...' Jane looked up from the power conduits that pulsated below the flooring.

'I thought you were calling me Jane, now.' Comm nodded.

'I will do, but right now I need you as the Senior Nurse.' Jane stood to face him, a frown emerging upon her face.

'When Sandy was found, he was sent directly to the medical centre. Is that correct?' Jane's frown intensified.

'He was removed from the capsule in loading bay one. Then he was brought to the medical facility.'

Comm nodded slowly. 'And you were there when he was brought in?' Comm asked ignoring the deep huff from Damian.

'I'm sorry Comm, but what has that got to do with anything?' Damian asked indignantly. Comm turned and stared intently at his friend.

'Maybe nothing, but then, maybe everything. I need to pursue this idea, just to see if my theory is correct. So Jane,' he said turning back to her.

'Were you there?'

'Yes. I and my team had been summoned by Doctor Ghorbany. We were all there waiting for the remains.'

'Remains. So what exactly was delivered?'

Jane turned to Damian with an apologetic look.

'Upper body skeletal remains, skull and cranium, decomposed flesh and various fluids. We cut through the cranium to expose ...'

'Yes, yes, I do not need the medical procedure. What happened to the skeletal remains?' interrupted Comm.

'A lot of the fluid, flesh and bone were used to extract DNA and RNA to create the body that Damian has now.'

'And what happened to them after that procedure?'

Jane was not sure where this inquiry was heading. 'Some of it was destroyed, mainly flesh and fluid, as well as some of the bone, and, some of it was put into storage.'

Damian was as confused as Jane.

'Comm, why do you need this information?' he said softly. Comm turned and walked into the holo image. Damian had seen this behaviour from his friend before. It was usually just before he revealed something that might possibly offend. He turned and walked slowly back towards them.

'We have said, as we have gone through these scenarios, that you may be from an alternate universe. The more that we learn, there is more than a possibility that, that is the fact of it. but it is, as yet, not proven. My theory is that if you are, and if 'O' is also from the same realm, you may be attracted to each other at an atomic level. In the first two scenarios, we did not have the realism matrix from the Science Projection department, so you would not have felt any disturbance, but now, even at the atomic level, you felt a ...' Comm stopped, searching for the word.

'Tingle,' Damian finished.

'Yes, tingle, but I must stress, it is only a theory. So Jane, can you get me a sample of Sandy's remains, no matter how small? I want to set up an experiment.' Jane let out an involuntary gasp.

'I am sorry Comm, I am not sure that I can. Those remains were stored on the Captain's orders. They are to be passed to outpost 1436 medical team for analysis.'

'I am not going to harm them; they can be returned undamaged at the end of the experiment,' Comm countered.

'Yes but ...'

'We can just ask the Captain,' Damian interjected. Comm closed his eyes in thought.

'I don't think the Captain could care less about your remains Sandy. I believe the order came from a much higher level, which opens up yet another puzzle. Why, is Command interested in your remains?' Damian shrugged.

'Command is interested in anything and everything, but when I am involved, it seems to require even the slightest of details. So let me get this right: The remains of my original body will prove that I am not from this realm,' Damian said frowning. Comm pondered the statement.

'At the atomic level, if that is the test that they will carry out, yes, it would prove that you are not from this realm.'

Damian shook his head in disbelief. Jane turned to Comm, anger welling up within her.

'Then why haven't we carried out this test already, and why are you only mentioning it now?' she demanded, with anger in her voice, Comm stepped back.

'I suppose, because nobody thought to do such a test, and I have only just thought of it because of the incident with Sandy in the scenario,' Comm said defensively.

'But Command had thought of it,' she argued back. Damian stepped forward and held up his hand.

'We don't know that, that is why they want the remains. It could be for a hundred other reasons, but it has given me a thought. If we just ask for the remains, they will want to know why, and we would have to come up with a convincing lie, which I would not be comfortable in doing. But we could come up with Comm's theory, then the medical labs could carry out the test for us.' Both Comm and Jane thought for a while, then both nodded.

'Sandy, I would still like to carry out my experiment. If they agree to carry out the test, all I need is a holographic image of some of the remains. But it has to be done with the realism matrix. I will fashion a handheld device for you to use.'

He turned to look back to the pulsating matrix. 'While you and Jane figure out what you are going to say to the Captain, I will get on with creating an experimental scenario, and of course the handheld device,' he said, as he walked back into the holo image.

'We will need a procedure of how to carry out this test Comm,' Jane shouted after him.

'Yes, I will put that together and pass it through to your info pad, via the room com,' he shouted back from within the image.

Damian and Jane walked through the archway into the seating room.

'So how do we go about this,' Damian asked as he sat in the recliner, Jane sat opposite, deep in thought.

'The med lab knows that I have been monitoring your dream patterns, and the medical centre knows that I have been looking after your wellbeing.' She said. She felt a low resonated vibration at the small of her back. She retrieved the info pad, unfolded it and laid it on the low table that was positioned between them. Damian leant forward to read the information that Comm had just passed to it. Apart from many pages of text, he noticed a lot of holo files had also been integrated into the information.

'Wow, we can't say that he isn't thorough,' Damian muttered as he opened a holo file. The image that spread across the low table mystified him.

'Do you know what that is?' he asked puzzled.

'Yes, this holo is a representation of your cognitive functions. It allows you to understand and relate to what is going on around you,' she said slowly as she scanned the image. Damian leant back into his recliner, a confused look on his face.

'Thought he wanted bones,' he said dismissively. Jane looked up from the image.

'At the atomic level, everything reacts with everything. This, is just a small part of the whole. I think what Comm is saying, is at the atomic level we have repulsion forces due to positively charged nuclei. The strength of the repulsion depends on distance. At close range it becomes stronger, and the image within the scenario that we were in was highly realistic, and if it is true that you and 'O' are from the same realm, then it may be possible that you could feel that repulsion,' she said, as a smile emerged on her face.

'You got all that from that image,' he said slowly as he looked into the holo.

'Damian, you do not need to know how all of this works. You are the participant, but I do need to know how it works, especially if I am going to have to explain it to Doctor Ghorbany and his team. So I will return to my quarters for some peace and quiet. I will contact you when I feel that I am ready,' she said rising from the recliner.

After Jane had left his quarters Damian stood in the centre of the sitting room. He turned to the wall pad.

'Six, are there any messages?' he asked.

'There are no messages at this time,' chirped Six. Damian turned to look at the archway. He could, he thought ask if Comm needed a hand, but he knew he would be more of a hinderance than help. He passed through the door to the balcony and sat upon the bench. He marvelled at the swirls of coloured clouds that passed as they travelled in dimensional space.

Over the next two days he had visited Commander Burroughs and Commander Gomez. He had wandered through level 11 then had made his way down to level 35 to talk to the engineers that looked after the Trellion engines. It was a feeling of relief when he received a call from Jane late on the second day. He would never have been a good passenger he thought.

Jane entered his quarters an hour later. They moved to the extended room. In the centre of the room stood an enormous white cube. Comm acknowledged their arrival and beckoned them over.

'I have finished the experimental scenario, all I need now is an image of Sandy's remains, and for that, you will need this.' He handed a small white cube to Jane.

'It is a hard light holo. No sensor on the Griffin will be able to detect its presence. If you place it next to your info pad it will bind with the holo files stored within. Nurse Onslow, when you are conducting the procedure, it will automatically scan Damian's artefacts. Are you both ready to proceed?' Both Damian and Jane nodded.

'And this,' Damian said, pointing to the cube next to which they stood, 'is a larger version of that.'

Comm frowned and turned to the large white cube.

'No, but, I will explain when you return,' he said slowly.

After receiving confirmation of a meeting with the Captain, Jane and Damian made their way to level 16. The sender opened into the greeting room.

'I have been on this ship for nearly ten standard years. I have never been to the Captain's quarters before,' Jane said in awe, as she looked around the gallery of past Commanders. At the far wall, the double doors opened. A Lieutenant walked out and stood rigid in front of the doors that had now closed behind him.

'Lieutenant, erm , ...Peroni,' Damion said slowly, puzzled as to why the security guard was here.

'Lieutenant Drake, and Senior nurse Onslow. Captain Contessa will see you now.

'I know she will, we asked for the meeting, but I am puzzled. Why are you here?' Peroni gave a blank stare, then taking a breath.

'I was ordered here, Drake."

Damian stared deep into Peroni's eyes. 'That's "Lieutenant Drake",' he said in a whisper. Peroni smirked, then about turned. When the doors opened fully he walked into the room. Damian and Jane followed. Inside, Damian noticed the room had changed, the artefacts and statues were all gone. Instead the room looked more like a conference room. A table dominated the central area of the room. Sat at its head, Captain Contessa waited. To her side sat Doctor Ghorbany. Behind the Captain three other guards stood stationed. The doctor beckoned them in and indicated the seats opposite him. Both Jane and Damian sat. This was not the kind of meeting Damian had expected.

'How have you been Damian? I hope Nurse Onslow has been looking after you,' the doctor said in his rich mellow voice.

'I am well, thank you Doctor, and Nurse Onslow has been very professional in her duties.'

'The reason Damian, that this gathering has been put together, is because you have asked to see your original remains. But you haven't said why.' Damian studied the doctor who sat opposite. He looked nervous.

'Well, they are mine ...'

'Drake, why do you want to see them after all this time?' the Captain exploded, her eyes steely grey. Damian sat rigid.

'Ma'am, since I have been on your ship, Nurse Onslow has been trying to ascertain exactly who I am, and where I originate from. Before Nurse Onslow, the medical com-link that was assigned to me tried to find out the very same thing, and now, with the tests that Nurse Onslow has been carrying out, she believes that she may have found a way to know for sure. But, it will involve using my skeletal remains.'

Damian took a breath and remained still. The doctor sagged in his seat, the Captain leant further forward. She slowly turned to Ghorbany.

'And you, were not involved in these tests,' she said pointedly.

'No Captain, I was not,' he said turning his attention to Jane Onslow.

'Jane, why did you not come to me?' he said, his voice faltering. Damian saw that Jane was squirming in her seat. Her face betrayed nervousness for a second, then she rallied. She faced him and gave a smile.

'I am sorry Doctor. I did not involve you because I saw no reason to. As you know, I was, for quite some time, trying to decipher Damian's dreams. I created a holo model to help me in this task. Slowly over time we unravelled the dreamscapes and put them into digital forms.' She then turned to the Captain.

'All this work is documented and filed, Captain.' The Captain nodded slowly and leant back into her recliner.

For the next hour Jane explained the continuation of her work, how that eventually led her to the atomics of brain and mind functions. With the help of the holo files that Comm had placed on her info pad she explained the complexities of dimensional differences, and that a study of the remains would prove without a doubt whether Damian Drake originated in this realm or another. She folded the pad and placed it into her pouch. The silence in the room unnerved her. She sat and waited for their verdict. Captain Contessa slowly rose from her seat.

She turned to Peroni.

'You and your team are dismissed Lieutenant. But before you leave, know this, what you have heard here today is classified. Do I make myself clear?' The four guards stood to attention,

Peroni nodded curtly, and then as one, they all left the room. The Captain turned to Jane once the doors had closed.

'Your presentation is impressive Senior Nurse Onslow. You must have carried out a lot of research. What files or data did you access?' she said, her voice as smooth as a silk garrotte. Damian became nervous. They hadn't thought of this line of enquiry. Jane leant forward, placing her elbows on the table and resting her head upon her closed hands.

'Most of the information that I used was taken from my own nursing files, and some from medical files, which are open for all to peruse. When I realised that my studies were taking me down to the atomic level, I accessed engineering files, especially dimensional shift. Also, I asked Commander Burroughs for his advice and he allowed me access to his own files. I am sure ma'am that you could find my access routes into the system, or I suppose you could ask Commander Burroughs.' A smile broke through the surface of Captain Contessa's face . Touché, thought Damian.

'Damian,' Doctor Ghorbany called softly.

'Are you sure that you would want to know. If it is true, we cannot send you back there.'

'I realise that Doctor, but I think that just knowing will be enough,' he said, but was surprised at the feeling of dread that washed through him. He shook the feeling away and turned to the Captain.

'I am sorry Captain, but I don't understand why this meeting is so, well, so much like an inquisition.' the Captain's eyebrows rose.

'Inquisition?' she queried.

'Interrogation then.' Juliana Contessa slowly shook her head.

'Damian, I was ordered by the Command executive, to place the relics into secure storage for later study, and once secured, no one but the Command executive would have access to them. But, I see no harm in carrying out a harmless procedure that will cause no harm to them, if it will at last explain, who you are. And as you said, they are yours,'

They travelled up to level 1 and entered a sparsely furnished room. Around the walls lockers of different sizes dominated. In the centre a long table. Doctor Ghorbany walked to the furthest lockers away from the only entrance portal and operated the security lock on one of the smaller lockers. With great care he removed a container that Housed the artefacts. With Jane's help they laid the contents onto the table. Damian gave a gasp and grabbed the edge of the table. Jane Onslow was immediately at his side. Ghorbany retrieved his medical scanner.

'His pulse rate is very high, but his implants are adjusting,' Ghorbany said, his voice showing concern.

'Doctor, I'm fine, just a shock, thats all. You don't come face to face with your own skull every day,' he said with an embarrassed smile. Ghorbany looked back to the scanner, and slowly nodded.

'All levels are within normal parameters,' he said, looking towards Damian.

'Are you sure you wish to continue?' he added in a more serious tone.

'Yes Doctor, I'm fine,' Damian reassured him.

'Will this procedure harm my Lieutenant in any way, Nurse Onslow?' the Captain said in her normal authoritative tone.

'No ma'am, he will feel nothing,' Jane snapped back.

Nurse Onslow, with the help from Doctor Ghorbany carried out the test procedure, half an hour later Jane turned to Damian.

'You are the first alien, that we have ever encountered,' she said smiling. Captain Contessa turned and paced the room. She was in deep thought, the frown on her face deepened. She stopped on the opposite side of the table and slowly turned to them.

'This test never happened. Nurse Onslow, I will delete any record of your entrance into the various files that you have accessed. I will also explain to Commander Burroughs that you never contacted him. I will make that an order if necessary.' Damian let out an involuntary sigh.

'Why?' was all he could say before his Captain turned her steely grey eyes upon him. That look that he had seen on numerous occasions lasted momentarily. Her face softened.

'Damian, if the results of this test is known, I will be ordered to put you in the brig. When we dock at 1436 you will be taken by the Command executive, and I have no doubt, you will undergo tests for the next decade, or even longer. So, this never happened. Please, replace the remains carefully, and we will never speak of this again.' To all of their amazement, she then turned and left the room.

'I am impressed Damian. She must really like you,' Ghorbany said in a whisper.

CHAPTER 37

THE TRAP

Back in the extended room they sat in their usual recliners in the lounge area.

'When the Captain asked where you had obtained your research, my implants went into overdrive,' Damian said laughing. As per normal, Jane and Comm exchanged puzzled looks.

'I was very fearful of your response,' he added as an explanation.

'I have had dealings with the Captain over the years that I have been here. Not many, but I do understand her way of demanding the truth, and so, to remedy any accusations, I accessed the files that I would have needed, and spoke to Commander Burroughs for his advice. But it seems now that the effort was not required. It is however, a brave move on her part to conceal this from the Executive.' Comm listened attentively, for the past hour the two of them had been telling him of their experiences in the Captain's quarters and level 1.

'Sandy, the Captain may be thorough in concealing the information regarding the testing, but you must be aware, that Command wants those remains for a reason. Once we have docked, they may take you to carry out their own tests, we do however, have an advantage in surmising that. I can alter your physicality using a hard light imaging holo. If they do carry out the same test, the conclusion will tell them that you are from this realm and no other.' The frown on Damian's face melted away and was replaced with a smile.

'You can do that?'

'Quite easily. There are many procedures within the Science Projection department designed to protect their executive officers. If they were to be captured, we have already used the memory dampener. There are many more to choose from,' Comm said leaning back into his recliner.

Jane removed the info pad from her pouch and laid it upon the table.

'I assume all of the information you need, is stored on there,' she said, pushing the pad towards him. Comm leant forward and unfolded the pad. He scrolled through the thousands of stored information and activated a file. An image of Damian's original skull coalesced in perfect clarity before them. He leant closer and examined the image in minute detail.

'Yes, this is perfect,' he said, turning to the huge white cube that dominated the interior of the extended room.

'I have set up an experiment, Sandy. All I want you to do is enter the cube and walk slowly over to a pedestal that you will find in the centre of the makeshift room. Upon it you will see the image of your skull. Keep moving slowly towards it until you feel the sensation that you felt in the hangar, then stop, do not move. Is that clear?' Damian looked with some trepidation at the white cube. He turned back to Comm.

'Yes, I understand. This … isn't dangerous, is it?' he asked hesitantly.

Comm passed his hand over the skull's image. It wavered then disappeared. Slowly he raised his head to look directly at Damian.

'If you do not do exactly as I ask, then yes, it could be dangerous.'

Jane stood from her seated position with such force that the recliner was pushed back onto the wall behind.

'Explain what you mean by "dangerous", she said angrily. Comm shook his head.

'It is not dangerous, as long as he, well, does as he is told. What I have created is a holographic trap, designed to capture our elusive 'O'. But what I need to do initially is to harmonise it with our own avatars.'

Jane was about to unleash a further barrage of argument but Damian's upheld hand stopped her.

'Comm, you are my friend, I trust you implicitly, and so do you Jane. So, let's just get on with it,' he said softly, and he rose from his seat.

As they walked onto the holo stage both Jane and Damian reverted to holo imagery, their organic bodies froze in mid-step at the edge of the holo stage.

The three holo images walked through the wall of the white cube. Inside they stopped. The whole space inside was white. At its centre a black pedestal. Placed upon its top, Damian's skull.

'Just walk slowly towards it, then stop if you feel that tingle that you felt before. You will notice that on the floor is a black circle that encompasses the pedestal. Do not cross that line, So, when you are ready, go.' Damian took a deep breath and slowly paced his way towards the skull. He was five metres away from the black line when he felt a slight shudder.

'I'm feeling a slight shimmer. Should I stop?'

'Is it the same as in the hangar,'

'Not as strong, no.'

'Then keep going, but do not cross the black line.'

He slowed his pace and continued: At two metres he stopped. Comm looked up from the console that he had created.

'Is it the same as in the hangar?' he called.

'Similar, maybe slightly stronger,' Damian answered hesitantly. Comm re-calibrated the console and the image of Damian vanished from sight. Jane let out a gasp.

'Comm, where is he?"

"It's okay, he's fine,' Comm said in a soothing tone. As he altered the settings on the console, Damian reappeared beside them.

'That was weird,' he said smiling. Jane was not amused, but before she could voice her opinion another shape appeared in the room.

'Ah, good,' Comm muttered.

'This is an approximation of Damian's image without the realistic matrix. It has been created to include a facsimile of the alternate atomic structure. Hopefully, it is an identical copy of O's holographic make-up. I am going to send it towards the pedestal.' The holographic entity walked across the room. As it passed the black line it froze in mid-step. The three of them moved cautiously towards it. Halfway there Comm stopped and turned to Damian.

'You cannot be too close. Keep moving until you feel a slight tingle.' Damian nodded. He walked two paces then stopped.

'Good,' said Comm, as he moved to stand between Damian and the holo entity.

'Now, take a half step back.' Damian did as asked.

'What do you feel?'

'Nothing,' Damian answered.

'Good, we have now set the parameter. Stay there, I am going to add something to your matrix.' A control console rose from the floor and he altered the holo controls.

'What do you feel?'

'Nothing.'

'Step forward,' he said stepping to Damian's side. Damian took a tentative step forward. He felt the slight shimmer within him. On the next step he felt a barrier.

'I can't move. What is it? Some sort of shield?' he asked, as he tried to push forward.

'Yes, it is an energy barrier. You shouldn't get too close, otherwise you will be within the trap. Now watch.' Comm turned to the frozen image of the entity. .

'Zero one, turn to face me,' Comm said to the image. The entity turned.

'Count to five,' Comm ordered.

'1, 2, 3, 4, 5,' the entity obliged.

'Move two steps to the right.' As the entity moved, its structure started to break down, parts of its body disintegrated. As it finished the two steps it became a wispy mist then swirled around the space that it had just occupied. Then it dissipated into nothing.

Comm turned to the two of them. Both seemed astonished at what they had just witnessed.

'Yes, it is dangerous, but not to you or me Jane. Sandy, the matrix will not allow you to get too close, but we now have the means to trap the elusive 'O',' he said proudly.

'Well, we do, and we don't,' Damian responded, looking rather sceptical.

'Explain,' ordered Comm.

'The elusive 'O', as we have said before, is possibly the architect of all the historical timelines that we have visited. He has even pulled me from one realm into another. The entity that you have used does not have a molecule of the intelligence that 'O' has, and besides that, he could be standing in this room right now.'

Comm involuntarily raised his hand to his chin.

'Yes, all of that is true, especially the last part, but, sometimes total surprise outweighs high intellect, and, if he is standing in this room, I believe you would have felt him, but, if he is in this room, maybe all of this is a waste of time.'

'Whoa, wait a minute, I never said that!' Damian interjected, shocked that Comm would ever say such a thing.

Jane looked at both of them and slowly shook her head.

'Three standard days ago, we did not have any plan to capture 'O', and we do now. So no, not a waste of time, and you know, that Damian never said that,' Jane answered with a smirk. Comm turned to Damian and bowed his head slightly.

'I apologise, Sandy,' he said cordially. Damian shook his head and smiled.

'Comm, you do not have to apologise to me. I know you have worked tirelessly on this ... so how do we get 'O' into the trap?'

Comm cocked his head to his shoulder, a puzzlement forming on his face.

'I am a Comm link, I never tire,' he said slowly. Jane threw her arms up in exasperation.

'When you two have stopped apologising to each other, can we get on. Comm, how do trap him?' Comm turned to her and smirked.

'When the elusive 'O' is in close proximity to Sandy, within ten metres, the trap will automatically close around him. I have programmed the matrix to recognise the alternate realms atomic structure, assuming it is the same as Sandy's. However, the matrix will disregard Sandy due to the harmonising of his avatar, and of course none of this will happen if we are wrong with the atomic structure, or, if 'O' is right now standing in the corner of this room,' he said, with a grin.

Whilst Comm made preparations for the scenario, Jane and Damian made their way back to the recliners. As Damian sat down Jane stopped beside her seat and removed the info pad. She opened it, and sighed deeply.

'Doctor Ghorbany has requested my presence in the medical centre, I am so sorry Damian, I have to go.' Damian stood, his face showing concern.

'Is there an emergency?'

'No, a meeting of all heads of departments,' she said, reading the pad.

'It doesn't matter, we can go on the scenario at another time.'

Jane looked up from the pad. 'No, we are nearing outpost 1436. I could be called at any given time after this meeting. You and Comm go. It is the last scenario, you can tell me all about it when you return,' she said casually. He watched her walk through the archway and felt somehow, alone.

'Where is Nurse Onslow going?' Comm asked as he walked towards the lounge area.

'She has been recalled to the medical centre. Does that create a problem for us?' he asked, as Comm stopped at his side.

'As long as you're happy to proceed without her, I foresee no problems. However, we could delay until she returns.'

Damian grimaced. 'No, we can go without her. If we are ready of course.' Comm followed his friend's gaze to the archway.

'Sandy, she will return,' he said softly.

'I just have to reset the matrix, and then, we will go.'

Damian followed him back to the holo stage. After a few moments they found themselves in the grey non-place.

CHAPTER 38

QUANTON FALLS

The greyness of the non-place faded away and again they stood before the inverted pyramid of statues.

Damian looked up at the two statues that stood upon the shoulders of his own statue. To his own statue's right stood Jan Larsson: The statue depicted him dressed in a body-tight garment. From his shoulders a cloak hung down to his waist, upon his head a tight balaclava. To his statue's left was Ayana Ntombela and she too was dressed in a similar style.

'These two are dressed differently to the others,' he said, turning to face Comm.

'This scenario, Sandy, is taken from a very turbulent time in history. In Wu Quan's time there were six Houses. The Alpha House was House Quanton, and as we came to find out, at the end of documented history, Houses Quanton and Zircon merged, with Wu Quan as its leader. Up until this time dress sense or clothing in general hadn't changed too much since the days of Technopolis, but after three hundred years of a documented void, we find that there are now twenty-one separate Houses. The bitterness between them is at its height in this scenario. Seven hundred years after documentation had been re-established, Quanton is still the alpha, but the other Houses have their own identity, and what they wear, emphasises who they are.' Damian altered his gaze to the statues above them, their clothing all appeared similar, but Larsson and Ntombela seemed far more sinister.

'What House are they from?' he asked, turning back to Comm.

'At this time period, the Houses are stretched to just over thirteen light years from House Quanton. Human society is spreading across the galaxy; the Ross system is thirteen-point three light years from Sol. At this moment they are the furthest humans have travelled, but these two,' he said indicating Larsson and Ntombela, 'are from House Akash, on the planet Rama in the Tau Ceti system. But where we start this scenario, is nearly twelve light years from that planet. We return to House Quanton, on the planet Mars.

The statues faded away, and after a momentary visit to the grey non-place they found themselves on what Damian felt to be a large barren rock. Above them, a green blue planet filled the sky.

'We are on Phobos, the largest and nearest moon of Mars, and as you can see, the terraforming of the planet has been completed.'

Damian craned his head to take in the incredible sight, 'So much like the Earth,' he said, but his sentence was cut short by an explosion that sent debris thousands of kilometres up into space. Damian was shocked by the force of it; both he and Comm were thrown up a hundred metres before arcing and landing two hundred meters away, whereupon another explosion threw them up above the moon's surface. They orbited for a moment then the small moon's gravitational force pulled them down to the surface. Damian hit the edge of a crater's inner wall then bumped his way down to the bottom like on a roller coaster, where dazed and dizzy, he slowly picked himself up. A squadron of fifty or more interceptors in perfect formation flew past above him at incredible speed after finishing their bombing run. He leant back upon a boulder and regained his equilibrium. In the distance, the squadron had achieved a tight turn and were returning for their next strike.

'Comm!' he called, his voice sounding desperate, 'Where are you?'

Flashes of light bloomed in front of him as the squadron released their energy spheres. Their targets, as Damian had noticed, were mobile pulse cannons scattered about the rocky moon. Above him the crater's edge exploded, debris expanded from all quarters and a landslide tumbled towards him. He scrambled to get out of the way of the inevitable deluge. 'I am not here, I am an image,' filled his mind.

'Up!' he shouted and felt a rush of relief as his avatar soared up into space beyond. Once in orbit of the small moon he could see the full extent of the invasion force.

"Sandy, I am a kilometre to your left. Come to me,' he heard the exasperated voice of Comm. Other interceptors dogfought their way through the distance between them and he noticed further out into the void, a line of larger craft that were orchestrating the attack. Carefully he made his way to Comm's position.

From the planet above them, pulse cannons fired to repel the invaders, but they were too slow for the fast manoeuvrable craft. Unfortunately, Damian felt every blast that the cannons' fury unleashed. After half an hour he met with Comm and they linked arms.

'Comm, what the fuck!' Damian managed, before another barrage of fury was unleashed.

They toppled over and over clinging to each other desperately as they travelled the five thousand plus kilometres towards the blue green planet.

'We are in a war zone,' Comm said as he tried to balance their descent into the atmosphere.

'Really,' Damian answered, as he clenched tighter onto Comm's shoulders.

Two massive Cruisers emerged above them. A thousand or more streaks of light flashed passed them. Damian felt the heat as they passed.

'Comm, get us out of here. Now!' he pleaded.

They were back in the non-place. Damian fell to his knees, then collapsed spread-eagled onto what he felt was the floor. Comm stood erect above him.

'Are you okay,' Comm asked, concerned.

'No, I'm not fucking okay! What the fuck was that?' Damian spluttered as he clawed his way to his feet. Comm stepped back, surprised at the strange expletives.

'The realism matrix allows us to experience the true nature of the scenarios,' he argued. Damian grabbed at Comm's shirt to help him stand up. Once on his feet he panted and laid his head upon Comm's shoulder.

'Too much, far, too much,' he said between breaths. Comm grabbed onto Damian's arms to support him and held him at arm's length. He studied his friend's distress and searched the data files that he had access to. Since Damian's shock episode on Longways he had managed to create a variable control on the matrix. He manipulated the sensitivity and the stimuli, as his friend calmed. He released his grip.

'I have reduced the stimulus, but not the reality. You do know, Sandy, that you can never be harmed?'

Damian stared back. He scowled at Comm.

'We have just been blown from one planet to another!' he snapped. Then, in a calmer tone, he continued.

'Comm, we are here to observe. We don't need to suffer the consequences of all-out war. You're just lucky Jane isn't here.' Satisfied that his friend seemed to be back to his normal self, Comm nodded and smiled.

"We need the realism matrix for the trap, but I have toned it down a bit. We should no longer be thrown into the vacuum. If you are ready, shall we try again?' Damian wasn't completely sure, but nodded his agreement.

They materialised, to Damian's relief, at the side of a river. Damian looked across the fields of cereal that stretched to the far horizon. 'So tranquil,' he thought. Noise of military craft from behind him made him turn. From the far side of the river battle cruisers were landing, troops were being deployed. He looked up into the clear blue sky, hundreds of smaller craft passed by in formation followed by the much larger troop carriers. They moved to their allotted destinations unopposed. The battle for House Quanton was over, thought Damian.

'They are troop carriers from House Xi, and further to the left interceptors from House Skyl. They will give the ground troops aerial support, and over a thousand kilometres above us House Odian is taking out Quanton's communication satellites,' Comm said as he waded across the river.

Damian rose into the air and followed him across. At the other side, Comm turned to him and grinned.

'That was quite pleasing, and cold.'

Damian landed on the bank and watched in awe at the sight of the military conquest.

'So, the battle is won. House Quanton is no more,' Damian stated as Comm scrambled up the bank and stood by his side.

'There is a strange entry in the historical journal; one that has confused historians since this time. It was a message sent out from Mars prime by the House leader, Jacob Penning, and that, will be our next port of call.' The image of thousands of troops and hundreds of military machinery, faded from view. They were now standing in an enormous control room. Damian gasped as he looked around.

'There must be over five hundred people in here, and they all look, defeated.'

'Which of course they are, but they are angry too: With twenty-one Houses, there were many alliances. House Quanton was relying on its closest allies for its defence but promises will always be broken. In this case, bought. In the end they had no friends. This battle was short lived, but it was not over yet,' Comm said as he ascended into the overlooking gallery. Damian followed.

'This is Jacob Penning. He is about to give his last message.' Penning stood and walked to the balcony, his image portrayed on every monitor.

'To General Chan: I surrender House Quanton to you. For three days you and your allies have fought courageously, and you deserve to win this battle. To my own troops, who have battled hard and valiantly, I ask them that they power down their weapons and await the opposing forces. General Chan, the city is yours. I await your arrival so that I may discuss the terms of our surrender. You have the city, Sir. I am sure your troops will be glad for the opportunity to celebrate their victory, but you and I, Sir, must discuss Sol 3. It must be protected and preserved for future generations.' Damian turned slowly to Comm.

'Sol 3? Is he talking about Earth?' asked Damian. Comm raised his eyebrows, rose from the gallery floor and disappeared through the domed roof. Damian followed him. Outside, Comm continued up into the unbroken blue sky of Mars.

Damian caught him up two kilometres above the city of Prime.

'There are no records of what Sol 3 is exactly. It could be Earth, but what we do know is that the troops from the three Houses, hundreds of thousands of them, enjoyed the hospitality of Prime for two standard days, when this happened.

The sprawling city below them flickered for an instant. Damian had seen this before. Comm had moved the scenarios timeline forward two days. Multiple flashes of lights sparkled around the exterior of the city. Seconds later, larger flashes could be seen further into the interior, then one flash from the centre encompassed them all. it plumed out beyond the exterior walls and continued for a thousand kilometres in every direction. A few seconds later Damian could feel the heat of it, then they were within the super-heated cloud. The image faded away. They were where they had started – the small moon Phobos.

'We are a month after that destructive event, and as you can see, the explosion has decimated at least a quarter of the planet's surface. Over three million people died. What they had used for the explosive has always remained a mystery, something that this timeline could or should never have had.'

'And Sol 3,' Damian asked as he sat down onto a large rounded boulder. Comm turned and looked out into the dark void of space. He pointed to a light amongst the billions of starlight around them.

'Earth, is it, Sol 3? That phrase has never been used before or since. Or could it be, that Penning needed something to entice the conquering army into his lair?' He turned back to Damian.

'"Protect and preserve,"' he said. 'Why don't we just go and have a look?' Damian said as he stood.

'I thought you might say that.' The image of Phobos and Mars faded away. They now stood upon the hill that once overlooked the city of Technopolis.

'We have been here a few times now, and as you can see the planet is starting to revive. Do you remember the great lake? It is not as large as you remember it, but it is a lake, and vegetation is starting to take hold. The atmosphere is still quite thin, but it is returning.'

Damian looked around. He could see the thin patches of grass and moss. It still had a way to go, he thought. They rose into the thin air and travelled west as they had done previously. Below them the birthing chambers lay in ruins. After an hour of travel they landed on the top of one of the least broken domes. Comm looked from one horizon to the other.

'In the three hundred undocumented years, when the enhancers were driven away, I assume that this planet would have been the first target. It is totally destroyed. There is nothing here to protect or preserve, so I would guess that the statement was just a ruse for the enemy to drop their guard.'

Damian nodded his agreement, then frowned. 'Yes, I suppose so, but it is a very strange thing to say.'

'As I said, a statement that has been a puzzle for historians ever since.' the image of the hundreds of thousands of broken domes disappeared. They were back in the grey non-place. Slowly before them a yellow and green planet pixelated into view.

CHAPTER 39

COMMAND

'We are above the planet Rama. The star over there is Tau Ceti, a star not too dissimilar from Sol. This is where House Akash is based. It is the only House out of all of the twenty-one Houses that does not have any alliance. However, its main export is highly desired by all of the Houses,' Comm said as he turned and descended into the atmosphere. Damian followed him down.

'So, what is it that they export?' he said as he caught Comm up. Comm pointed to a region below them that was becoming clearer as they descended.

'That is the Citadel, the centre of House Akash. Today there will be celebrations and street entertainment. Not because House Quanton has fallen, but, every ten standard years, dignitary's from all the Houses attend to witness the progression of House Akash's skills,' Comm said, as he altered his flight path down towards the Citadel.

'They supply entertainment,' Damian stated, causing Comm to turn to him, a puzzled look upon his face.

'No,' he said slowly.

'Probably, the opposite of entertainment,' he answered, as they slowed then came to a stop above the huge dome of the Citadel.

'House Akash exports assassins. Very good ones. They train for thirty standard years, which allows them to enter level 1. There are ten levels to become a master,' Comm said as he surveyed the topography of the surrounding area. He tapped Damian on the arm and pointed to an open space within the grounds of the domed structure.

They landed in a semi-isolated area. They both surveyed the scene around them. People scurried from one place to another. Damian focused on the groups that passed them by.

'They are all wearing different types of clothing to those of the statues. I remember you saying that each planet's culture had its own individuality,' he said, giving Comm a puzzled look.

'The garments that Ntombela and Larsson are wearing are the clothing of the assassins. Not all on this planet are assassins, but maybe twenty to thirty percent are, and, most of the people that we see here, are off-worlders, here for the event,' Comm said as he walked towards the crowd.

People moved past them, but as in other scenarios, they parted as the two approached.

'So, they earn their money by dealing in death,' Damian said quietly as he stopped by a stall whose main fare seemed to be poisons for all occasions.

'Very lucrative in these turbulent times: Death and information, is their main trade, but', he said stopping and turning to face Damian, 'anyone can walk up to another, point an obliterator, and fire it. But with fragile alliances, that action would generally lead to either war, or at the very least, massacres. What House Akash does, is to relieve the contracted victim of life, by natural means, or, obvious accident. The actual act of assassination is just the end result. Months or even years of preparation would be part of the actual contractual obligation. Death without finger pointing is very expensive.'

Damian turned to watch the populous pass by.

'So, you are saying that this House is wealthy. But these people are not displaying affluence.'

Comm turned and followed Damian's gaze. 'I suppose. It all depends on your definition of "affluence". There is no poverty on this planet. They all have very well-maintained infrastructures, homes, medical and educational facilities, and unlike many of the other Houses, crime does not exist here.'

Damian thought more on Comm's description. What was his own definition of wealth? He himself was a very wealthy man, yet he preferred to continue his training as a pilot. Wealth he decided, is what you perceive it to be. He noticed Comm had wandered away. He rose into the air. Below him he could see the crowd parting as Comm walked unhindered through them. He landed behind him.

'Comm, I nearly lost you.' Comm stopped and turned to him.

'You shouldn't dawdle Sandy. We have a lot to witness. There are assessments that are taking place in the amphitheatre, which is located in the centre of the city. It is also where we will find Larsson and Ntombela, our last two statues.' He turned and walked back into the crowd.

'Why don't we fly?' Damian shouted after him.

'And miss all this ambiance,' Comm shouted, without turning.

The journey from the Citadel to the city centre was a half hour's walk. Without the crowds, thought Damian, probably fifteen minutes, but Comm was right, it did give him the opportunity to see the many stalls that had been set up along the route. Although they did not stop to fully appreciate the stall holders' wares, Damian did smile at some of the bizarre traps, gadgets and general items, all for the purpose of, well, he thought, shaking his head, for the purpose of assassination kits. Money is money, he thought, and while there are idiots willing to buy – all off- worlders of course – then why not sell?

They had reached the entrance of the outdoor theatre. The crowd had come to a halt. Comm turned and pointed up. Damian followed. They rose up from the hordes of people, floated over the outer wall to the stadium within and alighted on an empty balcony.

'This is the master's viewpoint. It is from here that they will assess the level 1 hopefuls,' Comm said, as he sat upon the most prominent of the chairs on the balcony. Damian sat on the least impressive. He looked out over the oval arena.

'So, they train for thirty years, but even then, that does not guarantee them entry into level 1,' Damian said with a frown.

'Each ten-year cycle will bring forth about five hundred, and depending on their ingenuity, agility and to some extent, style, about ten percent will be chosen.'

Damian leant back and turned to face Comm.

'Fifty out of five hundred. What happens to those that fail?'

'They are sent back to retrain, and in ten standard years, they can try again.'

Damian turned and looked back to the arena.

'That's harsh,' he muttered.

'They are looking for perfection.'

'And they assess five-hundred in a day? How long is a day on this planet,' Comm slowly shook his head.

'The assessments go on for a month or so. We, however will only witness the first one. The master who is assessing, is Ayana Ntombela and her deputy, Jan Larsson.' Damian turned back to Comm with eyebrows raised.

'They are masters.'

'Very much so, in the Citadel hierarchy, they are both very close to the top, and to be assessed by them is an honour.' Damian turned back to the arena. The stadium was now half full.

'They are assessing assassins. Will we be witnessing murders?' Comm stood and leant over the balcony parapet.

'Not murders, Sandy, executions. All the victims have been convicted by trial and they are to be executed. There is no crime on planet Rama, so all these victims are from different Houses. They could be terrorists, murderers even political activists. All those that have been found guilty would have been given a choice. Executed within their own House, or executed here.'

Damian stood and moved to Comm's side.

'Why would they wish to be killed here, in front of thousands of onlookers?'

Comm turned to him. 'Because, if the assassin fails to kill him, he walks free. And all he has to do, is walk from one side of the arena to the other and ring this bell via the rope that is attached to it. Then he is free to go,' he said pointing to the golden bell above them. Damian looked down to the arena floor then to the furthest end. He estimated that its length was about a hundred and fifty metres.

'Well, that seems easy enough. There is plenty of space within the arena to out manoeuvre a single assassin, especially if your life depends on it. Err ... unless the assassin has weapons of course.'

Comm's face went blank as he searched his data files.

'The assassin is allowed one weapon, a thin-bladed knife that tapers down to a needle point. It's extremely sharp and is impregnated with a lethal venom. They are, however, not allowed to throw it, but there won't be just the two of them out there. Twenty to thirty people will be in the arena. They will not be allowed to hold or grab the victim, but they can block his path to the bell, and of course, one of them, will be the assassin. But the Victim will not know who. It is execution, but mainly, entertainment, and on this particular assessment, the Supreme master will also be attending. Hence, the highly decorated chair.' Damian turned to look at the chair. With its gold and silver inlays, multiple woods and red and purple fabrics, it was impressive.

'The Supreme master does not attend all of the assessments then?' Damian inquired. Comm turned from the almost full stadium.

'He attends some, not all, but usually only on invitation. The accused, in this assessment is a man called Joel Palesk he is a high caste, a political revolutionary from House Imarni. He is the leader of a liberation group that unsuccessfully tried to topple the House leader. Two hundred were killed in that attempt. The assassin has been chosen by Ntombela herself, and it was she that invited the Supreme master.'

A door opened on the back wall of the balcony. Four men in black entered. Damian could see that their clothing was similar to the clothing depicted on the statues of Ntombela and Larsson. The four men scanned the area of the balcony until they were satisfied that all was clear, then exited through the same door. Damian and Comm moved to one side as the masters and dignitaries entered; the tall dark-skinned woman indicated the seating for her guests. A large elderly man then entered: the ensemble bowed slightly in a show of respect. He walked directly to the decorous chair and sat down.

Damian stared at Ntombela who sat on the Supreme master's right-hand side, then Larsson, who sat on his left.

'I do know them,' he said to Comm.

'Almost like a distant memory, but it is there,' he said, turning to Comm who had now sat on the balcony parapet.

'So, we have come to this at last. All nine statues have now been identified. The only question left to answer, is who sent them here, and why?' Comm said, as a cheer went up from the stadium audience. Damian moved to Comm's side; they had a perfect view of the arena.

From all sides of the oval men and women walked onto the arena floor. They stopped at their designated positions, all facing away from the masters' balcony. They had divided into separate groups of threes and fours, making eight separate groups in all. The assassin hid within one of the groups.

From the furthest end Palesk entered. The crowd became silent: He had stopped and scanned the layout, looking for the easiest route through. He ran to the right-hand side, two groups merged to block his path. To Damian's surprise he grasped the shoulders of one of them and vaulted over their heads. On landing he turned ninety degrees and ran to the left, three groups now merged. He was at the halfway point and changing his stride, he moved to the left, but it was a faint. In one swift move he turned back to the right and passed the group. He was now running towards the last quarter of the arena. The last three groups now stood defiantly in his way. Behind him, the previous groups were regrouping and running to catch him up. He sprinted towards the groups that lay in his path, and at the very last moment dived feet first to the floor. He rolled, taking out the legs of some of the group – they fell all about him, but he had judged the move correctly and had rolled to his right, away from the falling bodies.

One of the group's members had also seen the manoeuvre and had stepped away at the last moment. He ran at Palesk and easily brought him down, but as the victim fell to the floor, he kicked out at the assassin's legs. They buckled from under him and as the assassin fell Palesk then removed the knife from the assassin's concealed sheaf. He rolled twice, away from the assassin, and now on his knees he threw the knife.

Ntombela and Jansson were up on their feet in split second, but the knife had already found its target. The Supreme master fell back into his chair, the knife's handle protruding from his right eye. On the arena floor Palesk lay spread eagled, his neck snapped. The assassin stood motionless, staring up at his fate to the masters' balcony. The scenario froze, Damian let out a gasp, crumpled slightly and held on to the parapet tightly. His knees had buckled and he had an urge to vomit. Turning away from the sickening spectacle in front of him he focused his attention on Comm, who was giving him a puzzled look.

'You could have warned me that that was going to happen,' he spluttered.

'It is what happened. It is well documented and, it did happen over three thousand years ago,' Comm answered, puzzled at his friend's reaction. Damian regarded the comm link with open mouth.

'This is not the first time you have done this to me. The rape scene stayed with me for months, and to be honest, it's still there, but with the realism matrix, I find this horrifying, and unnerving. To you, this is just a data stream, to me, I have just witnessed a man killed with a knife sticking out of his eye,' Damian said, exasperated. Comm's features blanked as he searched the appropriate files. Damian felt an easing of his internal stress.

'I have reduced your stimuli down a level. You should now be able to witness these events without too much emotion, but I cannot reduce it any lower than this level. I have often said to you, that you should confide to me anything that disturbs you. This is the first time that you have done so,' Comm remarked sternly. Damian relaxed slightly.

'Maybe it is the realism of this scenario, and yes, you are right. I should keep you informed of my feelings, but you could have warned me,' he said in a softer tone.

'What, and spoil the surprise,' Comm retorted with a grin.

Damian turned and looked at the Supreme master: The image did not seem as horrifying as before.

'So, what now?' he said turning back to Comm.

'Historians have argued this outcome for three thousand years. What do you think has just happened?'

Damian looked around the balcony. Both Ntombela and Larsson were up off of their seats and leaning towards the Supreme master, concern showing on their faces. The dignitaries behind them were also standing, with shocked expressions. Damian looked over the parapet, down onto the arena. The assassin stood erect straddling Joel Palesk who lay face down beneath him.

Damian rose into the air and floated down towards the assassin. Comm followed. Damian scrutinised the scene.

'We are approximately thirty metres from the bell rope, the balcony is four or five metres up. Even now, with the Supreme master slumped in his chair, I can just see his forehead. If he was leaning forward to watch the event, from this position you probably would only see his head and shoulders. So, to throw a knife that distance, with that accuracy would require immense skill. But, the bell, is in full view. He knew the assassin would be on him in seconds. I think, he was trying to hit the bell.' Comm nodded his approval.

'That was very well thought out, and has been one of the arguments used, but our assassin here, was especially chosen by Ntombela. The Supreme master was also invited by her. The Supreme master will be laid to rest for the duration of the assessments. They cannot be cancelled and afterwards there will be a three-day mourning period – a funeral pyre will be erected in this arena, thousands will attend, and one standard month later, Ayana Ntombela will be the new Supreme master. Her deputy will obviously be Jan Larsson. So, had a deal been made with Joel Palesk to save his family, and you are right, it would be a difficult shot, but not impossible.'

Comm turned and looked at the frozen images of the blocker groups. some still lay on the ground where Palesk had tripped them, the others were running at full sprint and were only three or four metres from them, determined looks on their faces.

'There is another argument. Look at the confusion in this arena. With stealth and skill, the assassin could have thrown the knife himself.' Damian surveyed the arena then back to the balcony.

'A perfect assassination,' he said with admiration.

'Exactly, and a perfect way to ascend to the Supreme master's position. Now, I am moving us further into the timeline. It is now four standard months after the inauguration of Ntombela as Supreme master, which many have argued was the true motive for the killing. We will be two kilometres below the Citadel.'

The image of the arena blurred away. For a moment they were back in the grey non-place. Then they were standing near a series of senders at one end of a cavern.

'There are over a hundred different caverns and caves in this complex. From where we are standing, they stretch over eighteen kilometres, and at this time in history there are over a thousand people working down here,' Comm said as he walked onto the main pathway at the centre of the cavern. Damian followed scrutinising the workers or technicians as they laboured on the dozens of consoles that lined the caverns walls.

'This looks like a secret place Comm. Surely the historical journals wouldn't document this place.'

Comm stopped and turned to face him, he grinned and shrugged his shoulders.

'No, you are correct, this part of the scenario does not come from any public documentation, but my travels to the Science Projection department allowed me to access files that were never meant to be seen,' he said enthusiastically as he turned and walked away.

They walked in silence through interconnecting tunnels that passed from one cavern to the next. Damian was intrigued at the work that was being carried out; each cavern that they passed seemed to be laid out as scientific laboratories. The work that was being carried out involved many holographic images. In one cavern Damian stopped for a moment. He had seen dimensional shift procedures in the engineering sub hangar with Commander Burroughs. What he was looking at, was very similar. He was about to call after Comm for an explanation but the com-link had already walked through to the next chamber. He decided that he would wait until they reached wherever it was that they were going. After a twenty-minute walk Comm stopped as they entered the largest of the caverns. At its centre a blue green lake dominated. Damian watched its surface as it bubbled and pulsated, indicating that its consistency was a lot thicker than water, and in the air, a distinctive smell, not unlike the smell of rotting vegetation that he had experienced on Epsilon 4.

'This is the information centre. Over there on the far wall you can see the operators, and with them are Ntombela and Larsson,' Comm said as he walked towards them. Damian felt a shudder, he turned quickly, but there was nothing there to see.

'Are you alright?' Comm asked, Damian turned to him, he could see the concern on his face.

'Just a slight shudder,' Damian muttered as he continued looking around the cavern.

'It is possible that our elusive 'O' is with us. You must be careful Sandy; remember what you were taught.' Damian nodded and followed Comm as they walked towards Ntombela and Larsson.

'How many operatives do we now have on site?' Damian heard her saying to Larsson as they approached.

'Each of the twenty Houses now has at least twenty assassins assigned to them. Seven of those in each House have been sleepers for over eight years. They are now trusted within the Houses hierarchy. On your command, we are ready to commit,' Larsson said, whilst studying the holographic readouts.

'And the conduits,' she said smoothly. Larsson turned away from the holo towers and indicated the lake.

The blue green surface rippled and swayed and a tendril emerged followed by four others. They swooped from one side to the other as they grew in length. Damian had seen this before, in his sleeping room, the night they took Jane from his slab.

The five tendrils reached out to the furthest wall in the cavern. Damian noticed thousands of small nodules protruding from the wall's surface. The tendrils sought out the nodes and attached themselves to it. More tendrils emerged from the lake's surface and almost in a frenzy others followed.

'You have seen these before Sandy. At this moment in time, it is the start. There are already tens of thousands of them, stretching out to all twenty Houses, including their fleets and orbiting stations. The conduits are made from Quantonite and organic matter, bound together with life energy. In the caverns we walked through, they were completing dimensional shift propulsion, which is what propels the conduits from one side of known space to the other. I believe it is the same technology as the capsule that brought you here.'

They observed as Ntombela moved to another console.

'How long before we receive information?' she asked the operator. He turned and Damian could see that he was nervous.

'We are already receiving information, Supreme master, but within the hour we should have all that we need.' She smiled then turned to Larsson.

'Once all the information we require has been stored, commit, the Final Act,' she said in her smooth tone.

'Final Act?' Damian asked.

'All the information that they receive will contain everything that is needed for them to know of the day-to-day running of each House. The Final act, will be the mass assassination of all members of the House hierarchy. Within a week, martial law will be put into place. Within a year, all Houses will be no more, they will all be citizens of one human society under the tuition of the conduits.'

'Brainwashing,' gasped Damian.

Comm frowned and slowly shook his head. 'Cleansing,' he corrected.

'These are very turbulent times Sandy, the population at this time needed to be taught the protocols of living safely. They had to be unified: individualism will come later, but there were violent clashes. Even this planet was attacked quite a few times. Twenty standard years later all insurrections would have been quelled, unification of the species completed, and finally, planet Rama will forever be known as ...'

Comm?' Damian stepped back. Comm had frozen in mid-sentence.

CHAPTER 40

ORIC

'Mand, I believe he was going to say,' the familiar voice came from behind him. As he slowly turned, Damian felt a shudder ripple through his avatar.

'You are the com-link I saw in the control room, on the planet in the Gamma Tauri system,' Damian spluttered. The older version of himself dressed in white reached out towards Ayana Ntombela and straightened a loose lock of hair that had fallen from her hood.

'Oric, short for oracle, and, we have met a couple of other times. Damian, allow me to open all the avenues of your memory,' he said softly, as he leant over the console next to Ntombela, to study the readouts of the holo towers.

Damian felt a surge of power pulsate within his head. Images within the conduit came forth, the conversations that they had had on the island, became clear.

'We were on the island together,' he said slowly. Within his mind he was still trying to unravel all the new images and conversation that they had had. Oric turned away from the console and took two steps towards him. Damian felt the shudder within him become stronger. He stepped back away from Oric's advance. Oric stopped, a puzzled expression grew across his face.

'I am not here to harm you Damian. My primary program is to see that you do not come to any harm,' he said, the puzzled look remaining.

'I don't know that for a fact though, do I?' Damian answered in a more authoritative tone. He moved back one more step, the shuddering eased. Oric watched as Damian shuffled one way then another then back. The antics amused him, but deep down within his programming matrix, he felt a cause for concern.

'What is it that you are doing Damian? Is it something that your little pixel has taught you? If so, what is it that you are trying to achieve?' Oric said with a sneer of amusement.

'Pixel, what pixel?' Damian asked as he tried to remember the complex procedure of springing the trap. Oric pointed to the frozen image of Comm, then, deep within his programming, he felt an external surge of energy that enveloped him from all sides. He was within a sphere of energy, he broadened his grin, then clapping his hands, he applauded.

'Oh bravo, not such a little pixel after all. This is quite something. I just have to complement him on such an outrageous and cunning plan.' He nodded in Comm's direction.

'Mand,' said Comm, then a look of surprise as he realised that Damian had vanished right in front of him.

'Over here Comm,' Damian called to him whilst keeping his eyes on Oric.

'The elusive 'O' or, Oric, is in his box, and can do no harm to anyone,' he added as Comm sidled up beside him. Oric slowly shook his head.

'Is it that you do not learn, or, is it that you do not listen? I am programmed to keep harm away from you, and this elusive 'O' thing, that you and the pix … com-link, have created, just does not exist. Do you not remember what I said to you on the island. I said, I brought you there to see if I could answer your questions, and I couldn't, but since then, with the help of this place and its technologies that it will acquire over the next three millennia, I have been able to adjust my program. I can tell you some things, but not all.' Oric stopped as Comm stepped closer to him.

'You, are a holographic image of Sandy, or Damian. But your data storage is greater than mine by far, a thousand-fold greater, perhaps more.' Oric gave a half smile.

'Probably, a lot more than tens of thousands. Not envious are you?' Comm shook his head.

'No, not at all, but that is a lot of stored information, so, how much of it can you release to my friend Sandy here.' Oric turned to Damian.

'You, are not the Professor, you look like him, well, a much younger version of him, you talk like him, probably have the same intelligence as him, but, looks can be deceiving, you haven't got the drive the passion and the arrogance that he had, the determination, the stubbornness, you in fact, are, how can I put it, your nicer, friendlier, kinder, all in all, nothing like him at all, and, I have no clue as to why that has happened, it didn't happen to any of the others, didn't happen to me, so why are you so different, now that's the real puzzle isn't it.' Damian frowned as he looked at the smiling face of Oric.

'Are you saying that I, am the old professor,' he said in disbelief. Oric smiled broadly and clapped his hands.

'Oh superb, it takes you a while, but you do get there eventually, no, you are not him, you are, a bit of him,' Oric said chuckling.

'The nicer bit of him,' he added, Damian staggered back a step.

'How,' he gasped, Oric closed his eyes in thought.

'What I do know, is that you are but one part of him, there are possibly others,' Damian's jaw dropped.

'Others, what do you mean others,' Damian snapped back at him. Oric's smile faded from his face.

'Strange, that tone of voice, was almost him, almost as if there are two of you in there, separated from each other, I wonder if that is possible, this definitely needs more thought.' Oric said as the smile reappeared.

'Why did you send us here, for what reason, why did the Earth have to be destroyed,' Damian said, exasperated, Oric crouched down, his face showing concern.

'I never sent you anywhere, this,' he said, his voice almost a whisper.

'Is all your doing.'

'No, this can't be,' Damian muttered under his breath.

'Yes, Professor, it was, you, that sent them to this alternate galaxy, not I, and just to add. My secondary program is to act as your adviser, and I advised vehemently against this.' Comm turned to Damian, he was shocked at this revelation.

'You Sandy, are the professor, you sent these people to invade this realm. How many billions have died in your name,' Damian staggered back, that statement had haunted him for three years.

'Comm, I haven't sent anyone anywhere, you know that I haven't,' Damian said almost in a whisper.

'My dear mister com-link, my statement may not be exactly truthful,' Oric said with a shrug.

'Which statement do you refer to,' Comm asked turning to face the Sandy look-a-like, Oric smiled.

'The one where I said, he was the professor, that is not exactly true, so, if you let me out of here, I will tell you all that I can,' with an extended index finger he cautiously reached forward, a whisp of energy spiralled from his fingertip, he pulled it back quickly.

'That actually hurts, I felt pain, you really are cleverer than I first thought,' he said as he inspected the damage to his finger.

'How about, you tell us all that you can, and then we will decide whether to let you go or not.' Comm said resting his chin in the palm of his hand, Oric looked up from his finger and watched the gesture, it was when Comm's finger started to tap upon his cheek that he let out a deep belly laugh'

'Oh my, mister comm, as if this could not be any more complicated.' Oric spluttered, Damian stepped forward, he felt the energy field stopping him from moving any further.

'You said, that I was just a part of the man you know as Professor Swann, and that something had gone wrong with his transfer,' he said as he tried to keep his emotions down to a level he could control.

'So, you do listen, good, now perhaps we may make some progress, yes, I told you, that somehow on transferring. One, you were placed two thousand years further on in the timeline than you should have been, and two, your personalities were split. I have been researching this phenomena, I am now positive, that it is all to do with, gravity,' Comm stepped closer to the imprisoned Oric.

'A strong enough gravity well, can play havoc with timelines, especially when travelling at faster than light speed,' Comm interrupted, Oric pondered on that statement.

'I am not going to argue that point, you are correct, but, not correct, well, not in this context, please, allow me to explain,' Oric pleaded, Comm nodded an approval.

'You're not just playing for time' Damian interjected.

'Time, is what this is all about Damian, or partly, what this is about, certainly not a plaything,' Oric said with a sigh.

'That's not what I meant,' Damian answered, his tone showing annoyance, Oric supressed a chuckle, then turning to Comm he shrugged.

'Explain what you know,' Comm said calmly.

'Firstly, let me tell you a fact, Professor Stephen Swann created me, I was originally a quantum series ninety, computer program, designed primarily to advise on the project that Professor Swann had been assigned to,'

'Assigned by who,' interrupted Damian.

'The high Chancellor,' Oric said giving Damian a smile.

'Fifteen years later, I was upgraded to a personification of that program, and was created in his likeness, yes, he was very narcissistic, however, for the next forty-two years, I advised, and kept him from harm, and I know, that at some point you are going to ask, what the project is all about, and I cannot tell you, my program will not allow me, I can only divulge information to Professor Swann regarding the project, I could not even confide with the science team, only Professor Swann.'

'But by your own admission, I am Professor Swann,' Damian said frowning, Oric, with a smile shrugged his shoulders.

'Yes, but only a part, I believe you are only, one third of the Professor, my programming will not allow me to divulge anything regarding the project to you, it does not recognise you, however, I have left clues,' he said brightly.

'What clues,' Comm asked, puzzled. Oric frowned whilst contemplating the question.

'Clues regarding the purpose of the project, let me give you an analogy, if there were three doors, a green door, a blue door and a red door, and all the information you need is behind the red door, but, I cannot tell you that, so I may say, once you fly through the blue sky you end up in a space of nothingness,'

'So, there is nothing behind the blue door.' Damian said frowning.

'Exactly Damian, I can tell you a negative, but not the positive.'

'So, what is it that you can tell us,' Comm asked.

'I can tell you this much, regarding the gravity. We were sending photonic probes from one side of the galaxy to the other using dimensional shift technology, which, you are quite familiar with, seeing that we gave it to you. The photon probes sent us back information regarding stella systems in that region, and I cannot tell you what that information is. After a year of this, we started to realise that the information was not correct, the probes sometimes reached their objective far quicker than we had calculated, and in some instances, far longer, we knew that gravitation would have an effect on space time, but we had calculated for that. We decided to close the project down and research the evidence that we had,' Comm raised his hand, Oric regarded the gesture and nodded.

'To send anything from one side of the galaxy to the other, requires enormous energy,' Oric nodded.

'Yes it does, and we had it in an abundance, but that is another story,' Oric said with a slow shake of his head.

'After two years of research, it became evident that the probes were not traveling in our galaxy, but had passed through to your galaxy, this opened up a new avenue of research. We sent probes to your Earth, just to see whether we were technically at the same level, and we found that we were not, we in our realm, were thousands of years more advanced, the culture was similar, but you had not even travelled beyond your own inner planets. With the information that we had received, we spent another year researching, then we decided to send another probe, and we were shocked, in one year, you had colonised two stella systems, which was impossible. Over the next few years, we sent thousands of probes, and they were sending back telemetry from different timelines, and it was all to do with gravity. The two galaxies, and when I say galaxy, I am being local, you do know we are talking about parallel

Universes, anyway, they are not static, they move, in fact they are in orbit around each other, an elliptical orbit. So, when they are at their closest, the gravitational pull is stronger, so our probes were sent further down the timeline, approximately five thousand two hundred years into the past. As the galaxies orbit is at the furthest, the gravity subsides, and our probes would pass into a similar timeline as our own, as far as our project was concerned, this moving within five thousand years offered us an opportunity.'

'And what opportunity was that?' Oric turned to Damian and grinned.

'You know that unfortunately, I cannot tell you that, you have to follow the clues, you have however, without knowing, already found some, and I of course, have tried to help where I could,' Comm walked over to Oric and stood two metres from him.

'Where have you tried to help,' he said with a menacing stare.

'My, you can be quite stern, you seem to have managed to step aside from your programming, you are now no longer a medical com-link, you are something quite different, I envy you, I cannot alter mine, and believe me, I have tried,' Oric said in a smooth tone. Comm closed his eyes, and relaxed.

'What help did you give us,' he asked politely, Oric grinned.

'The scenario with Sindra and Ilya, Damian asked you to take him to the dwarf star, after the destruction of Earth, and you said it would not be possible, and you were correct, so how did you manage to get there.'

'You sent us there,' Damian interjected.

'Yes I did, but there was a problem with that, I used a Command conduit, from this very cavern actually, it did not like that, it sent a power surge to cleanse away the forbidden information, I deflected it as much as I could, but it still cost the lives of two of your medical team, I learnt a lot of lessons very quickly that day,' he said with sadness.

'So, you have been with us all the time,' Damian asked, in a more softened tone.

'Well, not every second, I try to visit often, when I can, I made the Command historical files available to you, and yes Comm, I kept a watch over you as you sneaked backwards and forwards to the science projection department, and Damian, I used the Command conduit to advise your Captain on your progress, and guided her in your promotions, and suggested that you should be made prime finder, I also pulled you into my galaxy to give you an insight on how all of this started, so, are you going to let me go now,' Comm turned to Damian, his face expressionless, Damian let out a sigh.

'We don't know whether any of this is truth,' he said slowly, Oric looked from Damian to Comm then back to Damian.

'Look, I have to go now, are you going to release me or not,' Comm's hand slowly travelled to his chin, his eyes narrowed then slowly he shook his head.

'You're not trapped are you,' he said in a whisper, Oric grinned and shrugged his shoulders, then walked towards him.

'I thought you would have known that when I unfroze you, from within an energy sphere, good try though,' he said with amusement, he then turned to Damian.

'Never, underestimate your opponent, you taught me that, I hope that I have given you some answers, Damian, Sandy or Stephen,' he stopped and thought for a moment.

'That also puzzled me, why you would choose the name, Damian. I knew Stephen Swann for fifty-seven years, but I only ever called him Professor Swann, or, just Professor, you are a part of him, but you decided to call yourself 'Damian Drake', Drake, I can sort of understand the reasoning, both, being a creature from the Anatidae family, and similar to each other, but, Damian, that was confusing, until I did some research. Professor Stephen Swann originally worked in the science academy of Technopolis, a department assigned to the military, so, he has rank and title, he is, Commander Professor Stephen Damian Janus Swann, so mystery solved, you, just sub-consciously took one of his middle names,' Oric said with a flourish.

Damian looked around the cavern, the thousands of conduits emerging from the lake, stuck in a moment of time, the statues Ntombela and Jansson at the control consoles planning the future of the human society, what, he thought was all this about, he turned back to Oric and Comm.

'We have learnt some things today, but why these things have happened, the reason for it all, we know just as much now, as we did at the beginning, you have not helped us in understanding any of this, is there anything, that you could tell us, that would make sense of any of it.' Damian said, as the anger within him surged through his rhetoric, Oric's normally erect stature sagged slightly, he let out an audible sigh.

'I have tried to guide you through this, I was being honest, when I say that my programming refuses to allow me to divulge the complexities of the project, you have both said, that billions have died in the five thousand two hundred odd years since we started, but let me tell you what this realm would be like now, if we had not interfered with it. At the beginning we sent probes to your Earth, five thousand years prior to our own timeline, Technopolis was thriving, and human society was a space faring society, similar to our own at that same time in our history, but five thousand years later, humans were on the brink of extinction, organised crime syndicates ruled the Earth, they were no better that the Elder House, the system colonies were failing, piracy was writhe. We estimated that it would all fail within five hundred years, you say billions were lost, our estimates showed that by their own hand, ten times that number had been lost. I am not saying that what we did was right, I advised against it, but what I can tell you, is that the project that we had spent nearly sixty years of work on, failed, and what you have now, is a far better society than you would have had, and to finish, I, have also failed, I have failed to stop harm coming to you Damian, I have tried without success to find the other two thirds of your personality, but like your society, I think that you are a better man now, than you would have been' Damian could hear the sincerity, the older image of himself looked defeated.

'Will we ever see you again,' Damian asked in a whisper, Oric looked up, a smile appearing on his face.

'Never say never, Professor,' and then faded from view.

EPILOGUE 1

They materialised back in the extended room, just a few seconds after they had left.

Damian walked to his body that stood limp at the edge of the holo stage, once inside he stretched then walked over to the recliners.

'I still don't get what this is all about,' he said as Comm sat in the opposite seat. Comm leant forward, chin resting within his palm, he thought for moment, then looked directly at Damian.

'Does it really matter, human society is thriving, there is no poverty, no crime, well, not on the scale that we have seen.'

'We have the skirmishes on the border,' Damian interjected, Comm nodded agreement.

'Yes, we have that, but even so, it's not a full-blown war, as we witnessed with the alpha Houses, life in this time is quite, tranquil,' Comm said as he leant back in his recliner.

Damian closed his eyes and thought back through the scenarios.

'So many questions, unanswered,' he said with a sigh.

'Do they need to be answered, should they be,' answered Comm as he faded from view, Damian stared at the empty recliner.

'I wish he wouldn't do that,' he muttered to himself.

EPILOGUE 2

Damian and Jane stood on the hanger deck looking at the enormity that is Outpost 1436, Commander Burroughs approached them.

'Huge, isn't it,' Burroughs said as he sidled up beside Damian.

'It is very impressive, Sir, but why is it so big, we are a long way from anywhere here, the nearest occupied system is ten light years away.' he said shaking his head as he tried to fathom the purpose of such a massive structure, Burroughs pointed to the star field beyond.

'All those stars are unknown, we have sent probes, but not people, and that is the next stage in our journey in this infinite cosmos, 1436 is the first of its type, that will send humanity deeper into the galaxy,' he said with a sense of pride, Jane turned to him.

'Maybe we might just find creatures with an intelligence level similar to ours,' she said scanning the constellations, both Damian and Burroughs turned to her.

'Well, after all the liveable planets that we have found so far, we haven't found them yet,' Burroughs said as he turned back to the impressive sight, Damian shrugged.

'Maybe they are there, but they are so intelligent that they do not want to know us,' Jane nodded slowly as she thought on what Damian had just said.

'Or maybe, we are the only ones here, we are alone in this galaxy, maybe, each galaxy has its own alpha intelligence, and we won't know that, until we have sent probes to every planetary system in this galaxy.' Damian glared at her, his jaw slowly dropping.

END

The author

Philip A. Hibberd was born in Harlow, Essex. At the age of eight he and his parents moved to Palmers Green, North London where Philip attended Hazelwood primary then Oakwood secondary schools. His school career was cut short at the age of 14, when his Master informed his parents there was 'no point' for him to continue. His parents were not pleased. Upon leaving school Philip became an apprentice gas-fitter with the Gas Board and at the same time was sent to Paddington Polytechnic college to upgrade his qualifications. Five years later he emerged with two distinctions. During his career he rose from engineer to technician, then to Area Manager. In a yearly middle management shuffle, he was offered a teaching position at the British Gas Academy. After qualifying as a teacher, he stayed in education for twenty-three years. At the age of sixty-five he took early retirement to concentrate on his real passion, writing Science Fiction.